C000149677

Contents

Title Page

Copyright

Chapter 1   1

Chapter 2   9

Chapter 3   19

Chapter 4   28

Chapter 5   37

Chapter 6   48

Chapter 7   58

Chapter 8   68

Chapter 9   77

Chapter 10   87

Chapter 11   99

Chapter 12   107

Chapter 13   119

Chapter 14   131

Chapter 15   146
Chapter 16   155
Chapter 17   166
Chapter 18   173
Chapter 19   184
Chapter 20   195
Chapter 21   203
Chapter 22   216
Chapter 23   231
Chapter 24   241
Chapter 25   253
Chapter 26   264
Chapter 27   276
Chapter 28   286
Chapter 29   298
Chapter 30   308
Chapter 31   320
Chapter 32   336
Chapter 33   341
Chapter 34   351
Chapter 35   356
Chapter 36   368
Chapter 37   372
Chapter 38   379

Wolfish Charms

Jenna Collett

Epilogue   388
Acknowledgement   401
Books In This Series   403

Chapter 1

ARGUS

Deep in the woods
The Kingdom of Ever

The old woman smacked my hand with a wooden spoon. "Don't touch those. They're for my granddaughter."

Shaking off the sting across my knuckles, I eyed the fresh scones cooling on the counter, then flicked my gaze to the offending spoon. Winifred lifted her brow, daring me to try again. She was enjoying our stalemate, taking pleasure in my hesitation. It must run in the family. Her granddaughter had the same devilish nature.

My fingers hovered over the scones so close their heat grazed my skin. "Vivian and I have met. She won't mind."

Winifred grunted. "According to my granddaughter, you're not well-liked. She'll mind."

"Ah, Winnie, your words wound me."

She narrowed her eyes and took a creaking step in my direction. Her bony finger jabbed my chest with surprising force. "It's Oracle James to you."

Shadows danced over the long, silky strands of white hair that fell to her waist. Everything about her was pale and in stark contrast to the black sheath hanging from her slender frame. Only her lips were colored, painted red like blood from an open gash. Her eyes were gray as if the years had washed away their pigment. I guessed knowing the future did that to a person. I might have seen a fair share of horrors in my life, but at least I hadn't been able to see them coming.

Leaving the scones untouched, I circled the dim cottage. Outside, the wind dragged bare branches across the windowpanes, and the shutters rattled on their hinges. A fire crackled in the hearth, doing its best to ward off the winter chill. I added another log to the flames, causing sparks to spit into the grate.

Winifred insisted on a balmy temperature before she performed her work. According to her, the cold made it hard to read the future. I wasn't convinced; it seemed like a ploy to get me to chop wood. I caught her watching me from the window once, a wicked smile plastered on her face as I swung the axe, splitting the log in two.

There was always something that needed fixing before the future became clear. But manipulation was a trait I could respect, and it was another thing grandmother and granddaughter had in common.

The last time I saw Vivian, she was with the witch trying to scam information out of me. I still remember the challenge in her brown eyes as she downed my best bourbon. She'd labeled me a haunted man, and she wasn't wrong. You don't go from gutter rat to kingpin by only making friends. Since that night, my past wasn't the only thing that haunted me. Sometimes, I closed my eyes and saw thick, glossy hair spilling over her slender shoulders as she leaned forward, her mouth set in a devious red smirk that promised defiance. Defiance in my men wasn't tolerated, but hers might be the exception.

Satisfied with the temperature, I examined the large mirror hanging next to the hearth. The glass had splintered at the center, creating a spiderweb of fissures that spread outward. My fragmented reflection stared back as I traced a finger over a crevice.

"Visions getting the better of you, Winnie?"

She moved behind me, the top of her head barely reaching my shoulder. "Only when I look into your future. The mirrors can't handle it."

I grinned, the smile a crooked slash in the mirror's shattered surface. "You need better mirrors."

"No. I need clients who aren't gangsters and thieves. Though, you pay better than most." She popped half a scone into her mouth and dotted the corner of her lips with a napkin, clearly pretending she hadn't just scolded me for trying to take one.

"I'll buy you a new mirror." It was the least I could do. She'd broken three in the last week alone, and we weren't any closer to finding the Grimm's blade.

At the rate things were going, we'd go through every mirror in the kingdom and still need to import a batch from overseas.

Winifred cocked her head and began to name kingdoms with the best mirrors on her skeletal fingers. "Don't overlook the Thistleton Empire. Their craftsmanship is exquisite. They come highly recommended and rarely shatter during transit."

"They're overpriced," I grumbled. Winifred spared no expense when it was my money on the line.

"You can afford it. Except for your half-sister, you're all alone in that giant mansion built for ten times as many. A man your age should get married and start a family, but since your line of work attracts only less than desirable matches, someone else has to spend your blood money. Might as well be me."

Her sarcastic barb hit closer to home than she knew. I scowled at my reflection, seeing exactly what everyone around me saw. Take a word and add *less:* ruthless, reckless, heartless. They all fit like a second skin, and even masks can become permanent if you wear them long enough.

"I'll send a ship in the morning. You'll be up to your ears in plated glass in less than a month. Courtesy of my blood money."

The light faded from Winifred's eyes, and she drew a wheezy breath. "A month? Argus..." Her voice weakened, and she dropped her gaze to the floor. Whenever her eyes turned shifty, I knew she was remembering one of her visions. She'd grown more secretive lately, reluctant to share everything she saw. My gut told me it meant trouble, but seeing as how I was already neck-deep in that very thing, a little more didn't seem like a big deal.

"What is it, Winnie? Change your mind about Thistleton glass? Not expensive enough for you?"

She shook her head, sending her white hair swinging like a pendulum, then focused her gray eyes on me. Their intensity made unease expand behind my rib cage.

"Argus, you made me a promise when we started this search. I need to hear you say it again."

I froze, the mirth dying on my lips. What had she seen? My gaze darted to the cracked mirror, and guilt uncoiled in my stomach. I smothered it like a tiny flame deprived of oxygen. There was no place for guilt in our transaction. I paid her well. Whatever she saw in the mirror was insignificant if it meant finding the Grimm's blade. Nothing mattered more than that. It was my last chance to fix things.

Still, I had agreed to her promise and intended to keep it.

"You can rest easy, Winnie. I'll keep my word."

Worry deepened the lines on her face. My vow did little to relieve her tension. But what did I expect? When the devil makes you a promise, you don't smile.

"It's getting late. We should get started." Crossing the room, she lifted an oval mirror from the wall and placed it flat on her worktable. Candlelight illuminated her features as she leaned over the glass, staring into its depths.

I settled in a chair across from her and gazed into the mirror, wondering what it would be like to see more than my face. Nerves churned in my stomach as they always did while I waited for her visions to manifest. I might control the shadowy underworld in the kingdom of Ever, but I didn't control the future. No one could.

It still wouldn't stop me from trying.

Her hands trembled as she placed them palms-down on the glass. The room grew silent, and the walls seemed to close in. Outside, the branches increased their rhythmic thumping against the windows. Waves of heat scorched my back, and beads of sweat broke out on my skin. It was bloody hot in here!

"Do you see anything?" I asked, impatience thick in my tone. I tugged at my neckline, desperate for a cool breeze.

"Hush." Winifred's eyes snapped open, and she flattened her lips into a frown. "I'm working here."

"Please, continue," I grumbled, waving her on with my hand. "Time isn't of the essence or anything."

She ground her teeth and muttered under her breath. I couldn't make out the words, but it wasn't necessary. I'd provoked the soothsayer. Not ideal.

Refocusing her attention on the mirror, Winifred began to chant. The chilling cadence of her words rose the hair on my neck. A minute passed, then two.

The wind battered the cabin, trying to break inside as if it too wanted a glimpse of the future.

Tension clenched my muscles when her chanting ceased and she stared transfixed into the glass. The wind grew still. It felt wrong to breathe, the natural reflex too much of a disturbance in the soundless moment.

Winifred gasped. Her bony hands curled into fists, and her mouth went slack. Emotion welled in her eyes, and for a second, they flashed blue, then green, then back to gray. Her shoulders slumped, and she inhaled a harsh breath.

The mirror splintered.

A giant crack raced from one end to the other. She flinched and cried out, her voice ricocheting into the rafters.

"What is it? What do you see?" I leaned forward and caught her cold hand in mine. The iciness spread up my arm, dousing the heat radiating from the hearth. We were so close. Whatever she'd seen, I knew it was vital to the search.

Winifred tried to drag her hand away, but I tightened my grip, refusing to let her retreat inside her mind. She'd told me once, the only safe place from her visions was behind the barriers she'd created in her head. Those walls couldn't be breached. It could be hours, maybe days, before she clawed her way back out.

I squeezed warmth back into her fingers. "What did you see?"

Her skin was deathly pale. She parted her lips, and

I inched closer to hear her rasp, "You must keep your promise."

My brow creased. I already said I would. What did my promise have to do with her vision? She rambled the words again, her eyes losing focus. I snapped my fingers in front of her face.

"Winnie, what are you talking about?"

She straightened, altering her hold until she grasped my wrist. Her blunt fingers dug into my skin. "Keep your promise to me!" Fear overflowed in her gaze, and her breath hitched. "I'm so sorry, child," she moaned as her head lolled to the side, her body going limp.

I lurched from my chair, catching her before she hit the floor. Her white hair fanned around her like a soft blanket. Something resembling resignation filtered over her features. I'd never seen her like this.

"Argus..." she whispered.

"What can I do?"

Winifred rested her head on my knee. Her breath shallow, she said, "There's nothing you can do." She gave a weak cough, and her eyes fluttered shut. "It's already too late. The wolves are coming."

Chapter 2

VIVIAN

The ghost pointed to a spot on the board, and I slid his rook forward. He had me on the run. My queen was vulnerable—again. I hated chess, but I hated losing more, especially to a ghost who knew about my poor chess skills yet continued to choose it as our activity for game night.

I might need to cheat.

A throat cleared to my right, and I darted a glance at Ruby. Her shimmering hand passed through the table, then flashed me a signal. *Right. Like I have any idea what that means.* My fingers hovered over my remaining knight. Ruby's throat cleared louder. *Okay, not that one.* I switched to the bishop.

"No cheating, Vivian," grumbled the ghost across from me. The candles flared, punctuating his accusation, illuminating the room in bright light. His eyebrows drew together, and he slung his arms over his chest.

"Honestly, Fredrick, you should have picked a dice

game."

Fredrick lifted his shoulders and smirked, his image wavering like the candle flames circling the table. "You cheat at dice games too."

Ruby snickered. "And cards. Remember the time we caught her with an ace up her sleeve? It slid past her wrist and landed on the floor when she tried to deal."

"So, I cheat at game night. You're the two fools who keep showing up. Besides, you both have won plenty of times. There's a jar in the corner filled to the brim with your winnings. If I don't cheat every once in a while, you'll bankrupt me."

The ghosts turned to admire their cumulative winnings. They were saving up for something. I was afraid to ask what.

Ruby and Fredrick were what we in the ghost hunting business called "lifers"—an ironic label for ghosts who enjoyed the haunting lifestyle too much and had no intention of crossing over. They couldn't care less about unfinished business, preferring to haunt local villages or, in Ruby's case, the kingdom's moors. The young woman had perfected the whole white flowing gown and billowing hair look. Her pale features glowed, and her voice was like a siren's, echoing through the mist-shrouded landscape.

I was constantly getting letters about her. Letters we read aloud at game night. There wasn't much a ghost hunter could do if the ghosts refused to co-operate, and I couldn't stomach the solution of trapping their spirits inside a magic bottle. That wasn't how I ran my business. Besides, Ruby was a fantastic charades partner.

Tonight's game night was an impromptu get-to-gether. My grandmother, Winifred James, had canceled plans with me for the second night in a row. If that wasn't bad enough, my best friend Tessa was holed up in her magic shop "testing potions," which was a term she'd made up years ago that actually meant, "If the magic shop is rocking, don't come knocking."

Lucky girl. Men usually ran for the hills when they learned I could communicate with ghosts. Apparently, three's a crowd even if one of them is invisible.

Tessa had been scarce ever since she started her investigative business and fell in love with the Royal Agency's lead detective. It didn't bother me…much. I was happy for her. She deserved it, and I always had game night with dead people as my fallback.

Fredrick had me move his rook again, and I considered my dwindling options. That was when I saw an opening; a legit move that would put me back in the running for a win. Keeping calm, I slid my bishop diagonally. Nerves tingled across my skin, and I curled my fingers into fists to keep from tapping the table in excitement.

"I can see you bouncing in your seat."

I went still. "I'm not bouncing."

"You're bouncing." Fredrick grimaced and chose his final move, which I countered with my bishop.

"Checkmate!"

Ruby laughed and floated out of her chair. "My

turn."

I stood and stretched my aching muscles, then refilled my glass of wine. It was going to be a long night.

Ruby settled into the seat across from me while I rearranged the board. "You know," she said as I took my first sip of wine, "I heard a rumor a man has been visiting your grandmother all hours of the day for weeks now." She rubbed her hands together. "Spill it, Vivian. Is your grandmother seeing someone?"

I eyed her over the rim of my glass. "No way. Where did you hear that?"

"A phantom told me."

"Phantoms are liars!" I thumped my glass down next to the chessboard.

Fredrick floated his elbows over the table and rested his chin in his palm. "I heard it too, except he's much too young for Winifred, and he's not exactly her type, but he is rich enough. I'd certainly look the other way for a criminal if the price was right."

Ruby grinned and sent Fredrick a thumbs-up. *Unbelievable.* My gaze narrowed on him.

"Who is it?"

"Argus Ward. You know, the—"

"I know who he is." My fingers tightened around the base of my wineglass. Why was Argus Ward visiting my grandmother? He was a full-time con artist, a gangster, and my grandmother had strict clientele standards. At least, she used to.

"I wonder why Winifred didn't tell you?" Ruby asked, pointing to a pawn.

I pushed her pawn forward with too much force, and the little piece toppled over. "Probably because I'd disapprove."

Except that wasn't entirely true. I'd been slandering the man to anyone who'd listen ever since he threatened Tessa. Trouble was, the ghost hunter doth protest too much. Even Tessa had started to look at me odd whenever his name came up. Usually brought up by me.

The thing is, he made me curious. What was he hiding behind his overly confident smile? We'd only met once, but there'd been a moment when I saw the things that haunted him, and it made me want to learn more.

There was also the fact I found him irritatingly attractive. Not that I would let anyone find that out.

Ever.

"You're blushing," Fredrick said, stifling a grin.

"I am not." I pushed out of my chair and took a cleansing breath. The clock on the mantel read a little after eleven p.m. Was he there now? Was he the reason my grandmother canceled?

There was something in the letter she'd sent that felt off. For one thing, it was more than a couple of sentences, and she'd finished by telling me I made her proud. I'd figured that was her trying to butter me up after canceling, but now? Winifred didn't dole out compliments on a good day. Unease spread through my body. My grandmother was keeping a secret.

Tricky wench.

"It's getting late, you guys. I think—" A wave of dizziness passed through me, and I pressed my fingers to my temple. My vision blurred, my knees giving way until they landed hard against the floorboards.

What's happening?

I breathed through the vertigo, feeling every ounce of energy flush from my body like water funneling through a drain. Then, as swiftly as it came, the disorientation passed, leaving me trembling, hands braced on the floor. My hair hung in front of my face, and I pushed it aside.

"That was weird." I forced a laugh. "I think I might have had too much wine. I'm not feeling great." Climbing to my feet, I faced the table.

The ghosts were gone.

"Ruby? Fredrick? Where did you go?"

An eerie silence met my answer. It was never this quiet. The candle flames shed light over their empty seats, and I moved closer, searching the shadows.

"This isn't funny. You're scaring me." Which was a strange thing for a ghost hunter to say to a bunch of ghosts. "I mean it… Show yourselves. Don't make me pull out my sage."

That should at least have gotten a laugh from Ruby. She hated the stuff, said she could smell it even in death.

Nothing.

I turned in a slow circle, the realization taking longer than it should. They really were gone, and I was alone.

***

They didn't show up in the morning either. None of the ghosts did. Penny didn't materialize at breakfast, and Joe wasn't trailing after the milkman. In fact, none of the people walking down the street appeared haunted at all.

Something was very wrong.

It didn't matter why my grandmother had canceled our plans; this was an emergency. I picked up my pace, narrowly missing the scrawny urchin who thrust a paper into my hands.

"Hey, lady, don't go into the woods." His ink-darkened fingers wiggled, expecting payment. "Read it yourself. They found another body."

I withdrew a coin, exchanging it for the day's news. The boy bounced on his heels in the cold before snagging another paper and searching the thin crowd for his next customer.

The headline jumped off the page in thick black letters.

Animal Attack or Murder? Body Found at the Edge of the Forest has Authorities Puzzled.

Returning his attention to me, the boy scrunched his nose and wiped the sleeve of his jacket across his face. "It says the body was covered in claw marks. That's the second one they found this week. Both men were antiquities dealers. Tough way to go." He clucked his tongue and gave a solemn shake of his head.

I scanned the rest of the article. No known suspects. Little to no evidence. Tessa would have her hands full with this case. It wasn't long ago she'd solved her first murder, and it looked like this latest development would keep her and her partner, Derrick Chambers, busy.

I tucked the newspaper inside the wicker basket hanging from my arm and adjusted the ties on my long red cloak. A chill forced me to pull the hood over my head. The newspaper boy cleared his throat, realizing I hadn't moved on and was crowding his corner. He crooked his finger and signaled me closer.

"They named him, you know?"

My brow wrinkled. "Named who?"

The boy rolled his eyes and slapped a paper against his knee. "The creature."

"The article says the authorities don't know what killed those men."

"They can't print it yet. The agency doesn't want to cause a panic. They still named him though. It's gonna sell a lot of papers." He rubbed his hands together in anticipation and flicked his tongue over his cracked lips.

"So, what's his name then?"

He scoffed. "I ain't gonna tell you, lady. You gotta buy tomorrow's paper."

Irritation shot up my spine. I should have known he was baiting me. I didn't have time for dead antiquities dealers or murderous creatures, not when every single person I saw on the street was alive.

"Keep your paper, kid."

A carriage approached, weaving down the narrow

cobblestone street. I hailed it with my empty hand, and it pulled to a stop.

The driver called down from his perch, "Where to?"

"The fork at Blackbrook forest. I'll walk from there."

The driver sized me up, then cast a wary glance at the boy. "Is she serious? That's close to where they found the body."

The boy shrugged. "I already told her not to go into the woods."

"It's fine," I grumbled, yanking open the carriage door. The interior was freezing, and I huddled deeper inside my crimson cloak, sparing a final glance at the boy who looked back in concern. He tapped his heel against the stone and fiddled with his overlong coat sleeves. Finally, he came to a decision and raced forward, knocking on the carriage window before speaking through the glass.

"They're calling him the Red Wolf. Half-man, half-beast. A creature that claws its victims until they're painted in red. Be careful out there."

I pursed my lips and shook my head. "Creatures like that don't exist. They're fairy tales to scare little children."

The boy frowned. A stream of new customers poured out of a nearby tavern, and he cast a torn look in their direction.

"Don't say I didn't warn you, lady." He dashed back to his post as the carriage pulled away, and I heard his cries echoing down the street. "Get your paper here! Second body found in the woods this week. Will there be a third?"

Chapter 3

VIVIAN

Winifred's cottage was nestled between a copse of trees. The small clearing seemed to appear out of nowhere after nearly a mile-long trek through the dense forest. A well-trampled path led over babbling brooks and jagged boulders. Snow from the night before clung to the naked branches and dusted the pine trees, giving the woods a quiet tranquility.

I shifted the heavy basket to my other arm and picked up my pace, debating whether I should dip into the stash of elderberry wine if only to warm my insides. If I thought Winifred wouldn't grumble over the loss, I'd probably do it.

The thatched roof peeked through the trees, followed by the rough-hewn logs and worn shutters. A large stack of split firewood was piled at the foot of the flagstone steps.

Someone had been busy.

Winifred often made her clients do her chores

before she looked into their futures. It was genius. I had half a mind to adopt the plan. Imagine getting someone to wash my dishes before I agreed to scope out their haunted barn or ghost-infested attic? It had merit and would save a ton of time. I passed the axe lodged into a tree trunk and stifled a grin. *Sucker.*

Various sets of footprints already marred the fresh snow that covered the steps, which meant Winifred likely had visitors. I paused on the top step, my teeth sinking into my bottom lip. Was Argus inside? No way. It was probably the milkman or some socialite's mother desperate to learn when her daughter would marry, and if he'd come with a fortune.

Still…

I angled my head toward the darkened windows. Muffled voices sounded from inside. A man's voice.

Nerves fluttered in my stomach.

Here I was, in front of a house full of mirrors, and there wasn't a single one outside. Finger-combing my raven curls, I arranged a few so they'd cascade down the front of my cloak, then pinched my frozen cheeks. Hard. Because I was an utter fool, primping myself for a gangster. As if anything that wasn't holding a sack full of coins would catch his attention.

Not that I wanted to catch his attention. A sack full of coins, though? I'd take that.

I squared my shoulders and tamped down my nerves. I was Vivian James, for crying out loud! Unflinching among the dead; cool in the face of specters. A human man?

Please, I speak to ghouls over breakfast.

Well…not this morning, but that's why I was here. Winifred would know what to do, and Argus? If he was inside, I wouldn't spare him a second glance.

But I'd make my first glance count.

With a wicked smile, I reached for the handle, but the door opened before I could get a grip. A face appeared out of the shadows, and I stepped back in surprise.

"Tessa? What are you doing here?"

She crossed the landing onto the porch and shut the cottage door behind her. I could still hear muted conversation coming from inside. Derrick must be visiting too. I knew things had gotten serious between them, but Winifred was as much family to Tessa as she was to me, which meant things might be further along than I thought.

I pulled a bottle of wine from my basket and waved it in the air. "Do we have something to celebrate, Tess? You know I always come prepared. I can't believe you took Derrick to meet Winifred and didn't tell me!"

"Viv—" Tessa swallowed and took a shuddering breath.

I frowned, noting Tessa's red-rimmed eyes and slight tremble from her chin. My grip tightened around the bottle. It didn't matter if he was a detective—if Derrick had made Tessa cry, he would answer to me.

"Where is he? I'll kill him."

"Vivian, no." Her hand wrapped around my arm, and she took the bottle, setting it to rest on the porch. "You can't go inside."

"Then he'll have to come out here. Either way, he's a dead man."

"That's not what's happening." She closed her eyes, and tears leaked from beneath her lashes. When she opened them again, I saw the pain reflected there. "Viv, it's Winifred. She's gone."

My mind reeled. *Gone?* She'd just returned from an extended trip last month. Where would she go without telling me?

Tessa's fingers closed over mine, and she squeezed, biting back a sob. "I'm so sorry, Viv."

No.

The realization of what she was saying forced its way to the front of my mind, but I wouldn't let it take root. *NO.* I stepped around her, determined to prove to myself that what I was thinking wasn't possible.

"Vivian, stop! You can't go inside. It's an official crime scene. They're collecting evidence." She grabbed my arm and spun me back to face her.

I wrenched out of her hold, my head shaking in denial. It didn't make sense. I sucked in a breath, then another, too fast, until the ground tilted, and I reached for the railing to stay upright. Nausea churned in my stomach, sickness spreading like oil through my body.

"It's not true." I slid to my knees, the snow melting and seeping through the fabric of my cloak. *An official crime scene? Evidence?* That could only mean one thing…except it wasn't true. Winifred couldn't be dead. I'd know, wouldn't I? *I always know!* Horror constricted my chest as the pieces clicked into place.

Last night wasn't a fluke or a glitch in my powers. The ghosts were gone, and that could only happen if —

Tessa touched my shoulder, and I flinched. A warm jolt of soothing energy filled my body. She whispered an incantation, and my panic ebbed as her magic pulsed into me.

"What happened?" I croaked, my throat so tight it hurt to speak.

"The milkman found her before dawn. I won't go into the details."

"Tell me everything, or I'll go in there and see for myself."

Tessa's hand felt like ice against my neck. "Her injuries are consistent with the victims we've found over the past few weeks." She paused.

"Say it."

"Similar to an animal attack." Tessa knelt at my side and wrapped her arms around me. "Derrick and his men are in there now. We'll find out who did this, I promise. You know how much Winifred meant to me."

Past tense. It sounded so final. I wasn't ready! Years of training fled. Everything I'd said in the past to countless grieving family members rang hollow in my mind. Tessa guided me to my feet, and as her brief spell faded, a heavy numbness crept in.

"Let them finish here. Come back to the agency with me. I'll tell you everything we know. We'll get through this together."

"I need to see her." I glanced over my shoulder at the closed door.

"There will be time for that. But first, I need you to tell me everything you know about the clients she was seeing."

My mind stalled on a name. It reached the tip of my tongue, but I held it back. Why I hesitated, I wasn't sure. He was a criminal after all.

I only knew one thing for certain.

Argus had visited my grandmother, and now, she was dead.

***

All eyes were on me as Tessa and I walked through the agency lobby. Conversation halted, and the knowing glances speared me through the chest.

"That's her," someone whispered.

Another pointed then spoke behind their hand.

A memory surfaced. Me, at twelve, surrounded by a circle of children. They laughed, pointed their grubby fingers, and shouted, "That's her! That's the girl who talks to ghosts." Their laughter morphed into jeers, and a stone hit my cheek. Then another. A thin trail of blood ran down my chin. I closed my eyes and shielded my face, still seeing their accusing fingers. Their taunting shouts echoed in my ears.

"Vivian?"

"I'm sorry...what did you say?" I blinked, bringing

Tessa's concerned face into focus. Somehow, we'd reached Derrick's office, and she held open the door.

"Are you okay? Can I get you anything? Water?"

"No."

Tessa nodded and gestured for me to sit in the chair in front of Derrick's desk. "You were mumbling something when we came in. What was it?"

"Everyone was staring. They know, don't they?" I sank into the chair and pressed my fingers against my temple. Of course they knew. Word of Winifred's death would spread fast. It would be in the papers in a day, two at tops. The kingdom's oracle was gone.

And a new oracle would rise.

Tessa sat across from me, pulling my hands into hers. "No one outside the agency knows yet. But they will." She sighed and inched closer, her voice dropping to a whisper. "Has it started?"

I never imagined I'd have to answer that question. It wasn't supposed to be this way. We didn't prepare for it, always believed my firstborn would inherit the oracle's gift. There'd always been time.

Until there wasn't.

Until my ghosts vanished, along with the person I cared about most.

"I think so. Last night. But I can't deal with that now. I need to know what happened. Who did this?"

"We aren't sure yet. I went through her client book, and only one name stood out." She met my gaze, held it, possibly afraid of my reaction. "Do you know why Winifred was meeting with Argus Ward?"

"No. She didn't mention it when I saw her last week, but I heard rumors. Do you think he's involved? Has Derrick said anything?" My gaze shifted to his desk and the piles of case files. A thick folder rested on top of the stack labeled with Argus's name.

"We don't know that yet either. But it's possible. Some other victims had connections to his organization. Viv, I need you to stay away from him. Let the agency handle this. Whether or not he's involved, he's dangerous."

Tessa gave me a look. The one that said she knew what I was thinking and wanted to put a stop to it before I could act. But this was Winifred, a mother figure to both of us. What was I supposed to do? Go home and sit in my empty house and wait for her killer to be caught? I needed to do more than that. I owed my grandmother that much.

"You know, maybe a glass of water would help."

"Sure. I'll be back in a minute." Tessa slipped quietly from the room, leaving the door open a crack.

I hesitated, then rounded Derrick's desk and flipped open the folder on Argus Ward. I skimmed the pages, looking for anything that might help.

When footsteps sounded in the hallway, I quickly shut the folder and went back to my seat. Hushed voices leaked through the crack in the door.

"He's the only suspect. But it won't matter. Argus Ward always slips through the cracks. Even if they make an arrest, he'll probably get released on a technicality."

The second man chuckled. "All it takes to get away with murder in this kingdom is the right amount of coin, and he has plenty. Hell, maybe he paid someone to off the oracle."

My hands gripped the rails of the chair. They were right. If Argus was responsible, could justice be served? And could I live with my grandmother's killer roaming free?

No. I couldn't. It wasn't that I didn't trust Tessa and Derrick to put the person responsible in prison; it was that I couldn't be sure they could keep him there. Which meant I'd have to take matters into my own hands, and thanks to the file on Derrick's desk, I now knew where Argus lived.

Chapter 4

ARGUS

The merchant looked bored. He studied his boots as if they were the rare antiquities instead of the numerous items filling his shop. I scowled at Gregor, the man I'd sent to handle the situation. He shrugged his hulking shoulders, and I clenched my teeth. Idiots. All of them. What was the point of having a skilled gang of thugs if they didn't do their job? Gregor was my best man. He radiated intimidation, yet there stood Andrew Billings, owner of Relics and Rarities, looking obnoxiously unfazed.

If you want something done right…

"Where's your latest shipment?" I edged forward, forcing Andrew back a step.

He bumped the counter, rattling a pair of twin pewter statues. "I already told that guy over there. I haven't received anything new all week."

"I see. That's unfortunate."

"It is?" Andrew raised his brow.

"I'm afraid so. I have it on good authority an un-documented crate was delivered here yesterday."

Andrew flexed his jaw, his gaze darting to the storeroom. "You're mistaken, I assure you. I'm very careful with my records."

I grinned, flashing my teeth. "Am I mistaken?" Turning to Gregor, I asked, "Do I make mistakes?"

"No, boss."

"And why is that?"

Gregor didn't miss a beat. "Because you're the king."

"That's right. There might be a king who sits on his throne in the middle of his fancy castle, but I'm the king of these streets. I own the docks, I own the alleys, and until you pay back what you owe, I own this pile of bricks and everything in it. So, if you have undocumented goods, it's my business to know about them."

Andrew paled, his eyes bulging in their sockets. "You're Argus Ward? I didn't realize—"

"Crowbar." I held out my hand and waited until Gregor produced the steel object. We'd wasted enough time with formalities. After my last meeting with Winifred, I had to move fast. Her warning churned in my gut.

The wolves are coming.

Actually, they were already here. The shadowy creatures dogged my footsteps, leaving dead bodies in their wake. Unfortunate souls who found out the hard way the antiquities business could be deadly. Especially when we were all looking to get our hands on the same thing.

Andrew Billings needed to leave town within the hour. It was a miracle I'd found him first. He didn't realize it, but I'd saved his life. Death stalked his shop. It lurked in the shadows, waiting to strike.

Crowbar in hand, I gestured for Andrew to open the stockroom door. Inside, floor to ceiling shelves held statues, pottery, and glass-blown trinkets. White sheets were draped across furniture, keeping dust off the fine craftsmanship. Every item was ordered and arranged by type. But I wouldn't find what I was looking for on those shelves. Undocumented goods would be hidden until they could be sold.

I tapped the crowbar against the wall, listening for the hollow sound that betrayed a hidden compartment. Nothing yet. That left two options. My gaze ran along the rafters, then settled on the floor. Slowly, I walked the length, waiting for a telltale creak. It sounded near the back of the room. The floor bowed slightly beneath my boot.

Using the crowbar, I pried up the boards and tossed them aside. *Jackpot.* A crate rested beneath the floor, its lid stamped with the word "fragile."

"It's not what it looks like," Andrew stammered.

"Really? Because it looks like you're holding out on me."

"I already have a buyer for the items in the crate. I'll split the proceeds with you."

"I don't want your money." *Wait.* I winced and cursed my phrasing.

"You don't?" Andrew cocked his head in surprise.

"What I meant was, I have no interest in selling what's inside the trunk." At least, not everything. Once I'd gotten my hands on what I came for, the rest could sell for a princely sum. I'd take my share then. I gestured to the lock sealing the crate. "Open it."

Andrew scrambled forward, nearly tripping in his haste. He pulled a leather strap from around his neck. A key dangled on the end, and his fingers trembled as he inserted it into the lock. It clicked, and he rocked back on his heels, making room for me to examine the crate's contents. Sounds dimmed as all my attention focused on the crate. I pried open the lid, using my weight against the rusty hinges.

Inside, a glint of gold gleamed in the low light—but I hadn't come for gold. Not this time. I tossed aside a filmy teal swath of fabric and pulled a wooden box out from the depths. Deep claw marks scarred the rough surface, and a circular symbol had been scored into the wood.

The sign of enchanted steel.

After weeks of searching, I'd finally found it. I held the box reverently, afraid it might crumble in my fingers before I had the chance to retrieve what was inside.

Gregor spoke over my shoulder. "Is that it, boss?"

"Yes. It's the Grimm's blade." I placed the box on the floor and lifted the cover. Air lodged in my throat, and the sound of blood rushed through my ears. Someone groaned. It sounded more animal than human. The denial repeated, over and over.

It came from me.

The box was empty.

Andrew cleared his throat and tugged on his collar. "Uh, if you're looking for what was inside, it went to another buyer at auction. He only wanted the blade. I kept the box thinking it might be worth something on its own."

I climbed to my feet and growled, "Who bought it?"

"I'm not sure," Andrew stammered. "It was by proxy. The sellers would know."

"Their names?"

Andrew's face turned gray. "I don't know those either. They'd just arrived by ship and went straight to the auction."

Glancing at the crate, I noted the name of the shipping company. If I could get my hands on the ship's manifest and get the names of the sellers, I'd know where the blade went next.

I tossed the box to Andrew. "Get out. Don't touch anything. Pack a bag and leave town."

"My buyer will be furious!" Andrew sputtered.

"Would you rather be dead?" I fixed Andrew with a sobering stare. "Leave now, or you'll end up in tomorrow's paper like the others." I stalked from the room, motioning to Gregor to make sure the owner followed my instructions. I didn't need another murder on my hands; I needed the Grimm's blade. We were so close. Winifred had seen the blade inside the box, she just hadn't seen it get moved.

And now, time wasn't on our side.

***

A trio of gargoyles snarled from their perch on the roof of the Lennox mansion. The midday sun highlighted their stone-toothed grins, mocking me as I took the steps two at a time and threw open the door. It was as if they knew I didn't belong, that I was an impostor playing king of the castle.

My half sister Adella Lennox might have grown up in the vast mansion and acres of land stretching deep into the forest, but my money kept it running. I had considered getting rid of the gargoyles. The thought of shoving them off the roof until they cracked against the drive gave me a lot of pleasure, but then so did keeping them, knowing they had to watch the tarnished son of one of the kingdom's oldest families come and go every day.

Spite won. Spite would always win.

The gargoyles got to stay.

A fire snapped in the great hall, giving off welcoming waves of heat. I warmed my hands by the flames as I watched the orange flicker. The hypnotic dance allowed my mind to wander. If only Winifred had seen the blade had been removed... But that was the funny thing about visions: they didn't always give you the full story. If it was as simple as picturing where the blade was at the exact moment you were looking for it, I'd already have it in my possession.

Visions weren't that accommodating. You never knew exactly where you were in the timeline, and

I was confident fate liked to play games, dangling your wants in front of your face while holding back crucial information.

I checked the clock on the mantel. It was early afternoon, a perfect time to visit Winifred. I might not have an appointment, but we had an ongoing arrangement, and maybe if I offered to chop more wood, she wouldn't send me packing.

The clock chimed the hour as if in agreement. That settled it. I would drop in on the oracle. Hell, she'd probably see me coming.

"Excuse me, sir?" My butler, Hastings, appeared from a side door. His polished boots clicked over the parquet floor. He had a newspaper tucked under his arm, and he slowed, transferring it to one hand before holding it out to me.

"I don't have time for the news, Hastings. Put it on my desk—I'll get to it later."

The man's eyebrows drew together, his weathered features hardening. "You need to make time for this. There's been another murder."

Impossible. Andrew Billings was alive this morning, and even if something had happened in the time since I left him, the papers weren't that fast. I took the newspaper from Hastings and scanned the front page. The room tilted, words becoming blurry as their meaning took form in my mind.

It couldn't be.

Not Winifred.

Her murder was splashed across the front page. She'd been found dead two days ago by the milkman who had summoned the authorities.

My insides turned to ice, and regret sliced through me. In a daze, I stumbled toward my office, Hastings' concerned voice following close on my heels. The door opened in the shadowy room, and my gaze narrowed on the decanters of dark liquid behind my desk. I needed a drink. I needed…

The promise Winifred had wrung from me echoed in my ears, becoming a raging tide. It was more important than whiskey. Two days had already passed.

"Hastings, locate Vivian James. Have her brought here."

Hastings hesitated in the doorway, his brows drawing together. "About that, sir. She's already—"

The whisper of fabric captured my attention, and a feminine scent flooded my senses. It was a heady mix of lavender and some undefinable essence that belonged solely to its owner. Had I not been stunned by the news of Winifred's death, I'd have noticed it.

A voice sounded near my ear, the tone as sharp as the dagger she placed at the back of my spine. "Tell me, Mr. Ward. What do you intend to do with me once I'm here? Are you planning to kill me too?"

"Hello, Vivian."

"Murderer," she snarled. "You'll pay for what you've done."

"Those rumors are greatly exaggerated." The dagger bit into my skin, and I grimaced. "Hastings, what have I told you about checking guests for weapons at the front door?"

Hastings straightened the cuffs on his tailored jacket, oblivious or possibly unconcerned about my predicament. Knowing Hastings, my guess leaned toward unconcerned.

"Are we still doing that, sir? I figured Miss James was an exception."

"There are no exceptions."

"I'll be certain to check the next guest appropriately."

"See that you do. You're dismissed."

The door closed. Placing the newspaper on the table, I took a deep breath.

"All right, Vivian. You made it this far. Might as well finish the job."

Chapter 5

VIVIAN

My grip tightened around the hilt of the dagger. Damn my nerves. It had been easy enough standing in the shadows watching Argus enter the room. He'd moved with the confidence of a man unaware of a threat in his midst. Funny, how his demeanor hadn't changed when I pressed the blade into his back.

He must be used to it.

This gave me pause. Did I seriously think I could confront the man who might have killed my grandmother? I really was losing it. *Deep breaths.* All I had to do was question him, and if I didn't like the answers, one clean thrust, and it would be over. It wouldn't bring my grandmother back, but it would be something. Control where there'd been none. Justice he couldn't escape with a bribe or technicality.

If only mechanics were the problem. It was hard to concentrate when he seemed to expect death as if it was a long time coming. Seconds stretched into minutes, punctuated by the snap and crack of the fireplace in the corner. Where did one start with a deadly interrogation?

"Everything all right back there?" His voice was laced with a hint of amusement. "Can I make a suggestion?"

"No. Stop talking."

"Right. Carry on." He stood still as a statue, granite shoulders encased in a linen shirt. Narrow hips, legs braced apart, waiting for me to strike.

The hilarity of the moment hit me like an arrow between the ribs, and a hysterical laugh built in the back of my throat. I held it in for as long as I could, but what came out wasn't a laugh—it was an aching sob, the sound clanging in my head and hollowing out my stomach. It stole my courage and made my grip loosen.

Argus shifted and turned to face me. The blade that had been pressed into his back now threatened his abdomen. His hand closed over mine, and our gazes met in an airless moment. Concern overflowed from his eyes.

I felt myself waver. I was such a fool. Six feet of rigid muscle and bone towered over me, and I flattened my lips to keep them from trembling.

"Give me the knife, Vivian."

"No."

I could still do it. Except now, I'd have to look him straight in the eye and watch the moment his life ended. I might not make it out of the house, but what did it matter? Winifred was gone. My ghosts were gone, and I was facing an existence I never wanted.

"Why did you do it? It's cruel, even for you."

His jaw tightened. I half-expected him to rip the knife from my hand and plunge it into my heart before I had time to react. Instead, his thumb brushed over my skin, surprising me with the gentleness of his touch. The blade remained where it was—a sign he was letting me keep the upper hand for now.

"I'm sorry for your loss. Winnie was an exceptional woman."

"My grandmother never let anyone call her Winnie."

"She let me, mostly. Vivian, I didn't kill your grandmother."

My head shook in response. "There are witnesses who claim you've been visiting her for weeks and you were there that night. You're the agency's number one suspect."

The corner of his mouth lifted. "I'm the agency's number one suspect when a cat gets caught in a tree."

"Don't mock me! Your file was on Detective Chambers' desk. Stop denying it, or I'll—"

"Or, what? You'll kill me?" All traces of humor vanished from his face. Argus's body tensed as he moved forward, testing my bluff.

I failed miserably, sucking in a horrified breath as I jumped back a step.

My withdrawal inflamed his anger. With a flick of

his wrist, he captured the knife and rammed the tip into the surface of his desk, leaving it to vibrate as he stalked closer. I retreated, nearly tripping over my feet. My back bumped the wall, trapping me between the wooden panels and his formidable frame.

The concern was gone, wiped clean, and replaced with an emotion that made my stomach flip. He snarled, his hands slamming the wall on either side of my face.

"Are you insane?" His mouth dropped close to my ear, and the rasp of his voice sent a shiver up my spine. "Never stick a dagger in a man's back if you're afraid to use it."

"What?" I choked. "You're mad I didn't stab you?"

"Yes. Next time, don't hesitate." He grabbed my hand and pressed it against my right side. "Aim here, between the ribs."

I struggled to speak, thrown by his aggression and the warm pressure against my rib cage. Was he seriously giving me pointers? My gaze narrowed. He'd know best.

"Is that where you—?"

"Don't say it," he growled, kicking my legs apart with his foot.

I tensed as he searched me for more weapons. I couldn't move if I wanted to. The part of my brain that told my limbs to work malfunctioned. It started to tell me other things, like maybe if I remained motionless, he might keep sliding his hands over my body.

Yeah, stuff like that. My brain was a traitor.

His search ended, and he cursed when he didn't find anything else. "You only brought one knife? Winifred knew exactly what she was doing when she asked me to..." His voice trailed off, then he cursed again, this time harsher and more explicit.

"Asked you to what?"

He didn't answer. I wasn't getting anywhere. My knife was currently lodged in his desk, and he was angrier I hadn't used it on him than he was about my murderous accusations.

Well, that wasn't true. He wasn't happy about those either.

Had he really called her Winnie? Had she let him? He still had all his fingers, so she must have. Which meant...

I groaned and scrubbed a hand over my face. *Way to go, Vivian. You just threatened the one man who might have a clue.*

It was way too late to start over. My gaze darted to the blade stuck vertically in the polished wood. Was I supposed to apologize for bringing it, or for not bringing more? Argus was the most confusing man I'd ever met.

The silence grew awkward while I reviewed my options. Interrogation at knifepoint was out of the question, and he didn't look like the type who responded well to tears. Not that I had any. Something had broken off inside me, a disassociation leaving me unable to grieve in the way that made the most sense.

"Why were you going to see her?" I asked softly.

He leaned against the desk, resting his palm on the hilt of the dagger. "Your grandmother and I had a business arrangement."

"What arrangement?" At his continued silence, I grew frustrated and pushed away from the wall, invading his space. Argus didn't even flinch. "Do you know who did this to her?" My voice cracked. "I need to know who."

"Why? So you can charge after him with your pathetic dagger you have no intention of using?"

"I'll use it next time, I promise." My voice was laced with sugar and barely contained patience. "Tell me what you know."

Argus weighed my question, then came to a decision. "It was the Red Wolf."

The creature from the newspaper?

I backed away, shaking my head in denial. "She would have seen it coming. You can't sneak up on an oracle."

"I think she did see it coming. You're right, I was there two nights ago, and Winnie saw something in her mirror. She refused to tell me what it was, but now, I'm positive it was her death."

I felt sick at the thought. But if she'd experienced such a horrific vision and knew it was imminent...

"She would have come to me. She wouldn't have stayed out there in the woods alone." I lifted my gaze and pinned him with an accusatory glare. "You left her alone."

Argus's grip tightened around the hilt, the only sign my barb had made an impact. "Winifred wouldn't have put you in danger. Whatever she saw, I think she knew she couldn't stop it. Maybe trying would've had worse consequences."

"No. This is your fault. *You* did this. Whatever you were using her for is what got her killed."

"She knew the risks."

"That's not good enough!" I spun toward the bookcase, focusing my rage on the cracked spines lining the shelves. They blurred, and I blinked to clear my vision as guilt wormed its way under my skin. I should have gone out there more. Maybe if I had, I would have seen this coming. But that was absurd. Winifred had seen it coming and did nothing, told no one. I walked to the edge of the room, pausing in front of a large mirror that hung over a wooden sideboard.

"Let me pour you a drink. You look like you could use one," Argus spoke over my shoulder. I hadn't heard him approach. He reached past me, brushing against my sleeve, and lifted a bottle of amber liquid, then began to pour the liquor into a crystal glass.

I watched him perform the task in the mirror, his actions fluid and purposeful before he placed the drink in my hand. Did anything faze him? Maybe ineptitude. My mind replayed his fierce reaction when I'd retreated instead of made good on my promise to kill.

Who acts like that?

My side burned where he'd pressed my hand. *Aim here.* The glass I held trembled, sloshing liquor over the side of the rim. Argus wrapped his fingers over mine, halting their movement and allowing the whiskey to settle.

The moment felt suspended as our gazes met in the mirror, out of sync with the ticking clock in the corner. His lips moved, and I stared transfixed, not hearing his words at first.

"No matter how many times I saw your grandmother consult her mirrors, I only ever saw my reflection. What do you see?"

His question caught me off-guard. There was something in his tone, an expectation, or maybe it was hope. Did he know what was happening to me? How long could I deny it? Even to myself?

"I see nothing."

Argus dropped his hand, his lips curling in disappointment. "That's too bad."

"Why were you having her consult her mirror?"

He crossed the room and removed a key from his desk. "It's probably better for you to know." Inserting the key into a crevice in the side of the bookcase, he swung open a hidden panel. Another row of shelves appeared, holding a series of leather-bound volumes. He selected one and flipped through its pages, stopping somewhere in the middle. "The answer is right here."

I peered at the yellowed page, trying to decipher the handwritten scrawl. "You're searching for a Grimm's blade?"

"Yes. Tell me what you know about it."

Pacing the floor, I tried to remember what I'd heard. "They're exceedingly rare, mostly because enchanted steel is prohibitively expensive and can only be forged by someone who possesses elemental power."

"And what are they used for?"

I scoffed. "Decoration. Anything else is a fantasy. Creatures of the night, half-man, half-beast, they're fictional."

Argus turned the page to reveal an inked drawing of a jewel-encrusted dagger. Beneath it was a second image depicting a full moon, a raging beast, and a man wielding the blade.

"It's not fiction."

"You're mad. Creatures like that don't exist."

A scowl formed on his features. "That's ironic coming from you. Witches exist, ghosts exist, oracles exist, but the Red Wolf and others like him, that's too much for your reality?"

"I've never seen one," I said lamely, knowing the argument was weak but not caring. It was too much to contemplate. "You're talking about werewolves! It's ludicrous."

"It's not. They're real, and I've spent the last few weeks with your grandmother searching for a Grimm's blade so I can destroy one. We tracked the blade to a shipment delivered to an antiquities shop near the docks, but when I got there, it had been sold to another buyer. I was going to visit Winifred again today and see if she could track it."

I returned to the sideboard and refilled my glass, this time to the brim. Throwing back my head, I choked down the fiery liquid. Tears stung my eyes, and I gazed at myself looking frantic in the mirror. This was insane, and yet the newspaper articles describing the dead bodies with claw marks, and Tessa's reluctance to reveal the details of Winifred's wounds...

Maybe it wasn't crazy?

Argus said something else, but I couldn't tear my focus from my reflection. It stared back, unmoving.

Then, something shifted. The reflection rippled like a wave of water under the glass. I leaned closer, stretched my fingers toward the mirror. It rippled again, and gray, smokelike tendrils swirled and converged in the center.

Argus's voice dropped away, and so did his image.

I gripped the sideboard, nails digging into the wood, stomach churning in time with the mirror. *No! I'm not ready for this.*

"Sir!"

The office door burst open, breaking the spell. The glass became smooth as the smoke faded, revealing my stunned reflection. Over my shoulder, the butler lurched into the room, an apology exploding from his lips.

"I'm sorry, sir! This couldn't wait."

My attention snapped to the object in his gloved hands. "What is that?"

He held what appeared to be an iron cuff, with a thick chain trailing from the end. The chain had been shredded apart, and the iron bent at an impossible angle.

The butler stammered another apology. "I'm

sorry, sir, but your sister has escaped."

Chapter 6

ARGUS

I f I was the king of the streets, Hastings was the king of poorly timed arrivals.

"I can explain," I said, motioning to him. To Hastings' credit, he looked guilty and quickly hid the suspicious cuff behind his back. "I know how this looks, but trust me, it was for her safety."

"Her safety?" Vivian blanched and edged closer to the door, prepared to bolt.

"And the safety of others," I muttered. My temple throbbed as an ache spread behind my eyes. It was hard enough to disarm her and explain my association with Winifred, and now, Vivian was scowling at me like I was the worst kind of criminal. Maybe I wasn't up for a sainthood, but I didn't go around keeping innocent people in chains—usually. There was that one time, but they deserved it.

Vivian darted a glance at the door, her intentions written across her face. She wouldn't get far, but I didn't relish chasing her around the house. It would only give her more fuel for the low-life dossier she'd built about me in her head. The thing probably had chapters by now, bookmarked with each of my nefarious deeds.

"Hastings, could you, please?" I cocked my head toward the door, and the butler lunged into action, slamming it closed. He slid the locking bolt home and spun with his back to the handle, guarding the exit.

Vivian huffed an angry breath as her escape route vanished. "What's next? Are you going to use chains on me too?"

Maybe, if I thought it might work. But chains wouldn't do anything to save us from her wrath. If looks could kill butlers following orders, Hastings would be a memory.

"Don't be dramatic. You're not a hostage. Consider yourself a captive listener. It won't do me any good if you run to your witchy friend spouting nonsense about how I keep relatives chained in the basement."

Hastings cleared his throat. "Actually, we don't keep Lady Adella chained in the basement. She prefers her suite of rooms in the west wing."

Vivian's brow rose, and her mouth parted in stunned silence. "So, you do keep her chained?"

I grimaced. "You're not helping, Hastings."

"Sorry, sir." The man fiddled with the clasp on the iron cuff and bowed his head.

"Somebody better start explaining." Vivian's voice rose in pitch, her patience dwindling.

I held up my hands and moved closer. "Relax. Before Hastings arrived, I told you about the Red Wolf. My sister is one of his victims. She was attacked in the courtyard of the Remington estate a few weeks ago. The Remingtons are our closest neighbors, and Adella is good friends with their daughter, Sarah."

"I don't understand." Vivian cast a wary glance at Hastings, who still clutched the restraints. "What does that have to do with chains?"

"When we found her, Adella was in bad shape. She'd been bitten, but thankfully, she was still alive. Over the next few days, her wound healed completely. Faster than it should have. Then, the impulses started. Her appetite changed—"

"Lady Adella has always been a strict vegetarian," Hastings interrupted. "After the attack, she'd only eat meat. The rarer the better."

"What are you saying?" Vivian asked, visibly shaken.

I paused, reluctant to utter the words everyone in the room already suspected. Vivian might not believe it, but she knew where the conversation was headed. It wasn't fair she'd been dragged into this mess. I wasn't happy to be involved either, but choice rarely had anything to do with it. We could only move forward.

"Adella has the killer instinct. She's turning into one of those creatures. They're bound to do the Red Wolf's bidding, and until they adapt, they're mindless with bloodlust."

"The chains were originally Adella's idea," Hastings added. "She was worried she'd hurt one of the servants. It worked at first, but those things are drawn to the moon phases, and they become desperate to break free. Tonight, the moon is full. It's when they hunt."

Vivian grew quiet, and from my limited experience, that wasn't a good sign. She walked toward the hearth and stared into the crackling flames.

I made eye contact with Hastings, trying to gauge my next move. By the rigid line of Vivian's back, I could tell she wasn't taking my explanation well—which wasn't a shock; she'd been through a lot. I still couldn't believe she'd hidden in my office, knife in hand, ready to avenge her grandmother. At a basic level, it was admirable, but that didn't stop my blood from boiling at her wretched attempt. She'd hesitated, and it could have cost her her life.

The fact Vivian's blade was meant for me didn't matter. In anyone else, I would have exploited that weakness, but a haze had come over me; an instinctive need to rage at her and protect her at the same time. I'd landed somewhere in the middle until I realized she'd only brought a single weapon. Who did that? Of all the ill-conceived, foolhardy plans...

"So, that's why you're hunting for a Grimm's blade?" she said, breaking me out of my rage spiral.

"That's right. The blade is the only way to kill a werewolf and break the connection he has over his lineage. Anything less might kill the creature, but enchanted steel can sever the tie. Without severing the tie, any wolves he sired would be enslaved to a dead master and kill in his name. Apparently, that's worse."

Vivian stilled, becoming a marble statue in front of the fire as the light bathed her skin in a soft glow. "Then we'll have to stop her and find the Grimm's blade."

"I didn't ask for your help. Go home. You'll be taken care of."

"I'm not waiting to be asked." She stalked toward me, eyes flashing with emotion. "My grandmother is dead because of you." Unshed tears glistened beneath her lashes. "I'll find the thing that attacked her, and if I need a Grimm's blade to kill it, then I'll find that too, with or without you. It's your choice."

My gaze traveled down the gentle curve of her cheekbones, taking in the slight dusting of freckles on the bridge of her nose. She was a wisp of a thing, barely reaching my shoulders: unskilled in fighting, easy to disarm, reckless. All marks against her. But there was defiance in her eyes and stubbornness in the firm press of her lips, which meant trouble.

It might be my choice, but she wasn't really giving me one. When you have nothing to lose, you'll do anything to win; risk everything with no regard for your safety. She'd already proven that point today. Keeping her close would at least enable me to watch over her and clear my conscience where Winifred was concerned.

"All right. It looks like we have similar goals."

Her jaw clenched. "For now."

"You'll follow my lead? No questions?"

She bristled, her nose scrunching in obvious displeasure. "No promises."

Eh, it was a start. All great partnerships started with a level of distrust. Ours was no different.

She swept past me, and I felt the cold jolt of her dismissal. "So, how do we find your sister? Do you know where she'd go?"

Hastings stepped forward. "Adella has been talking for weeks about the winter festival at the Ashworth estate. She planned to attend with Sarah. It's one of the main social events of the season and would make for a good hunting ground."

"Ashworth?" The name was familiar. "You mean, the Ashworths who own the shipping magnate?"

"Yes, it's the same family."

"That can't be a coincidence," I muttered. The Grimm's blade had traveled on their ship, and I needed the manifest to track the blade to its next location.

"Is there a problem?" Vivian asked.

"We're not the only ones searching for the Grimm's blade," I mused. "The wolves want to find it first. We can't let them get control of the only weapon with the power to defeat them. The Ashworths might have information in their records that can help, and there's a good chance the wolves know about it."

Hastings stepped aside and unlocked the door so Vivian could pass through after she stopped pacing. "Then we'll have to watch our backs," she said. "I'll meet you at the festival around nine. And I suggest you bring along a bigger pair of shackles." She strolled through the door, her skirt fanning around her ankles.

The woman was a whirlwind to the senses. I wasn't sure how she'd entered my house an assassin and left a partner.

Rounding my desk, I removed her knife from where I'd embedded it in the wood and sighed. She'd left behind her weapon.

Unbelievable.

"Would you like me to return it to her, sir?" Hastings asked, barely containing a grin.

"What's the point?" I sank into my chair and massaged my temples. "She has no intention of using it."

Hastings lingered in the doorway while I rifled through a stack of messages piled on my desk. They overflowed across the ink blotter, one problem after another cropping up throughout the kingdom. I shoved them aside and downed the rest of my whiskey.

"I can see you, Hastings. Is there anything else, or do you just enjoy hovering?"

"I enjoy it, sir."

Cheeky bastard. For as many years as he'd been in my employ, he'd never mastered the fearful distance I tried to instill.

"Don't think I won't send out a dispatch looking for a new butler, one who checks guests appropriately for weapons, because I will."

A thoughtful look crossed Hastings' face, and he moved closer to my desk. He tugged the corners of his tailored vest and smoothed a hand over the silver buttons. Expertly polished, they gleamed in the light.

I picked up my quill, intending to ignore him, but his presence grated. Eventually, my head dropped against the back of the chair.

"All right then. You obviously aren't leaving until you've said your piece. Go on."

The jovial expression vanished from his face, wrinkles deepening, betraying his age. "Have you told Miss James about your agreement with the oracle?"

"That's what this is about? I'll tell her when the time is right."

"And would that be before or after you use her to search for the blade?"

"After," I snapped, unable to control the wave of irritation flooding my veins. My tenuous control was slipping. The events of the day were bad enough; I didn't need Hastings' condemnation as well.

He made a discontented sound with his tongue. "So, you believe the rumors she'll develop the gift? If she does, this kingdom will eat her alive. There's a reason oracles live like recluses in the middle of the woods."

His tone chipped my steel exterior. I pushed out of my chair, hands itching with pent-up anger, and stalked across the room to reach for the decanter of whiskey, then poured the amber liquid until it sloshed over the rim. A wet ring formed on the mahogany end table, and I lifted the glass to my lips, breathing in the fiery scent, but I didn't drink.

"She denies seeing anything in the mirror."

"And you think she's telling the truth?"

"No." I laughed softly, placing the drink back on the sideboard. "Winifred knew it would come to this. I see that now. She wasn't a fool, though I question her sanity in asking for any vows from me."

She'd made me promise to watch over Vivian in the event of her death, knowing the few who were blessed with seeing the future were always at risk from an unsavory crowd. What better than a villain to keep other villains away? The promise was easy to make; a necessary evil. Even if the worst came to pass and Vivian became my responsibility, I had a legion of people who could handle the infuriating woman, and enough money to make it happen.

But now, after a single encounter, I resented leaving the task to anyone else. Maybe it was the way she'd looked at me when she thought I killed her grandmother—that reckless determination encased in vulnerability—or maybe it was the way she looked when she realized I hadn't. It didn't matter. The weight of my promise squeezed like a vise inside my chest. Whether Vivian realized it or not, her new powers made her a target, especially for someone like me.

"We need to focus on finding Adella and tracking the Grimm's blade. If Vivian develops the gift, and if it becomes an issue, I'll handle it."

Hastings didn't respond, but his silence spoke volumes. He disapproved of my plan but knew well enough I wouldn't be swayed.

"As you say, sir." He returned to the role of the dutiful butler though his true sentiments remained just below the surface.

This wouldn't be the end of our discussion, I was sure of it.

At the entrance, he paused. "One last thing. You may be known as the king of the streets, but even kings can be dethroned if they're not careful. Don't make the same mistakes your father made."

The door closed softly behind him, trapping his words in the room. They slithered inside me, trying to take hold. I refused to let them. Nothing would destroy what I'd built. Not the Red Wolf, not the promise I'd made, and not the young woman who had looked at me for a second like maybe I could be trusted.

Chapter 7

VIVIAN

The full moon hung low in the sky, a giant ball of silver against the black night. It cast an eerie glow over the Ashworth estate, creating deep shadows.

Standing in the doorway that led to the courtyard, I took in the wintry scene decorated with twinkling lanterns and hanging crystals. A bonfire in a stone basin billowed flames in the center of the courtyard, pushing back the chill. Guests congregated around it, laughing and sipping champagne from slender flutes. Hidden from view, an orchestra played a lively tune, and servants wandered the grounds carrying trays of caviar smeared on golden crisps.

The festival was in full swing.

It was so strange being among people who acted like they didn't have a care in the world. You didn't notice when you were one of them, but when you were on the outside looking in, everything felt unnatural.

I scanned the crowd in search of Argus. Irritation made me tap my heel against the stone terrace. He was late for his own sister's abduction. If we were calling it that. I couldn't believe only a few hours ago we had stood in his office developing a plan to capture a budding werewolf. And where there was one, there were probably more—which meant the place could be crawling with the murderous creatures.

The gathering of laughing, blissfully unaware guests didn't seem so appealing anymore. They were lambs unaware of the literal wolves in their midst.

"Where is he?" I muttered, plucking at the tight bodice beneath my cloak. Argus should be here by now, but I'd searched everywhere, inside and out, and nothing.

Venturing back into the ballroom, I snagged a champagne flute from a passing tray. Was it just me, or were people staring? A pair of elderly matrons whispered behind their fans, and I slipped past them, pulling the edge of my hood up to cover my face. The last thing I wanted was to draw attention as Winifred's granddaughter. I couldn't handle the condolences or the numerous questions I wasn't ready to answer.

It was still too raw. Too devastating. But what scared me the most was the hollowness; the empty feeling that desperately needed to be filled with something, and so far, all that had been available to me was retribution. A bloodlust of my own. Did that make me any better than the wolves we were hunting? I wasn't sure.

Beneath it all was a new affliction I was trying to hide. A seductive whisper. *You know what comes next.* It was a lure that tugged on my insides, visceral, like a siren's voice calling sailors to their doom. I knew what it was, and I refused to answer the call.

Until it answered for me.

The crowd parted, and I caught my reflection in the mirrored wall. It was happening again. The strange sensation I'd felt while looking in the mirror in Argus's office flooded my system. I tried to turn away from it, but it held me in a trance. A smoky film formed over the glass, and the room darkened. Everyone dropped away.

An image formed. Tall hedges dusted with snow. They towered above my head, melding with the black sky. The glow of a lantern disappeared around a corner, and I followed it, leaving a trail of footprints on the frozen path. From somewhere deep inside the walls, a growl broke the silence. The vision wavered, diffusing until it was nothing but indistinct shapes and the echo of a beastly snarl.

Music swelled, and the ballroom came back into sharp focus. Conversation resumed as if it had never stopped, and I squinted, surprised to find the image in the mirror gone. I exhaled long and slow. I didn't want this. Never mind that I couldn't control it; I just needed to stay away from mirrors until I was ready to deal with them.

Turning away, I brought my attention to the task at hand. Where was that blasted man?

Another walk through the ballroom turned up

nothing, and I went back onto the terrace. I took a deep sip of champagne, letting the fizz bubble on my tongue.

"Did you miss me, love?" The low rumble sounded near my ear, startling me, and I inhaled my drink.

Argus slipped the glass from my hand while I cleared my windpipe, painful tears stinging my eyes. He gave me a little smirk and drained the rest of the fruity liquor.

"I wasn't finished with that."

He shrugged and placed the empty glass on the marble railing.

"Where have you been? You're late," I said through gritted teeth.

His gaze tracked over me from head to toe, taking in my satin slippers and the black lace gown peeking out from between the opening of my crimson cloak. I shivered, pretending it was from the cold when his stare was anything but.

"You told me to bring a bigger pair of restraints, and it took hours to go through my vast collection of handcuffs." He winked. "I'll show you sometime."

Heat blasted my cheeks. "Very funny."

"Who's laughing?" His smirk widened into a full grin, sharpening the rugged angles of his face. He looked every inch the villain against the wintry fairy tale backdrop. Dressed fully in black, his jacket was belted at the waist, and the sleeves clung to his muscular frame. As did his dark breeches encased in a pair of leather boots. The stubble covering his jawline only accentuated his roughened features, and the wicked glint in his eyes made me question the sanity of our arrangement.

Somehow, I'd made a deal with the devil to hunt enchanted blades and kill werewolves. This was not normal.

"The least you could do is show up on time. This is *your* sister who's about to go on a killing spree."

"I'm never late. You're the one who can't keep up. While you were busy dabbing lavender water behind your ear, getting ready for this evening..." He paused, leaning forward to whisper, "Smells great, by the way. I was busy collecting the Ashworths' ship manifest."

"I think you mean stealing."

"Semantics." He leaned against the marble railing, crossing a booted foot over his ankle. A dark lock of hair tumbled into his eye as he angled his head, cocking a grin. "I climbed a trellis, scaled a narrow ledge, and picked a lock on a storage cabinet, all while avoiding detection from the guests below. What have you done?"

Oh, I only witnessed an uncontrollable vision surrounded by a room full of oblivious people. Of course, I couldn't tell him that.

I blinked coyly, sweetening my smile until my cheeks ached. "I drank half a glass of champagne, and it was delicious."

Argus chuckled, pushing away from the railing. He placed a hand at my back to guide me down the granite steps lined with flickering torches.

"Half a glass of champagne? What an adventure.

The stories you'll tell your children."

I elbowed him in the ribs, which only made him laugh harder, his breath warm against the base of my neck.

"So, now we have the manifest, all we need to do is find your sister."

"That's a lot of 'we' coming from someone who's only had a few sips of champagne."

Oh, he is infuriating. "Will you be serious? We don't have a lot of time, and she could be anywhere."

"Not anywhere. I spotted her friend Sarah in the crowd. The two are thick as thieves. If Adella's here, Sarah will know." He pointed to a young woman in heated conversation with a tall, expensively dressed man. She swatted his hand away, then turned on her heel, coming up short when she spotted Argus.

The smile that lit her features could have out-shone the moon. I tensed as she started forward, the adoration in her eyes making me uncomfortable. How close were they? He'd said they were neighbors, but was that as far as their relationship went? I shook away the question. It didn't matter, nor was it any of my business.

"Argus! I can't believe you're here. You never come to these sorts of parties unless Adella drags you, and even then, you're usually off playing cards." She curled a lock of brown hair around her finger, still smiling up at him. It only dimmed when her gaze shifted to me.

Argus's hand was still pressed at the small of my back. I could feel the heat between my clothes.

"Sarah, this is Vivian James."

Sarah nodded at the introduction. "It's nice to meet you. How do you know—?"

"Have you seen Adella? Is she here?" he interrupted, earning a frustrated pout from Sarah.

She sighed and stood on her toes. "Yes. Last time I saw her, she was getting ready for the scavenger hunt. It's already started, you know?" Sarah stepped closer, twisting the ties on her eggshell blue cloak. "I still need a partner."

"That's a great idea." The man who'd been talking to her stepped into our circle. He bowed slightly and reached for my hand. "Jason Ashworth. It's a pleasure to meet you, Miss James. I need a partner as well, and I'm hoping you'll do me the honor." His lips grazed my knuckles, lingering over them for too long, and I resisted the urge to snatch my hand back.

A cold feeling spread across my skin. He had the eyes of a predator, sharp and calculating.

Argus made a sound beside me, and then he barreled through our hands, breaking the contact. He snapped his fingers at a waiter, snatching a glass of champagne from his tray and a caviar crisp from another. Returning, he handed them both to me, one for each hand. At least now, they were full.

Sarah frowned, then forced a laugh. "It's settled. Vivian will partner with Jason, and I'll partner with Argus. We'll keep an eye out for Adella while we're inside."

"Inside?" I asked, not liking the way Jason sidled closer. He was leering, and I wanted to toss the drink into his face, except it would be a waste of excellent champagne.

"Inside the garden maze. The hunt is the highlight of the festival. Each set of partners has to find a hidden medallion and make their way to the center of the maze." She hooked an arm around Argus's elbow, gazing up at him, the adoration back in full force.

He wasn't paying attention, too busy watching my hesitation. It was difficult to hide considering the vague vision I'd had took place inside a hedge maze.

I bit back my nerves.

"What's wrong?" He tried to extricate himself from Sarah's serpent grip, but I waved my hand, forcing a smile of my own.

"Nothing is wrong! We'll find your sister faster if we split up." Stuffing the crisp into my mouth, I latched onto Jason's outstretched arm, recoiling a bit from the touch.

Argus's scowl deepened. He'd already charged through us once, and I could tell he was scouting for another way to do it again.

"Let's hurry before we miss her." I started down the well-lit path.

Other guests stood in line at the entrance to the maze. An older gentleman handed out slips of parchment with an image of the medallion containing the Ashworth insignia. When it was our turn, he handed Jason the paper and said, "Good luck, son." The man's attention shifted to me, and there was that predatory gleam again.

Like father, like son.

I took a lantern and held it up to peer into the gaping entrance of the maze. Moonlight carved a dim tunnel through the narrow passage, and dread unspooled in my stomach even as the sounds of laughter echoed from somewhere inside.

The brief scene from the mirror replayed in my mind. My grandmother had often talked about her visions, the flashes of movement, strange objects, and mysterious surroundings. They painted a picture of the future and, in many cases, served as a warning. Different paths diverged from there. In her readings, she would smile and leave the choice to the customer, but she didn't tell them that occasionally it didn't matter; there was no avoiding the future. Once a path was chosen, it didn't always lead in the opposite direction. Sometimes, it circled back, leaving you in your original track. She called that fate.

Entering the maze, we came to our first fork in the path. Behind me, Sarah giggled.

"Let's go right. Jason and Vivian can go left."

A hand fisted my cloak, and I tensed before I heard Argus's whisper against my ear. He'd moved so quickly, pulling me back against him.

"I don't like this," he murmured.

"I can take care of myself. Go find your sister so we can get out of here. I'm sure by the time I've finished half my champagne, you'll have figured out the maze, tracked Adella, and found your medallion. I'll just try to keep up."

I couldn't see it, but I knew he smiled. "You do

that." His head dipped, mouth grazing the shell of my ear. "And by the way, you still smell good."

"Argus, let's go!" Sarah stamped her foot and huffed a breath of frozen air.

"Be careful." He let go of my cloak, then followed Sarah down the darkened path.

I watched them until they disappeared, my body humming from the way he'd pressed up against me.

"This way." Jason nudged me to the left, and I danced out of his reach when he went to wrap an arm around my waist. I clenched the glass flute. Maybe I'd toss the precious liquid in his face after all.

Instead, I drained it, then thrust the empty into his hand. Liquid courage coursed through my veins.

All right. Let's go find us a werewolf.

Chapter 8

VIVIAN

I trailed my fingers along the manicured hedges, looking up as we tunneled deeper into the maze. Jason droned on behind me, sometimes stepping too close. Those were the moments I picked up my pace and used the weak glow of the lantern to light my way.

He talked about the ship he captained and the cargo he ferried to the many islands surrounding the kingdom, and I pretended to listen. Every once in a while, we heard voices coming from another direction, muffled through the thick foliage. When we came to a dead end, he chuckled, the soft laugh sending shivers of foreboding up my spine. Jason reached for the lantern and placed it on the ground.

"Let's stop for a moment. There's no need to rush when I'm in such lovely company." He let the scrap of paper describing our medallion flutter to the ground.

Apparently, our search was over. No wonder Sarah

had swatted him away when we saw them talking. The man was a complete libertine, quick with the hands, and without any notion of my desire for personal space.

"I think we should keep looking. This place creeps me out."

"I don't know." He shuffled closer, the bulk of his frame leaning forward. Capturing a lock of hair that had fallen loose from my topknot, he tucked it behind my ear. "I think it's romantic. We're all alone, and you look beautiful in the moonlight."

I angled my head away, stepping back. My shoulders brushed against the coarse leaves of the hedge.

"We should keep looking."

The curve of his mouth twisted. "I'm not here to look for a stupid medallion. You want to win? Here." He withdrew a bronze medallion engraved with the Ashworth Shipping emblem from his jacket pocket and thrust it into my hand. "Now, we can move on to other activities." He gripped my waist, fingers digging into the flesh, and shoved me back against the spongy hedge. My body sank but didn't fall through the thick branches.

Surprise quickly turned into fury as I grappled for leverage in his hold. "You're despicable. Get off me."

"Come on, you know you want it. You're here with Argus Ward—I know the kind of women who flock around him. Don't play coy."

The thick, pungent scent of his cologne assailed my senses, making my stomach turn. He tore at the ties keeping my cloak together. The knot was almost too much for his fumbling fingers.

"Stop!" I pushed his hands away.

"That's it, I don't mind if you're feisty. I can play rough too." His harsh breath was like acid against my skin. He twisted the fabric of my cloak, frustration at the knots making him impatient.

"I'm warning you..."

Gaze darkening with lust, he was beyond listening, and when his palm roamed over my abdomen, reaching higher, I'd had enough.

Jackass.

"Hey, I'm up here."

He looked, and I rammed the heel of my hand into his nose, thrusting upward until I heard the cartilage crack. Jason's head snapped back, and blood gushed from between his hands as he clutched his nose. My knee connected with his groin, and he went down hard into the snow, wheezing in tortured gulps of air.

Skirting around him, I swept up the lantern and tossed his medallion to the ground.

"You bitch! You'll pay for that." He climbed unsteadily to his feet and lurched toward me, blood streaming down his face.

I ran.

The first turn came up fast, and I went right. My slippers slid, losing traction around the bend. I grabbed for the hedge to keep me upright, but it bowed beneath my weight. Off-balance, I dropped the lantern, and the flame extinguished, plunging me into darkness.

Jason was close behind, grunting in pain and cursing with each thundering step. I kept moving, using the hedge to guide me around the turns until my vision acclimated to the dim moonlight. Where was everyone? The maze was deathly still, and every path I chose was layered with fresh snow, a sign no one had gone that way. Fear toyed with the edges of my mind, telling me I'd gone too far, that I'd never find my way out.

A yelp of pain echoed behind me, then stopped short.

I came to a staggering stop, breathing heavily. A branch snapped, and my head jerked toward the sound. Jason or someone was still out there. Another branch cracked, then came the low, throaty rumble of a growl.

Not someone.

Some...*thing.*

Blood rushed through my ears, and my heart raced. The rustling drew closer, and I stepped backward until I came to the next split in the maze.

There! The soft glow of a lantern disappeared around a distant corner. I followed it, glancing over my shoulder, afraid of what might appear behind me. When I finally reached the spot where it had been, the light was gone. Choosing a series of other paths, I quickly came to a dead end.

Damn it.

I was hopelessly lost, and that thing was still out there.

Swallowing a frustrated whimper, I turned to go

back the way I came when footsteps began thudding down the path. There was nowhere to hide and nowhere to run. The walls towered on either side of me, and the only option was to face whatever was coming.

I needed a weapon.

Reaching up, I unwound my hair to release the topknot. Cascades of dark waves fell around my shoulders. I clutched the jeweled spike that held it all together, pointing the sharp end out between my knuckles. Okay, so it wasn't a broadsword or a razor-tipped dagger, but the only weapon I owned was probably still lodged in Argus's desk.

The figure loomed closer, right around the next bend. Besides the spike, I had the element of surprise. Sending up a wish that I wouldn't be mauled inside a hedge maze, I ran toward the sound.

Something hard collided with me at the intersection of the two paths. Arms banded around my waist, my feet flailing in the air as they left the ground. The jeweled spike slipped from my hand and landed in the snow. Frantic, I jabbed with my elbow, connecting with hard flesh. Someone grunted in pain, and then I was free, scrambling on my hands and knees. I found the silver pick and spun around, thrusting the sharp end forward.

A powerful hand grabbed my wrist, and my momentum slammed to a halt.

"If you're aiming for my heart, love, it's a little to the left."

Air whooshed from my lungs. Argus leaned over

me, his body pressing me into the snow. Our faces were inches apart, icy breaths mingling. His eyes were reflective pools in the moonlight, and the harsh planes of his face were cut with shadows.

But I didn't miss the quirk of his lips.

"What are you doing here?" I rasped, relief making my head spin.

"Trying not to get stabbed by you for the second time." He lifted a brow. "Though, I am impressed with your follow-through."

"Yeah, well, I learned my lesson. You were quite demonstrative."

"I can be."

His gaze dipped to my mouth, and heat pooled in my stomach. I could only guess what his next lesson would be, and from this angle, I could see myself as a willing participant.

"Is that from your hair?"

"Huh?" I blinked, tilting my head back to see my jeweled spike still caught in his grip.

"Oh, yeah. You still have my favorite and only dagger, so I had to be resourceful."

"I only have it because you went home without it."

"You should have brought it with you and given it to me here."

He scoffed, shifting his weight, but kept me pinned to the ground. "No way, love. I'm keeping it. It's not every day a woman like yourself threatens to kill me in my own home. You can pick out a new one. Actually, you can pick out two because I'm generous."

It was my turn to laugh. "Generous? Then you won't mind if I take three."

"Ah, now there's my limit." He rolled to the side and held out a hand, waiting to help me up. When I reached for him, Argus went still, focusing on the dried blood smeared across my palm. With a curse, he rolled up the sleeve on my cloak in search of the injury. "You're bleeding. Did I hurt you when we landed? You should have said something."

"It's not mine." I tugged out of his grip and grabbed a fistful of snow, trying to scrub the stain from my skin.

"Whose is it? Wait… Where's Ashworth?"

"There was an incident. Don't worry. I didn't stab him, but his nose is broken, and he might walk funny for a while."

Argus's features hardened. "Did that bastard touch you?" He rammed his fist into the ground. "I knew I shouldn't have let you go with him."

"It's fine. I'm sure he'll think twice about doing something like that again." My mood had soured thinking about Jason, but it soured further when I remembered Sarah. "What happened to your shadow? Don't tell me she tried to kiss you too?" I muttered under my breath, "Is it too much to hope she's nursing a busted nose somewhere as well?"

"I heard that. You're exceptionally ruthless."

"Says the felon."

He pulled me to my feet and straightened the cloak over my shoulders. My hair had tangled in the ties, and he gently unwound the strands.

"Sarah's a good kid. But no, something was following us, so I foisted her off on a group leaving the maze and then came to find you."

"Something was following me too. It's just like I saw in the mirror."

With his fingers still working to free my hair, Argus paused. "The mirror? I thought you said you don't see things in the mirror."

I brushed his hands away. "I don't."

"You're lying."

"No." I was omitting. There was a difference.

"Vivian—"

A scream pierced the night, ending in a guttural moan that made the hair stand on the back of my neck. It sounded close.

"Stay here," Argus said.

"In your dreams." I held onto the back of his jacket as we raced through the passage. There was no way in hell he was leaving me alone inside the maze. Not after that!

The entrance to the clearing appeared. Moonlight spilled into the center of the maze, turning the white landscape silver. Snow-covered benches were aligned in a circle converged around a raised circular platform.

Jason Ashworth lay unmoving in the middle.

Deep slashes covered his body, and blood had soaked through his clothes, trickling down the stone. His eyes were open and stared lifelessly at the night sky.

The hair pick slipped from my fingers.

We were too late.

Argus moved to inspect the body while I stood at the base of the platform unable to close my eyes to the horrific scene. Only minutes ago, Jason was alive. Insufferable, but alive.

"There are clawlike tracks in the snow. They don't look human," I said softly.

"Not entirely. Do you believe me now?"

"Your sister?"

He held my gaze. "Maybe. I don't know. It could have been another."

How many were there? I was afraid to find out.

Voices echoed through the maze, moving in our direction.

"Argus…" I scanned the clearing. There was only one way into the center. We were going to be found with the body. Icy panic spread through my system.

"Don't say anything to anyone. They can't hold us."

Easy for him to say. I didn't want to go to prison, whether they could hold us or not!

A group of men entered the clearing, their gazes landing on Jason's ravaged form. It was utter chaos. The men advanced, grabbing Argus and shoving him to his knees. One of them approached me, and I lifted my hands, sinking into the snow.

My heart pounded at the words that reverberated in my head.

"Arrest them!"

Chapter 9

ARGUS

"Y ou know, glaring at me isn't going to get you out of here." I shifted my weight, trying to find a comfortable spot on the stone floor. The cramped cell was no bigger than one of my closets, and don't get me started on the smell. Dank air, ripe with the stink of rotting meat and mold. Somewhere in the shadows, a steady drip tested my sanity, followed by the clawing sound of scampering rats that refused to stay in the walls where they belonged.

Vivian's gaze burned through the slits in the metal bars. She didn't appear fond of the accommodation either. Her bitter tone proved my suspicions.

"No, but it makes me feel better. You said they couldn't hold us!"

I had said that, and I still believed it. Things were just taking longer than I anticipated.

"At least you're talking to me again. That's progress."

She rolled her eyes, looking more princess than prisoner sitting in the cell across from mine. Her dark hair flowed in tousled waves past her shoulders, gleaming in the light from a nearby torch. Layers of lace pooled around her slipper-clad feet, which were streaked with mud from her trek across the dungeon floor.

"We lost your sister, Jason Ashworth is dead, and I'm in a filthy dungeon! I don't want to talk to you; I want to strangle you. This was the worst plan." She slumped against the wall and slung her arms across her chest, lips flat with disgust. If her frown went any deeper, it would dig a hole.

I stifled a grin. Now wasn't the time to smile, but her pout could rival the queen's. I half-expected her to snap her fingers and make the rats scatter in deference.

"This is temporary. They don't have any proof. Besides, I'm sure your witchy friend is doing everything possible to get us out. Once she convinces that self-righteous detective of hers we're innocent, we'll be free in no time."

Vivian straightened, angled her head up a notch, and her eyes flashed with indignation. "Derrick isn't self-righteous. He cares about people and the cases he works on. He's a good person. A model citizen."

Her unspoken words hung in the air like a challenge. *Good, unlike you.* My jaw ached from clenching it too hard.

"It must take one to know one then."

"As long as you know it." She sighed, dismissing

me with her whole body. The chill in the murky chamber was a tropical paradise compared to the icy front Vivian displayed. If only she could freeze the water wherever that dripping noise was coming from.

It grated.

But so did our circumstances. The night hadn't gone to plan. Understatement of the century. Ashworth was dead, and we'd been taken in for questioning—except there hadn't been any questions, only a straight march into the confines of the prison. It had been hours since we'd seen anyone. Hell, it had been hours since Vivian acknowledged my presence. Though, I preferred her sullen silence to her fiery defense of my least favorite detective.

Footsteps echoed down the long corridor, and a set of iron keys jangled in the lock. The rusty door opened on its hinges. I pushed away from the wall and gripped the metal bars. A man came into view carrying two covered trenchers. I wasn't sure which was worse: the smell coming from him, or the one billowing from under the loose lids.

Nope, I knew. It was definitely the food.

"Breakfast," the guard grumbled. He dropped the trenchers outside our cells, and they landed with a thunk on the stone. Bending over, he lifted the lids and slid the trenchers through a narrow opening before trudging back down the passage.

The iron door clanged behind him, and the lock turned.

Vivian eyed her food warily. She moved closer

to the steaming bowl, and her stomach growled. Hope morphed into revulsion on her face. Her nose scrunched, and she covered her mouth with the back of her hand.

"I think I'm going to be sick." She dipped a grimy spoon into the viscous sludge. The stew made a slurping sound when she withdrew the utensil. "Yeah, I'm definitely going to be sick."

My meal was less offensive. As expected. The trencher held an apple, crusty bread, and a large chunk of cheese. Vivian followed my gaze and gasped, pressing herself against the bars to get a closer look.

"Hey! How come yours is different?"

I scratched the nape of my neck, feeling guilty. "I know a guy."

She deflated into a pile of limbs and lace on the floor only to gag when her hand slid in something sticky. "Of course you do. Why am I not surprised? You probably have dirt on the jailer. Let me guess, he owes you money."

"Close. His brother owes me money."

Tossing her hands in the air, she snarled at her steaming trencher of goo. "Unbelievable. Is there anyone in this kingdom who doesn't owe you something?"

"You don't." I watched her reaction from across the corridor.

Vivian took a breath and twisted the folds of her skirt, startled by my statement. "That's right. I don't owe you anything, and I never will."

Her tone tightened my insides. *Such certainty.* Was I that wicked? And so what, if I was? The way I did things was necessary—roaming the streets had taught me that. Firsthand experience with death and squalor had molded me, not a fancy set of philosophical morals. She'd probably never gone a day without food. I peered at her bowl of gruel. If she was going to be surly, then maybe it was only fair she should experience hunger.

Vivian groaned and pushed her food away, slinking further into the shadows of her cell. Silence blanketed the dungeon except for the cursed sound of water hitting stone. And the rats. They were still lurking.

I grabbed the apple from my trencher and tossed it in my palm. The tart fruit made my mouth water and long for one of my cook's lavish meals. I lifted it to my lips, an inch from biting into its thin skin, and hesitated.

Damn it.

My eyes drifted shut as I exhaled. The devil on my shoulder cackled and called me an idiot.

Lowering the apple, I shrugged out of my jacket and placed the fruit in the satin lining. The bread followed, and I broke off a piece of cheese, then wrapped them all in the coat.

"Here. I'm not hungry. Someone might as well eat it, and since you're the only other person here..."

Vivian poked her head into the light, her eyes wide. "Are you serious?" Her stomach growled, loud and angry, impatient for me to answer.

"Jeez, take it before the earthquake in your stomach causes the whole place to fall around our ears. Catch." I maneuvered the bundle of food through the bars and tossed it over the aisle.

She caught it in both hands, blushing furiously. "Sorry. I can't control it. I've barely eaten anything since..." Her voice faded, and she pressed her lips together.

She didn't need to finish. Winifred's memory filled my mind.

Unwrapping the bundle, Vivian used my coat as a makeshift picnic blanket. "Are you sure you don't want any?"

I showed her the remaining piece of cheese and swallowed it whole. "I'm good."

She ripped the bread apart and chewed slowly, not meeting my gaze. "At least your mother taught you to share."

"I'll let her know you approve of my manners next time I visit."

The bread lodged in her throat, and she coughed. "What? You have a mother?"

"Well, I didn't crawl out from under a rock, if that's what you're asking. Shocking, isn't it?"

She ducked her head, hiding behind a wave of thick hair. "I meant that she's still living. Obviously, you have a mother. That came out wrong."

"No, it didn't. It's clear what you meant."

Brushing her hair over her shoulder, she fixed me with a thoughtful stare. "Look, I'll admit, I'm curious. You're not exactly what one would consider a family man, yet you're doing all of this to help your half-sister, your servants aren't living in fear, and now, you have this elusive mother. It's unexpected."

"What can I say? I'm a man of mystery."

She scoffed and stuffed more bread into her mouth, speaking between bites. "Does she approve of your lifestyle?"

"You mean, my life of crime and debauchery?"

Vivian nodded.

"Who do you think taught me to pick pockets, then *share* my findings with her?"

The hint of a smile quirked her lips before she contained it. Food definitely made her more agreeable. It was as if she'd forgotten she wanted to strangle me earlier.

"Where is she now?"

"Tormenting a neighboring kingdom. I'll let you know next time there's a family reunion."

An odd silence descended, and she turned her attention to the apple, running her fingers over the fruit. I probably shouldn't have mentioned family reunions. It was too soon, the pain too raw.

I let her eat quietly, trying to find the right time to ask the question that had been on my mind since the maze. Vivian might be attempting to hide it, but she'd started to develop the oracle's powers.

Clearing my throat, I took a shot. "Tell me about the vision you had in the mirror. Was it your first one?"

She stopped mid-chew and visibly swallowed. "I don't know what I saw, and I've only had one other experience. It's…disturbing."

"Do you think you could do it again?"

Vivian dropped the apple core onto my jacket and shook her head. "I knew it."

"Knew what?"

"You want to use me to find the Grimm's blade, the same way you did with Winifred. That's all this is." She gestured toward my shared meal. "It's why you agreed to let me help in the first place."

"No. That's not—"

The iron door swung open and banged against the wall. Tessa charged down the passageway.

"Viv? Where are you?" She stopped in front of Vivian's cell and crouched on her ankles, slipping her hands between the bars. "I'm getting you out of here."

The witch looked over her shoulder as Detective Chambers approached. He pushed a key into the lock and opened Vivian's cell, then stepped back as Tessa rushed inside.

"Ew, what is that awful smell?" The witch covered her nose.

"Breakfast," Vivian murmured.

"Let's go. I'm taking you home."

Vivian cast me an unreadable look and reached for my coat. The witch snatched it out of her hands and dropped it on top of the foul stew. There was no getting the smell out now. Hastings would be furious. Vivian winced but followed Tessa out of the cell.

"Thank you for coming," she said, giving the detective a watery smile.

I bristled when he placed a hand on her shoulder and returned it. A gentleman to the core. A knight in shining armor. *Blare the freaking trumpets already.* He walked them to the door leading out of the prison.

"Can you take it from here?" he asked the witch.

"I'll get Vivian settled." She squeezed his hand and mouthed a thank-you.

Vivian paused in the doorway, looking at me over her shoulder. "What about Argus?"

"Yeah, what about me?"

"You can rot." Tessa scowled, then grabbed Vivian's hand and pulled her through the gate.

I craned my neck as they disappeared down the long hall.

Detective Chambers remained in the doorway, spinning the key ring around his index finger. He approached my cell, a half-grin plastered across his face.

"Prison suits you."

I gripped the bars until my knuckles ached. "Open the door."

"You're not going anywhere. I have two recent murders, and you're connected to both victims. Not to mention, a few of the others." He leaned closer. "I've been waiting a long time to put you away, and you're making it too easy. It's almost disappointing."

"Well, we don't want that, do we?"

The detective's jaw clenched, and his voice dropped. "Your first mistake was ever going near Tessa. Your second mistake was showing your face around her friend. You won't be making a third."

Rage made my words clipped. "You can't keep me in here. I didn't kill Jason Ashworth or Winifred James. There's a killer out there, and Vivian could be in danger."

"Vivian doesn't concern you."

Denial ripped through my chest. "Vivian is mine —" I took a breath. "My responsibility."

"Not if I can help it." He reached for the torch flickering outside my cell. "You won't be needing this anymore."

"Send someone to her house."

"Give it up, Argus. You lose." Turning on his heel, he stalked toward the gate, taking the torch with him.

"Open the door!"

The metal grate slammed shut.

I closed my eyes and rested my head against the iron bars, feeling the icy chill against my skin. Control slipped through my fingers, making my chest tighten like a vise. When I opened my eyes, the darkness closed in, sucking me under.

For the first time in a long time, I tasted the bitter flavor of defeat.

Chapter 10

VIVIAN

Tessa grabbed my key and jammed it in the lock. "If I catch you looking over your shoulder one more time, you're coming home with me."

To say she was irritated at having to break me out of prison was an understatement. She hadn't stopped berating me since we left the agency. At my silence, Tessa circled back to the beginning.

"What were you thinking, getting involved with Argus Ward? I told you to stay away from him. You're lucky I was able to convince Derrick's superior he should let you go. This is serious. A man is dead—"

"I know how serious this is, Tess. And I'm grateful for everything, but I had to do something."

"Okay, but that doesn't mean you partner with Argus and go hunt werewolves. It's dangerous, and I'm not sure which one is worse."

"I'd say the werewolves are worse."

Tessa wrinkled her nose and shoved the door open. "It's a toss-up."

I stepped into the entryway and looked around. Everything was in its place, which seemed impossible considering how much had changed in the last few days. How dare my sitting room mock me with its sameness?

Before Tessa could shut the door, I looked over my shoulder a final time, fully expecting to see Argus lurking in the shadows or dogging my heels spouting arrogant remarks. His presence had begun to feel like an anchor in a storm, and now that it was gone, I felt adrift.

Which was more ridiculous than me hunting werewolves! It was insane. If Tessa found out, she'd have me committed. I'd be sipping tea in a whitewashed room at the kingdom's Home for Lost Souls before the day was done.

Barely containing a full-body shudder, I slumped into a plush chair. Tessa sat across from me and folded her arms in her lap. She cocked her head like a mother hen and all but clucked.

"Stop hovering."

"I'm not hovering; I'm catering to your every need. There's a difference. My thing is less annoying."

"No, they're about the same." I sighed and rested my head against the cushion. I needed a bath. My clothes and hair stank like the foul air in the dungeon, and I was definitely throwing out my shoes.

"Are you hungry?" Tessa asked, leaning forward.

"I can fix you something to eat. Anything you want."

"No, I'm not hungry." Guilt washed over me. I wasn't hungry because Argus had given me his meal. I don't think he intended to, but for whatever reason, he did. And then I left him down there, alone. A second wave of guilt crested. He wouldn't have done the same to me, I was sure of it.

In a strange sort of reversal, I felt like the villain.

My gaze drifted toward the window overlooking the bustling street. "You know what you can do for me?"

"Anything—just name it."

"Run me a bath? I smell like I took the dungeon home with me. It would help me to relax."

Tessa bounded out of the chair. "Of course! That should have been my first offer. Stay here, I'll get it ready." She slipped through the beaded doorway, and the long strings swayed back into place.

I craned my neck, counting to ten before dashing toward a small end table. Reaching inside a drawer, I retrieved a piece of paper and a pen.

"Did you want me to use lavender oils?" Tessa poked her head back through the beads.

Startled, I slammed the drawer closed on my finger. "I was just looking for something," I stammered, wincing at my terrible acting and high-pitched tone.

She made a face. "Okay...did you find it?"

"Ah, no. It must be in the other room. Lavender oils sound great."

A beat of awkward silence passed before Tessa nodded. She looked like she wanted to question me further but instead left to resume her task. I exhaled in relief and rubbed my throbbing finger. It served me right for going behind her back, but it wasn't going to stop me either.

I dipped the pen in a well of ink, the nib hovering over the page while I tried to form the right words. They should be simple and to the point. Emotionless and brief. I didn't want anyone reading into my meaning.

Hastings,

Argus needs your help. He's being held in the kingdom's dungeon.

Sincerely,
Ms. James

There. That was perfect. I blew on the wet ink and listened for movement inside the house. The last thing I needed was Tessa returning to ask about water temperature or candle placement. Folding the note, I sealed it closed with a drop of wax and climbed to my feet. The beads were my next opponent, and I cursed as I slipped through them. They made a rippling noise, and I froze in place, waiting to see if I'd alerted Tessa.

The sound was met with silence.

Breathing in relief, I found my coin purse, then painstakingly slipped back through the beads and out the front door. Carriages rumbled past, kicking up loose gravel. The lane was thick with people tucked deep into their coats. I caught the eye of a young boy playing with marbles in the street and called out to him.

"Hey, kid!"

He studied me, then sauntered over with a noticeable limp. I palmed a couple of coins, offering them to him when he approached. The boy's eyes widened, and his lips went slack.

"I have a job for you. Can I trust you?"

The boy nodded, features solemn. "Yes, Miss. I'm as trustworthy as they come. You can ask anyone."

"What's your name?"

"Timmy."

"Well, Timmy, this is important. I have a letter I need delivered as fast as you can."

"There's no one faster, Miss."

"I hope so, Timmy. This letter needs to be delivered to the Lennox mansion. Do you know where that is?"

Timmy laughed and scuffed his shoe in the dirt. "'Course, I do. Who doesn't know the Lennox mansion?"

"Good. You're to give this to the butler. His name is Hastings." I placed the letter and the coins in Timmy's calloused hands, then leaned in and whispered, "There's more money for you after you deliver the note. Tell Hastings that Vivian James said so. He'll make sure you're properly rewarded, but be quick about it."

Timmy bounced on his heels. "You can count on me."

With a curt wave, he took off down the street,

hobbling as fast as his feet would carry him. When he disappeared around the corner, I went back inside, feeling less guilty. Hastings would take care of everything. My conscience was clear.

"Bath's ready," Tessa called from the other room.

I followed her voice, smelling the hint of lavender as I moved through the house. Steam hung in the air, and the tub was filled to the brim with heated water. The scented haven melted the strain from my muscles before I even had a chance to climb inside.

"Toss your clothes in the hallway. I'll get them washed." Tessa buzzed around the small room lighting candles. "Oh, and one other thing. I wasn't sure if I should mention it earlier." She tapped her foot and darted a glance to the wall, clearly hesitant to come out with it.

"Just tell me," I said, bracing for more bad news.

"Derrick mentioned the prince ordered a public memorial for your grandmother tomorrow. He wants the kingdom to be able to pay their respects. They're holding it in the town square. If you're not ready, you don't have to go."

I felt gut-punched. A memorial? It shouldn't have come as a surprise, but I wasn't ready to say goodbye. Tessa droned on, but all I heard was a humming inside my head. Grief was such a strange thing. There were moments where I almost believed none of it had happened and my life was normal. Then, the next moment, it all came crashing in.

"I know it's morbid, but Derrick thinks it's a good idea," Tessa said.

I snapped to attention, catching the last of her words. "What's a good idea?"

She looked uncomfortable again, preferring to stare at the walls. "I guess it's not uncommon for someone's killer to attend their memorial. Derrick is planning to have agents posted around the square. There's a chance we might be able to determine who it was or maybe uncover more clues. Like I said, you don't have to go."

"I'm going." I took a deep breath, letting hot steam fill my lungs. It burned, adding to the heaviness already inside my chest. "Tell Derrick I'll be there. If there's any chance of finding who killed her, I want to take it. No matter what."

"It's your call, Viv. I'll be with you the entire time. We'll do it together." She pulled me into a hug.

The numbness inside me spread even as Tessa's arms tightened.

"I'd like to be alone for a while."

Tessa nodded, wiping at the tears spiking her lashes. "I'll be in the kitchen. Take as much time as you need." She retreated from the room, closing the door softly behind her.

I stood in the swirling steam feeling disoriented. Loneliness clashed with the anger in my heart. I caught sight of my reflection in the mirror above the vanity, my image partly obscured by an opaque film. It taunted me, called me to look deeper, and I had the sudden urge to smash it.

I didn't want to see the future. I wanted to bury myself in the past, where the world made sense. The lump in the back of my throat ached, and the longer I stared, the harder I tried to cry. I needed to purge the well of grief lodged deep inside me, but the tears never came.

Maybe that was a good thing. I feared once they started, they'd never stop.

***

"Do you feel better?" Tessa asked from her seat at the kitchen table. She lifted a pot of tea and poured the steaming liquid into a cup.

"Yes." I tucked my damp braid over my shoulder. "The bath helped with the smell."

She pushed the cup and saucer closer to me. "The rest will get better with time. I put some powder in there to help you sleep."

"Thanks." The tea tasted bitter, but I drank deep, longing for the oblivion that could be found at the bottom of the cup.

"I can stay with you tonight, if you want?" Tessa sipped her tea, watching me closely over the brim.

"It's not necessary. I'll be fine by myself. Besides, I know you and Derrick have plans."

Tessa's cheeks flushed pink. "I can change them. He won't mind."

"Don't be silly. I'm happy for you. You deserve it. There's no use staying here when I can already feel the effects of the tea. I'll be snoring in no time."

"You do snore like a bear." Tessa winked.

"Yeah, well, you talk in your sleep," I grumbled.

Finishing her cup, she pushed out of her chair.

"Dinner's on the counter if you're hungry. I brought in more wood for the fireplace, and there's fresh water in the basin. I'll be here first thing in the morning to help you get ready. We'll go over to the memorial together." She hesitated. "Are you sure you don't want me to stay?"

"I'm sure!"

"All right, fine. You don't have to get cranky about it. Keep the door locked. Derrick's sending an officer to watch over your house tonight, so don't be alarmed if you see someone outside." Her features softened. "Get some rest. It will help."

"I will. And Tessa, thank you for everything. I mean it."

She rolled her eyes to the ceiling. "Why have friends if they can't get you out of jail? See you tomorrow."

The front door closed, and I sighed, pouring myself a second cup of tea. Another dash of Tessa's sleeping powder was warranted, and I sprinkled it liberally into the cup. Whatever was in it was doing its job. My bones felt spongy, and my head was heavy on my shoulders. A few sips, and I swayed in the chair, blinking to keep my eyelids open.

Leaving the kitchen, I trudged toward the bedroom, my feet stone blocks that got more difficult to lift with each step. The bed beckoned, and I collapsed into it, tossing the covers over my body. My breathing evened out as the potion dragged me under until finally, I slept.

***

A strange sound woke me.

I peeled my eyelids open, letting my vision adjust to the dark and the spill of moonlight coming in through the window. Groggy and confused, I listened for the sound I'd heard.

There it was. The creak of a footstep echoed in the hallway. Fear pooled, then froze like ice inside my veins.

Someone was in the house.

Sleep deserted me, replaced by an alertness that made my heart thud behind my rib cage. I pulled back the covers and swung my feet over the bed until they touched the cold floor. Reaching for the nightstand, I wrapped my fingers around a heavy iron candlestick. My palm was sticky with sweat, and I tightened my grip.

Another footstep crept closer to my room. The door was slightly ajar, and the faint glow of a candle flame spread through the crack.

I pressed my back against the wall. Mouth dry, I tried to swallow and bit the side of my cheek to keep from making a noise. The figure on the other side of the door paused, and for a terrifying moment, I held my breath, raising the candlestick in the air.

"You're going to hit me when I open this door, aren't you?" Argus's voice punctured my fear, and I nearly dropped the candlestick.

I whipped open the door, extinguishing his flame. He grunted, and I heard him fumbling in his pocket.

A match ignited, then the flame caught, illuminating his hardened features.

"Are you crazy? Why are you skulking around my house in the middle of the night? You scared me!"

"In my defense..." He stopped, his lips twitching as if he was working out the words in his head before saying them.

"You have no defense! You're supposed to be locked up."

He leaned against the doorjamb. His clothes were different, and he looked hastily dressed. It shouldn't have done him justice, but he wore disarray well. Argus cocked his head and lifted a brow, curling his lips in a devilish smirk.

"I didn't know you cared so much."

Flustered, I took a step back, putting some much-needed space between us. "I don't."

"Then why send Hastings your note? You could have left me to languish alone in the dungeon. Most people would have."

I refused to answer, thankful for the low light that hid the flush of my cheeks. Argus seemed to notice anyway because his grin deepened.

"Either way, Hastings sent along a care package. I left it in the kitchen. Not that he let me have any. I promise you, there were always only three scones."

My eyes closed as I counted to five, trying to calm my racing heart. "What are you doing here?"

"Hastings worked his magic. You know, for a butler, he has a lot of pull. In the end, your favorite detective had no choice but to let me go. I'll never forget the look on Detective Chambers' face. In fact, I'm remembering it right now."

"That doesn't explain why you're in my house."

"No? I thought it did." He pushed past me into the room, peering around. "This is not what I expected. I thought you'd be messier."

"Get out."

Argus raised his hands. "Easy. I'm here because I think it's time you and I had a little talk about those new powers you inherited."

"I don't want to talk about them."

"Not even if they could provide a lead on the Grimm's blade? Maybe even find your grandmother's killer?"

I gritted my teeth. "What lead?"

"That's where you come in." He flourished a small hand mirror from the depths of his jacket. "Let's take a look, shall we?"

Chapter 11

ARGUS

Vivian eyed the mirror as if it were a snake coiled around my wrist. Slowly, her gaze lifted to mine, and suddenly, I felt like the snake. I'd seen fear in the eyes of merchants, shop-keepers, and hardened sailors, but it wasn't fear darkening her gaze. It was disappointment.

Fear, I knew how to handle. Disappointment, on the other hand, made my throat close up.

"I'm not—"

"You're not what?"

She seemed able to read my thoughts, judging them before I said them out loud; before I'd even made sense of them myself. "I'm not using you, if that's what you're thinking."

Her disappointment morphed into disbelief.

Neither was helping my cause.

"What I mean is, I am using you, but it's not solely for my personal gain. Which, I'll have you know, is rare."

"Lucky me." Vivian brushed past me down the hallway. Her abrupt departure nearly extinguished my candle for the second time.

I tucked the mirror back into my jacket and cupped my hand around the flickering flame. "So, is that a no?"

Her silence was my answer.

A cold and very telling silence.

I should have eased into the mirror. Dealing with Vivian was a twisting jungle of dead ends. Usually, I'd just hack my way through, but with her, bluntness only made the jungle more impenetrable.

Rubbing the bridge of my nose, I sighed as exhaustion flowed through every limb. I'd never felt so bone-tired in my life. It was stupid to come here. I don't know why I did. She'd left me sitting alone in the dungeon, hadn't even tried to plead my case. She hadn't looked back. The fact she'd sent a note to Hastings was…surprising. In a good way.

There was a guard outside her house standing to attention, hand on the hilt of his decorative sword. At least the detective had listened to my suggestion—even if it was a poor excuse for protection. It hadn't taken much to sneak past the guard and climb in through the kitchen window, which only went to show how much she needed me. Any number of villainous scoundrels could have broken in.

I know because one did.

I followed her down the hallway, poking my head inside darkened rooms. My curiosity about Vivian grew stronger by the second. The place suited her. It was well-kept, with a cozy interior. Swaths of color-ful fabric gave each room a bohemian feel, and eclec-tic statues lined wooden shelves.

"What's the rent on this place?"

"There isn't any," Vivian answered. She bent over the kitchen hearth stoking the fire, then swung a kettle over the flames. "I inherited it. You'd be amazed at what people leave you in their will when you help their loved ones to cross over." She turned her back to the fire, and the orange glow framed her body, making her look like one of the phantoms she was so fond of helping. A sad smile curved her lips. "The truth is, I haven't seen any ghosts since the night my grandmother died. I think they're gone and they're not coming back."

I leaned against the kitchen table. It seemed to me that being free of spirits would be a good thing, but not to her.

"You miss them?"

"Very much. That probably sounds strange to you, but they were my life." Eyes downcast, she bit the side of her lip. "Want to know a secret? Tomorrow is Winifred's memorial. I've spent my entire life able to see ghosts, and I've never been to a funeral. I've walked alongside death, but I've never said goodbye to anyone I care about."

I remained still, startled by her confession. I'd said goodbye to so many it was almost second nature.

"So, I guess your parents are still around?"

Vivian shrugged and checked on the boiling water. "No, but to be fair, I hardly knew them. My mother died when I was a baby, and my father tried to stay, but he couldn't handle my gift. He was horrified that my first words were spoken to the dead. I was three when he sent me to my grandmother's house. Winifred raised me, and I haven't seen him since."

Deadbeat fathers. I knew a thing or two about those, but Vivian had been lucky to have someone like Winifred in her corner.

I stifled a yawn and scrubbed a hand over my face. "Sounds to me like you ended up in the best place possible. You didn't have a typical upbringing."

"How so?"

"Because anyone raised by Winifred James wouldn't turn out to be typical. I can see a lot of her in you, mostly her stubbornness."

"I'm not stubborn. I'm tenacious."

"There's no difference."

"Yes, there is. Tenacious makes me sound passionate and noble. Stubborn makes me sound like a mule. Are you calling me a mule?" There was a twinkle in her eye, a devilish glint I couldn't help but respond to. She wasn't like any other woman I knew. She was silk and steel. Vulnerable and unwavering.

Tenacious.

I lifted my hands. "Never that. I don't want to get stabbed a third time."

Her lips pressed together, containing a grin. "That's too bad. I think the third time might be the charm."

"I've changed my mind about letting you pick out

a dagger. I can see now, it isn't wise."

She tossed her hair back and crossed her arms. "You said I could have two. Besides, I don't know how you can see anything with your eyes drooping like that. You look dead on your feet. You've almost fallen over twice since you came in here."

Tired was an understatement. My hand gripped the back of a chair as a rush of dizziness washed through me. Every bone in my body felt leaden. It was all I could do to stay standing. Determination and my desire to keep talking with her were the only things that kept me on my feet.

Vivian bent over the hearth and poured boiling water from the kettle. "I'll make you some tea. It'll help."

"No." I waved the water away. "I already had some."

She paused, her brow wrinkling. "When did you have some?"

I swayed and tightened my hold on the chair. The room had started to tilt.

"Does it matter?"

Her gaze swung to an empty teacup on the table, and her lips thinned. "It might. You didn't drink from that cup, did you?"

"Well…"

She gasped and moved toward the basket of baked goods Hastings had made me bring. There was a hole where one of the scones should have been.

"You did, didn't you? You ate a scone too."

Cursing, I rubbed my grainy eyes. "I was starving!

If you remember, I gave you my meal back in the dungeon. I didn't think you'd miss a single scone or a cup of cold tea to wash it down."

Her lips twitched, then she laughed. Huge bouts of laughter that caused her to clutch her sides.

"What's so funny?"

Tears leaked down her cheeks. "I'm sorry, I can't help it. You've poisoned yourself."

My knees buckled, and Vivian reached out to steady me, ducking under my arm to hold me upright. I shook my head to clear my muddling thoughts even as the edges of my vision grew fuzzy.

"What do you mean, I poisoned myself?"

"Tessa gave me one of her sleeping potions. I only drank a few sips before it knocked me out. You drank the rest." Her lips trembled as she tried to suppress another laugh. "I'm afraid you don't have much time. Minutes at most."

I blinked, trying to make sense of her words. A sleeping potion? The realization hit me in the gut, and I grappled for her arms.

"No. I can't go to sleep. What about—?"

"Using me to search the mirror for something other than personal gain? I'll look in the morning."

She pulled me forward, and I stumbled, nearly careening into the wall. *No!* My mind shouted in denial, but it didn't get past my throat. It was hours until morning, plenty of time for someone else to slip past the useless guard. Someone like the Red Wolf.

I ground my heels into the floor, but Vivian had

the momentum and tugged me down the hallway, kicking open a door next to her bedroom.

"You can sleep it off in here."

I landed with a hard bounce on a firm mattress. Her hands delved into my jacket pockets, then she pulled out the hand mirror and set it on a side table. Next came my jacket, which she slid past my shoulders and folded at the edge of the bed.

"Vivian, you can't let me fall asleep." I tried to catch her wrists, but my fingers slipped over her skin, numb with fatigue.

"Shh... That's exactly what I'm going to do."

"No, you don't understand. I made a promise. I have to keep it." Words jumbled inside my head, confusion muddling them together.

Vivian peered down at me, moonlight painting her face in silver. Her brow creased.

"What promise?"

"The one I made Winifred before she died," I mumbled, unable to keep my eyes open.

The mattress shifted, and she shook my shoulders—harder when I didn't wake, my head rattling against the pillow.

"What did you promise her? Hey!" She snapped her fingers in front of my face.

Sleep dragged me under, and I tried to shake her off, pulling the blanket up to my ears. I'd almost forgotten why it mattered so much to stay awake.

"I promised to keep you safe."

Vivian's hands stilled against my shoulders. "From the Red Wolf?"

I blinked, her features coming into focus. My hand lifted and cupped her cheek. *So beautiful.*

I exhaled the answer. "From everything."

She leaned over me, the tips of her thick hair grazing my jaw. Her scent flooded my senses, and I breathed it in, wishing she'd stay long after my eyes closed.

For a moment, Vivian didn't say anything.

"Stop," she whispered. The question must have shown on my face because she answered her own statement. "Stop doing things that make me not hate you."

Chapter 12

VIVIAN

Everything.

The single word, delivered almost as a whisper, echoed in my mind. I wrapped a shawl tighter around my shoulders and huddled at the kitchen table. Morning light peeked through the curtains, unmoved by the fact I wasn't ready to face the day. Argus was still asleep in my spare room, and I should be angry. He'd barged in, evaded the guard stationed at my door, and proceeded to demand my cooperation.

He was controlled chaos, and I was still trying to figure out how he commanded attention yet sent everything else spinning at the same time. It was obvious he was used to getting his way, and this situation was no exception, but there'd been something in the way he gripped my hand before he fell asleep that made me question his motives. All that chaos compressed into quiet desperation, as if his promise to my grandmother meant more to him when he realized he might not be able to keep it.

Why had she asked him for such a ridiculous promise? She knew the kind of man he was. There were two types of people in this kingdom: those who wanted a piece of his empire, and those who were trying to stay out of his way. Tessa was the latter of the two, but my grandmother hadn't pushed Argus away. She'd helped him and had probably witnessed the risks of doing so.

Whose instincts should I trust? And what if my instincts told me there was more to Argus than I originally thought? Maybe a lot more.

Dropping my forehead against the table, I exhaled a pained breath. The silence was deafening, and my internal questions remained unanswered. I stared at the empty teacup that was his undoing, and laughter kindled in the back of my throat.

"Even giants can fall."

I traced the curved handle with my fingertip. It felt cathartic to laugh. The emotion caught me by surprise, but it didn't feel wrong. That surprised me too. There shouldn't be room for laughter in the middle of grief. The two emotions were opposing forces.

But maybe that was the point. In the darkest moments, it was the opposites that provided light.

Everything.

The word forced itself to the forefront again, and I squeezed my eyes shut, trying to banish the dangerous train of thought.

Everything was messed up.

Everything had gone wrong.

Those were the facts, not a single word laced with urgency and promise.

I groaned and pushed the teacup away, rattling it in its saucer. I wanted to break it, smash it against the wall into pieces in the same way I felt broken, but that wouldn't do any good. One mess didn't clean another. Instead, I pulled the hand mirror Argus had brought closer. I'd taken it from the nightstand while he slept. He'd be furious if he knew I planned to use it without him. But my curiosity was too strong, and I wanted to try without any influences.

It was time.

Peering into the glass at my reflection, I swallowed the nerves that tightened my throat. My dark hair hung in messy tangles, the tips brushing against the glass. I hardly recognized the young woman staring back at me. She looked haunted, unsure. She looked like the scared child with a set of powers she didn't want. Powers that made her a freak. I wasn't that little girl anymore, yet it felt like I'd been thrown back to the starting point. Except this time, instead of power people feared, I had power people coveted.

Talk about polar opposites.

The longer I stared at my reflection, the more uncertain I became. How did one go about seeing the future? Was I supposed to summon it the way I used to summon ghosts, or would it come to me on its own when it was ready? Winifred had made it look so easy. It was almost an extension of her, a natural occurrence, like breathing, yet nothing felt natural about this to me.

I tried to summon it first, placing my fingertips on the glass as my grandmother had always done. I focused my energy, growing frustrated when nothing appeared. At the party, the mirror had changed on its own.

Maybe I was trying too hard? Yes, that was it. I needed to become one with the future, let it flow through me. Oracles were calm in the face of all things; portals of what was to come. They were transcendent.

I relaxed my fingers and wriggled my shoulders, getting more comfortable in my seat. "Okay, mirror, do your thing."

Nothing happened.

"I hate you!" I snarled at my reflection. Any thought of transcendence flew into the rafters. Had I lost my ghosts for this faulty, sad excuse for a power? "Do your part of the deal."

My reflection winked.

I jumped, my chair scraping across the floor. Horrified, I flipped the mirror over and yanked my hand away as if whatever was on the other side intended to pull me through.

Flaming haunted asylums, that was close. Was the mirror supposed to do that? I shuddered. And people thought ghosts were creepy... They had nothing on sentient reflections trapped behind glass.

Blowing out a harsh breath, I eyed the mirror's ornate metal handle. Tension constricted my muscles. This was ridiculous—it was only a mirror! It couldn't hurt me. I wiped my damp palms on my skirt and slowly turned it back over.

See? Harmless.

I leaned over the reflective surface and whispered, "Good mirror, play nice. I'm still getting the hang of this, and we wouldn't want you to end up in the fireplace."

This time, when my reflection winked, I didn't run screaming.

So, progress.

I gently touched the glass, and tendrils of white smoke obscured her image until she faded into a dense mist. The smoke swirled, and the edges of my vision grew dark, becoming a tunnel that pulled me in. Sounds faded, and the kitchen dropped away.

When my vision cleared, I stood in the middle of the forest, boots planted deep in snow. A bitter chill sliced through my cloak, and I rubbed my arms, trying to kindle some warmth. Moonlight illuminated a pair of tracks that led through the trees. Blood dotted the path like bread crumbs showing me the way.

Shouts pierced the night, calling a name. I tried to locate their direction, but they seemed to be coming from everywhere.

I followed the droplets. They grew in number, becoming a slash of red against the pristine white. Near the base of a tree was a small object nearly buried in the snow, and next to it, a figure lying motionless. There was so much blood. Too much.

I choked on a scream.

"Over here!" a voice cried. It was mine, but it came from further away. A blur of motion raced toward the tree, and I saw myself slide in the snow. Tear-stained and terrified, she yelled over her shoulder, "Over here!"

I wanted to step closer and help somehow. Her cries were pleading and desperate. The sound affected me deep in my core, but I was frozen in place, merely a spectator to the unfolding horror.

Other people emerged from the trees. Their faces were shadowed and unrecognizable, and they dropped to their knees beside her. She picked up the strange object in the snow, pressed it to her chest, then buried her face against the still form.

"Vivian?" My name echoed from above the tree-tops. It shook the ground beneath me, making the trees appear like they were caving in. White smoke rose around my feet, climbing higher, clouding the scene.

"No—wait!"

"Vivian, answer me."

The woods vanished, and my reflection returned, peering back with wide eyes. Her lips moved, and the words wrapped around me, almost entrancing in their tone.

"You can't stop it, no matter what you do."

"Vivian! Snap out of it." Rough hands grasped my shoulders, breaking my connection with the mirror. Argus's fierce gaze drilled into mine.

"You're awake?" I mumbled, dazed as I blinked away the mist that clung like cobwebs in my mind.

Argus's jaw tightened with fury. "What were you thinking? You should have waited for me. Do you even know what you're doing?"

I shook him off and stood on wobbly legs. "I'm fine. You should be happy. It's what you wanted me to do, and it worked. I saw something."

He held himself in check, fingers curling into fists as if to stop from grabbing me again. "What did you see?"

Death.

Grief.

Failure.

The vision replayed in my head. What had I seen? I only knew I'd been in the forest and whoever had died was someone I was searching for. Someone who'd probably counted on me coming sooner.

"There's going to be another murder."

"Who?" he asked, voice thick with dread.

I held his gaze, feeling a tug of inevitability. "I don't know who. I saw my future self in the woods. She found the body, but I couldn't get close enough to tell who it was. There was something buried in the snow, and then other people arrived. Someone tried to hold her back. There was so much blood. She was screaming." I squeezed my eyes shut as her wrenching cries filled my ears. "I don't know. It happened so fast. I...I couldn't—"

Argus reached for me and pulled me against his chest. His arms wrapped around my shoulders, his palm cupping the back of my head. I could hardly believe what was happening. My thoughts scattered as his fingers sifted through my hair, and his soft words washed over me.

"It wasn't you. Thank God, it wasn't you."

Had he thought I witnessed my death like Winifred did? I shivered. Argus's grip tightened, anchoring me to him, and it was such a grounding sensation I didn't want it to end.

"What are we going to do?" I mumbled, breathing in his clean, masculine scent.

His chin rested on top of my head, and he exhaled a slow breath. "We're going to stop it."

I didn't ask how. It didn't matter because I wanted to believe him. Even knowing my grandmother wasn't able to change her fate and that my reflection had said the same thing, I had to trust Winifred had a greater plan and that Argus was a part of it.

Somehow, we'd figure it out together.

Pulling back, I looked up into his face, and I was struck by what I saw there. Gone was the arrogant twist of his smile, and he didn't try to—or maybe he couldn't—hide the tenderness in his eyes. It was as hypnotic as the swirling mist in the mirror and just as confusing. His words from the night before echoed in my mind.

Everything.

He meant it.

And maybe it was reckless. Maybe I was making the biggest mistake of my life by assigning emotions that weren't there. But I couldn't be that bad at reading things, could I?

Only one way to find out.

Going up on my toes, I trailed my hands up the firm wall of his chest and brushed my lips against his.

Argus went completely still. He did *not* kiss me back.

The embarrassment was swift and stabbing; a mortal wound. How was it possible I didn't witness my death in the mirror?

You idiot!

I dropped back on my heels. He still hadn't moved, and I refused to look up. Nope. I planned on staring at my feet for the rest of my exquisitely short life.

Ruby and Fredrick, I'll be joining you soon. We can haunt the kingdom's moors together.

Honestly, there was rock bottom, and then there were the fifty feet of dirt that encompassed the next three seconds, followed by a volcanic—

His fingers gripped my chin. My gaze flew up, and, *whoa*, why was I looking at my feet? *Sweet spirits, save me.* The breath caught in my throat as his mouth came down on mine. I was an idiot, but not for initiating. I was an idiot for thinking the light peck I'd given him was a kiss.

Because it wasn't. I had proof.

Argus held me in place, locking his other hand at the base of my neck, and then angled his head deeper. The heated draw of his lips made me desperate to match his intensity. My tongue swept against his, and he groaned, fingers digging into my skin. The sound clenched my stomach with delicious pressure. His hands dropped to my waist, and he guided me backward.

The chair tipped over. The small of my back bumped the table.

Rough stubble scratched my cheek as his mouth trailed along my jawline, then lowered to the pulse point in my neck. My heart raced, and I bit my lip as his teeth skimmed my collarbone.

Another thud broke through my disjointed thoughts. Was I still knocking over chairs? It made sense to me.

Wait.

That was the door. Footsteps creaked down the hallway, and I sucked in a panicked breath.

"Viv? It's Tess. Are you in the kitchen?"

Argus tensed, his mouth hovering over the exposed skin of my shoulder.

Damn it! Icy awareness spread through my body. What was I doing? I shoved at his chest, pushing him off me, as Tessa entered the kitchen.

Argus staggered back a step, and the flash of hurt that appeared before his cool mask of indifference fell back into place shredded my heart. What had I done? Dread plummeted in my stomach.

"What is he doing here?" Tessa sneered. Her eyes narrowed into slits, and she clenched her hands. For a second, I thought she was going to shoot magical daggers straight into Argus's back.

"Everything is fine, Tess."

"It doesn't look fine. Why is this man in your house? Was the hole he crawls out of filled for the night?"

"Good morning, witch." Argus tore his gaze from mine and focused on Derrick, who came in behind Tessa. "Incompetence must run rampant in your agency. Your guard still doesn't know I'm here."

Derrick stepped forward, features hardening, but Tessa raised her hand. "Don't let him bait you. He's not worth it."

"Tessa, don't," I pleaded.

She looked at me, and disappointment washed over her face. I felt it in my toes. Tessa had never looked at me that way before. The feeling gutted me, and an apology raced to the tip of my tongue.

"I'm sorry." I mouthed the words, but her look didn't change.

"The memorial starts in an hour. We're meeting the prince there. He wants to give you his condolences in person." Tessa glanced at Argus, then back to me. "We'll wait in the carriage. Get rid of him." She spun on her heel.

Derrick gave Argus an unreadable look before following her down the hallway.

I picked up the fallen chair and slumped into the seat. The silence was unbearable. My eyes felt grainy, and the lump in my throat thickened, becoming painful.

Argus grabbed the mirror and tucked it inside his jacket. His movements were stilted and tense. He leaned his fists on the table for a minute, hanging his head.

I have to fix this!

"I'm sor—"

"Don't you dare say it." He scowled as he pushed away, the force moving the table's wooden legs an inch, and he strode toward the back door. "I'll send one of my men to the memorial to keep watch."

"You aren't coming?" Why did it sound like I was speaking over razor blades?

He paused, his hand on the knob. "I have a business to run. I don't have time to monitor your every move."

The brutality in his tone made me flinch. Argus's jaw worked as if he wanted to say more, then decided against it. He stalked through the doorway, slamming the door behind him.

I reeled, caught between my best friend's anger and the whiplash from my intense moment with Argus. My fingers wrapped around the porcelain teacup perched on the table, and I threw it against the wall. It shattered, jagged edges scattering across the floor.

Everything...*hurt.*

Chapter 13

ARGUS

That wasn't handled well.

I stormed down the back steps inhaling a breath of frigid air. The sharp sting was a welcome sensation in my chest. Right now, physical pain was the only thing that made sense.

What happened back there? I woke up to an eerily quiet house and found Vivian entranced in the mirror. Her face was pale, lips moving in a silent plea. It was like watching someone enthralled in a nightmare, and I had to stop it. I just didn't anticipate what would come next.

When she kissed me, it was like stepping into a waking nightmare of my own. I knew it wasn't real, that it wouldn't last, and I would jerk awake haunted by the feel of her against me, her taste and scent; ghosts of a moment that shouldn't have been mine.

She was vulnerable and had acted out of character—a rebellious attempt at control I should have let end there. Because I knew it for what it was. It didn't take an oracle to know how she'd react when she came to her senses. People wanted my money, power, and influence, but they didn't want to be associated with the man who provided it, and they definitely didn't want anything deeper.

An honorable man wouldn't have taken advantage of her lapse in judgment. He wouldn't have returned feelings years of experience told him he wasn't capable of having.

I wasn't honorable. Though, for a few hard-won seconds, I'd tried to be.

I could still feel the silken strands of her hair between my fingers and smell the faint scent of lavender that clung to her skin. Her soft lips were the razor's edge of addiction. Vivian didn't shy away from my aggression, and I'd wanted her to, hoping to scare her off before she could convince me I was wrong.

She'd almost done it. I'd never wanted to be so wrong in my life. The world had narrowed down to just the two of us, and it suddenly didn't matter who I was or what I'd done in the past. Maybe in another time or place, things could be different. But that was the consistent thing about expectations: they had a funny way of being met. Vivian might have lowered herself to welcome my touch, yet the second there was a chance we might be discovered, she'd shoved me away.

And it damn well hurt.

I maneuvered through the tight alley at the back of her house and into the street. Carriages rumbled down the cobblestones, and people rushed by wrapped up inside their coats. I joined them, stepping into the current. Overhead, clouds blocked out the sun, turning the morning gray and miserable, a reflection of my darkening mood.

I walked until I came to the docks. Salt filled the air, washing away any lingering memories of lavender. The docks were more of a home to me than the Lennox mansion. That house fit me like an ill-made suit—borrowed but not designed for me—yet I wore it all the same. You couldn't rule from the bottom, so even though I might have preferred to, claiming my birthright was a necessity.

Shouts of laughter spilled from the open door of the Laughing Raven. Two sailors lurched into the street, their eyes squinting against the daylight. They shuffled toward their ship using each other to stay upright.

Entering the tavern, I stood in the threshold assessing the room. The usual drunks were facedown at their tables, while others nursed hangovers in front of steaming bowls of porridge. The establishment reeked of misery from too much liquor, not enough money, and wretched circumstance. A home, if I'd ever had one.

The barkeep looked up and caught my eye. Wordlessly, he angled his head toward a table in the corner, where a barmaid met me. Her tight corset didn't interest me as much as the bowl of porridge she placed on the table. I dug in, savoring the sweet taste of brown sugar. The pounding in my head receded, leaving only the gnawing ache in my stomach I began to realize wasn't hunger. At least, not the kind you could alleviate with food.

"You look like death," Wade grumbled, sliding into the chair across from me.

"It hasn't come to that yet, but wait a while," I muttered, scraping another spoonful of porridge from the bowl. "Have you found anything on the names I sent over from the manifest?"

The barmaid returned and plunked a steaming bowl in front of Wade. He waited until she wandered off before answering my question.

"As a matter of fact, I have." Wade slid a scrap of paper across the table. "The two men who sailed with the crate are returning home on the Black Eagle. The ship's docked for another hour." He spooned porridge into his mouth, then made a face. "This is too sweet. I need to hire a new cook for this place."

"Well, you can't have mine." I palmed the slip of paper, glad for a course of action to distract me from the disastrous morning. An interrogation might lighten my mood. "I need you to do something else for me. But it has to be kept quiet."

Wade pushed his bowl aside and leaned back in his chair. "What a coincidence. Quiet favors are my specialty. What do you need? Intel on a merchant? Someone to case out the brothel? My afternoon's free for that last one." He smirked.

"Adella's missing."

"Damn it, Argus." Wade dropped his head into his

hands, cursing under his breath. "Did that chit run off with the stable boy again? I swear, if you ask me to chase her across the kingdom like last time, I'll lose it. This place doesn't run itself, you know?"

"You said you had the afternoon free."

"Not for that."

"Afraid of getting another black eye?" I stifled a grin at Wade's disgusted expression.

"She throws punches for the strangest things," he grumbled.

"Well, you did try to kiss her. You're lucky that's all you got."

Wade grimaced. "I won't be making the same mistake twice. She's a hellion."

"She's in trouble."

This got his attention. He straightened, and a dark look furrowed his brow.

"How long has she been missing?"

"Three days. We followed her to the Ashworth estate but lost her in the crowd, and then I ended up in jail. I need you to find her." I paused, lowering my voice. "She's been bitten."

"Hell, is she...?" His voice faded.

"I don't know what state she's in. That's why we have to find her. I can still fix this, but I need your help and your discretion. Jason Ashworth was killed the other night, and she was there."

"I heard about Ashworth. I'm not saying the lowlife deserved it, but I'm not surprised. He never liked to be told no, if you know what I mean?"

I nodded, the taste of porridge souring in my

mouth when I remembered the way he had his hands all over Vivian. The wolves had done me a favor.

"Don't worry," Wade continued, "I'll find Adella. You concentrate on finding the blade. We'll meet in the middle." He pushed away from the table, eying his uneaten breakfast with a grimace.

"Has Gregor been in yet?" I asked.

"No. But he should be soon. Want me to leave a message with the barkeep?"

"Yeah, have Gregor go to the town square. I want him to make sure things go smoothly at the memorial today."

Wade frowned. "The memorial for the oracle? What does that have to do with you?"

I sighed, smothering the little flame of guilt that had been trying to catch fire since I left Vivian's. "I have a...responsibility for her granddaughter. Gregor can handle it. It's a simple job—he only has to watch her."

My jaw tightened as my parting words to her echoed in my ears. The flame of guilt ignited scorching a path through my chest. I grit my teeth. She'd be fine for a couple of hours. How much trouble could the woman get into surrounded by palace guards and her revered detective? I scowled and pressed the heal of my hand against the fiery ache behind my rib cage.

The corner of Wade's mouth lifted. "I'm guessing it's not that simple."

"It is. Get going. I have to head to the Black Eagle

before it sails."

Wade nodded, still smirking. "Whatever you say, Argus." He gave me a mock salute, then stopped to leave the message with the barkeep on his way out the door.

I lingered by the table, reluctant to get started even though I didn't have much time. Gregor would show. He'd get the message. I was worrying over nothing, prioritizing things that had no business being first. Enough of this. I headed for the door.

"Ashworth's paying a small fortune to make it happen."

I froze as I caught the end of the hushed conversation. Two men sat hunched over a nearby table, shoveling food into their mouths.

"I should have accepted the job, but it's risky with all those palace guards roaming the street." The man wiped his beard with his sleeve. "I'll leave it to some other fool to get rid of the girl. Though, I wouldn't have minded dragging it out a bit. The oracle's granddaughter is a looker."

My fists clenched at his lewd suggestion. The urge to wipe the sleazy look off his face was only outweighed by my need for more information.

"You're disgusting, Frank." The other man chuckled.

Both stopped talking when they noticed me standing over their table. The one with the beard dropped his spoon.

"A—Argus, I didn't see you there. I still have a few days before my next payment. You'll get it in time. I already have the money."

"Who did Ashworth pay to get rid of the girl?"

Frank expelled a relieved breath. "I don't know. Some guy."

"When?"

"The memorial. Ashworth wants it done immediately. She must have really crossed him." He nudged his partner.

"You didn't hear?" The other guy shook his head and rolled his eyes. "The girl's a suspect in his son's death."

"Damn," Frank muttered. "I didn't know. I bet I could have got him to pay more. Maybe I should head over there?"

I gripped the table and thumped it against the floor to get their attention. Frank's bowl fell off the edge and smashed to the floor, porridge oozing under his seat.

"The girl is off-limits to you or anyone else. You go after her, and you answer to me."

"Jeez, Argus." Frank eyed his ruined breakfast with a frown. "You can have the job if you get there in time. I'm sure Ashworth will pay whoever can get it done the fastest. We'll spread the word that she's yours."

"Make sure you do." I backed away from the table, clenching the ship information in my pocket. I had to make a choice: the blade, or Vivian. Either way, I was going to lose one of them.

When I hit the street, I ran.

***

The route leading into the town square was packed. Mourners jostled each other for a prime view of the procession, while others watched from second-story windows. A heavy mantle of grief hung in the air. I elbowed my way through the crowd until I could see the ceremony route.

Even though the procession hadn't started, a drumbeat pounded in the distance. I searched the onlookers, a ball of dread in my chest. Ashworth could have paid anybody. Knowing the old man, he'd be here too, making sure the hit went according to plan.

It was careless to assume we wouldn't face retaliation for what happened in the maze. Ashworth might think twice about coming after me, but he wouldn't hesitate with Vivian; she was an easier target. The nausea of a near-miss coated my insides. If I'd left for the ship sooner, I might not have discovered his plan.

I needed to get eyes on Vivian, and then, once I did, I wasn't letting her out of my sight. She could push me away all she wanted. Until this was over, she was stuck with me.

"Argus!"

A slender arm wrapped around mine and pulled me close. I looked down at the young woman wrapped in a fur coat. Her cheeks and nose were red from the cold.

"Sarah? What are you doing here?" I tried to extricate my arm, but she gripped it tighter.

"I was so worried about you after what happened at the Ashworths' party. To think, if you hadn't forced me to go with that other group, I might have been inside the maze when Jason was murdered. I was furious with you at the time, but you were only looking out for my safety." She swept her lashes down, lips trembling.

"You weren't in any danger, Sarah," I said absently, scanning the crowd over her head.

"Because of you." She shuddered and pressed closer against my side.

"Yeah, sure."

Where was the best vantage point on the route? Would he take her there, or wait until she'd reached the square? What about the windows? A long-range attack? Ice formed in my veins. There were too many possibilities.

"Did you find Adella? Was she inside when it happened?" Sarah asked, squeezing my forearm to try and regain my attention.

"Adella's fine. I sent her to the countryside for a while until things cool down." The lie was easy, and I hoped the story would keep Sarah from stopping by the house for a visit. Maybe it would buy us some time.

She pouted. "I wish she would have come by before she left. Now I won't get to see her for ages. You either, I bet." She went up on her toes. "Promise me you'll come to dinner this week. My parents always love it when you're around. I insist."

The drumbeat grew louder, and tensions rose in the crowd.

"Ugh, what a dreadful occasion. Everyone is in mourning. I can't believe the oracle is dead."

"Her name was Winifred."

"Hmm?" Sarah looked up at me and blinked. "Did you know her? I don't like to speak ill of the dead, but I heard the woman was very temperamental. You know, I didn't realize it at the time, but that friend of yours, Vivian James—she's the oracle's granddaughter. I heard rumors about her too. They used to call her 'ghost girl.' No one would talk to her except some witch. Can you imagine?"

I bristled and removed Sarah's arm from mine. "You don't know what you're talking about, and don't call her that."

She lifted her shoulder and made a little harrumph in the back of her throat. "Either way, you never answered my invitation. Please, say you'll come. I'll have the cook prepare your favorite. Argus? Are you listening?"

A man weaved through the crowd, head hanging low as he moved away from the mourners. I caught his profile and tensed. It was Ashworth.

"Stay here, Sarah," I said, already on the move before she could protest.

The crowd made it difficult to keep him in sight. I cursed, coming up short when someone blocked my path. By the time I broke free, Ashworth had vanished. A horn blared, and the pit of dread in my chest widened. The procession was about to begin.

I needed to find Vivian.
Now.
Before it was too late.

Chapter 14

VIVIAN

Worst carriage ride ever.

I returned Tessa's glare inch for inch. She hadn't said a word since we left the house, preferring instead to skewer me with dagger eyes and condemning silence.

"I thought you were supposed to solve murders, not commit them. Keep looking at me like that, and I'll keel over in my seat."

Tessa sputtered and jerked the filmy black veil out of her eyes. "What do you expect when I walk in and find you two together? You refuse to let me stay with you, but you have no problem opening up to him over breakfast. I can't believe you let that man into your house."

"I didn't let him in. He sort of crept in."

"You mean, he broke in, like a criminal. I'd count your silver if I were you." Tessa's face turned a shade of red, blending with the rouge she'd applied to her cheeks, until I couldn't tell what was makeup and

131

what was anger.

I leaned forward, swaying with the bumps in the road, and jabbed my finger in her face. "I prefer gold —you know that. And you're one to talk! Didn't you tell me Derrick went through your things the first day you met? He thought you were a suspect in a murder! Not only that, he confiscated your potions and leveled fines against you. How is that any better?"

Tessa gasped. "Don't you *dare* bring Derrick into this!"

We both turned as Derrick shifted uncomfortably in his seat. He pulled a woolen cap down over his eyes and feigned interest in something out the window.

I slumped against the cushion, irritation coursing through me. An uneasy silence blanketed the carriage, and none of us wanted to be the first to break it.

Fine by me.

A needle of guilt had been doing damage to my insides ever since Argus stormed out of the house. I could still see the flash of hurt in his eyes when I pushed him away. My rejection turned our moment in the kitchen into something sordid and shameful when it felt the opposite.

I struggled to put into words the elusive thing I saw in him. Tessa had a point: he was everything she warned about. But there was something else lurking beneath his rough exterior.

A heart?

Maybe.

He might be selfish, arrogant, and dangerous, but wasn't he also kind? Concerned for my safety? There was something captivating about him, and whatever it was had me going out of my mind picking fights with Tessa and hoping he might show up at the memorial after all.

The carriage jolted to a halt, and Tessa grumbled, "We're here."

Derrick nearly fell out of the carriage trying to put distance between us. "I'll go see if the prince is ready. Wait here."

The door clicked shut, locking us in our silent stalemate. Minutes passed, and my anger drained from me, turning into an ache that tightened my throat. The last thing I wanted was to be at odds with Tessa. It wasn't like I had many friends left. At least, not any I could see.

"You're different," Tessa said, looking out the window.

"I know." What did she think would happen when my life flipped upside down?

"It scares me," she whispered.

"It scares me too."

Tessa sniffled and pushed the veil out of her eyes. It slipped back into place, and her nose scrunched as she tugged it from her head and tossed it onto the seat.

"I know I've said this before, but you need to stay away from Argus. He'll drag you down with him. He can't be trusted, and he won't be there for you when you need him."

"Maybe not."

She sighed. "But you're going to get involved with him anyway? Why? Explain it to me, so it makes sense."

My fingers fisted the fabric of my mourning gown, crinkling the black satin. "I don't know. I lost Winifred and my ghosts in exchange for something I never wanted. I feel like I've lost everything."

"You didn't lose me."

"I know that." I rubbed my eyes, covering my face with my hands, and exhaled a long breath. "I don't think I can explain it so you'll understand." My involvement with Argus was undefinable. It went against logic and at the same time was the only thing that seemed to make sense. Maybe I was rebelling at the universe for taking my grandmother from me, but working with him felt tangible; like a way forward. There was also a part of me that felt a connection to him, almost as if he was missing something too. "Look, I just want to get through today, say my goodbyes, and make sure everyone in attendance knows how amazing my grandmother was."

Tessa slid forward and clasped my hands. "I know. I'm sorry. I'm just worried about you, but you're right—today is about Winifred."

I gave her a watery smile. "Still friends?"

"Always." Tessa squeezed my fingers. "Even if I don't approve of your choices. I won't pretend to like him though. He has to earn that, and right now, I don't see how that's possible."

I wiped the wetness from my cheeks with my sleeve. "You know, I didn't approve of Derrick the first time around either. He was too rigid and very grumpy."

Tessa stifled a laugh and wiped at her own tears. "He still is. You'll love this. Last night, I made him cook dinner while I played with my herbs. It was only beef stew, but he acted like I asked him to make a four-course meal."

"How'd it come out?"

"It was terrible. I faked enjoyment until his back was turned and then magically made it disappear. Only, I messed up the spell, and the food reappeared in my shoe closet. Now, my best slippers smell like over seasoned beef."

I bit my lip, a laugh warring with my grief. *Some things never change.* I could hold on to that.

The door opened, letting in a blast of chilly air. Derrick ushered us into the street, where the prince waited with his entourage.

"Is everything okay?" he whispered to Tessa.

She nudged him in the ribs and scoffed. "That? That was nothing. You should have seen us when we were younger. Once, Viv pretended a ghost was haunting me for an entire week because I ate the last of her grandmother's cookies. She's vengeful."

I smoothed the wrinkles from my gown and lifted a shoulder. "At least Winifred's cookies tasted better than Derrick's stew."

Derrick's eyes widened. "You said it was good!"

"It was good...ish. I may need new shoes though."

"Ladies!" Prince Marcus approached before Derrick could respond—which was probably a good thing because he looked ready to defend his inedible stew.

"I'm so sorry for your loss, Miss James. Winifred was a remarkable woman, and she'll be greatly missed. I want you to know, you have the full support of the royal family during this time. If there's anything you need, please ask."

"Thank you, Your Highness." I curtsied low, bowing my head. "It's a pleasure to see you again. I believe the last time we met was at Tessa's reward ceremony."

He took my hand and placed a light kiss on my knuckles. "I remember you. You look as lovely now as you did then."

Tessa leaned in, her voice barely above a whisper. "See? I told you Prince Marcus was charming. He's not a killer either."

I spoke through clenched teeth. "So, my standards have fallen that far, 'not a killer' rates as a positive trait?"

Tessa shrugged. "He also has a castle."

A horn blasted, signaling the start of the ceremony, and a solemn feeling settled in my stomach. The moment I was dreading had arrived.

"It's a short walk to the square," Prince Marcus said. "I'll give my remarks, and then you're welcome to say a few words. I realize the ceremonial walk is difficult, but it's a kingdom tradition. If you'd prefer a carriage, it can be arranged."

My back stiffened, and I shook my head. Winifred would be horrified if I defied tradition, especially at her memorial.

"No, I'll walk."

"I'm sure she'd be proud." His features darkened. "We have the entire agency searching for her killer. We will bring that person to justice."

"Thank you, Your Highness."

He bowed and turned on his heel before mounting his horse and moving to the front of the procession.

Tessa took my hand. "Are you ready?"

I scanned the growing crowd over my shoulder. Argus wasn't there. *He won't be there for you when you need him.* Maybe Tessa was right, but I couldn't help feeling a rush of disappointment.

Squaring my shoulders, I gave her a determined nod. "I'm ready."

We followed the prince to the front of the procession. The crowd was thick, standing in a solid mass along the ceremony route. Many hung their heads and dabbed handkerchiefs at their eyes. Others shook their heads in pity when they saw me take my place in line. I buried my emotions, keeping my head high and my eyes forward. There wasn't any use studying the crowd for a familiar face. Argus had made his choice.

The processional started, and my feet dragged like heavy weights. I tried to think of what I should say when it was my turn to speak. Words and eloquent phrases crowded my mind, but nothing seemed good enough. Winifred wouldn't want a flowery speech, I knew that much. Her raspy voice filled my head: *I'm dead, get over it. Get a good price for my house. You know, for an ex-ghost hunter, you're awful weepy over the deceased.*

The line moved slowly toward the square. Processional music played, and the horns sounded raw against my ears. Wreaths had been laid across the path, and mourners tossed sprigs of greens at our feet. They crunched beneath our boots, becoming a scented carpet.

Somewhere further down the line, a commotion captured my attention. The crowd surged. Bodies pressed in close, a blur of faces and growing confusion. I tried to find the source of the disturbance as the procession stopped.

"What's going on?" someone hissed. A murmur swept through the gathering, and people jostled each other to see ahead. I tripped, losing sight of Tessa as the crowd swelled around us.

"Tess!" The crush of bodies, tightened my throat, making me panic. Whistles pierced the air as Royal guards pushed their way through, breaking up the onlookers, but it wasn't enough to set things back in motion.

"Come with me, Miss James." A royal guard grasped my elbow.

"Wait! I need to find Tessa." I stood on my toes, but the crowd rocked forward, making me lose my balance. The guard tightened his hold, squeezing my elbow in a painful grip.

"Now, Miss James, until we can regain control." He hauled me through the crowd, and then we broke free, but he didn't let go of my arm. I twisted in his hold, the ache in my elbow making me wince.

"Keep walking," he murmured.

"Let go." My shoes skidded over gravel as he continued to drag me away from the procession. Alarm bells rang in my head as the mouth of an alley appeared. This wasn't right.

He's going to pull me inside!

"Help! I need—"

He clamped his hand over my mouth, and his other arm snaked around my waist, lifting me up. My feet lost purchase on the ground, and we were still moving, the alley swallowing us in shadow. The deeper we went, the quieter it became.

My panicked lungs worked overtime, but the guard's seal over my mouth made dragging in air almost impossible. Dizziness washed through me, and when he finally let go, I stumbled, unable to keep my balance.

"Good work."

I looked up as another man appeared from where he leaned against a brick wall. Familiarity tugged at the edges of my mind. He was older, with fine lines around his eyes and hair that was more salt than pepper. With one flick of his wrist, a weighted bag sailed through the air, and the guard caught it one-handed. He hefted it in his palm, then nodded. Without giving me another glance, the guard turned on his heel and left the alley.

My heart pounded in my ears. I wanted to run the opposite way, but fear rooted my feet to the ground.

The older man stood over me. His hand shook as he reached into his tailored jacket and withdrew a small dagger. But it wasn't frailty that made him tremble; it was anger.

"Who are you?" I asked.

He chuckled low and deep. "You think you can come into my home, murder my son, and get away with it? That's not how this works. Get up." His fingers dug into my bicep, pulling me from my knees.

Recognition exploded in my mind. The man was Jason Ashworth's father.

"Lord Ashworth, I didn't kill your son. It was—"

He shoved me against the wall, cracking my head against solid brick. Darkness seeped into my vision, and I blinked to regain my focus. Ashworth pressed into me, running the flat side of his blade down my cheek.

"You were the last person to see him alive. You were his partner in the hunt, and you lured him to a secluded spot. They never should have let you out of prison. If justice won't be served that way, I'll take it myself."

I recoiled as the knife slid past my chin, flinching when it drew closer to my neck. How ironic. Only days before, I was the one with the knife declaring vengeance. Except this encounter wasn't going to end in the same way as the other one. I had to do something! I couldn't stand here and be skewered in an ally. Not on the day of my grandmother's funeral.

Talk about stealing her thunder...

My hands splayed out in search of a weapon. Ashworth leaned in, his hot breath fanning my face. His eyes were wild and bloodshot, tinged with malice.

"He was my only son."

"I'm sorry," I stammered. The tips of my fingers connected with a plank resting on a stack of crates. I stretched, and the beam teetered, threatening to fall out of reach.

"Why did you do it?" His jaw ticked, and veins protruded from his neck.

"I didn't!"

"Don't deny it!"

Stretching as far as I could, I made contact with the plank. It was now or never.

I cast my gaze over his shoulder. "Help! Over here!" I shouted.

This distracted him enough. Ashworth shifted his weight, giving me enough room to fully grasp the plank. In one smooth motion, I swung the board and connected it with the side of his head. The crack was sickening, and his knife slipped from his hand.

Lunging from the wall, I ran for the entrance to the alley. He was right behind me. My adrenaline spiked higher.

I'm going to make it! So close!

Fingers tangled in my hair, wrenching me back. I landed hard on my backside in the dirt, then on my hands when he kicked me to the ground with a booted foot.

"Get off me!" I rolled, jabbing my fingers in his

JENNA COLLETT

face.

He ducked and gripped my hands like a vise over my head. Without any leverage, I was losing the fight. I struggled harder, bucking my entire body to dislodge him. His fist rose in the air, and I braced for impact.

It never came.

Instead, Ashworth's body was lifted off me and thrown against the wall. I sucked in air, too stunned to move, until the sound of bone crushing bone spurred me into action. Scrambling to my feet, I heard Ashworth moan as he slumped to the ground, his head lolling to the side. Blood dripped from his mouth into the dirt.

Argus lifted the man's head and reared back to deliver another vicious blow, one I feared would snap his neck.

"Don't kill him!" I cried, limping closer.

He was blinded with rage, oblivious as I reached for his arm. When I touched him, he froze, his fist in mid-air.

"You have to stop. Please!"

His eyes frantically scanned my body, and whatever he saw there only ratcheted the intensity of his anger. I'd never seen anything like it.

"He dies," Argus growled, moving to scoop up the knife Ashworth had dropped, but I beat him to it, planting my foot on the hilt.

"No, he doesn't."

He seethed, his chest rising and falling on huge lungfuls of air. "Move, Vivian. Now."

142

"No." I ground my foot into the blade and kicked it further down the alley, where it disappeared into the shadows.

His bark of laughter echoed off the walls. "You think I didn't bring my own? I just didn't want to get it dirty." He reached for a sheath at his waist, and I dropped to my knees, throwing my arms around his shoulders. Every muscle in his body went rigid. He let out a breath but didn't take another one in.

"You can't," I whispered furiously in his ear. "Don't give them another reason to put you away. What about the Grimm's blade? Your sister needs you." I paused, my voice thick and tight. "You can't because...I need you."

For a heart-stopping minute, he didn't react. Tension radiated from him, vibrating with a force I wasn't sure any words could soothe. The ache sharpened in my chest. Finally, I felt him relax, and I breathed in relief.

Behind us, Ashworth stirred, groaning in pain. Argus set me back and stood, facing the man who'd attacked me.

"If you or anyone else you pay ever goes near that woman again, I will kill you." He bent and fisted the collar of Ashworth's shirt. Argus's voice rumbled low, too quiet for me to hear, but Ashworth's skin paled to a deathly pallor. He dragged the man to his feet and shoved him away. "Go. Before I change my mind. It won't take much."

Ashworth spat blood into the dirt and sent me a ravaged look. He nodded once, then stumbled out of the alley.

"Are you okay?" Argus asked, coming to my side.

I brushed the dirt off my clothes, wincing at the abrasions on my hands. Tracks of blood and grime marred my palms, but it could have been so much worse. Except for some sore muscles and bruises sure to show up later, I was unharmed. Not that I could convince Argus. He pushed the hair off my face, then ran his hands down the sides of my neck, grazing my shoulders, examining my ribs.

"I'm fine." I caught his fingers and forced a smile onto my face. "You said you weren't coming. You said you were sending someone else."

"I found out about Ashworth. You shouldn't have stopped me. He deserves—"

I pressed my finger against his lips. "Stop. He's grieving. I'm not defending him, but I can't blame him either. Not after what I did."

"It's not the same thing."

"It's exactly the same."

"That's another thing we disagree on."

My lips twitched. "I'm glad you're here."

His features softened, and he leaned forward to rest his forehead against mine. We fell back into that comfortable moment, the one from this morning before it all went to hell. It shouldn't be so easy. Nothing was solved between us, but I didn't care.

"Let me take you home," he said.

"No way. I'm speaking at the ceremony."

It took all of two seconds for Argus's scowl to return. "Not after this, you're not."

"Yes, I am.

He wrapped a hand around my arm and started to lead me out of the alley. "You were attacked. You need to rest."

I yanked my arm out of his grip, dancing back a step when he reached for me again. "You're wrong. I need to speak."

"Vivian—"

"I'm all she had. Someone has to stand up for her and let the people know the type of woman she was. If you can't understand that, you can go. It's your choice." I crossed my arms over my chest, refusing to back down.

Argus looked conflicted. Getting his way came naturally to him, and having someone resist his direction was clearly a new experience. Anger and disbelief warred across his face.

I held my breath while I waited for his decision, knowing in my heart this one mattered. Whatever he chose would determine the course of our relationship. I hadn't lied when I told Tessa I was scared. I was out of my mind with the fear I was making the wrong choices.

He reached for me, and I tensed, certain he was going to drag me kicking and screaming from the alley. But instead, Argus cupped the side of my face, his thumb smoothing over my cheekbone. I froze, dumbfounded, afraid to think what it meant.

Our gazes locked.

His voice was a husky rumble. "Then I choose to stand with you."

Chapter 15

ARGUS

"You will?" Vivian blinked, and confusion knotted her brow. It almost made me smile. Was she expecting resistance? Of course she was.

On any other day, in any other situation…

My thoughts stalled. In what felt like slow motion, Vivian stepped forward and wrapped her arms around me. Her head rested on my chest, tucked beneath my chin. The faint flowery scent of her hair reached my nose, and a few errant strands tickled my jawline.

I stood awkwardly, arms hanging in the air like a puppet on a set of strings. A puppet waiting for instructions on how to react.

"Thank you," she murmured, her arms tightening around my back.

Any carefully construed words I might have uttered fled. When was the last time someone willingly hugged me? Had it ever happened? Certainly not for something as insignificant as words. Yet they hadn't felt insignificant.

When I lowered my arms around her, she relaxed deeper into our embrace. The oxygen in the alley evaporated, and my lungs burned, reminding me to breathe. I clawed for something to say, anything to stop the strange tide of emotions rolling through me. Instinctual phrases such as "back off" and "leave me alone" formed in the back of my throat.

"I think you should come and stay with me at the Lennox mansion."

Okay, so I took the opposite direction.

She didn't answer, and my insides shriveled. Heat climbed the back of my neck. *What a stupid thing to say.* But I kept on talking.

"Only until we track down the Red Wolf and make sure Ashworth doesn't come after you again. You could stay in Adella's wing of the house, use all her servants. Hastings will love it. He thrives when he has people to dote on, and my cook always complains there are never enough guests to try her meals."

Kill me now. The rambling wouldn't stop! I wanted to skulk into the corner of the alley and die. Some poor soul would find me, take one look, and say, "Here lies an idiot."

An unbearable silence stretched between us, and I nearly let out a string of curses. Forget the future; I needed to change the past and revoke my impulsive invitation. As if she'd want to live with a criminal! The fact she hadn't stumbled out of the alley screaming for the authorities already was a complete miracle.

"Okay," she said, leaning back to look up at my face.

"Okay?" The woman must have hit her head. My fingers sifted through her hair, probing for a bruise.

"What are you doing?" She leaned into my hand and gave me a quizzical look.

"You're concussed."

Vivian pursed her lips to contain a laugh. "I'm not concussed. It's a good idea. Temporarily, of course, until we straighten things out. I'm sick of looking over my shoulder, and I don't want you sneaking into my house anymore."

I narrowed my eyes, trying to guess her angle. I expected a fight, not an easy win. That usually meant there was a catch.

"How are you going to explain our living arrangement to the witch?"

Vivian frowned. "Her name is Tessa."

"That's what I said."

She pinched me. Hard.

"That hurt!"

"Then don't say stupid things. I know there's history between you two and most of it isn't pleasant, but enough is enough. Find a way to get along."

"She came to me first looking for money, not the other way around."

"And she paid you back. A clean slate."

My teeth ground together. "Fine. If she makes an effort, so will I. But my goodwill doesn't extend to

Detective Chambers. He enjoyed keeping me in jail way too much, and I know he's dying to put me back in there."

Vivian sighed. "I guess it's a start."

"Are there any other concessions I need to make? Do I have to invite the entire agency over for tea and biscuits?"

Her mouth hitched. "No. That seems like overkill."

"Good, because there are conditions at my place too, mostly relating to my business. Not to mention, rooms you're not allowed to enter."

Her brow lifted, and a playful light gleamed in her eyes. "Rooms where you keep victims chained to the walls?"

"No," I scoffed. "Rooms where I keep my riches."

This time, she couldn't hold back her laughter. The lush sound made me grin. I liked her laugh and wanted to hear more of it—a lot more. My irritation dissolved as if it had never been there. I tugged her closer, her body pressing up against mine.

"You don't know how to pick locks, do you?"

She nodded solemnly, her fingers tracing a line down my back. "I do. I'm quite good. But I promise not to rob you blind."

"It's not my gold I'm worried about."

The air felt charged, and some of the humor left her eyes. Another stretch of silence followed as our kiss from earlier filled my mind. This was a risky plan. I shook my head, trying to clear my thoughts. Lines that had always been crystal clear were starting to blur.

"We need to go. The ceremony has probably already started. They'll be wondering what happened to you." I unwound her arms from my waist, acknowledging the coldness that crept in where her hands were.

"What are we going to do about Ashworth? Do you think he's really gone?"

"He won't bother you again, I'll make sure of it."

"I believe you." There was trust in her tone; a certainty I wasn't sure I'd earned or deserved. She straightened her cloak, fixing the ties around her neck, then brushed dirt from the fabric.

She believes me?

Vivian took a deep breath and walked out of the alley. I followed close behind as she weaved through the crowd toward the town square, keeping an eye out for anyone suspicious. The chances were slim for another attack, but I didn't want to risk being blindsided.

The procession had ended, and Prince Marcus's voice boomed through the square, addressing the mourners. As we drew near, he spotted Vivian and gestured her forward.

"And now, a few words from Winifred's granddaughter."

The crowd parted, opening a direct path to the raised platform. Vivian hesitated under the scrutiny of so many expectant faces. I placed my hand on the small of her back, and she jolted.

"Would you like me to speak instead?" I whispered, leaning in.

"Winifred would roll over in her grave."

I chuckled. "I don't know, she and I kind of had a thing going on. She almost let me try one of her scones."

"You nearly lost your hand in the attempt, didn't you?"

"Maybe. But don't you think a hook for a hand would only make me more dashing?" I nudged her forward. "Come on, let's go together."

Some of the tension drained from her as we climbed the steps to where Prince Marcus waited. At the top, Vivian slowly turned and faced the crowd. Staring straight ahead, she remained completely silent. She was either gathering her thoughts or preparing to faint. The longer she stood there, the higher the scales tipped toward fainting. I moved behind her, so she wouldn't end up facedown on the wooden planks. That was no way to conduct a eulogy.

Through the crowd, I located the witch. Her mouth hung open, but she snapped it shut when we made eye contact, then stood on her toes to whisper something to the detective. The devious part of me wanted to wave, but I'd promised to make an effort.

Though, waving was a social gesture...

I wriggled my fingers. The witch looked like she was going to have a stroke in the square.

Prince Marcus cleared his throat, signaling Vivian to start her speech. The crowd began to murmur. It seemed I was going to have to speak after all.

Finally, Vivian began, and a hush fell over the

gathering. "Thank you all for coming." Her voice was thick and unsteady. She paused again. The silence grew uncomfortable. A minute passed, then she reached behind her and found my hand, squeezing it for all it was worth. She didn't pull away, simply held on like I was her lifeline.

Me.

Argus Ward.

What a fool.

I gripped her hand tighter, my throat constricting as her voice rang out over the crowd, stronger, surer.

"My grandmother meant a lot of things to the people in this kingdom. Her wisdom and sight guided many of you, and now that she's gone, it feels like we're all a little lost."

The pain in her voice held the crowd in a somber trance. An ache expanded in my chest as I listened to her speech. Winifred would have been proud. *I* was proud. They didn't listen to her out of fear, but out of reverence and respect.

A novel concept.

"The future is never certain, though my grandmother tried to make it so. We live our lives with the expectation of another day. We make plans and we design our futures oblivious to fate having other intentions. It seems odd coming from an oracle, but the most important thing Winifred ever taught me was to live life in the present. The people we love are here today, and we should let them know how we feel in case they're gone tomorrow. So, that is how I want you to remember her. Don't be fooled by the promise of the future. Her gift was never to show you the end; it was to show you the way."

She wiped tears from her eyes and released my hand. As she descended the platform, the crowd bowed their heads, some reaching out to touch her shoulders. Vivian spent time with each of them, letting them offer condolences.

I remained rooted to the platform. Her words lodged themselves deep inside my bones. Nothing I did was in the present; my entire existence was a form of preparation. Each day passed into the next while I anticipated other people's strikes against me. I valued nothing worthwhile, discontent with my surroundings, and shut myself off from those who tried to get close. Self-preservation was my excuse, but it was beginning to feel more like cowardice.

"What are you doing here, thief? I thought we'd gotten rid of you." The witch climbed the platform, frowning at me from beneath a black veil. Her voice wavered. Was she affected by Vivian's speech as well?

"I'm here to pay my respects."

"Laughable." She pushed aside the veil. "Where did Vivian go earlier? She wasn't in the procession when it arrived."

"There was a situation. I handled it."

She bristled, and a dry laugh escaped her lips. "There's always a *situation* with you. You can't change who you are."

Her words cut like razors. "No, I can't change who I've been."

"There's no difference," she grated.

"Not according to Vivian. You heard her. The future isn't certain."

"Don't twist her words. You've brought heartbreak into her life and put her at risk."

"That's the past again."

Vivian worked her way through the mourners. A small child clung to her skirt, and she smiled, patting the top of his head.

The witch visibly swallowed, her chin trembling. "You need to understand, she's my best friend. Winifred was like a grandmother to me too. I can't lose them both."

"You won't."

She searched for something in my features while unshed tears glistened in her eyes. "You just said the future isn't certain."

I returned her stare, noticing her distrust. "As far as Vivian's safety is concerned, it is."

Chapter 16

VIVIAN

"Are you sure you want to do this?" Tessa asked for the tenth time in as many minutes. She wasn't thrilled with my decision to move into the Lennox mansion. Though, she'd handled it well, all things considered. Telling her about my attack in the alley helped. Now, she just looked worried. She'd already packed and re-packed the same dress twice.

"I'm sure," I said, tossing more clothes onto the pile.

"You can stay with me. The magic shop might not have twenty bedrooms or a ballroom the size of my entire property, but it's a solid option. There might be a barrier spell I could cast."

I tucked a pair of satin slippers into the bag and shook my head. "No way. You'd probably cast it in reverse, and we'd be stuck inside for months."

"At least we wouldn't run out of wine," she grumbled, shoving my garments aside and slumping onto the bed.

"Tess, I know it sounds crazy, but Argus's home is the safest place for me right now. I'm vulnerable here alone, and I don't want to put you in danger too. Besides, this is a temporary arrangement. The faster we track down my grandmother's killer, the faster I can come home."

Tessa grunted and crossed her arms. "Admit it, you're only doing this because you'll have access to a personal cook."

She had me there. There were other reasons—a few I wasn't ready to analyze—but the extravagant meals would be a perk.

"His cook's culinary mastery has nothing to do with my decision."

"Liar."

"Maybe a little." I smiled, trying to reassure her. "Look, I know you don't trust Argus."

"Ha! Don't use that word and his name in the same sentence."

I breathed through my irritation. The two of them were impossible!

"Winifred trusted him. I don't take that lightly. She made him promise to watch out for me if anything happened to her. We'll never know what she saw in her mirror before she died, but I have to believe whatever it was proves he's worth a chance. Your past with him is exactly that: the past."

Tessa sighed and fiddled with the corner of the bedspread. "Great, now you sound like him." She deepened her voice, doing her best Argus impression. "The past is past. I can change. I'm a good person now. *Blech.*"

I barely suppressed a laugh. "He did not say that."

"He did! And he was looking at you all googly-eyed when he said it. I thought I was going to toss my breakfast. I might now just thinking about it."

Warmth flooded my cheeks, and I pulled my hair forward to hide the blush. "Don't be silly. I'm a burden to him at most. Your breakfast is fine right where it is."

"I wish I was being silly." Tessa narrowed her eyes. "Something's going on between you two, I can tell. I have a sensitivity for these kinds of things. Don't get me wrong, I get it. He's rich, handsome, and has that whole dangerous appeal going on, but he's not stable. What would a normal night with Argus even look like? Dragging you around while he extorts money from business owners? Dinner with a side of thievery?"

A carriage rumbled to a stop in front of the house.

"Well, whatever it is, I think I'm about to find out." I peeked through the window as a driver dressed in the Lennox livery descended from his seat.

"You can still change your mind. I'll send the driver away." Tessa leaned over my shoulder and whistled. "Damn, that's a nice carriage." She jabbed me in the shoulder. "Don't be swayed by nice things. You still have to come back to all this."

"Don't be jealous," I shot back.

"I'm not...much."

I took a calming breath, which did little to settle

my nerves, and gathered my bags. I'd be lying if I said I wasn't terrified of my decision. It felt like stepping out of my old life and into something strange and new. I wasn't sure I'd be able to find my way back when this was over.

Argus's house wasn't the problem; it was him. Something *was* happening between us. I knew it in the alley when I was certain he'd pull away, and instead, he stayed. Then again, on the platform, when my throat closed up and everything I wanted to say evaporated in my mind. He was a source of strength, grounding me, and the words had appeared. I'd thought it would be impossible to say goodbye, yet the moment was cathartic.

Tessa's reservations made sense, but they didn't change anything. I had to see this through. I wanted to.

She walked me to the carriage, where I handed my bags to the driver. "I'll stop by the magic shop tomorrow so you can see for yourself I'm still alive after a night under Argus's roof."

"That's not funny." Tessa wrung her hands and pulled me into a hug. "Be careful," she whispered.

"Everything's going to be fine." I hugged her back, then climbed into the carriage.

As it drove away, she called out, "It had better be fine, or Argus is a dead man. Oh! And bring some of his cook's pastries when you visit!"

***

Hastings met me at the door. A wide smile lit his

face as I tilted my head back and hovered on the steps studying the gargoyles. They looked about as forbidding as their master.

He whisked my bags away, and still, I stood on the stoop staring at the intricate iron railings and priceless stonework. I was definitely out of my league, but nobody could say Vivian James didn't know how to adapt.

Ushering me inside, Hastings' white-gloved hands gestured to a foyer with vaulted ceilings and a giant fireplace that crackled with warmth. "Miss James, it is such a pleasure to have you stay with us. I admit, I was thrilled when I was informed of your impending arrival."

"Are you sure you don't have to check me for weapons this time, Hastings? I wouldn't want you to get in trouble with Mr. Ward."

He threw back his head and laughed, the deep sound rumbling through the foyer. I couldn't help it. I liked this man, and it was so refreshing to see a kind face who didn't act like I was made of glass.

"I still maintain you're the exception to the rule." He winked. "Come with me. Your room is ready, and I'm sure you'd like to relax before dinner. You've had a trying day." He leaned in and spoke as if he was revealing a trade secret. "Fiona, our cook, has been hard at work in the kitchen. I hope you're hungry."

There was no use fighting his infectious attitude or the horrible rumble in my stomach. His bushy brows raised in mock horror.

"I'm actually starved, and please, call me Vivian."

"Wonderful! I'll leave a more extensive tour of the house to Mr. Ward when he's available. I hope you don't mind, but he's currently out of the house on business. He won't be here for dinner, so, if it's all right, I'll have your food brought up to you."

"Thank you, Hastings. I'd like that." I added an extra note of brightness to my tone, trying to hide my disappointment. Naturally, Argus wasn't here. It wasn't his job to monitor my every move—his words, not mine. Maybe it was for the best. I needed some time to decompress and get used to my new surroundings.

Hastings glossed over my fake enthusiasm. "If you need anything, I'm at your service. Please, consider this your home, as ostentatious as it might be. Some rooms can be quite cozy."

We walked through the foyer and up a grand staircase. Plush red carpet covered the steps, and the white banister gleamed under an enormous crystal chandelier. Along the wall, family portraits hung in large gilded frames.

"Is that Adella?" I asked, pausing to study the young woman depicted in the painting. The image was striking, a beautiful mix of light and color. She wore a flowing emerald gown that complimented her sun-kissed features. Seated on a marble bench, she looked ethereal among a garden of ivy and roses.

Hastings nodded. "Yes, that's Adella when she was fifteen or so. Her mother, Isabel Lennox, painted it before she passed."

"It's lovely. Her mother was incredibly talented."

I gazed at the other paintings lining the wall: more portraits of Adella through the years, and a few other family members I didn't recognize. There was one notable absence. "Are there none of Argus?"

"I'm afraid there aren't." Hastings continued up the stairs, forcing me to catch up.

"Why not? There are so many of Adella." I checked again, not believing Hastings' word. "I'm sure there's a painting of him somewhere. He's the family heir." It bothered me that there wasn't one.

He paused on the landing, his jovial expression gone. "There is a lot you don't know about Mr. Ward. Suffice to say, he hasn't led an easy life. Don't let the opulent house and all of its trappings fool you."

His words stung even though his tone wasn't harsh. "I'm sorry. I didn't mean to pry."

The corner of Hastings' lips twitched. "If you don't pry, my dear, how will you ever see below the surface?" He took my hand in his own, his skin soft and papery, but there was strength in his grip. "Mr. Ward is a private person. He can be difficult at times, but the fact you're here speaks volumes."

I swallowed past the lump in my throat. "I'm only here to bring my grandmother's murderer to justice."

He patted my fingers. "You're here because you want to be. Don't hide your actions behind excuses. Now, let's go see your room."

The second floor was as lavish as the first. I had to keep my mouth closed tight to stop from gaping like a fool. Velvet drapes hung from huge paneled windows that cast sunlight onto the polished hardwood floors, and ornate rugs splashed reams of color along the hallway. It was almost a shame to walk on them; they were works of art in their own right. My gaze roamed over the elegant scrollwork in the crown molding where even the ceiling had been given special attention.

"Here we are." Hastings pushed open a door, and I sucked in a sharp breath. "That's the reaction we hope for." He grinned.

"I've never seen anything this beautiful." Stepping inside, my feet sank into the thick carpet. The walls were covered in light floral paper, creating the illusion of petals falling from the sky. A large canopy bed took up one corner of the room, where panels of sheer fabric created a luxurious haven.

"Your bags have been placed inside the bureau. Relax, get some rest, and I'll have dinner brought up to you soon. If you need anything, pull the bell chain."

Hastings backed out of the room, leaving me to gawk at my surroundings. This was a far cry from my tiny bedroom in town, and I almost felt like a fraud running my fingers over the silk sheets and satin duvet. Any minute now, someone was going to burst into the room and drag me away, I was sure of it.

Guilt wormed its way through my heart at the thought of what I'd had to lose to gain so much splendor, but Winifred would disapprove of me wallowing in my losses. It was a good thing I couldn't see her ghost—she'd haunt me with a frown on her lips and pity in her eyes. The James women did what needed to be done, whether it was helping a stranger at the end of their life or delivering a dark future.

I unpacked my toiletries, arranging the stoppered bottles on a gold-plated vanity. The mirror revealed my reflection, and I stared into it for an uneasy second before deciding it was probably best to cover the blasted thing for the time being. Draping a light blanket over the frame, I blew out a breath and nervously paced the room.

A short while later, a soft knock sounded on the door. I looked over to see a woman wheeling a cart into the room. She bobbed her head, and a gray ringlet escaped her white cap.

"Miss James? I'm Fiona, the cook. I hope you don't mind the intrusion. I wanted to bring up your dinner myself, so I could meet you."

"Not at all. Call me Vivian, please." My gaze landed on the cart. "Is that all for me?"

The three-tiered display held a variety of meats and cheeses, the bottom tier loaded with fruit arranged in intricate designs. The smell of roast chicken and vegetables wafted from beneath a silver lidded plate. There were other dishes, some I didn't recognize, but they all made my mouth water.

"I wasn't sure what you liked to eat, so I brought an assortment." Fiona grinned, lifting the lid on the chicken.

"It smells amazing."

She prepared a plate and set it on a small table,

then whipped out a cloth napkin and laid it across my lap. While I took my first bite, she hovered over me, her eyes wide with expectation.

"How is it? If you don't like it, I can prepare something else. We don't get a ton of guests, so I want to make sure it's perfect."

The moist, flavorful chicken melted in my mouth, and I all but swooned. "It's delicious. Be careful—I might get used to this."

Fiona laughed and patted the hair at the back of her cap. "I'm hoping you do." Moving closer, she bit the side of her lip. "Can I ask you a question?"

"Sure," I said between mouthfuls.

"Can you really see the future in the mirror? Hastings said I shouldn't ask you about it, but I'm very curious. I've never known anyone with special powers before."

I frowned and set my fork down. "It's okay. The answer is yes, but if I'm being honest, I'm not very good at it. Right now, it seems like I'm not very good at anything except getting myself into trouble."

"Goodness, that sounds familiar. You know, before I was a cook, I was a maid. Not a good one either. I can't tell you how many shirts I burned holes in with the iron, or how many times my employers slipped on the floors I over polished. I was fired three times before I came to work for Mr. Ward."

"You were? And he still hired you?"

Fiona waved her hand. "I lied and got my friend to act as a previous employer for a good reference. Mr. Ward found out, of course. I wasn't aware of it at the time, but my friend mentioned how much I love to cook. Well, after I accidentally dropped a bucket of dirty water all over the floor in the great hall, he had me reassigned to the kitchen."

"And you discovered your great talent?"

She clucked her tongue. "Lord, no, child. I almost burned the place down baking a loaf of bread. But I kept trying. I was determined to keep this job, and so I practiced. Poor Hastings was my taste tester, and eventually, the more I cooked, the better I got. Now, I'm a culinary queen." Crossing the room, she picked up a hand mirror resting on the vanity and brought it back to the table. "What I'm trying to say is, it's okay if you're not good at the moment. You just need to keep trying. Practice makes perfect."

Chapter 17

VIVIAN

Practice did not make perfect.

I groaned and slid the hand mirror away. It was more than a week since I'd arrived at the Lennox mansion, and no matter how hard I tried, the mirror was stuck on the vision of the next murder. Over and over, I watched myself find the body, and each time, her cries made me feel helpless.

Besides the forest, I wasn't able to tell where we were or who the victim was. I tried to focus on the object buried in the snow but could never get close enough to make out what it was, and the faces around me remained blurred and indistinct.

Basically, I had nothing.

Something was holding me back from harnessing my new powers in a way that would be helpful. Which was ironic, considering how hard I'd resisted using them. Now that I wanted them to work, the mirror was being difficult. What was the point in seeing the same vision fifty times over if I couldn't find any clues that would help?

To make matters worse, the mirror wasn't the only one acting difficult.

Argus was avoiding me.

When he was in the house, he was locked in his office, and if we happened to cross paths in the hall-way, it was an awkward dance of polite greetings and unreadable glances. The reserved distance made me want to scream after those few stolen moments of connection. It made me feel lonelier, and not even visits from Tessa or afternoon tea with Hastings filled the void he'd created.

I wanted to pin it all on his frustration at losing the blade. Maybe he blamed me? I found out later, the ship carrying the men who'd sold it set sail the same day as the memorial. He'd had to choose be-tween going after it and rescuing me.

Argus's decision had set us back days while he sent one of his men to track them down. There wasn't any news on his sister either. It was as if she'd vanished that night in the maze.

Each day that passed held us back further from finding the Grimm's blade or the Red Wolf. That alone should be enough for his aloof attitude, but I sensed it ran deeper than that. Some of it was surely related to the way I pushed him away the morning of our kiss, and I didn't know how to bridge that gap or make amends.

"Time for tea, Miss James." Hastings entered the conservatory carrying a silver tea set and placed it on a narrow sideboard. He prepared two cups with extra lumps of sugar and took the seat across from mine. "You look lovely this afternoon, as fresh as any flower here." He waved his hand, gesturing to the vast greenery that decorated the conservatory.

The bright and airy space with giant windows and sweet-smelling florals had become my favorite spot in the house. It was an indoor garden where I could while away the hours with my mirror.

"You're such a charmer, Hastings." I smiled at him over the rim of my teacup.

He made a sound in the back of his throat. "Nonsense. I'm simply stating what every one of us can see."

"Not every one of you," I muttered, taking a deeper sip and letting the hot liquid burn my tongue.

He frowned, his white bushy eyebrows drawing together. For a moment, he was quiet, then his warm smile returned, and he gestured to the hand mirror.

"Any more luck with your visions?"

Making a face, I peered out the window. "No. It's still the same. I even went for a walk around the grounds this morning to try and clear my head."

"Don't go too far. The paths around the house are safe, but the woods are deep, and it's easy to get lost."

I shivered as I remembered standing at the edge of the forest that morning. I'd considered following the path that led further inside, wondering if being surrounded by dense trees would jog something in my mind, give me a clue to the vision. There was a moment while I stood there that I felt something staring back. The unseen eyes prickled my skin and tightened the ball of unshakable dread in my stomach.

"You should take Mr. Ward with you next time you go for a walk. I'm sure the fresh air would do you both some good."

I laughed into my tea, and it almost went up my nose. "The last thing Argus wants to do is spend time with me. He'd probably run in the other direction if he saw me coming. Fiona would find him hiding in the pantry."

Hastings poured himself a second cup and nodded. "You're probably right. I think you make him nervous."

"Well, I'm not trying to. I don't know how I'm supposed to act around him. Things got...complicated, and it feels like my fault."

"It's not your fault." He stirred his tea, glancing around in unease, then lowered his voice. "You see, the thing you need to understand about Mr. Ward is he's always led a solitary existence. It's all he knows, reinforced by an upbringing from an emotionally absent mother. He doesn't talk about her much."

"He told me about her. I kind of stuck my foot in my mouth then too. I was just surprised."

"Edie Ward isn't a bad woman. She's a grifter and a loner, but in her way, she loves her son. She taught him to survive, though you and I both know survival isn't all there is to life." With another glance over his shoulder, Hastings continued. "As a result, Mr. Ward holds himself apart from people even while surrounding himself with the very thing he thinks he doesn't need. The servants here and his half-sister, we all try, but it only gets us so far. I think there's always been a part of him that longs for something deeper, but he doesn't know how to open up to it." Hastings patted my hand. "We all need someone to love us. Mr. Ward, for all his faults, is no different."

"So, what should I do?"

"Start by having dinner with him. I think if you two spend some time together, the tension will naturally resolve itself."

"You'll have to chain him to the chair."

Hastings chuckled. "I hardly think that will be necessary. But I'm prepared to act if the situation requires it. Sometimes, you have to use force." He drained his tea and collected my empty cup. "Leave things to me. I'll have him collect you here at dinner time."

"That will give me more time with the mirror. I have to figure out how to make it show me something different." I sighed. "I wish Winifred was here. I wish I paid closer attention to how this works. Mostly, I just miss hearing her voice. I'd give anything to hear her scold me about what a terrible oracle I am."

"I never met your grandmother, but I think she'd be proud of the way you're handling things. The rest will come." Hastings gave me a stern look. "But don't work too hard. I'm not afraid of using force on you either, and I will force you to enjoy yourself while you're here."

"Thank you, Hastings. You're a good butler."

He winked. "I'm an excellent butler." Picking up the tray, he left me to my mirror gazing.

The light faded as evening fell. I lit the wall sconces and settled back into the chair, determined to finally get my visions to work. When I placed my hands on the glass, the familiar mist obscured my reflection, and there it was: the same vision I'd relived for days. It played through, and I slumped in my seat.

"I get it. You don't like being told what to do. Neither do I." Pulling the hand mirror into my lap, I stared at my reflection. "I don't want to let him down, you know? I don't want to let anyone down. If I can't help in this way, what good am I?"

The mirror offered nothing in response.

"And I don't care what Hastings said," I added. "I messed things up. You didn't see the look on his face when I pushed him away. Even after that, he still showed up. If the situation was reversed, I would have vowed to the spirits never to show my face in front of him again. So, I just need a little guidance. Some reassurance I'm not going crazy, that I—"

My reflection tossed up her hands and heaved a sigh. Slowly, the mist began to swirl.

Okay, so, apparently, you can annoy the mirror.

The smoke cleared, and just like before, I saw my future self from a short distance. She stood in the dining room, the table set with the remnants of one of Fiona's lavish meals. Dinner was over, and she sipped wine by the fireplace.

Argus approached. His charcoal gray dinner jacket was expertly fitted across his broad shoulders, and he looked relaxed, swirling whiskey in his rocks glass. At the fireplace, he took the wineglass from her hand and placed it on the mantel. He said something, but the words were muted and dull like everything was underwater.

Whatever it was made the air thick with expectation.

My future self answered, and the moment felt suspended until he reached out, fingers sliding behind her neck, to draw her closer. His head dipped, and he kissed her softly on the—

Thick, impenetrable mist rushed in, engulfing the scene. Darkness spread before I blinked, and the conservatory came back into sharp focus.

Oh, come on! I finally get a decent vision and it's fade to black.

Seeing the future was the worst.

Chapter 18

ARGUS

"You're hovering again, Hastings." I sighed and closed the account book I was working in. "Is there something you need?"

"It's dinnertime, sir."

"So, have my food placed on the sideboard. I'll eat later."

Hastings didn't move to do my bidding. Instead, he remained by the edge of my desk.

I pinched the bridge of my nose. "What?"

"Your meal is being served in the dining room this evening. Miss James is waiting in the conservatory for you to escort her to dinner."

"And why is Vivian waiting for me in the conservatory?"

Hastings had the nerve to look innocent as he said, "Because I told her you were looking forward to spending the evening with her, sir. The poor woman has been here a week, and you've hardly seen her.

She's been overworking herself practicing with the mirror, and she needs a break. I think it's fair to say, you need one too."

I scrubbed a hand over my face. Avoiding Vivian for the past week had felt like a necessity. I was getting too involved. Inviting her here seemed like the smart thing to do at the time, a decision made out of fear for her safety, but it was like jumping feetfirst into the fire. Her presence was everywhere. The faint scent of lavender drifted through the hallways. Her laughter echoed from abovestairs while she visited with Hastings or spent time in the kitchen with Fiona. A part of me was glad her visions weren't helping because it meant she wasn't any closer to returning home. So, I hid in my office, stayed out late, and pretended it was business as usual.

But leave it to Hastings to meddle.

"She's waiting, sir." He gestured toward the door, and I pushed out of my seat. "Wait—you can't go looking like that. Your shirt is rumpled." He handed me a freshly pressed shirt and a charcoal gray evening jacket. "Here, put these on."

I dressed in the garments and straightened the sleeves. A quick glance in the mirror over the sideboard had me scowling, and I ran a hand through my hair. "How do I look?"

"Excellent, sir."

"You're lucky decent butlers are so hard to find," I grumbled, leaving the office in search of Vivian.

At the entrance to the conservatory, I hesitated, watching her from the doorway. She hadn't heard me yet. Her attention was directed on the small hand mirror she'd placed on a wrought iron table. Potted ferns created a canopy over her head, and lush flowers bloomed in tiered planters climbing the walls. She traced her finger over the glass, deep in thought.

"Did you see something?"

Vivian's gaze lifted from the mirror, and she flushed, her cheeks turning the same shade of pink as the blossoms near her seat. "Uh, no," she said, flipping the mirror over. "It's still not working."

"You must have seen something. You're acting strange."

"How would you know how I act? You haven't seen me in days. Any word on the blade?" She switched topics so fluidly, I probably wouldn't have noticed, but her shoe bounced against the stone tile. Vivian looked guilty. There was definitely something going on.

"Gregor should return any day now. We'll know where the blade went then."

She bit the side of her lip. "I...uh..." Clearing her throat, she said, "I never thanked you properly for showing up that day. You lost the blade because of me, and I—"

"Don't do that."

"Do what?" Her brow furrowed.

"Make it seem like I struggled with a choice. There never was one."

Her flush deepened. "Yes, well, you chose to honor the promise you made to my grandmother, and it cost you. I'm grateful."

Ah, yes, the promise. Funny how the obligation never entered my mind.

I held out my arm. "Are you ready for dinner?" I was good at changing topics too.

She stood, which ended the nervous bounce of her toes, but for some reason, she kept glancing at my evening jacket. I was starting to feel self-conscious. Had Hastings picked out the wrong one? What did he know about fashion?

"Is something wrong? You're staring."

"What?" She jolted out of whatever trance she'd found herself in.

This was getting ridiculous.

"My jacket. Is there something wrong with it?"

"No, it's nice. Very fitted. Charcoal's a good color on you." Patting my shoulder, she continued without taking a breath, "I'm starving. Are you hungry? Let's go." Vivian sailed right past my outstretched arm toward the door.

In the dining room, she settled in the seat across from me, placing the napkin in her lap. A side door opened, and two servants entered carrying large silver trays. They served Vivian first, then placed a covered plate in front of me.

Hastings bowed and signaled the lids to be removed. "Fiona has prepared her specialty this evening. Beef Wellington with a shallot mushroom sauce, served with winter greens and sliced almonds." He lifted a wine bottle and poured us each a glass. "Enjoy your evening," he said, snapping his fingers as he followed the servants out of the room. Before the side door closed, he gave me the eye. His message was clear: *Don't screw this up.*

Vivian took a healthy drink from her glass. "The wine is very good here. So is the food."

"What did you see in the mirror, Vivian?"

Her face soured as she speared a mushroom with her fork. "Nothing. I already told you, it's on the fritz, and I can't make it work."

"You're lying."

She leaned forward. "How can you tell?"

I contained a smile at her quick surrender. "You gave yourself away in the conservatory. You were bouncing."

"Huh." She slumped back in her chair. "Fredrick said the same thing. I'm going to have to work on that."

"Fredrick?" My grip tightened on my utensil. Who the hell was Fredrick, and why was he watching her so closely?

"Wow." She whistled. "Are you planning to kill someone with your butter knife? Fredrick's a ghost. He says I bounce when I chea— I mean, take my turn at chess."

"Oh." I smeared a pad of butter onto a roll, only slightly relieved. "Now we've established you did see something, are you going to tell me what it was?"

She heaved a sigh. "Fine. I saw our dinner."

"What?" I laughed. That was why she was flustered? "Unless Fiona poisoned the beef, I don't understand why you lied."

She didn't answer, but I noticed she didn't try any more of her food either.

"*Did* she poison the beef?"

"No. It's safe to eat." At my skeptical look, she rolled her eyes and cut a small piece, then chewed it slowly. "See? Not dead."

"Okay, so, whatever you saw happens during our dinner. Is it dangerous?"

This made her pause, the fork inches from her mouth. "Not exactly," she hedged.

"Then I think you should try to change it."

"What?" The fork clattered to her plate. Vivian frowned, looking a little deflated, as if I'd told her she couldn't have any dessert.

"Think about it. We don't know how set in stone your visions are, which means we don't know if we can stop them from happening. This might be a good opportunity in a non-dangerous setting to try and alter your vision. We can even make it into a game if you want."

"How so?"

I sipped my wine, watching her over the rim. Her interest was piqued.

"If I can guess what you saw in your vision when it happens, I win. And if I can't, or if you successfully change it, you win."

Her lips curved at the challenge. There was a definite sparkle in her eyes.

"What do I win?"

I glanced around the dining room. "*If* you win, you can have anything you want in this room. Mind you, the gold candlesticks alone are worth a fortune, and if you choose the diamond-encrusted clock on the mantel, you'll be set for life."

"I thought I couldn't have your riches," she teased.

"Today, I'll make an exception. But I don't think you'll win. I've gotten pretty good at reading you."

She considered my offer for another second, then stuck her hand out over the table. "Deal."

My hand closed over hers, and we shook. How a simple handshake became my greatest temptation was startling. Vivian smiled at me, a sly little grin as seductive as it was confident. Then, she released my hand and dug into her dinner.

I couldn't remember the last time I had a dinner guest. Adella was rarely around, usually off causing trouble with Sarah while I ate in my office poring over account books. Dining rooms always seemed stuffy, a place where boring noblemen droned on about the price of wheat, or where primped ladies debated the latest fashions. But Vivian wasn't like that. She was witty and smart and completely oblivious to the way she held everyone's attention, including mine. Eating alone in my office felt like a horrible offense when I could be here, sitting with her. Maybe Hastings had the right idea.

We ate quietly for a while, both of us taking turns watching the other, neither of us sure how to break the silence. It wasn't uncomfortable, it just felt precarious, as if once that thin veil broke, there was no going back to the manufactured distance between us.

"Your house is beautiful. Did you grow up here?" she asked as she sliced her beef into bite-sized pieces.

"No, this is Adella's home. I grew up with my mother. We had a small one-room in town. I wasn't welcome here." I poured myself another glass of wine. "My father, Robert Lennox, never wanted a son. He never gave me his name."

"Why not? Every wealthy gentleman wants an heir."

"An heir would mean he'd have to give up his power someday. My father was a cruel man, and even though he was a peer, he was also the head of the most feared criminal organization in the kingdom. He didn't want to share any of his empire with me. In the end, he didn't have a choice."

"What happened?" Vivian asked, holding out her glass.

I topped it off and stoppered the bottle. "My mother taught me everything she knew. How to pick pockets, how to scam money with street games, and how to watch my back. I eventually started running with a shady crowd and rose through their ranks. It was the first time in my life I wasn't on my own. We might not have been pillars of society, but I built something that helped me survive." I rested back in my seat. "My father hated that there was a rival gang in his kingdom, especially one led by his son. There were a lot of dark days—blood spilled, money lost. He even tried to kill me."

"Argus..." Vivian stopped eating, her features

drawn with concern. "I don't know what to say."

"Well, he didn't succeed, and that only made him furious. It wasn't long after that, he got sick, and in an ironic chain of events, the man who wanted to live forever died, and I inherited everything. His empire, this house, and a sister I barely knew." I sighed. "This is the only life I've known. It's what I've worked toward, but lately, I wonder if..." My voice faded. I wasn't sure I wanted to say the words out loud.

Vivian filled in the rest. "You wonder if it still fits?"

"Yeah. Exactly."

She traced the edge of her plate with her index finger. "I can't believe I'm saying this, but you and I aren't so different. We were both born into a world where people weren't willing to accept us."

"How so?" I asked.

Her mouth twisted in a wry smile. "People have always been scared of my abilities. Maybe I reminded them of their mortality, but no one wanted anything to do with the girl who saw ghosts. I spent most of my time alone talking to dead people, which, as you can imagine, didn't help me to fit in. I would have given anything to be like everyone else. To be normal." Her gaze flickered to mine, and my breath held. She grew quiet as emotion drifted across her beautiful features.

"I'm glad you're not normal."

"What?" Disbelief tinged her voice.

"Normal is so boring! Would a normal woman

have tried to stab me twice? Have tea every afternoon with a butler? You're not afraid to say what you think, and you charge into every situation with a brave smile on your face. It drives me crazy, but I wouldn't want you to be any other way."

The silence that followed had weight to it. My words seemed to hang in the air, and even though they left me exposed, I didn't want to take them back.

Vivian's gaze dropped to her plate, and she bit the side of her lip, brow creasing as if she was struggling with a decision. She exhaled a small puff of air and mumbled something about fairness under her breath. Another minute passed, then she looked up. Reaching out, she leaned forward as if she were attempting to place her hand on mine, but her arm bumped my wine glass, knocking it over. Red liquid sloshed over the table and streamed down my jacket, staining the fabric like a bloody wound.

"Damn it, your jacket." She rounded the table with her napkin and dabbed at the soiled cloth. Her mouth formed a comical circle, and I suddenly realized what this was. I'd almost forgotten we were in the middle of a bet. At the start of dinner, she was worried about something that was supposed to happen, and according to the horror written all over her face, she hadn't been able to change her vision.

"I win," I said, shrugging out of my jacket and using it to mop up the wine that dripped off the edge of the table.

"You win?"

"The bet. Your vision was you'd spill wine all over me and ruin my most expensive jacket."

She wrung her hands. "Was it that expensive?"

"Nearly priceless. You can't purchase fabric like this in the kingdom; it has to be ordered from overseas."

Her skin paled. "Is it really ruined?"

"I'll never wear it again."

"I see." Her shoulders lifted. "Yeah, that was the vision. I guess I couldn't change it." With a sigh, she let her napkin flutter to the table.

"Don't be upset. I'm sure we'll figure out a way to change your visions. I should probably get someone to clean this up. Sorry about cutting dinner short."

A small frown formed on her lips as she eyed her near-empty plate. "Yeah, I think I'm finished for the night anyway. I'm pretty tired. Thanks for dinner."

She backed away from the table, but there was something in her eyes that left me off-balance, as if I was missing something important. Had I hurt her feelings by making a big deal out of the stain? I didn't even care about the stupid thing. I'd definitely screwed up.

"Hey, it's not a big deal."

At the entryway, Vivian paused. "Yeah, I know. I'm just sorry things turned out this way. Goodnight, Argus." She ducked her head, trying to hide a sad smile that wavered at the edges, and then she was gone, her soft footsteps fading down the hall.

Chapter 19

VIVIAN

I tossed and turned, kicking the sheets off my legs. Scenes from dinner kept replaying in my mind—in particular, a scene that hadn't happened. It was ridiculous to be disappointed, especially since I was the one who'd changed things.

Argus might not have known what he was betting against, but I did, and I'd felt things moving in that direction. It was like a river current pushing me along a predetermined path. Hearing his stories and sharing mine only brought us closer. Spilling wine on him was my last-ditch attempt at suppressing the urge I had to learn more; to quiet the voice in the back of my mind that whispered temptation.

What if I saw things through? What if he kissed me, and I didn't want him to stop?

It didn't matter though. My clumsy effort was a success. He'd thought that was the vision, and with his jacket ruined, it could never unfold in the same way. No jacket, no kiss. The plan worked.

So, why was I so restless? I should be happy.

I was happy!

Ugh.

I rolled out of bed and slipped on my dress from earlier. Maybe if I went down to the kitchen and made myself a warm glass of milk, I'd be able to sleep. I certainly wasn't having any luck in here.

The house was dark and silent as I crept downstairs. Coals glowed a faint orange in the fireplace, and I rubbed my shoulders against the slight chill, tiptoeing down the hall. Argus's office door was closed, but there was a weak flicker of light below it. Was he still awake? I moved slower, holding my breath, until I'd passed.

Exhaling a sigh of relief, I kept moving only to step on the wrong floorboard. The telltale creak sounded more like a high-pitched screech in the hallway.

Damn.

Maybe he didn't hear it? He could be asleep at his desk. But if that was the case, why didn't Hastings make sure he went up to bed? It couldn't be comfortable, and he'd probably be sore in the morning.

Get a hold of yourself, Viv. It's not your job to make sure the man gets a good night's rest.

"Can't sleep?"

I whirled around to find Argus leaning in the doorway. The top buttons of his linen shirt were open, revealing an expanse of tanned skin, and he'd rolled his sleeves up past the elbows. He looked disheveled—a look I appreciated more than the starched gentleman who escorted me to dinner.

"No." I cringed. Did my voice really just squeak like that?

Sheesh, you're pathetic.

"Me either. Want a drink?"

"Uh, sure. Whiskey will probably knock me out faster than warm milk."

He made a face and stepped back, allowing me to enter. "Warm milk? Sounds disgusting."

"Yeah, well, none of it works as well as Tessa's sleeping powder."

Argus nodded as he moved toward the sideboard. He poured the liquor into two glasses and handed one to me.

"That stuff was surprisingly fast-acting."

Sipping the whiskey, I watched the candlelight play over his handsome features. The fire in the hearth snapped, filling the silence. It was warm in here. Too warm. Why did I bring up the sleeping powder? Now, all I could think about was that night before he'd fallen asleep, when he promised to keep me safe from...everything.

I took a deep gulp from my glass and handed it back. "This is probably a bad idea. I should go." I turned toward the door, cursing myself for retreating like a spooked cat.

"Please, stay."

The rough edge to his voice made my stomach flip. My feet ground to a halt.

Don't do it, Viv.

"All right. For a little while." I reclaimed my glass

and swirled the inch of liquor in the bottom, keeping my gaze fixed on it like I'd walked through the desert and hadn't had a drop of liquid in days.

Argus leaned against his desk, crossing his feet over his ankles. "Hastings said you've been overdoing it with the mirror and need a break." He paused as if weighing his next words. "So, tell me, what does a typical night look like for you? You know, before you signed on to search for mystical blades and hunt werewolves?"

"A typical night?" My fingers drummed the rim of the glass. "It feels like forever since I've had one of those." I walked the edge of the room, stopping by a shelf containing a set of dice and a deck of cards, and smiled softly. "I used to host game night."

"What's that?"

"Well, Fredrick, the ghost I mentioned earlier, and my ghost friend Ruby would come over, and we'd play games. Chess, charades, dice, it didn't matter. We'd take turns picking. They'd place their bets with secrets and dirty gossip but make me play with money."

"What do ghosts want with your money?"

"That's an excellent question. They won't tell." I leaned in and whispered, "If you ask me, I think they're saving up to usher in the apocalypse."

He smirked and picked up the deck of cards. "Sounds like my kind of stakes. Do you want to play?"

"I don't have any money."

"That's easy, we'll play like the ghosts do. The winner gets to ask any question they want, and the loser has to answer it." A devilish smile curved his lips. "On pain of death."

"That could be risky. I might learn where you hide the bodies."

He winked. "Only if I let you win."

"Ha! That does it. Deal the cards."

Argus settled on the sofa and began to shuffle the deck. The muscles in his forearms flexed with the movement, and his long fingers dealt the hand with precision. I stared, transfixed, until he cleared his throat.

Moving into the chair across from him, I picked up my hand and studied the cards. It wasn't great. Actually, it was terrible.

"I'll take three." Removing the cards from my hand, I accepted three more from the top of the deck. This was worse! How could I not have a single pair?

Argus watched in silence from his seat. The boldness of his gaze unnerved me.

"Aren't you going to take any cards?" I asked.

"No. Are you planning to fold?"

A quick glance at my hand told me I should take the draw. But I did have one trick up my sleeve, and it technically wasn't even cheating.

Keeping my features neutral, I lowered the cards to the table and bounced my foot. His eyes followed the motion, then he studied his cards again, a worry line on his brow.

Sucker.

"I'm all in. Do *you* want to fold?"

The worry line deepened. "Maybe I should."

I lifted my shoulders in an innocent shrug, heel still tapping the floorboards.

His gaze locked with mine, and my foot slowed to a stop. *Uh-oh.* He wasn't falling for it.

"No. I'm all in too. Reveal your hand."

Damn.

Slowly, I fanned my cards out faceup. I had nothing, but he held a three-pair. He'd called my bluff.

That stubborn lock of black hair fell into his eyes as he cocked his head and grinned. "Now, what should I ask you?"

"Go easy on me," I grumbled. "Maybe you're dying to know what my favorite color is? Or if I prefer cats or dogs? I'll even give you two for one on those questions."

"You certainly know how to tempt a man, but no." He rubbed his hands together. "Tell me a secret you've never told anyone."

"What?" I cried. "No way! I'm not telling the head of the kingdom's crime syndicate any secrets. You'll use them against me, probably try to extort money out of me or something."

His eyes glinted with mischief. "Most likely. But you did promise on pain of death. You have to answer truthfully."

This was not happening. I squeezed my eyes shut so I couldn't see his face. Was I really considering it? Not even Tessa knew this secret. But what did it matter? It wasn't like I planned on spending the rest of my life with him. In a short time, we'd go our separate ways, and I'd probably never see him again.

"Okay, fine." I blew out a breath. "No one knows this because it's so mortifying, but...I tried to kiss a ghost once."

Argus choked on his whiskey. "You, what? Explain yourself."

"Oh, God." I covered my face with my hands, wishing the floor would open up and swallow me. "I was thirteen, and there was this farm boy who'd had an accident with a pitchfork."

"Wait, hold up—that's how he died?" Argus was trying so hard not to laugh, his whole body shook.

"Yes," I snapped. "He might have been a little accident-prone, but he was beautiful. Do you want me to finish the story or not?"

Argus nodded. "I can honestly say, there is nothing I want to hear more."

I scrunched my nose and continued. "You see, I read somewhere that on the night of the summer solstice, a ghost can take physical form. That night, we were together, and it was incredibly romantic. At least, according to my thirteen-year-old brain. The moonlight hit him just right, and I thought it was happening. I mustered up the nerve, went up on my toes, and kissed him."

"What happened?"

My features soured. "The stories weren't true. I passed right through him and fell face-first into a haystack."

Argus threw back his head and laughed. The rich, throaty sound filled the office, and it was hard not to join in. There was something so magnetic about him. I'd never seen this easy, relaxed side of him before, and even though it was at my expense, I didn't mind because he was sharing it with me.

"It's not funny."

"It's *very* funny."

Crossing my arms over my chest, I admitted, "All right, maybe a little. Deal the cards."

After a quick back-and-forth, I lost the next hand too.

"What are you most afraid of?" he asked.

Slumping back against the seat, I sighed. "Spiders. No—wait. What are those things with all the legs? Centipedes. It's definitely centipedes."

He stifled another grin and handed me the deck, his fingers brushing mine. "I'm learning so much about you."

The third hand was a draw. By the fourth, I was ready to win one. It was my turn to deal, and as I shuffled, I palmed three kings while he refilled our glasses.

Argus chose two cards, and I selected one. I didn't bother bouncing my foot because this time, I had a winning hand. Studying his cards, he took a sip from his drink and darted a glance at me over the rim. I wriggled my brows, and he shook his head, a small smile playing on his lips.

"Did you lose this much when you played with your ghost friends? The apocalypse must be imminent."

"Well, aren't you a jokester after a couple of winning hands?" I gestured to his cards. "What do you have?"

He placed them faceup on the table. A single pair of eights. I did a little dance in my seat as I displayed my three kings.

"I win!" Pushing out of the chair, I steepled my fingers and drummed them together. "Oh, I have so many questions I don't know what to choose first. I might be the most powerful woman in the kingdom right now if you think about it."

"How's that?"

Leaning over the back of the sofa, I placed my hands on his shoulders and whispered, "Because the formidable Argus Ward is at my mercy." Trailing a finger along the back of his neck, I felt him tense beneath my touch. "I'm going to draw it out a bit, if you don't mind. Let you wonder what I might ask."

"You don't play fair."

If only he knew the half of it. The rough edge to his tone was back, and it had the same effect as before. Picking up my glass, I walked toward the fireplace taking a deep, cleansing breath. I was playing with fire, and I liked it. I heard him move behind me, but I didn't turn. Making him wait was fun. What should I ask? I wasn't kidding—I had a million questions. If I won hands all night, I'd never get them all answered.

A soft sound reached my ears, and it took me a second to place it. Fabric shushing over fabric. My brow creased. I turned and blinked.

Wait...

What was happening?

Argus stood in front of me wearing the charcoal gray jacket from dinner. He smiled and smoothed a hand over the spot where I spilled the wine.

"Hastings got the stain out. He's a wizard with that kind of thing. You seemed upset earlier, and I planned on showing you tomorrow, but now seems like a better time, what with me being at your mercy and all. I thought cheering you up might take the sting out of your question."

Shock filtered through my system. My heart pounded in my ears as he moved closer, and the glass slipped from my fingers. A shadowy voice wove around me.

Once a path is chosen, it doesn't always lead in the opposite direction. Sometimes, it circles back, leaving you in your original track. That's called fate.

I hadn't changed anything! A laugh bubbled in the back of my throat. He wasn't even aware of the significance. I stepped back, dazed. My body trembled. I felt hot all over, and there was this strange smoky scent, as if...

"Vivian, your dress!" Argus lunged and yanked the bottom of my skirt from the flames. He batted it with his hand until there was nothing but a singed hole in the fabric, then gripped my shoulders, pulling me away from the fireplace.

"What is wrong with you?"

"You surprised me, that's all."

"So you thought you'd take a walk into the fire?" He was angry, but it was laced with an adrenaline that slowly faded, and soon, something else darkened his gaze. The look probably could have picked up where the flames left off, burning right through me. His jaw tightened. "You are the most frustrating, complicated puzzle of a woman I've ever known."

"Look at you doling out compliments."

The air thickened the longer he stared down at me. His hands slid up my shoulders, and then his calloused palms met the skin at the back of my neck. Gaze dipping to my mouth, he said, "I'm going to ask my question now."

"What? I won. It's my turn."

He shook his head. "No, you didn't. You cheated on the last hand. I watched you in the sideboard mirror. I was going to let you have it, but I changed my mind."

"You knew I cheated?"

"Yes, which means I win by default. So, I'm going to ask you one more question, and remember, you have to answer truthfully."

I could only nod.

His thumb stroked my cheek. "Are you going to push me away again when I kiss you?"

Chapter 20

VIVIAN

Not if, but when.

His question spoke to the essence of my dilemma. I could answer and walk away like I had at dinner. The choice was mine, but it wouldn't be a decision based on what I wanted, only on what I was trying to avoid. We'd end up in the same place, over and over, until I made a decision based on honesty. Like our game, I had to answer in truth.

"No, I won't push you away."

"I hoped you'd say that." There was a flash of a smile as he drew me closer. Argus's mouth brushed against mine. Slowly at first, almost as if he was testing my resolve. The tips of his fingers skimmed the column of my neck, a pressure so light it sent shivers racing to my core. He wasn't hesitant; he was careful. Deliberate. When I opened for him, his tongue was a caress, still achingly slow. It drove me crazy in the most delicious way.

The kiss was intimate, such a stark difference from our first impulsive attempt. I wound my arms around his neck and pressed myself close. My fingers threaded through his hair as the kiss deepened. Whiskey and spice flooded my senses. The liquor that was supposed to help me fall asleep instead tasted like flavored sin on his lips.

He pulled back on a ragged breath, and my heart stutter-stopped beneath his searing gaze. He'd asked me earlier if what I saw in the mirror was dangerous, and I'd said no. But this *was* dangerous. It felt like I'd walked to the edge of a cliff, and there was no going back the way I came. All I could do was jump.

I wet my lips. "And they say cheaters never win."

His mouth kicked into a smile. "There's nothing normal about you."

"And it drives you crazy."

"You have no idea," he said as he dragged me back for another kiss.

We stumbled a few steps until he pressed me against the wall, and I was surrounded by the heat of his hard body. This time, it wasn't slow. Like the moment in my kitchen, the kiss was filled with urgency and a little bit of desperation. I slipped my hands beneath his jacket and ran them over the solid wall of his chest. The sound he made in the back of his throat made my stomach clench. We were out of control as he slanted his mouth over mine, and the rough hands that framed my face roamed lower, sliding over my breasts, then lower still, circling my waist.

I never wanted it to end, but it was too much, too fast.

Too complicated.

"Argus," I whispered hesitantly as his mouth left mine to skim my jawline. I bit my lip hard when he found the sensitive spot behind my ear.

"I know," he breathed. He buried his head into the crook of my shoulder, and I held him against me as my heart rate slowed. For a long moment, neither of us moved.

"That was my vision," I said, breaking the silence. "The one from dinner."

A harsh laugh burst from his lips. "The one I asked you to change?"

"Yeah. You were supposed to kiss me then, but I thought if I spilled wine on you, it wouldn't play out like it was supposed to. Seems silly now."

He straightened and gazed down at me. "Warn me next time I do something that stupid." His fingers sifted through my hair, coming to rest on my shoulders. "Why didn't you try again just now? You could have walked away."

"Because I didn't want to, and I think that makes all the difference."

His mouth curved into one of his teasing smiles. "Well, thank God for game night." He leaned forward and brushed a soft kiss against my lips. "And for cheaters."

I shrugged off his hands and slung my arms across my chest. "You know, I would have won one eventually. If it wasn't for that damn mirror, you wouldn't have even known I cheated."

"I doubt it."

"Double or nothing?"

His brow rose in challenge. "Deal the cards."

***

Sunlight streamed through the windows, and I snuggled deeper into the feather mattress. The coverlet was thick and warm, and the silk sheets were heaven against my skin. Deep contentment relaxed my muscles. For the first time in a long time, I felt rested.

I stretched like a cat, curling my toes and reaching my hands out to each side. Even with my arms spread wide, I didn't touch the edge of the bed. Apparently, luxury meant the freedom to toss and turn without the fear of landing on the floor. I rolled to my side and tucked the downy pillow beneath my ear, smiling at the dress I'd draped over a chair before I fell asleep. The burn spot looked ugly in the daylight. My smile widened, becoming a cheesy, cheek-aching grin.

I'd stepped into the fire in more ways than one.

Game night had never gone like that before. In the end, Argus and I stayed up for another hour playing cards and telling secrets. Mostly mine. He was right to assume I wouldn't have better luck the second time around...

I really needed to stop gambling, but I'd discovered a secret about the visions: Choice didn't matter if it wasn't based in truth. Basically, it was a whole lot harder to change things than I realized.

Squeezing my eyes shut, I kicked my feet under the covers like the thirteen-year-old girl who thought she could kiss a ghost if the moon was right. Except last night's kiss was way better than any I'd had before, and to make things trickier, Argus was fun. I'd enjoyed playing cards with him. For a moment, I'd felt like my old self again. With everything going on, the uncertainty and grief, I hadn't realized how much I needed normalcy.

A knock on the door broke through my thoughts. It creaked open, and Fiona poked her head inside.

"Are you awake, dear? I brought you a bite to eat and some hot tea."

"Of course, Fiona." I hurried to slip a robe over my shoulders and tame my hair.

She entered the room wheeling in a silver cart. A tea set rattled on the tray next to a three-tiered stand loaded with pastries and fruit.

"You sleep like the dead, child. It's nearly afternoon."

"What?" I sputtered, pushing aside the drapes to peer out. "I never sleep so late."

Fiona stifled a grin. "Mr. Ward instructed us all to let you sleep in as long as you like. That lasted most of the day until he started to bark orders someone should check on you to make sure you hadn't escaped out the window in the middle of the night. I've never seen a man pace so much. I'm sure he wore a hole in the carpet." She poured tea into a porcelain cup and handed it to me.

"Thank you."

"We're all so happy you're here. I know the circumstances are dire, but it's nice to have another female presence in the house. Keeps Mr. Ward on his toes." She winked and filled a plate with a selection of fruit and a large croissant.

Her sly wink almost made me choke on my tea. It was a known fact gossip spread like wildfire among the servants. Did they already know what happened last night? Were they tucked away in the shadows discussing it?

She must have read my thoughts because she said, "Don't worry about the gossip, honey. I'm placing my bets on you."

"I have no idea what you mean." I picked at the croissant, afraid to make eye contact.

Fiona waved her hand and made a harsh sound. "You'd better not let me down either. I have a month's wages on you charming the pants off our employer."

"Fiona!" I tried not to laugh, but her blunt expression was too much.

"Hush, child. Hastings bet his favorite pocket watch. We have a lot riding on this." She snapped her fingers, and her face lit up. "Do you like oysters? I have a fantastic recipe. They're an aphrodisiac, you know? It could help swing things our way, and it's not cheating if it's food."

Oysters? The servants were placing bets? This was not good. I set my plate aside.

Fiona added a second croissant and more fruit,

then continued. "No one says you have to play fair in this house, not against Mr. Ward. Besides, you're a thousand times better than those floozies he brings back here."

Floozies! My hand tightened around the teacup, making the dark liquid ripple. Jealousy did not become me, but denial did.

"I hate to break it to you, Fiona, but I'm only here because he promised my grandmother he'd watch out for me. His invitation was guilt-driven."

Fiona's laughter filled the room as she tossed back her head, nearly dislodging her frilly white cap. "Oh, honey, do you honestly think Argus Ward does anything he doesn't want to? Mark my words, you're special. Just don't go breaking his heart, you hear?"

His heart? If floozies were involved, I was sure I didn't stand a chance. Besides, how did you break a villain's heart? A few kisses didn't mean he was mine, and they certainly didn't mean he was willing to give me anything more than that. Sure, kissing him curled my toes and made me wonder what other wicked things he could do with his mouth. But his heart...? Absurd. I didn't even want it.

Did I?

My teacup thunked heavily onto the cart, and I winced before crossing the room to the bureau. "Where is Argus this afternoon?" I asked.

"Holed up in his office. We're supposed to alert him when you're ready to come down."

I selected a dark green tunic dress and held it against my frame, surveying it in the mirror. "Don't worry, I'll alert him myself."

Fiona grinned and clapped her hands together. "Wonderful! I'll prepare snacks."

"No oysters!"

Her lips formed a pout. "As you wish."

Chapter 21

ARGUS

I stared at the deck of cards on my desk. Hastings must have put them there after tidying up the mess we left behind. Our glasses had been washed and placed neatly on the sideboard, and the end table where we'd played our game was straightened perpendicular with the edge of the carpet. Traces of the night before had been wiped clean, but they were far from gone in my mind.

Last night might have been normal for Vivian, but it wasn't for me. Maybe she didn't realize it, but people didn't tend to sit around playing cards with me. They didn't reveal embarrassing stories or trust me with their greatest fears. She'd worried I'd take advantage, and in any other instance, I would have. But the thought of using what she shared...hell, the thought of anyone else even knowing those private details about her made me edgy.

My gaze drifted from the deck of cards to the wall, where I could almost see her leaning up against it still. Her beautiful features flushed, lips swollen, and dark, glossy hair tousled around her shoulders. I almost missed all of that with my ridiculous suggestion for her to change her vision. What a mistake.

I scrubbed a hand over my face. These visions were something else. Life was a whole lot simpler when you didn't know what was coming.

Hastings appeared in the door, and my first thought was that Vivian was finally awake. It was early afternoon, but I could eat. Would she want to have dinner again? Something casual, maybe in the conservatory?

"Good. I'm glad you're here, Hastings. Have Fiona prepare—" I paused when I realized he was ushering Gregor into the office.

My informant stopped in front of my desk and waited until Hastings closed the door.

"You're back. Did you find them?"

"Yes, boss. I located the merchants who sailed on the Black Eagle. They gave me the name of the buyer."

"Who is it?" I asked, pushing out of my seat.

"Lord Bowen MacKenzie."

I cursed and braced my fists on my desk. "You're sure it's him?"

"One hundred percent. The merchants delivered the blade themselves."

This complicated things. I wasn't surprised Bowen had gone after the blade. He was an ex-treasure hunter turned reclusive weapons collector who stored his vast collection in a desolate manor on the cliffs. Trouble was, the last time he and I crossed paths, things didn't go his way. I conned him out of a weapon for his collection, and even before that, we always had a bit of a rivalry—until he all but vanished after a mysterious incident that ruined his face and earned him the nickname Bowen the Beast. Now, there were only rumors of his activities. Some said he took pleasure in torturing trespassers, locking them away in the catacombs beneath his house. Others claimed the scars on his face and body were forced upon him by his own blades, and he only went out at night, hunting those responsible.

Regardless of the rumors, if Bowen had the blade, I had to go after it.

"It won't be easy," I said. "We'll need a plan."

"Should I put together a team?"

"That won't be necessary. I'm going alone. Bring me everything you can gather on the inside of the manor, especially information on where his collection is stored. You have until the end of the week."

Gregor grunted his disapproval. "That's suicide. You know it as well as I do. Reconsider."

"It's done. I've already made my decision."

A commotion at the door drew our attention. It was flung open and crashed against the wall. I saw it happen almost in slow motion: Gregor reaching for the dagger at his waist, and Vivian charging into the room, her features set in a furious line. Rounding the desk, I lunged for Gregor, grabbed his arm, and placed myself between the two of them.

"Are you insane?" Vivian shouted. She ground to

a halt when she saw me restraining Gregor. Her eyes went wide at the edge of his blade.

I let out a slow breath, which did nothing for my anger. "What are you doing here?" I gritted out.

Gregor flipped the knife back into the sheath at his waist. "Is this the girl with the visions? She's going to get you killed if you're not careful, boss."

"Leave us, Gregor. You have work to do."

He smirked as he passed Vivian and muttered, "Saved by the devil."

The door clicked shut behind him, and I leaned against my desk. "Never barge into my office like that again. My men rarely introduce themselves before they react."

She had the nerve to act defiant, eyes flashing as she spoke. "Then don't make secret plans. I heard what you said."

My lips twisted in a condescending smile. "Eavesdropping, love? How much did you hear?"

Squaring her shoulders, Vivian notched her head higher. "You found the location of the Grimm's blade.

"It seems so."

"Were you planning to tell me about your mission before you went, or after?" She shook her head. "You know what? It doesn't matter. I'm going with you."

Pushing away from my desk, I stalked closer and came to a stop in front of her. It was as close as we'd been the night before, but this time, I didn't reach for her. This time, I had to push her away.

"Out of the question. You're staying here."

"I'll follow you."

"I'll lock you up." I leaned forward and whispered suggestively, "All you have to do is ask if you want to see my handcuff collection."

She ground her teeth, refusing to back down. "Ha! A useless threat. I already told you, I can pick locks. I doubt there's anything in your collection that would hold me."

I wanted to pull my hair out, she was so frustrating. If she thought for a second I was taking her with me, she was out of her mind. I moved closer, invading her space and forcing her back a step.

"Do you even know where I'm going?"

She visibly swallowed. "MacKenzie Manor. Bowen the Beast has the blade."

"Then I'm sure you've heard the rumors. Except they're far worse than you can imagine. He's a ruined man, and he ruins everything he touches. You still want to go?"

Her lips parted. There was something in her eyes that made me instantly wary.

"You need me," she murmured.

Her declaration was a punch to the gut that pushed me to analyze and question the truth behind it. I didn't need anyone. Spurred on by my silence, Vivian closed the distance between us, tangling her fingers in my shirt. I tensed, my hands reflexively circling her waist.

An airless moment passed.

"You can deny it all you want. It doesn't change anything." She lifted a palm and brushed it against my cheek. It took all of my willpower not to lean into her. "I'm not letting you do this alone. If you go, I go."

"It's too dangerous."

"Maybe so, but as it turns out, I'm an oracle. The gift doesn't only come with seeing the future. There's also intuition; a sense of danger lurking around the corner. If you want to sneak past Bowen the Beast, you'll need me to do it. Besides, there's one other thing you need that only I can get for you."

"There's nothing in this kingdom I can't get for a price."

The corner of her mouth lifted, and she patted my cheek. "It's adorable you think that. The thing is, we'll need a replica of the Grimm's blade so Bowen won't know it's missing when we switch it out. Lucky for you, I'm friends with a witch who dabbles in illusion. And trust me, your money is no good with her."

I cursed. "Fine. Summon the witch."

***

Tessa strolled into the library, a smug smile plastered across her face. "Today is my favorite day. The mighty Argus Ward needs *my* help. I knew it would happen, and it's exactly as satisfying as I thought it would be."

Vivian sat in the plush chair beside me refusing to meet my gaze. She examined the floorboards as if she found them fascinating. It was smart of her not to look up. She'd manipulated me quite successfully. Agreeing to meet with the witch went against everything in me. She was more likely to set me up than to help me retrieve the Grimm's blade, and based on the way she was gleefully rubbing her hands together, I wouldn't put it past her.

Taking Vivian with me to retrieve the blade was a bad idea. Gregor wasn't kidding: this was a suicide mission. Our chances of breaking into the manor, finding the blade, and sneaking away without detection were slim to none. The stakes were higher than they'd ever been. But Vivian had backed me into a corner, threatening to charge in after me if I went alone.

She'd do it too. We'd end up dead in that scenario. I'd spent the past few days trying to convince her to change her mind, but she refused.

Letting her come along either made me the stupidest man alive or the luckiest. I hated to admit it, but she had a point. An oracle's intuition could be the difference between living another day or ending up as target practice in MacKenzie's dungeon—which wasn't an enduring goal of mine. We also needed a replica, which meant we needed magic and the witch who came with it.

Vivian was right. I did need her, but I wasn't happy about it.

"If you're so fond of helping, witch, you can help yourself to the exit. Don't let Hastings hit you with the door on the way out. I'm sure I can pay another witch to do my bidding."

"Not if I blacklist you. Another witch won't even look your way."

Vivian placed her hand on my knee, her warm fingers squeezing gently. "Stop it. Both of you."

Tessa waved her hand in the air, dismissing me with cool indifference. "I'm only here because Vivian asked for a favor. If it was up to me, I'd let you do your thief-taking and then alert the authorities on your way out."

"Figured as much," I muttered.

The pressure on my knee increased, turning painful. Okay, so we weren't off to a great start. I bit my tongue to keep from pointing out the witch had started it. It might be petty, but it would be satisfying.

"Are we finished with the pleasantries?" I feigned a smile and located the worn volume of mystical creatures from the bookcase. The brittle pages crinkled as I turned to the hand-drawn picture of the Grimm's blade. "We need the dagger to look exactly like this, not a jewel out of place. Bowen will know."

Tessa examined the picture, her lips pursed in a frown. "You doubt my ability, thief? This is child's play. A baby witch could do it."

Vivian made a choking sound in the back of her throat that sounded a lot like a strangled laugh. The witch ignored her and began to search the room for a suitable object for the transformation.

"Use this." I laid an iron poker from the fireplace across my desk.

She eyed it with disdain and shook her head, still scanning the room.

"What's wrong? It's perfect."

"I don't work with iron, only gold." She stood on her toes and selected a pair of heavy golden candlesticks. Plunking one onto the table, she tucked the other one away in a bag at her feet.

"What do you think you're doing?" I reached for her bag, but she hissed and made sparks shoot from her fingers.

"One candlestick is for the spell, the other is your payment. Vivian's my best friend, but you owe a surcharge."

"Tess…" Vivian warned.

"What? It's the friends and thieves discount. I'll be stopping by the kitchen when we're done here too. That butler of his said I could."

Hastings was a traitor.

"Just cast the spell, witch."

She shrugged and took the book from me, running her fingertips over the blade's outline as if committing it to memory. Satisfied, she tossed the book aside and held her palms over the candlestick. Tessa focused her energy, lips moving in a silent chant. The candles illuminating the room dimmed as if she was sucking the energy from their wicks. The air grew hot as her magic power pulsed around us.

Vivian launched from her seat and placed herself at my back. Her fingers dug into my jacket, and she peered around my shoulder. Was she worried? A tightness constricted my chest. She'd run to me, trusting I'd keep her safe. That was oddly…pleasant.

"Don't worry, love. There's nothing—"

"Quit moving! If Tessa's spell goes haywire, I'm

making sure you turn into a rodent before I do."

"Wait, what?" I tried to turn, but Vivian gripped my arms and thrust me back into place, using me as a shield.

Unbelievable.

I wasn't her hero at all. I was her sacrificial lamb.

Chivalry sucks.

Tessa's eyes closed, and sparks rained from her hands. A crack of thunder boomed, rattling the decanters on the sideboard. Crystal glasses threatened to topple to the floor when another boom struck.

I resisted the urge to check for whiskers.

The candlestick glowed molten orange, then melted, rearranging into its new form. I stared at it, my mouth twisting in confusion.

"Uh, Tess…" Vivian said when the magic settled and my ears stopped ringing. "That's not a dagger. That's a flute."

The witch bobbed her head and chewed on the corner of her lip. "Yeah. I can see that." She drummed her fingers on the desk and muttered something about being grateful the candlestick wasn't a pumpkin.

"I thought you said a baby witch could do it? What are we supposed to do with a flute? Play Bowen the Beast a melody?"

"Give me a second," she grumbled, lifting her palms to try again. More sparks, a louder chant, and a curse for good measure. The witch channeled her magic, and the flute melted into a steaming puddle, then solidified into a dagger. Tessa blew out a breath, then tossed her hair over her shoulder. She preened and waved her hand over the newly formed blade as if she hadn't screwed it up the first time. "See? Told you I could do it."

To be fair, the candlestick-turned-flute-turned-dagger was an exact replica. Emerald gemstones protruded through the slender hilt, surrounded by rows of glittering rubies. The curved blade gleamed, narrowing into a jagged, razor-sharp point. There was even a magical aura infused into the piece similar to the essence of enchanted steel. A trained eye wouldn't be able to tell the difference.

"How long will it remain like that?" I asked.

"There should be plenty of time for you to make the switch before it changes back. With any luck, Lord MacKenzie won't notice for days, maybe weeks if he doesn't catalog his collection often." She smirked. "Though he's gonna be pissed off when the illusion fades and all he's left with is a candlestick."

"We'll be gone by then. Thank you, Tess." Vivian squeezed her friend's hand.

"Are you sure you know what you're doing?" she whispered, dragging Vivian out of earshot.

I held my ground and gave them space, part of me hoping the witch might convince Vivian to change her mind. The selfish part of me hoped she wouldn't. Vivian's gaze burned into my back, but I busied myself with finding something to transport the replica. There were still plans to be made and hours to go before we could travel to MacKenzie Manor. Gregor had provided information on the best way inside as well as some vague schematics. They were based more on hearsay than fact, but they were all we had.

It was difficult not to eavesdrop as the women whispered in the corner. I might be used to the witch filling Vivian's head with unflattering stories about me, but lately, my patience where that was concerned had worn thin. When the two broke apart, Tessa looked troubled. Vivian pulled her into a hug.

"Everything will be fine. Now, why don't I go see if Fiona can pack you up some of her famous scones for the road? Part of your payment, of course." Vivian winked.

Tessa laughed, but it sounded strained. "I always collect my fee."

Vivian headed for the kitchen, and I expected the witch to follow, but she lingered by my desk. Silence stretched while she shifted her weight from foot to foot, seeming to gather her thoughts.

"Speak freely, witch. We're alone."

Her chin quivered, and all of her bravado faded before my eyes. Gone was the snarky witch with a comeback for everything. In her place stood a woman with fear in her eyes and a healthy dose of bitterness.

"Let me be clear, Argus. I don't care what happens to you, but if anything goes wrong and Vivian—" She choked on the words, unable to finish. Unshed tears glistened in her eyes.

I took pity on her. "Relax, witch. If I don't come back with Vivian, I'm not coming back at all."

She took a shuddering breath. "Then I guess that's

the first time I'll be glad to see your face."

"I'll remember you said that."

"And I'll remember your promise."

Chapter 22

VIVIAN

No one said anything about going in through the tunnels.

I placed my hands in front of me, feeling my way to avoid taking branches to the face. It was a few hours before dawn, and the only light filtered through the trees from the half-moon. An icy wind slid down the collar of my cloak, and I rubbed my frozen fingers.

I carried the makeshift blade in a bag slung over my shoulder, and every few minutes, I ran my fingers along the hilt to make sure it hadn't turned back into a candlestick or a dreaded flute. The last thing we needed was for Tessa's spell to fade before we made it inside.

In the distance, I spotted the dark silhouette of the manor. It loomed like a giant iron and brick monstrosity at the edge of the bluff, but we wouldn't be approaching it head-on. The map Gregor had provided detailed the entrance to a cave that would lead us through an old shipping transport for the manor. It tunneled through the rock face in a series of twisting passages. Over the years, it had crumbled into disrepair and often flooded with the tide, making it unusable for long stretches of the day.

"Over there." Argus pointed toward a rocky path that led down the side of the cliff.

Stones rolled under my feet, threatening to pitch me over the edge and into the water below. The sound of waves crashing against boulders followed us down. Dressed fully in black, Argus was a shadow in front of me, his boots nearly silent over the rough terrain. I followed in his footsteps trying my best to be quiet.

When an icy patch caught me by surprise, I careened into his back. Stifling a yelp, I tried to regain my footing when his arm snaked around my waist. He steadied me, then pushed back the wave of hair that fell into my eyes, his fingers lingering along the base of my neck.

"You okay?" His voice was low, barely audible over the waves.

"Yeah. I'm good. Thanks." I gave him a weak smile I was sure he couldn't see. So far, I hadn't exactly proved myself useful. It seemed an oracle's intuition didn't extend to where you should plant your feet to keep from landing in a watery grave.

We kept moving until the cave appeared like a black hole cut into the face of the cliff. The opening was no taller than six feet and wide enough to push a cart through. As far as narrow passages went, I wasn't an admirer. Staring into the black hole made me wonder if once we went through, would we ever come back out?

Water swirled around our toes, lapping at the rocks. I shivered against the frigid wind and checked the blade again.

"How long before the tide comes in?"

"A few hours. We should have enough time to come back this way." He paused, staring at the frothy water. "You can swim, right?"

"Swim? Sure, but I'd rather not navigate this dark tunnel through freezing water if it's all the same to you."

"Then we'd better hurry."

I ushered him forward with a flourish. "Gentlemen first."

He smirked. "I may be unskilled in societal norms, but isn't it supposed to be ladies first?"

We both peered into the gaping hole. Somehow, it had gotten darker. I dug into my bag and retrieved the pair of moonstones Tessa gave me before we left. She'd infused them with light and showed me how the heat from my hands activated their power. When I wrapped them in my fist, they glowed, giving off a blue tint.

"Ladies first is only for pleasurable things, not traipsing through an underground passage into the lair of a deranged lord."

Argus laughed and held out his hand for the moonstones. "My mistake. Let me do the honors then." His grin widened, becoming suggestive. "Stay close and keep an eye out for any deranged lords."

The plink of water hitting stone filled the narrow tunnel. I followed Argus, and the dark swallowed us whole. At least the wind had disappeared, but I could still hear it howling near the entrance. Claustrophobia tightened my chest. Enclosed spaces were not my favorite, and I repeatedly stepped on Argus's heels, afraid any distance between us would cause him to vanish, leaving me lost in the tomb of my own making.

"Sorry," I mumbled, my toe scraping his boot for the tenth time.

He laughed softly, and the low timbre warmed my insides, a noticeable difference to the chill that cooled my skin. "You know, this isn't the first time you and I have walked down a dark passage together. Who knew we'd make a habit of this sort of thing?"

I smiled at the memory. "That's right, the night we met. We dodged the police raid by leaving through your secret escape route. I can't believe you remember that."

He reached back to guide me over a rocky step. "Oh, I remember everything about that night. You made an impression." His voice rumbled with amusement. "But you're as clingy now as you were then. Afraid of the dark, love? I'm starting to think the key to keeping you close is to drag you down forbidding tunnels."

"Hilarious, but I'm only using you as a shield in case any of MacKenzie's henchmen are lurking down here."

"You're very fond of using me as a shield. First, with Tessa's spells, and now, dangerous mercenaries. Here I thought it was because you enjoyed the view of my backside."

I scoffed and shoved him between the shoulder blades. "Be serious. The only views I'm interested in are the sunny beaches of the Sylvan Isles, which is where I'm headed when this is all over. Assuming we don't wind up in the Beast's dungeon first."

Argus turned and walked backward, careful to avoid the water-filled ditches. He lifted a brow.

"The Sylvan Isles, huh? I have a house there. Maybe we'll run into each other. Unless we're trapped in the dungeon, of course."

A strange flutter began in my stomach. Being trapped on an island with him sounded more dangerous than any dungeon. His playful banter was making me forget where we were.

Who would have thought Argus could make trampling through the dark somewhat enjoyable? But that was who he was. He joked easily, burying his worry and apprehension behind a rogue smile. He never wanted to appear vulnerable or show weakness for fear others would take advantage. Yet I sensed his desire to share that part of himself.

It must be very lonely to hold back, afraid to put your heart in someone else's hands. What would it feel like to be the recipient of something he'd never given to another person? And why had I begun to want that person to be me?

The passage opened onto a small, rocky alcove

with an iron door embedded in the wall. Argus examined the lock, running his thumb over the keyhole.

"Do you have the key?" I asked, kneeling beside him and making my own inspection of the lock.

"Do I look like I have the key to the door at the end of the creepy tunnel?"

I flattened my lips. "Well, I don't know. Maybe one of your underworld cronies picked it up."

Argus patted his jacket and dug into the deep pockets. "As a self-proclaimed master locksmith, you should know there's only one way we're going to get through that door." Frowning, he double-checked the jacket's lining, then spun on his heel, scanning the uneven floor.

"Did you forget something?"

He exhaled, seeming to count to ten, as patience slipped from his features. "I don't forget things. Hastings must have..." His voice trailed off, and his eyes widened when I reached into my boot and withdrew a rolled leather bundle. I spread it across the ground, motioning him to bring the light closer so I could select the rightsized pick.

"Where did you get that?" Argus hunched over, scrutinizing the picks.

"Hastings gave it to me. He said it was a gift and that it might come in handy."

Argus flipped the leather over to reveal his initials. "That's mine. Hastings gave you my lock pick set. Unbelievable."

"He did?" I angled my head, struggling to contain

a smile. Argus was no match for his butler. Then again, I had accepted it knowing who the rightful owner was. "It's a lovely set. Better than mine." I feigned innocence. "I guess I should thank you for the gift as well."

Argus scrubbed a hand through his hair. "Something has gone terribly wrong in my home."

He had no idea, and I wasn't about to tell him.

"Here—hold this." I thrust my bag into his hands and set to work on the lock.

The pick felt comfortable in my hand, and I flashed back to my more mischievous days when Tessa and I would try to break into my grandmother's wine cabinet. We'd steal sips from cordials and elderberry elixir, then put everything back where we'd found it, too young and oblivious to realize the liquid level was dropping or that our giddy, fuzzy-headed demeanors gave us away. Winifred blamed delivery boys and various clients, always changing and upgrading the locks, and every time, we'd rise to the challenge.

My hand stilled. Maybe it had all been for this moment? Was it possible she was preparing me, giving me the skills I'd need after she was gone? It might be a lot of weight to place on an old memory, but Winifred's sly smile every time I breached her new lock replayed in my mind. I shivered at the cold hand of inescapable fate.

"What do you have in here?" Argus asked, breaking me out of my stupor. He shook the contents of the bag. "Why is it so bulky? Didn't anyone ever teach you to pack light?" He pulled back the flap and dug around, his head jerking up in shock when he discovered what was inside. "Did you honestly bring snacks on our dangerous mission?"

"Well," I hedged, feeling heat climb my neck. "Fiona packed them. I didn't want to be rude and turn them away. They're mini beef pastries."

"I know what they are," he grumbled, taking one out and examining it with the light. "But why are they heart-shaped?"

I coughed to hide a bark of laughter. Fiona had struck again. He was lucky there wasn't a container of oysters hidden in the bottom.

"Put them back," I said, returning to my task.

Inserting the tension wrench into the lock, I fitted the pick above it and gently tested the pins. Applying a little pressure to the wrench, I fiddled with the pick until I'd set the first pin. A thrill shot through me as I worked. Our caper might turn out to be addictive. Tessa felt the same thing while investigating Ella Lockwood's murder. She'd solved a crime, and I was committing one, but we'd both stepped out of our comfort zones and found a surprising sense of purpose.

Argus leaned over my shoulder while I maneuvered the last pin. Something crumbled down the front of my cloak, and I brushed it away. Beef-scented flakes stuck to my fingers.

I whirled, catching him in the act. "Are you eating my snacks?"

He stopped mid-chew. "No."

"Give me those!" I tugged the wrapped bundle from his hands and hugged them to me, breathing in the heavenly buttery aroma. I placed them by my side and then went back to setting the final pin. "There better be some left in there, or—"

"Or what?" Argus asked, so close I could feel the heat from his body. If I leaned back, I'd find the solid wall of his chest. My heart beat double-time as I rotated the pick and heard the soft click of success.

The door swung open with a rusty whine.

I looked over my shoulder, a smug smile curling my lips. "Or I'll make you regret it." My smile dimmed as my gaze locked with his and I saw the smoldering heat reflected there.

He swept up the bag and slung it over his shoulder, then walked through the opening, his words echoing in the narrow chamber. "I hope you do."

***

The interior of Lord MacKenzie's manor was exactly as I imagined. Dark, moody, and cold.

While the decorations were sparse, they all served a running theme: weapons. The walls were dotted with metal shields and helmets with grand plumage, while intricate carpets ran the length of each hallway depicting woven battle scenarios. In the corners, suits of armor stood like sentries guarding the domain.

Argus gave me the moonstones, and I held them in my fists, letting little shafts of light peek through my fingers. It was eerily quiet. The manor's hallways were catacombs of twisting passages and hollowed alcoves. Somewhere down one of the gloomy tunnels, a beast roamed.

I tried to channel the intuition that supposedly came with my new powers. So far, I hadn't felt anything beyond a constant state of dread, and it didn't take an oracle to pick up on that instinct. Was danger stalking us from behind? Would I sense it coming before it was too late?

Argus pointed down another corridor, and there it was: a thin coil of foreboding that stood out from the rest. The sensation snaked over my skin, constricting the air inside my chest.

Someone was close by.

I pressed my hand into Argus's back, nudging him in a different direction. According to Gregor's information, there was a chamber beneath the east wing that contained most of Bowen's collection. We just needed to find it. Ideally, before someone found us.

Before we left, I'd tried to summon the location in the mirror but couldn't make it happen. All the reflection chose to reveal was a maze of mist-shrouded rooms, each one similar to the last. There had been one clue though. Somewhere, there was a painting of a giant elk with an arrow protruding from its side. I was pretty sure the way to Bowen's collection was behind that painting.

The clue was something, but considering the manor was rumored to have over one hundred rooms, it might be a while before we stumbled into the painting.

An hour passed while we searched, and the dread continued to build inside me, a brush fire waiting for a match. Something was going to happen. I massaged an ache in my shoulder that spread down my side, growing more painful with each passing minute. Argus must have noticed because he drew me into a nearby room and cupped his hands around my face, concern hardening his features.

"What is it? Do you sense something?"

Unease filtered through me. "It's hard to explain. Whatever it is, it's getting stronger. I think we're close."

His thumbs ghosted over my cheekbones, and the soft caress made my eyes close. The dark helped me focus, his touch grounding me as a wave of certainty washed through my body.

"It's in here," I whispered.

"Are you sure?"

"Yes." I stepped out of his grasp and held the moonstones up to light a large cabinet filled with stone statues. Their gruesome eyes seemed to follow my movement, reminding me of miniature versions of the gargoyles perched above Argus's mansion. "It's like they're watching us." I traced my finger over the stone face of one of the statues.

Click.

The sound made my heart stop.

"Don't touch that!" Argus lunged toward me, wrapping his hands around my waist.

We spun as a draft of air whistled past my ear. A razor-sharp bolt sliced through my sleeve and thudded into the wall behind us.

Too stunned to move, I blew out a breath. Argus's hands tightened around my middle. With our bodies pressed together, I could feel his heart pounding in his chest.

That was close.

"You're bleeding," he said, ripping a piece of fabric from my sleeve and pressing it against the wound.

I hissed from the fiery sting. "What was that?"

"A fury statue. It looks innocent enough until you touch it. One of the many items in Bowen's collection."

The bolt had embedded itself a few inches into the wall. If Argus didn't pull me out of the way, it would be sticking out of me.

A hysterical laugh bubbled in my throat. "See? I told you something was about to happen."

"Not funny." He pressed the wound harder to stem the flow of blood. "You could be dying right now. If something—"

"Shh." I laid a finger against his lips. "I'm fine. It's just a flesh wound." I smiled for his benefit even though my skin burned. "Consider it a battle scar. It'll make an impressive story. Tessa will—"

"Murder me."

"No. I won't let her. I've grown used to having you around."

His grip eased along with the tension in his jaw. The bleeding had mostly stopped. He drew me closer, wrapping his arms around me, careful not to jar my injury.

"Do you hug everyone you go on dangerous missions with?"

He smiled against my hair. "Only the pretty ones."

"Ah, I see. So, Gregor then?"

His soft laugh wrapped around me, making me feel safe from whatever lurked in the shadows. If only we could stay like this. It was selfish, but I wanted everything else to fade away. All the obligations, the retribution...everything except this comfortable feeling.

Over his shoulder, I spotted a mirror on the wall angled to reflect the hallway. A grim figure was approaching in our direction. The noise from my injury must have alerted someone.

"We need to hide," I whispered. "Someone's coming."

We broke apart and scrambled behind an enormous sofa. Argus unsheathed a dagger, poised to strike on the advancing target. Light filled the room as a man entered holding up a lantern. His boots creaked over the wooden slats, and I tensed, my fingers tight over the moonstones to block their blue-tinged glow.

A torturous minute passed, and my legs burned from my crouched position. Finally, the man retreated, and his footsteps moved further down the hallway. I nearly collapsed against the floor in relief.

"Looks like your intuition paid off." Argus slid his knife back into its sheath, then held out a hand to help me up.

"What? Oh, no. I saw him in the mirror."

"Exactly. Your visions saved us."

My brow creased. "No. I mean, I saw his reflection in the mirror the regular way."

"Oh." Argus frowned. "That works too, I guess. It's just mildly disappointing."

"Isn't it though?" I winced as I probed my cut. "What do we do now?"

"Keep searching, and don't touch anything." He moved on silent feet toward the door and peered into the hallway, checking to make sure the figure hadn't returned.

I'd lost my makeshift bandage in the scuffle and scanned the floor for it. The last thing we needed was to leave evidence lying around. It had fallen beneath a set of floor to ceiling drapes, and I bent to retrieve it.

"That's odd," I muttered. There wasn't a draft. It should be colder by the window. Carefully, afraid of setting off some hellish curtain weapon, I pulled back the drape.

The elk painting was underneath.

I sucked in a breath. We'd found it! The visions had worked! A gold tassel hung on the side, and I used it to pull the drape further away from the painting.

Another clicking sound made my blood run cold.
Seriously? Not again!

My stomach lurched as the floor beneath my feet rotated. The wall swung inward on a circular platform, taking me with it.

I uncurled my hands on reflex, causing the moonstones to slip from my fingers and roll out of reach. Darkness descended as the revolving wall locked into place. Running my hands up the paneled wall and around the painting, I desperately tried to trigger the reversal mechanism, but I couldn't locate the lever.

A whimper escaped my lips when something moved behind me in the dark. The light scrape of nails against wood filled my ears, followed by a low guttural growl.

I wasn't alone.

And whatever was with me wasn't human.

Chapter 23

ARGUS

"**I** think the coast is clear."

Whoever had come to check on the disturbance had moved on, but we needed to hurry. We'd already been searching for too long, and each minute made our escape harder, especially if our exit route flooded.

I eased back into the room. "Have you found anything?"

My voice faded as I stared at the empty spot where I left Vivian. I blinked, unable to grasp that she was no longer there. Anger was quick to form. Now wasn't the time for tricks! She'd almost been skewered through the chest, and the image hadn't stopped replaying in my head, so if she thought hiding was going to lighten the mood, she was sorely mistaken.

"Vivian, this isn't funny."

An unbearable silence filled the room, and the pounding of my heart became a physical sensation, threatening to crack my rib cage. It thundered in my ears, sending panicked signals to the rest of my body.

"Vivian?" Her name fell from my lips, more a plea than anything else. I rounded the sofa and spun in a slow circle. There weren't many places to hide, which meant...

What?

In these situations, I thrived on adrenaline. It honed my senses. But this time, everything dulled as if my body was solidifying to stone.

Seconds slipped past—valuable seconds I would never get back. Seconds that made our separation tangible, a living thing that threatened to become permanent. I tried to calm my rising terror only for it to swamp me inside and out.

When a faint glowing object caught my attention, I skidded toward it and scooped it up in my palm. The moonstone's twin was missing, which hardly blunted my fear but made me pray Vivian still had the other.

Where was she? The room only had one exit, and I'd been standing in it. There had to be something I was missing, another door or a secret passage... On my knees, I scanned the wall for a hidden panel. A floor to ceiling curtain covered a window. Had she gone through there?

I threw the drape aside, nearly ripping it from its mount, but there wasn't a window, only flat wood paneling.

Which was odd.

I ran my hands along the wall, feeling for a groove

or a lever. My legs almost buckled when I located a seam. Air rushed from my lungs in a loud *whoosh*. There was a passage here! Vivian must have activated it when my back was turned!

"I told her not to touch anything," I murmured, still searching for a way inside. "Does she listen? No. This woman really is going to be the death of me."

It wouldn't budge. I flattened my palms on the wood and dropped my head against the surface. Frustration built in my chest and bubbled in my veins.

What was I thinking of bringing her here?

I scoffed. That was the problem: I wasn't thinking. At least, not with my head. I let her seduce me with tempting words that made me think I didn't have to do things alone. But I knew better. Always work alone! Watch my own back, and never get close enough to someone who could become a weakness.

They'll either betray you or be used against you.

Slowly, I pulled away from the wall. Vivian had the decoy, and if the passage led to Bowen's collection, I'd have to find another way inside and trust she could handle herself till then.

Trust. A wretched word I had no experience with, but here we were.

"The lever's on your left."

The deep voice sounded directly behind me. Lifting the moonstone, I turned, and the light illuminated the razor-sharp end of an arrow protruding from a crossbow as well as the disfigured face of the man holding it. His twisted skin was pulled back in an evil sneer, and a jagged scar ran from his cheekbone down the side of his neck, disappearing beneath his shirt collar.

"Argus Ward," Bowen rasped. "It took you long enough to track down the blade. I've been waiting for you." His finger hovered over the trigger.

"Really? You should have sent a formal invitation. I would have come sooner."

Bowen grunted, his left eye twitching at the base of his scar. "That would have been too easy for you, and not enough fun for me."

Palms out, I slowly rose to my feet. "Now, Bowen, you're not still upset about the time I swindled you out of that battle-axe, are you? Because, to be fair, it hardly made me any money on the black market. I saved you the trouble of selling it."

Another man stepped out from behind Bowen. He held a wooden club. In three steps, he raised it over his shoulder and swung. It cracked against the side of my head, causing white-hot pain to explode behind my temple. The room tilted dangerously. My knees hit the floor, and shadows crept into my vision, promising to numb the agony.

The man jabbed the club into my abdomen. I sucked in a pained breath. Wooden floorboards rushed to meet me as I landed on my side.

Bowen leaned over me, the sharp end of the crossbow pointed at my chest. "I'd forgotten about the battle-axe."

Consciousness ebbed and flowed, and I coughed, the action making my chest throb in agony. "Well, no use bringing it up then. Forgive and forget. That's my motto."

Black dots swam in my vision as the club ground against my aching ribs. I bit back a savage oath. The numbness was coming, one way or another. I tried to hang on, but the pain was too great, and my eyelids slid closed.

Bowen's words clung to me as darkness dragged me under. "You always get what's coming to you. That's my motto."

***

I jerked awake and instantly wished I hadn't. A sharp thud behind my eyes churned my stomach, and bile climbed the back of my throat. My arms were shackled above my head. Even the barest movement sent spikes of pain through my shoulders.

The dimly lit workshop felt like an oven. Coals from the forge glowed, radiating heat. Stone block walls held lit torches that jutted out over racks of throwing knives, sharpened spears, and rusted tools. Metal hooks hung from the ceiling, some laden with chains, and an elaborate pulley system had been built along one wall.

Bowen stood a few feet away, running a sword over a whetstone. The sickening slice of metal being sharpened rose the hair on the back of my neck. He paused when he realized I was awake.

"That's gonna leave a mark." He aimed the blade at the side of my head. "It'll fade though, unlike these." His rough fingers stroked the jagged scars on his left cheekbone, leaving a dark trail of ash.

"How long was I out?" The question sounded muffled in my head, and fear of the answer made me dizzy. How long had Vivian been on her own? Had he caught her too, and if so, where was he keeping her?

Bowen chuckled and continued to sharpen the sword. "Does it matter?"

"How long?" I growled, yanking on the chains that bound my wrists. Pain sizzled down my arms.

"You're not asking the right questions. It's disappointing." The sword clattered against a wooden table, and he barked a command over his shoulder at his lackey. "Bring me the Grimm's blade."

"Yes, sir." The heavy reinforced door creaked open as the man slipped through.

Bowen approached a crucible hanging over a heated forge. He thrust the sword into the red-hot coals, and the metal soon glowed a molten orange.

"You and I go way back, don't we? We have a history of getting in each other's way. You reminded me of the battle-axe—which, you're right, did turn out to be low quality—but there were other times too."

"Hazards of the trade." Dry heat blasted my skin, and beads of sweat trickled down my neck.

He grimaced. "No doubt. But there's one encounter I want to make sure you remember." His fingers ghosted over his scars again, and his rasp deepened. "Because it's one I've never been able to forget."

"I don't know what you're talking about."

"Of course, you don't. Why would you? You were always so obsessed with ruining your father's empire, you never stopped to think about who else could get caught up in your plans. You know, it wasn't long ago that I was just like you, always looking for the next score, walking over anyone in my way as long as I got to the treasure first. As you can see, it didn't work out for me."

"Enough of your vague ramblings. If you knew I was searching for the blade, why did you buy it out from under me? Why go through all the trouble?"

Bowen hooked his fingers in the leather belt at his waist and leaned against the table. His half-smile was mocking, the curl almost vindictive.

"Because you ruined my life by setting fire to the one object I spent years searching for, and this seemed like the perfect opportunity to return the favor."

I wracked my brain to figure out what he meant. There was only one instance that came to mind, and I'd completely forgotten about it. It was right before my father died, when I took over his holdings.

"The warehouse fire?"

"Very good. You do remember. I'd just returned from overseas, and the shipment I brought back had been offloaded into your father's warehouse. He hired me to find the Incantus knowing I'd been researching its location for years."

I shifted positions, wincing from the sharp ache in my ribs. "The fabled treasure chest? What did my father want with it?"

"It wasn't for him. It was for the witch."

"What witch?" I asked warily, a sense of foreboding slithering down my spine.

Bowen lifted an eyebrow. "You didn't know? That's a surprise. Robert visited a witch to find a cure for his illness. The witch promised him immortality, but she wanted the Incantus as payment." He gave a smug smile. "That's where I came in. I found the chest. It was the greatest achievement of my career, and it wasn't even about the money. It was the prestige."

I watched as he selected a short, thin blade and pushed away from the table. His boots left imprints in the soot on the stone floor.

"The night of the fire, I went to retrieve it but found the building already engulfed in flames." He rolled up his shirtsleeve to reveal a swath of puckered, burned skin on his forearm. "I nearly died in that fire trying to get to the treasure. The building was a total loss, everything inside either burned or scavenged by the men who tried to put out the flames. The contents of the chest were gone. Robert blamed me for setting the fire. He thought I'd decided to keep the treasure for myself. He tortured me. He gave me these." Bowen swiped a hand down the side of his face, ending at the base of his scars. "It wasn't until much later, I discovered it was you who'd burned the warehouse."

Realization settled. I held my breath as he crouched over me, twisting the knife so the metal gleamed in the torchlight.

"Do you have any idea what it feels like when hot metal slides through your skin? The searing pain that stops your breath? The screams you can't contain? Screams that ring in your nightmares long after it's over... Pain like that does something to your soul. It corrodes it until there's nothing good left."

"I didn't know. You were never the target."

"Maybe not, but it doesn't matter. I couldn't let it go, and when I found out you were desperately searching for the Grimm's blade, I took it, and now, I'm going to destroy it while you watch. I lost my treasure, and you'll lose yours."

"Don't do this," I grated.

The door swung open as Bowen's lackey returned with the blade.

"Ah, it's here." He accepted the weapon and strode toward the forge.

The jeweled dagger glittered in the firelight. To see it finally in person after searching for so many weeks was a mixture of awe and dread. It was in sight but still out of my hands.

Bowen held the blade over the crucible. I rattled the chains, desperate for some way to stop him. Without the dagger, all was lost.

"You know, I planned on dragging this out. All this time, my revenge against you kept me going. It was all I wanted, all I could think about." He went still, the muscles in his jaw tightening as an unreadable emotion flashed across his face. "But life has a funny way of changing your priorities."

"What are you saying?"

Bowen's smile was real this time. It spread across

his features, and when he spoke, understanding dawned in his tone as if he was just discovering a truth.

"There's something I want more than this. I didn't think that was possible, but she's waiting for me downstairs."

My heart nearly exploded in my chest. Ice filled my veins.

He'd found Vivian.

"Don't touch her."

Bowen ignored me, his features hardening. "This ends tonight. It's time for me to let go and look toward the future." He released the blade.

I watched as it hit the molten iron, floating for a few seconds until it sank beneath the surface. It was gone forever.

"Your debt is paid." Bowen turned on his heel, his boots thudding toward the door.

"Don't touch her! I'll kill you if you do," I shouted at his back, straining against the chains until blood trailed down my wrists.

He didn't slow, tossing the declaration over his shoulder. "You'll be released in the morning. Don't show your face here again."

Then, he was gone.

Chapter 24

VIVIAN

T he beast lurked in the dark. It shuffled closer, exhaling a chuff of hot air. Nails scraped against stone, and the musky scent of fur filled my senses.

How large was it? Ten feet tall with blood dripping from elongated teeth? The terrifying image paralyzed my search for the moonstones. I was certain any movement would cause the beast to lunge and begin to tear at my limbs.

A scream built in the back of my throat. Why didn't any of my visions reveal my imminent death by mauling? I wouldn't have touched anything! I'd have borrowed a pair of cuffs from Argus's vast collection and chained my arms to my sides. Though, considering my luck at changing the future, I probably would have tripped headfirst into the beast's lair and ended up in the same predicament, only with less limb movement.

The beast snarled and snapped its teeth together.

I scrambled backward, and my boot rolled over a round object. The moonstone! It had cooled to the point of losing its light. I grabbed it and rubbed it between my palms, blowing hot air onto the smooth stone.

Light spilled from my hands, brightening the tunnel. Visibly shaking, I dumped the contents of the satchel at my feet, fumbling for the fake Grimm's blade. Argus was right: I had packed too much, and now, I would die among my pile of belongings. At least the dead were spared an "I told you so."

Wait! There was the blade, sticking out from beneath a napkin-wrapped beef pie.

Something cold and wet touched my leg. I screeched and focused the light, revealing a long snout and a pair of gold-speckled eyes. The animal growled, drool spilling from between its jowls.

Huh?

My nose and lips scrunched together. It wasn't a werewolf. It was just a big, furry, sloppy dog.

"Good boy," I murmured, reaching for the beef pastry instead of the dagger. "Here you go." I tossed the treat further into the tunnel, and the dog whined, spinning on its talons to dive after it. It devoured the pastry and licked its chops before trotting back to me. A pleading whimper was followed by a snout nudging my knee.

Relief made me weak. I rested my head against the wall, trying to calm my speeding heart. Opening my hand, I offered another treat. The dog lapped it from my palm, his tongue tickling my fingers. Satisfied, he rested his head on my thigh with a contend huff.

I chuckled and ruffled the fur between his ears. "See? Everyone loves Fiona's cooking. Too bad Argus isn't here to witness this. It figures he's not around when snacks save the day. He won't believe me when I tell him."

The dog whined in answer, pushing his paw into my leg.

"No more," I scolded, climbing to my feet. "You're as bad as he is, eating all my food. You're lucky there's any left."

I examined the wall, running my hands along the wood and around the painting. There had to be a way to make it rotate again. Pressing my ear against it, I listened for anything on the other side, but it was completely silent. How thick was this wall? I knocked three times and waited.

Nothing.

This was a waste of time. I could be here all night trying to figure out the mechanism that rotated it. Either way, Argus was going to kill me. He definitely wouldn't let me go on any other missions. I was supposed to watch out for him, and instead, I was literally stuck between the walls of the house. But I had discovered the elk painting, and while my methods were more accidental than intentional, I was on the right path. The best solution would be to keep going, find the Grimm's blade, and then find a way out. The faster I did both, the sooner I could get back to Argus and his probable wrath.

If this was going to be my first and last mission, I

might as well make the most of it.

"Stay," I instructed the dog, pointing to the floor.

He wagged his tail and gazed up at me, eyes pleading.

Moving away from the wall, I started down the tunnel. The dog followed, nudging the back of my thigh, likely looking for more treats.

We turned left, then veered right. The corridor seemed to go on forever, nothing but stone and darkness, until finally, we came to a set of stairs. I peered over the ledge, using the moonstone to see down them, but I couldn't make out the bottom.

"Looks like we're going down there," I whispered to the dog. "What do you think? Should we delve deeper into the beast's castle? Is this where the bones of trespassers are kept?"

The dog looked too happy to give a reliable answer.

He probably plays fetch with the bones.

I took the stairs slowly, running my hand along the wall to keep my balance. Cobwebs snagged between my fingers, and I wiped them on my cloak, shuddering as their sticky threads clung to my skin. The dog's nails clicked against the wood behind me. I was glad he was there. I had no illusions that my meat pastries had endeared him to me more than his master, but I felt braver with his company.

At the bottom, the space opened up into a vast cavern. I held the light above my head and surveyed the area. The room was a collector's treasure trove. Hundreds of weapons hung from the walls. Swords and daggers glinted in the blue glow of the moonstone. A row of spiked maces hung from hooks, some dotted with what appeared to be dried blood crusted between the razor-tipped peaks. Jewels sparkled from the silver and gold hilts of broadswords, and various other objects I couldn't name were displayed or mounted to best accentuate their dangerous purpose. Scattered among the weapons were statues perched on pillars, decorative masks, and an array of antiquities.

In the center of the room stood a glass case resting on top of a stone dais. Gruesome faces and strange symbols had been etched into the stone. Remembering the innocuous appearance of the fury statue that nearly took me out, I approached the dais with caution.

Inside the glass case was the Grimm's blade. Excitement hummed through me. I'd done it! I'd found the blade, and it looked exactly like the one Tessa created. The decoy was perfect.

My hands hovered over the case, ready to lift the lid, when I heard footsteps.

"So much for the guard dog. Brutus, come here." A woman's soft voice filled the space behind me.

The dog trotted toward her and sat at her feet, licking her palm. The woman's hair fell in soft blonde waves down her back, and she wore a powder blue gown with lace sleeves. She had a journal tucked under her arm, and a quill nestled behind her ear. A wary smile formed on her lips.

"Who are you?" I asked, stunned to find another

woman wandering Bowen's mansion.

She laughed. "Don't you think I should be asking you that, considering you're in my home?"

"You live here? With Bowen the Beast?"

"I do. For the time being. I'm Liana Archer. My father ran into a bit of legal trouble with Bowen, and I ended up taking his place. Of course, that explains why I'm here, but not why you're here, Vivian."

"I didn't give you my name." This encounter was getting stranger by the moment.

She adjusted the notebook under her arm. "No, you didn't. But you didn't have to. I've known for a while you'd come for the Grimm's blade. It was all part of his plan. Though, trap might be a more appropriate term. He really doesn't like your friend."

"Trap? You mean, Bowen planned this?" Worry made my stomach clench. If Bowen already knew we were here, Argus could be in trouble.

"Relax. I don't approve of what he's done." Liana crossed in front of me, placing her notebook on the stone dais, then lifted the glass surrounding the Grimm's blade. "Take it. You'll need a direct hit to the heart—nothing else will do."

I traced the hilt of the blade, then wrapped my fingers around it, lifting it from the pedestal.

"How do you know that?"

Liana's lips thinned as if she was recalling a disturbing memory. "I have some experience with weapons like this. The monsters you seek are drawn to the blade. They'll stop at nothing to reclaim it and secure their bloodline. I think they suspect it's here. Something was lurking around the grounds last night."

"I don't understand. Why are you helping me? What if Bowen finds out?"

"I have my reasons."

"If Bowen is keeping you here, then let us help you. Come with us."

Liana shook her head. "I can't leave. I made a promise, and I won't go back on my word. But he's not all bad. He's been kind." Her features softened. "Sometimes, I catch glimpses of the man he used to be, and I have hope."

I clasped her hand, not knowing what to say. We were both quiet for a moment until footsteps came thundering down the stairs. Brutus whined, nudging his nose into Liana's skirt.

"Quick! Someone's coming." Liana tugged my arm, but I held back, reaching inside my bag. I withdrew the decoy and set it on the pedestal, then replaced the glass enclosure.

"So neither of us get in trouble." I winked, then followed Liana into the shadows behind a cabinet of wooden spears.

A man appeared, slowing near the glass case. He wasted no time collecting the decoy before turning on his heel and heading back up the stairs.

"That was close," Liana whispered. Brutus seemed to agree, resting his furry head on her knee and wagging his tail. "You'd better hurry. If he sent someone to get the blade, it means he's found your friend. He'll be keeping him in his workshop. I'll show you the way and distract Bowen so you two have enough time to get out."

"Thank you, Liana. I don't know what to say except I hope one day, we'll be able to meet again. Under more pleasant circumstances."

"You mean, when we're not in a cavern full of weapons while the master of the house holds your friend hostage?"

I grinned. "Exactly."

"I'd like that a lot. Now, let's go rescue your friend."

***

The heat grew the closer I got to Bowen's workshop, and worry gnawed my insides as I followed the hallway down. It was so quiet. What if I was too late? What if Argus wasn't inside? Liana would distract Bowen and buy us some time, but there was no way I was leaving without Argus even if I had to search the entire estate.

At the entrance, I pushed open the door and squinted against the blast of heat. The air shimmered with it. Torches bounced light on the stone walls, making shadows dance like living creatures.

I slipped inside and clicked the door back in place. Tools were scattered across worktables, and black dust coated nearly every surface. The scent of coal was thick and mixed with the bitterness of tar.

My gaze landed on a slumped figure in the corner. Argus was chained to the wall, head down, unmoving. Horror clawed at my throat. I suppressed a cry as I ran to him, going to my knees in the soot. There was dried blood from a gash on his head, and the skin around his wrists had been scraped raw.

"Argus, wake up." I scrambled to the workbench and found a semi-clean rag, dipped it into a basin of water, then rushed back to his side. Pressing the damp rag to his wound, I tried to wipe away the blood.

He didn't move.

My vision blurred, and I blinked away a prick of tears as panic seized my lungs. I dug into my boot, pulled out the lock pick set, and crawled to where the chains met the wall. My fingers trembled as I tried to work the pins.

"You know, I didn't expect to get as much use out of this set as I have," I joked, almost choking on the words. The first lock broke free, and I gently lowered his arm to his side and began to work on the second.

Argus mumbled something, and I took my first real breath.

"That's it. You need to wake up so we can get out of here."

"Vivian?" He slowly came to, wincing as he turned his head.

"I'm here. Try not to move until I get this chain free." I maneuvered the last pin, filled with relief when I heard the click and the iron cuff popped open.

"Did he hurt you?" he asked.

Confusion wrinkled my brow. "Hurt me? Who? You mean, Bowen?"

Argus nodded, gritting his teeth as I removed his arm from the cuff.

"I haven't seen him. He doesn't know I'm here."

"But he said you were waiting for him downstairs." His voice broke. "I couldn't do anything. I couldn't—"

Comprehension dawned, and I lifted his chin with my hands, stroking his cheeks with the pads of my thumbs. "It wasn't me. There's another woman here. She helped me find you and is currently keeping Bowen distracted so we can escape. He was waiting for her."

He blinked, still dazed, as my words sunk in. "It wasn't you..." Something dark and wild flashed in his eyes, and then, suddenly, he dragged me into his lap, his hands cradling my face. He must have been wracked with pain, but he didn't seem to care. "Don't *ever* do that to me again."

"What?"

"Disappear." His mouth met mine, and he angled his head to drink me in. Confusion slipped away, replaced with a fierceness that made me shiver even in the baking heat.

I ran my hands along the solid planes of his chest, and he groaned, deepening the kiss, drawing my breath and taking it as his own. Somehow, I pressed even closer, afraid I might hurt him but wanting more. Argus welcomed it, trapping me in his arms even as he hissed in a pained breath.

"Stop—you're hurt."

"Then make it better."

He kissed me slow, with unhurried strokes of his tongue that made fire consume my senses. The entire mansion could have burned to the ground and we'd still be sitting there among the ashes, the spark that set the flame.

With reluctance, Argus released me and pressed our foreheads together. We stayed like that for a moment until I rubbed my hand along the back of his neck.

"Do you kiss everyone you go on dangerous missions with?"

"No. Only you."

"Good answer. Now, since we have what we came for, I'd love for you to take me home."

"Home?" A smile that could have melted steel curved his mouth. "I like the way that— Wait, did you just say we got what we came for? Viv, I'm sorry, but Bowen destroyed the blade in front of me."

"No, he didn't. Wow…you need to keep up. While you were messing around, I found a secret passage, survived an attack from a wild animal, and switched the blade before Bowen's lackey collected the decoy, all while looking this good." My fingertips teased his collarbone. "I have to ask, what have you done?"

His gaze burned into mine, the intensity making my heart stutter. It was a breathless moment before he spoke.

"I hung around a fire pit with my hands tied, and it was torture."

"Ah, a fire pit. What an adventure. The stories you'll tell your children."

He laughed. "Hmm, speaking of stories..." He ghosted a hand over my jaw, then tucked a loose strand of hair behind my ear. "Did you really fend off a wild animal?"

"Yes. You're lucky I'm alive."

His eyes narrowed. "I don't believe you. You don't look injured."

"Well, it's not a competition," I muttered.

He rolled his eyes. "I'm glad you're alive."

"It was touch-and-go for a while there. Things were dire."

"I'm sure it was. So, I guess it's back the way we came? Are you ready for a swim through a flooded tunnel?"

I scrunched my nose in horror. "You're welcome to try, but I have no intention of setting foot in icy water. There's another way out. You know, it helps to make friends while you're on dangerous missions. I'm learning lots of things."

"Oh yeah?" he drawled. "What have you learned?"

"One,"—I held up a finger—"I'm the finest lock-smith in the kingdom. You should hire me."

"Not a chance."

I pouted and lifted another finger. "Two, I make friends wherever I go. I'm extremely personable."

"Keep going."

"And three—"

He snagged my hand before I could hold up a third finger. Dipping his head, Argus brushed his mouth over mine and whispered, "What's the third thing?"

I smiled. "Always bring snacks."

Chapter 25

ARGUS

"You're right—this is much better than a flooded tunnel." I peered over the ledge, holding one hand on the window frame. There was a dizzying three-story drop onto a stone terrace, and the wind beat the side of the house like a battering ram.

Vivian's hand rested on my back as she looked over my shoulder. "All the other windows are secured, but the iron bars have rusted on this one. It's how Liana escaped after she came here."

"And yet she's still wandering the grounds."

"Well, obviously, Bowen went after her."

"Bet he used the front door," I muttered, testing the windowsill with my boot. Seemed sturdy. It was the thin ledge leading to the exposed brick we'd need to use as handholds that had me worried.

Soft laughter sounded near my ear. "I thought you liked this sort of thing. Isn't this similar to how you stole the Ashworth ship manifest?"

"Sure, but I only had to worry about breaking my neck at the time. Now, I have to worry about your neck too."

Vivian rolled her eyes and slipped the strap of the bag containing the Grimm's blade over her head. In one smooth motion, she reversed our positions, twisting her body flush against mine, then swung a leg over the ledge.

Instinct made me grab her around the waist, which caused her lips to curve in a wicked smile. My heart stutter-stopped behind my rib cage. The vixen was enjoying this, and I was going to end up in an early grave from heart failure.

"Whoa... What are you doing?" I refused to let her go, sure her first step would send her plummeting to the ground.

"Going first."

"No way. I go first. You said so yourself, earlier."

"That was then; this is now. You have a head wound. Someone has to catch you if you fall."

I scoffed and shook my head, which caused the thrumming ache to worsen. "You can't just change the rules whenever you want. Who'll catch you if you fall?"

She looked down, and her brow creased. "Well, I suppose the terrace will." Mischief flickered in her eyes. "Why? Would you miss me?"

Yes. I swallowed around the tightness in my throat.

"No. It would save me a ton of trouble and lower my food bill."

Her eyes narrowed into slits. The wind whipped Vivian's long hair around her shoulders, strands clinging to the sides of her face.

My lie lingered between us, a stupid sentence I suddenly wished I could take back.

"Huh. Maybe you should go first. I'm kind of worried you're going to step on my fingers now." She curled her lip in disgust and pried my hands from her waist, then lowered herself onto the ledge. Her boots slid along the narrow outcropping. She shivered as another gust of wind forced her flat against the wall. When she came to her first foothold, Vivian took a deep breath and began to climb down.

Inch by inch, she worked her way down the side of the house, her feet digging into the small crevices. I could do nothing but follow, horrified each time she paused to blow hot air on her numb fingers.

"You know, you're right about one thing," I called down to her.

"What's that?"

"I really should hire you, but I'm not going to." My arms burned as I moved another few feet toward the ground. This slow descent was murder on my sore ribs, and Vivian was right: my head wound was making the ground blur.

"Why not?"

I caught up with her, slowing down so I wouldn't trample her fingers and give her the satisfaction of being right even if it wasn't intentional. "Because I think you'd enjoy it too much."

She blew the hair out of her eyes and gazed up at me. "I think it's because you're scared I'm better at this than you."

I smirked, warming to her game. "Better than me? There isn't anyone better at this than me, love."

She made a face, scrunching her pert nose. "Arrogant to the end, as usual." Her gaze traveled the remaining feet to the terrace. "I think this is far enough."

Pushing off the wall, she landed on both feet on the stone tile. Like a cat, Vivian stretched her arms over her head and rearranged the bag to a more comfortable position.

"See? Nothing to it," she said when I joined her on firm ground.

Footsteps crunched down the path, coming around the corner of the house. Vivian paled, her eyes widening into saucers. I motioned for her to come toward me, but she froze in place.

"Nothing to it, huh?" I grabbed her arm and spun her around, pressing her back against the side of the house. "Don't move," I whispered as I buried my face close to her ear.

Deep in the shadows, we waited while the man came closer. He whistled a lazy tune and paused at the edge of the terrace, almost exactly where Vivian had stood. A match scraped across the stone, and the faint scent of cigar smoke filled the air. Vivian felt tense as a bowstring beneath me. Her breaths were shallow, and I could sense the fear coiling inside her body at being discovered. She could scale walls, fend off wild animals—her words, not mine—and plant a decoy blade, but almost getting caught was her limit.

"Relax," I breathed, cupping the side of her face with my palm. "He can't see us."

Her throat muscles contracted, and she jerked her head in answer. Some of the tension drained from her body.

The man shifted his weight, crunching snow under his boots. He dragged on his cigar, and air hissed through his lips. Long minutes passed before he dropped it and crunched the end with his heel. The whistling started up again, fading as he moved off the terrace and down a gravel path.

I leaned back, keeping her trapped between my arms and the brick wall. "Still want to join my team?"

Vivian winced. "I panicked."

"I know, love."

Her eyes flared at the endearment, or maybe it was the way I said it. Either way, I was surprised when I went unchallenged.

"I think I'll stick with what I'm good at, thief."

The nickname, which was laced with insult when the witch said it, sounded intimate coming from Vivian.

I liked it. *A lot.*

Dropping my arms, I put some distance between us and scanned the grounds. We'd cleared Bowen's house, but not his property. I needed to stay focused on getting Vivian and the Grimm's blade somewhere safe.

Back *home.*

"Let's go."

Vivian cast Bowen's mansion a final look, then followed me into the trees that thickened at the edge of the property. Moonlight slivered through the branches, casting spotlights in the snow. We weaved through the thick trunks, doing our best to cover our tracks as we went.

I couldn't help but replay the night and the troubling knowledge my father had been meeting with a witch to develop a cure before his death. What if he'd succeeded? The man had only wanted one thing: complete power. What was more powerful than immortality? I'd need proof, but if it was even remotely possible Robert Lennox had returned, he'd returned to take back what he believed was his.

"Did you hear that?" Vivian slowed, her gaze scanning the trees. She edged closer to me. "Liana said she saw something lurking around the grounds. She thinks it was one of the wolves. They're drawn to the blade, and now, we have it."

"Keep moving," I said, unease forming like acid in my stomach. The woods were eerily silent, a tomb of shadow and snow. We were too vulnerable. An attack could come from any direction or be hiding behind any tree. "Give me the blade."

Vivian dug through the bag and withdrew the dagger. She clutched it so tight her knuckles were white around the hilt. The stones would likely leave indents on her palm. I took it from her, assessing the weight of it in my hand. It resonated power, and the current transferred through my skin and flowed up my arm.

A low howl pierced the silence, sending a stream of birds into the air. I spun toward the sound, shifting Vivian behind my back.

"If I tell you to run, you run."

She searched through her bag again, pulling something else from its depths. Another weapon? I watched as she used both hands to twist a metal bar, locking the two ends in place. At the tip was a spiked ball. Its thorny surface glinted in the moonlight.

Waving the weapon in the air, Vivian said, "Yeah, well, if I tell you to duck, you duck."

"Is that a mace?"

She held the weapon at an angle, examining the razor-sharp peaks. "Is that what it's called? I named it Spike."

I opened my mouth in protest, but she silenced me with a swipe of her hand. "Before you say anything, you're not the only thief around here, and Bowen had a whole collection—I don't think he'll miss one. Besides, did you honestly think if we were in a house full of weapons, I'd let you have the only one? Amateur."

The curl of her lips was almost my undoing. I'd never seen anything more alluring than her swinging a mace in the moonlight.

Another howl ruined the mood.

Vivian lifted her weapon and pressed her back against mine, each of us straining to see in the dark.

Absolute silence fell, and as the minutes passed, the blade grew damp in my palm. I gripped it tighter.

The gruesome roar came from the right. A lithe body launched through the air, matted fur covering muscle and bone, but it didn't hide the sharp claws and elongated teeth.

Air whooshed past my face as I rolled, taking Vivian with me. We landed in the snow.

The wolf crouched low on two hind legs. Its eyes glowed silver, and it snapped its teeth.

"Do you see that?" Vivian pointed to the scar on one of its legs, a deep bite mark. "It's not the Red Wolf. It's one of his bloodline."

I held my breath, locking gazes with the creature. Could it be Adella? Fear slithered around my heart. Had my sister been sent to kill me? Would I be able to kill her? As I gripped the blade tighter, the questions I couldn't answer tormented me.

The wolf snarled, baring its teeth, and reared back for another attack.

"Run!" I shouted.

Vivian scrambled to her feet and lurched forward. I raced behind her catching branches in the face and sliding in the slick snow. The sting barely registered. Behind me, the ground thundered. Lungs burning, I spurred Vivian faster.

"Don't stop! Whatever happens, keep running."

She turned terror-glazed eyes on me, then her gaze lifted over my shoulder, and she did exactly what I told her not to do. She skidded to a stop, kicking up fresh snow.

The wolf was gone.

Frantically, Vivian searched the trees, the weapon in her hand shuddering.

"Where is it? Do you see it?"

Everything blurred together—the trees, the snow —and Vivian hunched over, gulping icy breaths. Her pale skin was dotted with perspiration, hair wild around her shoulders.

A flash of movement caught my eye. The wolf launched from behind a tree, targeting Vivian. She stumbled, swinging the mace and making contact with its leg in a sickening thud. Jerking the mace free, she landed hard on her backside.

The wolf growled and swiped a meaty paw, catching her in the side before she could roll out of the way.

"No!" My shout resonated through the trees. I dove, dragging her out of the way, as the wolf struck again. Agonizing pain blistered across my back. It stole the breath from my lungs, and my knees hit the ground.

The blade had slipped from my fingers, the top of the hilt just barely sticking out of the snow. It was too far out of reach. If I went for it, I'd leave Vivian vulnerable to attack.

She struggled beneath me, screaming, but I wouldn't let her go. I tucked her head against my chest, banded my arms around her, and kept the wolf at my back, bracing for the fiery pain of claws raking my skin. But it never came. The woods grew deathly still, and I braved a glance behind me.

Silver eyes bore into mine. Teeth gnashing, the wolf threw back its head and howled. When the cry ended, instead of finishing me off or going for the blade, the wolf whirled in the snow and barreled through the trees.

Breathing heavy, I closed my eyes in relief. That was too close.

"Let me go!" Vivian bucked her whole body against me, breaking free. She stood and nearly slipped on an icy patch, her eyes wild. "I can't believe you did that!" Biting back a horrified moan at the sight of my back, she dropped to her knees and gently probed my flayed skin. "I can't believe you did that," she said again, this time hardly more than a whisper.

I sucked in a harsh breath. Turmoil rolled in my gut, anger and relief mixed with fear, and I couldn't get it out. It was a wall of iron choking me from the inside.

"Why?" Her voice rose, high-pitched and urgent. "Why did you do that? You should have tried to kill it, not rescue me." Tears stained her cheeks, and she captured my face between her hands. "It could have killed you! What were you thinking?"

A million things all in an instant. People say their past flashes before their eyes when they're about to die, but I didn't see my past because that wasn't of any value. I saw my future. A future without Vivian, cold and alone. It wasn't worth living. Yet even as she asked for the words, I held them back.

"Argus," she pleaded, her frozen breath mingling

with mine. "I need to know why you did that. Please? I need to know if you feel the same way I—"

"I did it because I made a promise."

Even though I said it softly, the words seemed to echo in the forest. Lies were always the loudest, and this one was deafening. It threatened to shake the ground and the very foundation of what we were heading toward.

The light in Vivian's eyes faded. It was like watching a candle flame sputter, then extinguish. A dry laugh escaped her lips. The broken sound scattered glass inside my chest.

"A promise? That's right. I'm so stupid." Her hands fell to her sides. She breathed through an aching sob, and her voice cracked. "I guess I should thank my grandmother for dragging it out of you. The mighty Argus Ward makes a promise! We should all be so honored." She rocked back on her heels, scooped up her weapon and the Grimm's blade, and shoved them both into her bag. "Consider yourself released from it. I don't need it. I don't need anything you have to give." Her wrenching gaze held mine. "Which, apparently, isn't much."

"Vivian, you don't under—"

"Can you walk?" she asked.

"Yes."

"Good." She turned away, trudged through the snow, and didn't look back.

Chapter 26

VIVIAN

Argus hissed as Tessa slapped a medicated concoction against his back. It made a wet sucking sound and oozed a white substance. Tattered strips of fabric hung from the remnants of his shirt, the edges soaked in blood.

"Watch it, witch." His features contorted in pain, and the noxious smell wafting from the bandage made his jaw clench.

"You watch it," she mocked, turning back to the bubbling brew that made my stomach revolt even from across the room.

My gaze moved uncontrollably toward Argus to find him studying me. His quiet stare was twisting me in knots. The weight of it made my mouth dry and my skin feel tight. He'd been doing it nonstop since we returned. Wasn't there anything else he could focus on?

Tessa snapped her fingers in front of his face. "Hey, eyes up here. You'll need to apply more of this tomorrow, but the pain should already be subsiding. There won't be an infection. Much to my disappointment," she grumbled. "You're lucky I'm such a talented healer in addition to my many magical abilities, and since you brought Vivian back in mostly one piece, you get my charming bedside manner as well." She flashed her teeth, but the smile didn't reach her eyes.

"Tess, not now," I sighed, too emotionally drained to listen to them squabble.

"I know, I know. This is me making an effort. Now, Viv, lift your shirt a bit so I can see the wound on your side. I can't believe in addition to being nicked by a fury statue, you almost got mauled." She made a tsk sound with her tongue and picked up a different bowl of sweetly scented paste, then winked. "This one smells better and produces the same results."

I couldn't help but glance at Argus again to gauge his reaction to Tessa's preferential treatment, but he'd moved closer and was focused on my injury, trying to peer around her. She smeared paste onto half of the wound, and I shrieked. This wasn't medicine; it was molten lava! I slapped her hand away, hardly able to breathe through the excruciating pain.

"Are you trying to kill me? I thought you said this one was better!"

"I said it smells better."

Argus scowled, and in three steps, he swiped the bowl from Tessa's hand. "Bloody hell, witch, your bedside manner leaves a lot to be desired." He crowded her out, silencing her with a look that could have toppled three grown men.

Crouching down, Argus lifted my shirt. I went still as he dipped a finger into the bowl and gently dabbed at the wound. His touch was featherlight, but I still stifled a scream at the inevitable burn.

"Almost finished, love." Lowering his head, he blew cool air against my skin. The pain diminished, replaced with tiny shivers that raced to my toes. "Better?" he asked softly.

My throat closed. All I could manage was a nod. He was too close, his gaze too unsettled. I tried to hold on to my disappointment, needing to wrap it around me for fear it would dissipate like steam under Argus's heated stare.

There was no denying we had a physical connection, but that was all it was to him. Even after everything, I was still just a promise made in exchange for services rendered.

What a joke.

His revelation in the woods felt like falling into icy water. The shock then numbness threatened to paralyze my heart.

My mind flashed back to the night he drank the rest of my sleeping potion. I'd begged him to stop doing things that changed the way I felt about him. The request might have been useless, but I needed to ask again. If there was any possibility of us continuing to work together, I had to build a stone wall around him.

"Stop," I whispered, lowering my shirt and stepping back. "Please, stop."

He knew immediately what I meant. The single word caused his features to cave, his whole body taking my message like a blow to the chest. I wanted to take it back as soon as I said it, but I held firm.

Argus straightened, still holding the bowl, and his knuckles went white around the porcelain. There was a beat of silence while he searched my face, then his voice rumbled, "Viv, we need to talk."

"*Vivian* needs to rest." Tessa stepped between us. Placing her hand on my back, she propelled me toward the door.

I concentrated on putting one foot in front of the other. It felt like I was still on that walk through the woods, trudging through the snow, trying to keep my head high, refusing to let him see me cry. Just outside the door, I paused and spoke without looking over my shoulder.

"Now we have the blade, I'll restart the search for the Red Wolf in the morning."

"That's not what I want to talk about." He tried to follow us, but Tessa flicked her wrist and sent an armchair into his path. It slid across the floor as if on a gust of wind.

"There isn't anything left to say."

"Yes, there is," he said, sidestepping the chair. Argus charged toward the doorway like an animal stalking its prey.

Tessa lifted an eyebrow in challenge and drummed her fingers into her palm, curling them into a fist. The office door slammed shut, locking

Argus inside. He rattled the handle and pounded against it until the wood shuddered in its frame.

"Witch! Open the door."

"Tess, what are you doing? Let him out."

"Forget it. He needs to cool off." She dragged me down the hallway, and Argus's angry outburst faded. When we were far enough away, she rounded on me, crossing her arms. "What is going on with you two?"

"Nothing. We found the Grimm's blade, and now we're going to track down the Red Wolf. Soon, everything will go back to normal." Exhaustion flowed through my body. It was after dawn, and I needed sleep. I wasn't ready to analyze everything with Tessa—she'd see right through me.

Unfortunately, she wasn't going to give me the chance.

"Normal?" She scoffed. "Do you honestly think you can go home like nothing happened?"

"Yes," I hissed.

"You're being ridiculous. I'm not blind, but apparently, you are."

Anger spiked, sliding through my system like hot oil. "I'm not blind. I know exactly where I stand. I have no intention of staying here any longer than necessary. I'm still a stupid promise to him, nothing more. He said so tonight. To my face. In a super direct way." I bit my tongue, not intending to let that slip.

Tessa looked at me—really looked—and I saw the moment she read between the lines. "Viv, are you in love with him?"

"I don't know! Maybe. It doesn't matter how I feel if it's not reciprocated. I know you hate him, and it hasn't been that long. I just thought…" Wretched tears stung my eyes. I was so sick of the emotional ups and downs.

"He's such an idiot," she said.

"What?"

"You heard me. Argus is a colossal moron for making you think he doesn't care about you." She ground her fist into her palm. "Men are the worst. They act one way and tell you something else. Derrick does it too. He always says the wrong things when he's worried, and I always get bent out of shape and think about poisoning his dinner. But I don't, and do you know why?"

I sniffed to keep the tears at bay. "Because prison is awful. There are so many rats, and the food is terrible."

Tessa bobbed her head. "That is why. Honestly, if the conditions ever improve, the man had better watch his back."

A laugh burst from my lips, and Tessa clasped my hands in hers. "But seriously, even when he says things he doesn't mean, I still know he cares because he shows it in so many ways. That's just as important."

I shook my head. "It's not the same thing though. Derrick loves you. He has your best interests at heart and wants to take care of you."

Tessa groaned and covered her face with her hands. "I can't believe I'm saying this, but wow. You really are blind. That man in there just went up against a witch so he could help ease your pain. I'm pretty scary, you know? Plus, he asked you to live with him to keep you out of danger, which seems to me like he's concerned about your best interests and wants to take care of you." She sighed. "You know I don't particularly approve and it's because I worry about you, but I've seen the way he looks at you. It's like there's no one else in the room, hell, like there's no one else in the kingdom. Maybe just give him some time to come around?" She squeezed my hand. "And if he doesn't, I'll poison his dinner. Prison be damned."

"You make it sound so easy."

"It's not. It's difficult and confusing, and sometimes, it breaks your heart, but if you can figure it out, it's worth it. Don't tell him I said that though. I fully intend to go back to hating him. I have a lot of nasty zingers built up, and it would be a shame for them to go to waste." She gave me a little nudge toward the stairs. "Get some sleep. I'll let him stew a bit longer before I let him out—maybe it will do him some good. Besides, I'm kind of enjoying it."

"You're really vengeful." I wiped at my damp lashes. "I've always liked that about you."

Tessa pretended to buff her nails on her sleeve. "I mean, it's one of my best qualities."

"Thanks, Tess. For everything. I know this isn't easy for you."

"This isn't about me. For once." She smiled. "Now, go. I'll check on you later. Leave the thief to me."

***

Hours later, I woke to my stomach growling and rolled over to find a plate scones on the nightstand. Pushing aside the wispy canopy, I plucked one off the plate and collapsed back against the pillow. My eyes drifted shut as I reveled in the tart burst of cranberries and buttery pastry.

"Bless Fiona," I mumbled around another bite.

Maybe the saying was true and food did heal all wounds? Better yet, maybe I should give up men and learn to bake? If I left, I'd need to take Fiona with me —there were some things you just shouldn't have to live without. I'd come up with the funds somehow.

I finished the scone and sighed. The food was good, but it didn't stop me remembering every moment from the previous night in excruciating detail. Did I imagine Argus standing outside my room before I fell asleep? I assumed he'd come tearing up the stairs the moment Tessa freed him from his office and beat down my door. It didn't happen like that, but someone stood there for a long time. Soft candlelight was still bleeding through the crack near the floor when I finally drifted off.

Climbing out of bed, I got dressed and peered into the mirror over the vanity. It took a good pep talk before I summoned the courage to leave my bedroom. I crept down the hallway toward the stairs and was halfway to the conservatory when I heard the sound of laughter.

Tessa and Hastings sat around one of the wrought

iron tables sipping tea. I breathed a sigh of relief. If she was here, that meant Argus likely wasn't. I might have been brave enough to leave my room, but I wasn't brave enough to face him yet.

"There she is!" Tessa called out when she spotted me. "I figured I'd stay to make sure you were all right. Do you need me to have another look at your injury? I can whip up some more salve."

"Absolutely not. I've had enough of your healing to last me for a while." I sat down in a vacant chair, and Hastings poured me a cup of tea.

"Miss Daniels was filling me in on your adventure last night. Did you really fend off a wild animal inside the walls of MacKenzie Manor?"

Tessa bit into a fruit tart and pinned me with a look. "It was a dog, wasn't it?"

"No." I laughed, toying with the handle of my teacup. "It was huge. You should have seen the teeth, and the claws could have ripped me to shreds. Honestly, you're both lucky I'm still alive."

They stared at me. A full minute passed in silence.

"Fine! It was a dog. It ate Fiona's beef pastries and licked my hand. I think I made a friend for life."

"You owe me five royal coins, Hastings."

He shook his head and dug into his pocket, then slid the money across the table.

I slung my arms across my chest and sulked. "I did find the blade all by myself. That should count for something. I mean, sure, it was pretty much handed to me by the woman who lives there, and I only found the hidden passage by accident, but if you look at the bigger picture, I was an integral part of the mission."

"That's right. No one could have stumbled into the blade better than you." Tessa smirked and finished her tea.

"Don't you have someone's day to ruin with one of your spells?"

She grinned. "Nope! I cleared my schedule for you."

"How wonderful."

Hastings cleared his throat and reached into his jacket, then pulled out a slim gold envelope. "I hate to break this up, but this arrived for you this morning, Miss James."

"It came for me—here? Who sent it?" I took it from him, and the paper shimmered in the light. Turning it over, I saw my name had been scrawled in elegant script across the front.

"I'm not sure. It simply appeared in the correspondence basket. It wasn't there earlier."

Tessa gasped and plucked the envelope from me before I could open it. She slid her finger under the flap and pulled out the card. "It can't be. Do you know what this is?"

"Not unless you give it to me."

"It's an invitation from the High Council." Her eyes were as wide as saucers as she handed it over. "You've been invited to their summit in Winifred's place!"

"What's the High Council?" Hastings asked.

"They're only a collection of the most powerful supernatural beings in all the kingdoms. From witches and shapeshifters to oracles and mediums, they're the best of the best. Every year, they host a summit. It's invitation only. Winifred never missed one."

I scanned the page while Tessa nearly bounced in her seat.

"Viv, you have to take me with you."

"I don't know... This was Winifred's thing. It feels weird to go in her place. Besides, with everything going on here, it doesn't seem right."

"She'd want you to go! There will be other oracles there. Powerful ones. They can help you figure out your visions." Her eyes glazed over. "And the witches. Just think of the spells I could learn..."

I chewed the edge of my thumbnail, considering her point. I wasn't getting anywhere with the mirror, and now we had the Grimm's blade, it was more important than ever I figure out the final vision. An oracle with more experience might be exactly what I needed. There was also a part of me that wanted a little space. A couple of days at a magical summit would clear my head.

"All right. We can go together."

Tessa clapped her hands and shot out of her chair, wrapping her arms around me. "When do we leave?"

I checked the invitation and frowned. "A carriage will pick us up this afternoon. That's awfully quick. Are you sure—?"

Her hands came down on my shoulders, and she gave them a little shake. "Viv, if the carriage was waiting outside now, I'd be ready." She flashed me a smile. "Pack your bags. We're going on a trip."

Chapter 27

ARGUS

"So, you found the Grimm's blade." Wade shut the door to the back room at the Laughing Raven and took a seat behind his desk. He offered me a drink and gave a brief salute before downing his. "And how is our old friend Mackenzie? Still hiding away in that decrepit manor all by himself?"

Leaning back in my seat, I lifted an eyebrow. "Actually, he wasn't alone. There was a woman there, Liana Archer."

"Archer? Isn't that the surname of the man who sold the blade to Bowen? Do you think that's his daughter? I wonder how she ended up there..."

"I don't know, but it wasn't the only surprise." I sighed. "Bowen had information about my father. It seems Robert visited a witch before he died. He was trying to find a cure. What if he found one?"

Wade held up his hand. "Hold on... Are you suggesting your father is still alive? If that's true, where's he been for the past few years?"

"Good question." I scrubbed a hand over my jaw. "Here's another one: What if he's connected to the killings? Robert's thirst for power was unmatched. He would have done anything to stay alive. But it was more than that. He wanted immortality."

"You think he's the Red Wolf?"

"I think it's possible. In his final days, no one ever saw him, and we only had a secondhand confirmation of his body. There wasn't any reason to suspect differently because his organization crumbled, and everything was turned over to me. Now, here we are, years later, with a series of killings that started with known associates of mine—associates who used to work for him and traded sides."

Wade bypassed refilling his glass and drank directly from the bottle. He grimaced and wiped his mouth with the side of his sleeve.

"Hell, Argus. If it's true, we're not dealing with a frail old man grasping for power on his way out; we're dealing with a hard to kill, bloodthirsty werewolf determined to pick up where he left off."

Tapping my thumb on the rim of my glass, I stared into the amber liquid. "We need to find out, one way or another."

"And how are we supposed to do that? Robert isn't going to place a banner in the paper declaring his return."

"No, but that doesn't mean we can't find him. He might be immortal now, but he's not invisible. If he's here, someone's seen him." I shook my head as I recalled my conversation with Bowen. He was right: I wasn't asking the right questions. As long as I believed my father was dead, I wouldn't think to look for him. He could hide in plain sight building his army, and we wouldn't be able to stop him until it was too late. "I want everyone on this. Let's see what we can find."

Wade took another swig from the bottle. "What about the witch he consulted? Is there a way we can track him through her? Even finding out if a spell like that is possible would help. Give us something to go on."

"I don't have the witch's name, but…" I groaned, not liking my train of thought. "I might know someone I can ask. Trouble is, we're not on good terms."

"Well, you'd better get on good terms. We need all the help we can get. Pay her off. Seduce her if you have to."

"Ha! That would solve my problem. I'd be dead and wouldn't have to deal with any of this. Besides, it's more complicated than that." I drained my glass, wincing as the fiery liquor burned my throat.

"Well, you wouldn't be you if it wasn't complicated. Let me guess—it has to do with the pretty oracle staying with you? Rumor is, she's got you all twisted up. Now, I'm not one to believe in rumors, but I haven't even mentioned her name and you look murderous. Never thought I'd see the day."

My hand tightened around my glass. "Speaking of murderous, where's my sister, Wade? It's been weeks, and you haven't found her."

"Relax. I've been working a couple leads. I'll know more soon."

"Find her." I scowled and pushed out of my chair. "I have to go visit a witch."

***

There were more troublesome things than trying to get information out of a witch who hated your guts. I just couldn't think of any.

The bell above the door jangled as I entered the magic shop and surveyed the cluttered, rustic interior.

"I'll be right there!" the witch shouted from one of the back rooms.

Her workbench was littered with open spellbooks. I caught the lingering scent of the healing salve she'd forced on us the night before. It tested my gag reflex, and I nearly opened a window. I was sure she'd added something extra pungent on my account, which was fine, but seeing Vivian in pain had blown through my restraint.

Last night turned into a disaster, and it was all because I couldn't say the words that came so easily to other people. Instead, I'd ruined everything. In an ironic twist, the promise that brought us together had torn us apart.

Emerging from the back of the shop, the witch flashed a welcoming smile that withered the moment she spotted me. "Oh, it's you. I thought I had a paying customer. What are you doing here?" Before I could speak, she held up a hand. "If this is about Vivian, I don't want to hear it. I don't regret locking you in your office last night, and I'd do it again."

"I know you would. But that's not why I'm here. I need information. It's about the werewolf."

"Oh." She furrowed her brow and leaned against the workbench. "Look, we have our differences, but I want that thing caught as much as you do and not only for Vivian's sake. Winifred meant something to me too. Besides, the sooner this is over, the sooner Vivian can put all of this behind her."

All of this. What she really meant was, *all of you.* I ground my teeth.

"I need to know if a witch can turn someone into a werewolf."

She crossed her arms and lifted a brow. "Are you accusing me of something?"

"No, I'm serious. We know the wolf's bloodline advances through a bite, but the original of that line—how are they made?"

"Well, you're right about one thing: it's definitely magic. Not the kind you'd find in this shop. I run a reputable business, unlike some..." She flashed her teeth, getting in a dig before continuing. "But blood magic would do the trick."

"Blood magic? What's that?"

Sighing, she crossed to her bookcase and searched the volumes, then pulled a heavy book off and dropped it onto a viewing table. "It's more ritual than anything else. What I do here is based in illusion or delivered in potion form. Blood magic is much darker. It's also forbidden. Though, witches walk a fine line when it comes to forbidden." Flipping through the pages, she stopped and pointed to an entry. "You need all the right elements to make it work, and it's not as simple as casting a spell and *poof*, bloodthirsty wolf. It's about being reborn. The candidate has to be brought to the brink of death and then fed the blood of a wolf. At least, that's what the book says. I've never tried it. Seems pretty gross."

So, it was possible. I studied the illustration of a man restrained on a platform under a giant moon. She wasn't wrong; it looked gruesome.

"Are you aware of any witches who could have performed that ritual? Let's say, in the last few years?"

She shook her head. "No. I don't know anyone who could pull that off. Not in this kingdom. Though..." Tessa chewed on her bottom lip. "I could ask around tonight at the summit."

"What summit?"

The witch looked surprised. "Vivian didn't tell you? She's been invited to the High Council gathering in Winifred's place. The invitation came this morning. It's a great opportunity for her to learn more about her visions. She's taking me with her. We leave this afternoon."

An icy feeling spread through my chest. "She's leaving today? For how long?"

Tessa shrugged. "A couple days, maybe more. You never know with the High Council. I think Winifred didn't come back for six months once."

"Six months?" There was no way in hell she was

leaving for six months. Six hours, maybe. Six days if I could stand it, but... I clenched my jaw. "Is it safe?"

The witch waved away my concern as if it were a fly buzzing around her head. "There's a covenant in place during the gathering. No killing or maiming of any kind. It's all on the up and up." She narrowed her gaze. "And don't even think about trying to talk her out of going. She needs to be around other oracles right now."

"No, you're right. It's better for her if she can learn how to control the visions. I just..." Hated she was leaving with things strained between us.

"You just what?"

"Nothing."

She smirked and returned the book to the shelf. "Well, if you want to see her before she leaves, I'd hurry. The carriage is picking us up soon, and a High Council carriage waits for no one."

***

The sleek horse-drawn vehicle was already waiting outside the Lennox mansion when I returned. There was no driver, which was...concerning. I guessed the entrance to the gathering was a secret that couldn't be entrusted to a coachman.

"Where's Vivian?" I asked Hastings when he met me in the foyer.

"Upstairs, packing." His features hardened, and he swept his arm toward the staircase, the move severe enough to stretch the lining of his tailored jacket. "What did you do?"

A pair of servants carried a trunk down the stairs and placed it in the entryway. They didn't meet my eyes and swiftly departed down the hall.

"Fix this, or find yourself a new butler," Hastings grumbled, following in their wake.

I cast a glance up the stairs, then took them two at a time. There was more commotion at the top of the landing. Another trunk whisked past me. As fast as I went up the stairs, the walk to Vivian's room took forever. I hesitated before entering.

Inside, I could hear her moving around mumbling something to herself. She looked up when I walked in, pausing her attempt to buckle the strap on her satchel. I froze, my boots cemented to the floor. The wardrobe was empty, and the vanity that had been covered with her toiletries was bare. None of her personal items remained. If she wasn't standing in front of me, I wouldn't have believed she'd ever been here.

"This is more than a couple days." The words scraped through my throat.

"Yeah." She slung her bag over her shoulder and smoothed the wrinkle it made on the bedspread, another trace of her gone. "I guess you heard about the summit. The more I thought about it, I realized I had to pack anyway and figured I might as well get it all done at once." She swallowed and addressed her feet. "I'm not coming back here when it's over. I'm going home."

"Why?" Numbness spread. It started somewhere in my chest and worked its way to my limbs, keeping me in place though my mind demanded I rip the bag from her shoulder and hold it hostage.

"Because this was always temporary. Ashworth hasn't tried anything else, and you have the Grimm's blade now. When I get back from the summit, I'm sure I'll have a better understanding of the visions. There's no reason for me to stay here any longer."

"That's not true. Hastings—"

"Your butler? You want me to stay for your butler?"

"No. Of course not." I was scrambling, not making any sense, so I latched onto the only thing that did. "The killer's still out there. It's not safe for you to stay alone."

She pinched her lips together and tightened her grip on the bag, looking as if it wasn't the strap she wanted to strangle but my neck. "It's not your job to take care of me. I already released you from your promise last night. The agency can provide protection. Derrick's officers—"

"Aren't worth a damn!" I snapped, slamming my palm on the canopy post. "There's no way in hell I'm letting the agency take over. You're *my* responsibility." Gritting my teeth, I grated, "You don't get to release me from you."

Her laughter was harsh, eyes flashing with anger. "I don't want to be anyone's responsibility! Can't you see that? Especially not yours. Not after everything that's happened between us." Her chest rose on a heavy breath, and her fist covered her mouth as if it could hide the pained sound in the back of her throat. "I want...I want to be more than that to you."

Her words punched me in the gut and sucked all air from my lungs. Did she have any idea what she was asking? How much I wanted things to be different? The life I'd chosen wasn't a silly game where the loser had to spill a secret. The consequences were far greater; the losses unimaginable.

Vivian waited for a long moment. The most beautiful thing I'd ever seen, standing in the silence her confession created. A silence I ached to fill with the words she wanted to hear but couldn't.

Lifting her chin, she held my gaze and took a shaky breath. "I have to go. The carriage is already here, and I'm sure Tessa is waiting. I'll reach out to you when we get back and let you know if we learn anything. Goodbye, Argus." She walked past me toward the door, so close her floral scent flooded my senses. My eyes closed, fingers itching to reach for her.

Too late.

Her footsteps faded down the hallway, and my hand closed over air.

Chapter 28

VIVIAN

The whole way to the portal, Tessa couldn't sit still. She tapped her feet and flipped through the worn pages of her spellbook, making a list of everything she wanted to try. Her eyes danced with excitement, yet I couldn't capture any of her optimism. Nothing could banish the sight of Argus standing like a grim statue while I walked away.

Tessa nudged my shoe. "You're being awfully quiet over there. For someone invited to the inner circle, I expect more enthusiasm."

"I am enthusiastic. I just hide it better," I mumbled, staring out the carriage window.

"Did something happen between you and Argus before we left? You can tell me." She waved her hand in a circle, encompassing my presence in the seat across from her. "This is a judgment-free carriage."

"I don't believe you. You live to judge."

She closed her book and drummed her fingers on

the cover. "That's true. But seriously, Viv, I'll listen."

"I know you will." I sighed and leaned back against the cushion. "I told him the truth, that I don't want to be his obligation; I want to be more. And then I told him I wasn't coming back after the summit."

"Wow. What did he say?"

"Not much. He let me go, Tess. And the thing that hurts the most is, part of me believes he didn't want to, but he won't allow himself to try." I rubbed my hands over my face and groaned. "What do you do when the person you love can't love you back?"

Tessa leaned forward, elbows on her knees, and gave a curt nod. "That's easy. You go to a supernatural gathering and get drunk."

I laughed. "Well, what a coincidence. We're on our way to a supernatural gathering."

She sighed and made a face. "I'm sorry, Viv. I thought things would turn out differently. He came by the shop today and asked me if witches could create werewolves, and he seemed genuinely concerned about you when I told her we were leaving."

"Concern isn't the issue." I pressed my hand to my abdomen as if it could ease the horrible feeling in the pit of my stomach. "Look, can we talk about something else? Anything! What did Derrick say when you told him you'd be hobnobbing with a gang of powerful witches?"

Tessa grinned, happy to play distraction. "He told me to bring him back a souvenir. He also said not to accept magical rings as a form of payment for my spells." She scrunched her nose. "Honestly, you get haunted by a murder victim one time, and it's all anyone warns you about."

"Well, it is solid advice."

The carriage rumbled to a stop at the edge of a snow-covered field. I squinted through the glass at the lone hooded figure standing a few yards away like a scarecrow doing its best to ward off scavengers. Next to him, floating in the air, was a shimmering circle, the center whirling like a vortex.

"Is this it?"

Tessa peered over my shoulder. "Let's see...a grim figure holding a giant scythe in front of a mystical portal? I'd say we're in the right place. You brought the invitation, right? He seems like the type to check for identification."

I patted the folded parchment inside my bag.

We climbed from the carriage and took our first steps toward the portal. A fresh wave of nerves unleashed in my stomach. It was one thing to remember my grandmother's stories about the High Council, and another to attend one of their gatherings. Boots sinking into the snow, we crossed the field and came to a halt in front of the guard. He didn't speak, which multiplied the intimidation that radiated from the dark void beneath his hood.

"Show him the invite," Tessa said under her breath.

I withdrew the invitation and offered it to him, holding the slip of paper between two fingers. The wind fluttered the parchment and whistled across the field. For a long moment, nothing happened. Was I missing something? Was there a secret password or handshake I'd forgotten to learn?

"Tess, I think—"

The reaper reared back and swung the scythe.

My heart stopped pumping, and my eyes squeezed shut. *Welp, problem solved.* We were dead. I wouldn't be having any more uncomfortable conversations about my relationship with Argus after all.

When I realized he hadn't sliced us in two, I popped one eye open. The invitation was still in my hand, but the bottom half was sheared off.

"What's happening?" Tessa asked from behind me, gripping the back of my cloak. "Is that bad?"

"I don't know," I whispered. "It doesn't look good."

"Great. We're going to die in a field. I knew this was too good to be true. I won't even get to browse the illegal potions."

The top half of the invitation shook. It glowed, and the severed edge regenerated until the entire invitation had reformed. The hooded figure lowered his scythe and gestured with a crooked finger to the portal.

Okay, maybe we weren't going to be chopped into tiny pieces and fed to the birds.

"See? Like you said, he was checking our identification." I contained a full-body shudder and took a hesitant step toward the portal.

Tessa followed, still clinging to my cloak, and turned toward the guard. "Have a nice day. Good luck with your slicey thing."

I swear, the reaper frowned beneath his hood. Tessa might still get us killed. I grabbed her wrist and yanked her through the portal before we could give him another chance.

***

As far as portals went, it wasn't so bad if you didn't mind the sickening sensation of falling off a cliff. We landed on our hands and knees in the same field, except it was night.

Tessa breathed heavily through her nose. "I did not like that."

"It was our first portal. I'm sure it gets easier." I climbed to my feet, taking in the scene in front of us. Hundreds of floating lanterns covered the field, and colorful burlap tents fluttered in the breeze. A giant bonfire took center stage shooting flames high into the sky. Revelers danced around it, chanting and swaying their arms in time with a mysterious drumbeat.

"Looks like the High Council likes to party." Tessa nudged me in the elbow. "This will work."

"Yeah, well, don't get used to it. We can't stay too long."

"Uh, Viv, the summit lasts for three full days." She pulled out her list. "It will take that long to get the full experience."

"Tess, time is subjective here. Three days is, like, two weeks on the other side. Remember when my grandmother forgot to bring her pocket watch to one of these and lost track of time?"

"Ah, yeah. The six-month incident. So, you're saying we only have a couple hours here? That's highly disappointing." She pressed the list to her chest, her gaze roaming over the packed field. "We should divide and conquer. I'll speak to the witches and see if I can get any information on the spell Argus mentioned. You find the oracles. We'll meet afterward to party."

"Sounds like a plan. Just don't get us tossed out like the time you dragged me to that cooking with potions demonstration."

Tessa snorted. "That was a nightmare, huh? I still maintain they gave me a faulty cauldron." Walking backward into the crowd, she wriggled her fingers. "Come find me when you're done."

I stood at the edge of the field, unsure if I wanted to dive in. The air was alive with magic and foreign scents. It was as if every supernatural being had converged in the same location and their energy couldn't be contained. It burst at the seams, hypnotic in its pull. No wonder Winifred never missed one of these gatherings.

I followed the crowd past a raised platform, where a group of witches played a game of magical darts. One of the glowing bolts went wide of the mark, then twirled in the air, coming back around to find the bull's-eye. Weaving through tents, I came to a stop in front of one with a wooden post tamped into the ground. The hand-painted sign read: "Fortunes for Sale. Gold Only. No Soliciting."

"Don't just stand there, sweetie. Futures don't

read themselves."

I turned toward the musical voice and found a young woman staring back. Her green eyes sparkled with warmth as her lips curved into a dazzling smile. Long black curls cascaded down her back in untamed waves, and a purple and blue patterned sheath clung to her generous curves.

"I've been waiting for you. Come inside—I'll give you a reading." She held open the tent and ushered me through. When she dropped the flap, the chaotic noise from the revelers faded as if muffled by enchantment.

The air was thick and humid and contained the soothing scent of spices and incense. In the center of the tent was a table unlike any I'd seen before. The mirrored surface reflected the burlap ceiling, where an illuminated crystal scattered shards of light across the ground.

"Do you like it?" The woman ran her fingertips over the table. "I had it specially made. It's reinforced and guaranteed not to crack no matter how dark the future, and I've seen some dark stuff."

"It's beautiful." I took the chair she offered, reluctant to look directly into the glass.

The woman settled into the seat across from me and sighed. "You look exactly like Winifred when she was your age. I'd know you anywhere."

My gaze shot to hers. "Did you know my grandmother?"

"Know her? She was a good friend of mine, and she loved sharing stories about you. I'm Melody." She frowned at my lack of recognition, then rolled her eyes. "Oh, for fortune's sake, does the name Melodious ring a bell? I swear, your grandmother tested my patience with that nickname."

"Melodious! That's you? But you're so young." I bit my tongue at Melody's look of disdain. "What I meant was—"

"Sweetie, I sold my soul for youth and beauty ages ago. I can't say I recommend it, but it has its perks, and my favorite part was everyone thinking I was Winifred's daughter. It drove her crazy." She paused to arrange her vibrant skirt so it flowed around her ankles. "I miss her, you know? But seeing you here, it's almost like she's here too. She was so proud of you. Her little ghost girl."

The ache in my chest expanded, and I dropped my gaze. "I miss her so much. I hate that I didn't get to say goodbye."

"I know you do." She reached across the mirrored table and clasped my hand. "Goodbyes are often a luxury. Winifred knew how much you loved her." Frowning, she squeezed my hand. "I hate that you had to go through everything alone. You're probably still struggling with your new powers. I would have come to you sooner, but when you sell your soul, you kind of have to play by someone else's timeline."

I brushed my fingers under my damp lashes. "I never thought I'd have to take her place. I'm terrible at it. The mirror doesn't show me anything useful. It's the same vision over and over."

Melody smiled. "It's not you. These things take

time. You didn't know how to help ghosts right away either. If I remember correctly, you unleashed more spirits than you crossed over in the beginning."

I nodded my head. "Yeah, I did."

"The mirror's the same. You'll learn to harness it better, and eventually, the readings will make sense. Not all of them, because fate is a tricky bastard, but you'll get close. People think oracles have the answer to everything, that we're all-knowing, but it isn't true. No one knows everything. Occasionally, fate lets a little chance slip through just to complicate things." She winked. "We still charge the same though."

"What if you want to change something you've seen in a vision? Is it possible to prevent it from happening at all?"

Melody exhaled a long breath and looked down to pick at the corner of her thumbnail. "It depends. Sometimes, when you try, you end up exactly where you started. That's called—"

"Fate." I smiled. "I know. I ran into that one already."

"Well, not even fate is foolproof. But it's difficult to change. The mind isn't capable of changing a vision; only the heart can. Trouble is, most people don't know what their heart wants, or they're in denial."

"What does that mean?"

"It means you can't rationalize your way into a changed future. I'll go left instead of right. I'll buy a red dress instead of blue. But the red dress will go up in flames, and I'll take three more left turns until I'm heading right. The heart knows what you have to do if you listen to it."

I bent over with my hands on my knees, overwhelmed. Melody took pity on me and moved closer. She pushed a lock of hair out of my face.

"Why don't we look and see what we're dealing with?" She moved my palm onto the mirror, then rested her hand over mine. Her eyes closed, and she whispered something unintelligible.

There was a spark of connection between us. It ran up my arm and tingled in my fingers. When Melody's eyes opened, she peered into the glass.

The vision that had haunted me from the beginning played beneath our entwined fingers. My future self trudged through the forest, approaching the tree where the body lay in a pool of blood. I witnessed it all again: the screams, the blurred faces, and the mysterious object she pulled from the snow and pressed against her heart.

"I can never see who it is. The vision always ends there, and I'm too far away."

Melody squeezed my fingers. "Let me try something." She moved our hands across the glass, curving upward toward the top of the mirror.

Beneath my hand, the image rotated and moved closer.

"How are you doing that?" I asked.

"Lots of practice and the help of our combined power."

As the vision became clear, my heart pounded in

my ears. I could see his face. The cry on my lips was soundless, but in my head, it reverberated to every corner of my body, a scream of denial so strong blackness crept around my eyesight.

It was Argus lying dead in the snow.

A sickening crack filled the tent, and a fissure raced through the mirrored table. I snapped my eyes shut, but I still saw his lifeless body and unseeing gaze staring up at the treetops. This couldn't be happening. Not again! I refused to lose someone else I loved.

My heart twisted, and then, something strange happened. A bright light flashed behind my eyelids. It seared white-hot through my body, followed by a wave of peace and acceptance.

Melody gasped, her grip on my hand becoming a wrenching pain. "No," she whispered. "This can't be happening again."

When I opened my eyes, the image in the mirror looked different. It flickered in and out. Sometimes, it was Argus lying in the snow, and sometimes, it was me. Then it would flicker, and the ground was empty.

"Why is it doing that?"

"This is very rare. A decision you make alters the future, and it's showing you the unique paths all at once." Her voice was soft and filled with awe.

Something cold trickled through my veins. "But you have seen it before. What did you mean when you said this can't be happening again?"

She didn't respond, refused to meet my gaze.

"Answer me. Whose vision changed?"

A tear slid down her cheek. "Winifred didn't want you to know, but I won't lie to you. You probably assumed she witnessed her death in the mirror, and I'm sure you blame yourself for not being there to help her. But you weren't there for a reason. Before she died, Winifred saw the different paths and picked one. She sent you away, and it changed the future." Melody cupped my face between her hands. "Sweetie, Winifred never saw her death. She saw yours."

Chapter 29

VIVIAN

I jerked out of Melody's grip and stumbled from the chair. The ground tilted as I lunged for the opening of the tent, yanking it open just as my legs decided I'd gone far enough and collapsed beneath me. My knees hit the dirt, and I sucked in gasping breaths. Squeezing my eyes closed, I blocked out the swarm of revelers who stopped to stare.

Everything I thought I knew about my grandmother's death was wrong. It was difficult to accept she'd witnessed her death in the mirror, but I never imagined she'd seen mine and made the choice to face the killer in my place.

Her sacrifice broke my heart, but strangely, I understood it. How many times had Winifred drilled into me that the James women always did what was necessary no matter how dark the future? She would have known what she had to do to change things, and she would have accepted it the same way acceptance stole through me after witnessing

Argus's death.

I'd been trying to find a way to alter the visions without knowing the cost was extraordinarily high. How foolish to think something as trivial as spilling wine might be enough to change things. If it was that easy, Winifred would still be here.

Warm hands pressed against my shoulders, and Melody knelt beside me. Wisps of black hair clung to her tear-stained cheeks. I expected to see pity in her eyes, but there was none. She looked at me like someone about to enter a battle knowing they might not return. I imagined it was the same way my grandmother looked at the end.

"Come back inside. I'll explain everything."

I climbed to my feet using Melody's arm for balance. The crowd that had formed around us dispersed, moving on to more entertaining sights. Inside, she gestured for me to sit again.

I sank into the chair in front of the glass table and dropped my head into my hands. "I'm sorry about your mirror."

Melody made a noise of disgust and waved away my apology. "It's fine. I'll have a witch look at it before I leave. I'm half-inclined to get my money back. Reinforced, my ass. It cracked from a simple fate switch. Clearly, we're dealing with poor craftsmanship."

"Fate switch? Is that what it's called?"

She slid into the chair across from me. "It doesn't have a name, but I'm trying to see if one will catch on. The way it works is, you see the paths laid out in front of you, and you have to make a choice. In the original vision, your friend dies facing the creature, but down another path, you do when you take his place. That's the fate switch."

"What about the one where neither of us dies? How do I choose that one?"

"Well, that's where it gets complicated. Whatever decision you make either increases or decreases the likelihood of that happening. But you won't know in advance because, like I said, fate's a tricky bastard."

I pressed the heel of my hand into my forehead as I tried to make sense of it all. "What if I make the wrong choice?"

"There aren't any right or wrong choices, only choices you can live with. Some people make the wrong choice and sleep fine at night. I sold my soul. Sometimes, I regret it; other times, I count my blessings. You'll have to forgive my cliché advice—feel free to hate it—but you have to follow your heart."

A harsh laugh escaped my lips. "You're right. Your advice sucks."

"Yeah, it's pretty condescending under the circumstances."

I inhaled a shaky breath. "Tell me what happened to my grandmother."

Melody leaned back in her chair, and her gaze took on a faraway look. "I was with her when she first had the vision of your death. We were trying to track the Grimm's blade for your friend, and she thought the added power, like what I did with you, would help refine the scene. It was working, but then the whole thing changed. The night she died, you were supposed to go over for a visit. Somehow, the wolf found out about your friend using Winifred to track the blade and went to her cottage. In the first vision, Winifred survived the attack, but you didn't. In another version, she died facing the wolf alone. She canceled your plans and kept you away."

"She shouldn't have done that! There must have been another way."

"You're right. It's possible, but it's not for us to question her choice. She did what she thought was right, and you'll do the same." Shaking her head, Melody laughed softly. "I thought it was strange, but Winifred never blamed that man for bringing the creature into your lives. I asked her why, and she got all cryptic about how sometimes people bring in the good with the bad. I think she saw something she liked in him."

I swallowed around the lump in my throat. "He called her Winnie. Can you believe that?"

"Oh, God. Does he still have all his fingers?"

"All ten. You're as shocked as I was."

Melody stifled a grin, then leaned forward, concern filling her eyes. "I want you to know that even though she didn't think she could win against the wolf, she wasn't scared. You grew up with the ability to see ghosts, so you know death comes regardless of our plans. It takes what it wants when it wants, and for the most part, it's not the end. I think for people like us, it's not the fear that gets us; it's the sadness of being separated from the ones we love." She made a face. "And you don't want it to hurt if you can help it."

I hung my head in my hands, almost needing to laugh at the irony of it all. Death was a tricky opponent. Winifred had sacrificed herself for me, and now, I'd come full-circle and faced a similar choice. In the end, death could claim its original target.

Melody must have thought the same thing because she stroked her fingers through my hair and lifted my chin. "It's not a game you've lost. It might feel that way, but you're still in control. You have a choice."

"So, what happens now?" I asked.

She sat back in her chair and crossed her arms. "You go home. The visions will grow stronger and clearer. You'll know when it's time."

Pushing out of my chair, I gave Melody's mirrored table a final glance. "I should probably go find my friend. If we stay too long, it will be hard to drag her away. She's already angry we don't have the full three days."

"Ah, yes, the time difference." Melody chuckled and moved around the table to pull me into a perfume-scented hug. Her whisper skated past my ear. "Whatever you choose, face it head-on. Don't march quietly toward death. Remember, the decision you make decides whether you're worthy of the third path, and don't forget about chance. If you see an opportunity, take it."

The tent flap opened on a rush of air, and a trio of women staggered inside. They laughed and pushed each other to be the first to approach the table.

"Sirens." Melody rolled her eyes. "They love hearing which one will enthrall the most sailors. They also pay well." She turned to the trio. "One at a time, ladies, and I only take gold."

They giggled and dug into their bodices, withdrawing numerous golden coins. A brunette plunked enough money down to purchase a carriage and took the first seat. She swayed slightly in the chair and hiccupped.

Melody tossed the coins into a chest under the table. "They also have trouble staying away from the punch."

"Well, if there's punch, I know where to look for my friend. Thank you," I said, feeling my throat tighten.

She sniffed and turned her head to hide a well of tears, then waved me off. "I'm not good at goodbyes, so I won't say one. But I will say good luck and give them hell."

I left the tent and wandered into the crowd. At the far end of the field, merchants hawked their wares from makeshift stalls. Their shouts rose above the din, calling to anyone who passed. I skirted a stall filled with sizzling meats, then another draped with precious stones and glittering jewelry. Remembering Tessa's promise to Derrick to bring back a souvenir, I scanned the buyers. Sure enough, I found her leaning over a shelf of colorful jars. She dipped her finger into a creamy substance, then rubbed it over her palms.

"I'll take one of those, please," Tessa said to the old lady behind the counter.

The woman nodded and plucked the jar from the shelf, then placed it inside a basket already filled to the brim. Forget her spells—this was why Tessa had money problems. She was a compulsive shopper. As soon as a coin hit her pocket, it was in someone else's hand.

"Don't you already have a shop filled with this stuff?" I asked, sidling up next to her.

She jumped, and guilt splashed across her face. "I don't have *exactly* this stuff." She hid the basket behind her back and pulled me aside. "Don't give me that look. I haven't spent my entire time shopping. I spoke to the witches first. It seems Argus might be onto something. A few years back, there was a witch in a neighboring kingdom powerful enough to cast a wolf transformation ritual. No one's heard from her in years. Apparently, she was exiled, but whoever she turned might be the person we're looking for."

"That's great, Tess."

Shifting the basket to her other arm, she continued. "Yeah, and the timing works too. It takes a while to grow accustomed to the change and longer still until they're able to control it at will. It's likely our killer's been dormant until now because he wasn't strong enough. Derrick put together a profile on the victims. The early ones all have a link to Argus's organization or are directly related to his search for the blade."

"So, it's possible Argus or his organization is what

the wolf is after?"

"That could explain why his sister was targeted, but I think it's more than that. If you look historically at what the wolves do, they expand their pack, infiltrate villages, and overrun them. I think this is about gaining power. Argus is probably just breaking the surface. If you ask me, I think the entire kingdom is in danger." She gestured with the basket. "What about you? Any luck with the oracles?"

I nodded and ducked my head low so she couldn't read my eyes. "Yeah. I think I'll be able to control them better now. An oracle gave me a crash course."

Tessa nudged my arm. "See? I knew coming here would be a huge help. With any luck, we'll be able to track the wolf through the mirror. It's almost over, Viv. I can feel it. We're going to catch Winifred's killer."

The old woman cleared her throat, trying to reclaim Tessa's attention. She held up another jar, presenting the pink powder with a flourish. Tessa looked torn until I rolled my eyes and gestured for her to take a look.

"We still have time. You might as well make the most of it."

"That's right, we do." She winked. "After this, we're heading straight for the punch. I promised you a good time to take your mind off the man who shall not be named again this evening, and I always keep my liquor-based promises." Tessa wriggled her eyebrows and returned to the old woman's side.

Seeing her in her element, so happy and optimistic, made guilt crush my insides. I wasn't ready to tell her about Melody's revelation, and there was no use spoiling the evening. The future would come one way or another, so I might as well enjoy the present. Besides, I'd earned a night of mindless revelry.

With the two of them distracted, my gaze wandered over the table. I hardly recognized anything. I picked up a vial and read the handwritten label.

Elemental Flare. Hmm...

Wasn't this powder on Tessa's highly dangerous but effective list? If I remembered correctly, it was caustic enough to burn skin, and if you got it in your eyes, it caused temporary blindness. Melody's parting words replayed in my mind: *If chance presents an opportunity, take it.* Argus had taught me a lot, but one of the more important things was that two weapons were better than one.

My fingers curled around the glass vial. The blade might be the only thing that could kill the Red Wolf, but the actual danger lied in getting close enough to use it. Whatever happened, I wasn't going down without a fight. A fistful of powder could render him blind, possibly giving me that little bit of chance.

Glancing around discreetly, I slipped the vial into my pocket.

"Ready to go?" Tessa asked, slinging the basket over her shoulder. She'd added the jar of pink powder to her stash.

"Yup. I'm feeling very thirsty." I grinned like I hadn't just stuffed a stolen vial of magic powder inside my cloak.

"That's the Viv I know and love! Let's go have some fun." She spun on her heel and headed toward the food tent.

The old lady snagged my arm, her fingers biting into my skin. She dragged me to her eye level, and her cracked lips formed a knowing smile. Did she see me steal the vial? What did they do to thieves at High Council gatherings? Air wheezed out of the woman's lungs and brushed against my cheek. Visions of them roasting me over the fire pit formed in my mind.

I dug a hand into my cloak, preparing to return the vial and beg for forgiveness.

"Keep it," she rasped. "And don't miss."

Chapter 30

ARGUS

I pushed the food around on my plate, the fork clinking against the china. It sounded overly loud in the quiet room, but there wasn't anyone around to complain to. The chicken was dry, and the greens were wilted. Candlelight sputtered over the sad meal and the empty chairs around the table.

This was the fourth night in a row Hastings had served dinner in the dining room after I explicitly forbade it. He was punishing me, still threatening to quit every chance he got. The first two nights, I picked up my plate and went back to my office. The third, I hardly remembered because I'd had a liquid lunch and it hadn't worn off by dinnertime. By the fourth, I was punishing myself, remembering what it was like when she was here and things made sense.

Vivian had returned home a week ago and sent a note addressed to Hastings explaining everything the witch had learned at the summit.

Then, nothing!

According to the man I placed outside her house, she stayed inside practicing with the mirror. Occasionally, the witch would stop by for a visit. Fiona had started to deliver her meals, and yesterday, I caught Hastings sneaking out to meet her for afternoon tea.

But she hadn't come to see me.

Not once.

She'd put herself out there, revealed her feelings, and I'd let her go. It was stupid of me to think she'd try again. No. She was moving on and putting everything behind her, including me.

The witch got her wish.

Bloody brilliant.

Footsteps echoed down the hall. I mentally groaned, preparing myself for more of Hastings' condemning looks. But it wasn't Hastings who strolled into the room; it was Wade.

"What is with your butler? He took ages to open the door and then asked if I was carrying any weapons. When I said yes, he muttered, 'Good,' and walked off."

I speared an onion with my fork. "They're all on strike. Grab a plate. You'll have to serve yourself."

Wade mounded a plate full of chicken and vegetables from the sideboard and took a seat. One bite in, and he reached for the wine.

"The chicken is dry. This is awful."

"The cook's on strike too."

"What a mess. This is why I don't have servants."

I frowned at him over the rim of my wineglass. "You don't have servants because you're broke."

"That too." He chewed his meal, skipping the soggy vegetables. "The reason I'm here is because I have a lead on Adella. I paid one of Remington's servants to monitor Sarah in case Adella went to her. He came forward and said she's been acting strange and sneaking out of the house. He followed her but lost her in the village. She'd packed food and other items to take with her. It's a hunch, but I think she was taking them to Adella."

"You think Sarah knows the truth about what happened to my sister?"

Wade shrugged. "Who knows? Either way, we need to question her. It's late, but we can go now. The servant I paid will let us in the back. Sarah's room is on the third floor."

I tossed my napkin onto the table. "Good work. Let's go. I can't stomach any more of this meal."

Wade nodded and pushed his plate away. "It's highly disappointing." He grabbed a roll from a basket and cracked it against the table. "You'll lose a tooth if you try to eat this."

"I think she's counting on it," I grumbled as Wade followed me out the door.

We traveled the short distance to the neighboring estate and worked our way around the building to the servants' entrance. Wade knocked twice on the door, and it creaked open to reveal a short, squat man with bushy eyebrows. He flashed his teeth when Wade tossed him a bag of coins. Stuffing it in his pocket, he jerked his head toward the servants' passage.

"Go all the way up and take a left. It's the door on the end. Lord and Lady Remington are still out for the evening, so you'd better be quick about it."

"Wait here," I said to Wade, then headed up the narrow stairway.

At the top, a door opened into a darkened hallway. My boots were silent on the carpet as I crept toward the room at the end of the hall. The door was slightly ajar, so I peered inside. The bed was made, and she wasn't in there, but the curtains covering the threshold to the balcony fluttered in the breeze, letting in a blast of chilly night air. Moonlight painted the stone railing in shades of gray, and two torches cast a glow over the marble tile. The wind was stronger on the balcony. It made my eyes sting.

Sarah leaned against the rail, her face turned toward the moon. Dark hair whipped around her shoulders, revealing the pale column of her neck. She must have been freezing, yet she didn't move, more statue than human until I called her name.

"Sarah?"

Startled, she whirled around, brushing at her tear-stained cheeks. She took a step and stumbled into the railing, reaching to steady herself against a column.

"Argus, what are you doing here?"

"I need to talk to you about Adella."

She cleared her throat, her voice thick with unshed tears. "Oh… Is she back from the countryside?

Have her stop by."

"You know she never went to the country estate. That's why I'm here."

Her lips trembled, and she leaned heavily against the railing, keeping the weight off her right leg. "Go away, Argus. Leave me alone."

My gaze narrowed as I moved closer. "What's wrong with your leg?"

She refused to answer and turned her face away.

"Sarah, what is going on? Talk to me."

"Talk to you?" she rasped, limping along the rail. Angling her head, she peered over the side as if judging the distance to the ground. "You never talk to me. You don't even notice me." Her voice dropped to a whisper that nearly carried away on the wind. "He promised me you would. But he lied. He lied about everything. I can't do this anymore." Curling her fingers around the marble handrail, she slipped her foot between the grooves of the balustrade and climbed onto it.

I lunged, grabbed her around the waist, and swung her off the ledge.

Sarah whimpered. She pressed her back against a column, breathing heavily. Her brown eyes held mine, and when she blinked, they flashed silver.

"You're one of them." My gaze dropped to her leg, finding the edge of a bandage wrapped around her ankle. "It was you in the woods, wasn't it? You attacked us. Vivian hit you with a mace."

A guttural moan escaped her lips, and she thrust her hands against my chest with enough force I staggered backward. Her silver eyes glowed, mouth curling as she seethed and pushed away from the railing.

"I did it for you! It was all for you. He promised me if I became one of them, I'd be unstoppable; I wouldn't be overlooked anymore. You never notice me, always treat me like an annoying child. He said you'd see me differently."

I struggled to understand. Her words were coming so fast and broken they were difficult to follow.

"What happened in the woods, Sarah?"

She sobbed, and some of her fury drained away. "I went to retrieve the blade. I followed you after you escaped into the forest, but you were with her." Her fist trembled. "I was furious. I wanted her gone. It was like a haze, and all I could think about was maybe if she was dead, things would be different. The urge was too strong. I couldn't control it, and I attacked." Her voice broke. "But then you dove in front of me, shielded her with your body, risked your life for her, and I knew it was over. No matter what I've become, I could never hurt you, so I left." She sank to the stone floor, her skirt pooling around her feet and revealing her injured leg. She tugged at the bandage. "It's not healing properly," she said. Her voice dropped to a whisper. "I'm so sorry. Please, forgive me."

I knelt beside Sarah, surprised to find I wasn't angry. I felt partly to blame. I'd always known she felt something, but I didn't care. In a way, I understood how easy it was to be tempted by an offer of power, no matter how villainous, when it felt like there was no other choice. Sometimes, it was easier to blind yourself to the consequences if it got you what you wanted.

"Sarah, who did this to you? Who's the Red Wolf?"

A fresh stream of tears flowed beneath her lashes. "It's your father. Robert Lennox is the Red Wolf."

My eyes closed, and my lungs wouldn't fill. I knew it. The truth had been right in front of me all along, and now, I had proof.

"And my sister? Where is she?" When Sarah hesitated, I gripped her shoulders. "If my father's responsible, she could be in danger."

"I know. After what happened at the Ashworth party, she's been hiding from him."

"Does anyone know she was involved in Ashworth's murder?"

Sarah ducked her head and pressed a hand to her waist. "It wasn't her," she whispered. "Adella didn't kill Ashworth. I did."

"What?" My fingers dug into her shoulders. She had no idea what her actions had set in motion, giving Ashworth the motivation to go after Vivian instead of the actual culprit.

She winced and shrank into herself, stammering, "He was all over me at that party before I ran into you. I was glad he partnered with Vivian and not me. But when you left me with that group in the maze, I was so frustrated, I tried to follow you. I got turned around and found myself in the center of the maze, and that's where I saw him. He was bleeding and spitting mad. He must have thought I was Vivian because he launched himself at me, tore at my clothes. I couldn't get him off, and before I knew it, I'd shifted. It happened so fast."

"That bastard." I ground my teeth as I remembered the blood coating Vivian's hand. And then he attacked Sarah? He deserved what he got. "What happened next?"

"Adella found me and helped me to clean up. She didn't know I was one of them, but I told her the truth about her father, how he was responsible for her transformation and had approached me as well. She was terrified he'd use her against you, so she stayed away. I've been trying to keep her safe. That's why I went after the blade. I thought if we just gave him what he wanted, he'd leave us alone."

"You should have come to me."

"I know." Sarah dipped her head. "She's been staying in an empty storage building owned by my father."

I held out my hand and helped her to her feet. "Take me there."

***

The stairs creaked as we climbed to the second floor of the abandoned building. Rotting wood bowed beneath our feet, and the stench of mold was thick in the air.

"She's been staying in this dump the whole time?" Wade grated as we came to a stop in front of a metal door.

Sarah averted her gaze. "It was the only place I could think of. No one comes here, but it's close enough to the house I could bring supplies."

I reached past them and wrenched open the door, sliding the metal across the groove in the floor. The rumbling sound reverberated in the narrow chamber and shook the floorboards. My eyes adjusted to the dim light as I searched the space, and I spotted a straw mattress in the corner. Next to it was a small writing table and a set of chairs, where Adella sat reading a book.

She looked up, her eyes widening when she recognized me. Slipping a ribbon between the pages, she slowly rose to her feet.

"Argus..."

I drew a deep breath through my nose and let the air burn in my chest. We'd found her. All these weeks, and she'd been holed up in some hovel.

"Adella, we've been looking everywhere for you."

She chewed her lip. "You have?"

The air left me in a rush. "Of course, we have! Since you left. I searched for you at Ashworth's. Why did you run?"

Her gaze tracked to Sarah, then Wade. Twisting her hands, she tangled them in the fabric of her dress.

"Why don't we wait outside?" Sarah said, slipping from the room.

Wade followed, and then it was just the two of us. Adella's features were pale. With dark circles under her eyes, she looked exhausted, and her shoulders slumped.

"I'm sorry I've been so much trouble. I shouldn't have tried to escape, but that night, the pull was so strong, I had to get out. I thought it would be fine and no one would notice. But when Jason was killed, I panicked."

I moved closer and leaned my fist on the table. "I know you didn't kill Jason. You should have come home."

"I couldn't!" She spun on her heel and shook out her hands. "I didn't think you'd want me back after what happened, and when I learned the truth about our father, I thought you'd be happy to be rid of me."

My throat felt tight. "Why would you say that?"

Eyes watering, she sat in the chair and hung her head. "I know I'm a burden to you, another responsibility you inherited along with the house. I always hoped it would be different. We never really knew each other growing up, but when you came, I thought everything would be perfect. In some ways, it was. You're nothing like our father, and having him gone was a blessing. But I wanted more. A real family. You were always so closed off and distant. After a while, I stopped trying and just went about my life, but I still hoped one day we'd be close. Then, this happened, and I thought it would be easier for everyone if I stayed away."

Her words rang in my head. *Responsibility. Burden.* They were all so familiar. Had I pushed Adella away too? It was never my intention, but somewhere along the way, it had turned into a natural defense; a reflex to a truth I didn't want to face. Something was missing, and finding it scared the hell out of me.

Claiming the seat across from her, I cleared the rust from my voice. "I didn't know you felt that way. I guess I assumed you already had everything you needed and weren't interested in the stranger taking over your home. We were so different."

Her features softened. "Not that different, I expect. You always seemed sort of lonely, and I definitely was."

A taut, uncomfortable laugh bubbled in my throat. "You could tell?"

She nodded, lifting her gaze to mine.

"I'm sorry, Dell."

The corner of her mouth curved at the nickname. "I remember the first time you called me that. I hated it! But then you stopped, and I hated that more." She sighed. "I'm sorry too."

"I know I haven't always been very open—and believe me, you're not the only person I've hurt because of it—but you're family, and I don't have much of that." Blowing out a breath, I scrubbed a hand over my jaw. "I'll try harder."

She smiled, her eyes warming. "Me too."

"Will you come home now? We'll figure things out and find a way to deal with our father."

Her laughter was filled with relief, and her hands clasped together. "Yes. This room is awful. You can smell that, can't you?" She shuddered. "And I desperately miss Fiona's cooking."

I winced. "I should warn you, things are tricky

at home. Hastings is planning to quit, and Fiona is burning my food."

Eyebrows drawing together, she leaned forward. "What did you do?"

"I let something go I shouldn't have. It was a huge mistake."

"I thought Argus Ward didn't make mistakes," she teased.

"Yeah, well, don't tell anyone. I don't want it getting around. It'll ruin my reputation."

"Secret's safe with me. Are you going to get it back?"

"Yes." I set my jaw. *Whatever it takes.* "But it won't be easy. It's pretty temperamental. Extremely tenacious. A real handful."

Adella gave me a knowing smile and patted my hand. "I like her already."

Chapter 31

VIVIAN

The last rays of light speared through the trees as I walked the path toward my grandmother's house. Snow crunched beneath my boots, and the air froze my breath in white puffs. I wasn't sure how many times I'd walked the same path—hundreds, maybe a thousand—but it had never felt like the last time until today.

Ghosts were funny things. Sometimes, they were people who were lost or had something left undone. Other times, they were places with memories that haunted you.

Both needed to be set free.

Tessa and Derrick had already been to the house a few times to help with the cleaning and packing. With everything that happened, I hadn't allowed myself to go back, preferring to channel my energy into finding her killer. But now, I knew Winifred's secret, and I couldn't put it off any longer. I'd always gone to her when I had a problem, and even though she was gone, going home might bring clarity and a sense of peace.

The cottage came into view, and I slowed to commit the tranquil scene to memory. Fresh snow blanketed the ground, wiping away all traces of life. Nature had a way of reclaiming things; hiding the evidence we were ever there. Left long enough, the house would disappear behind overgrown trees and choking vines. But it couldn't erase what she'd done. Our actions lived on in so many ways, shaping our future, and we probably weren't even aware of half of them. That must be why people craved the mirror: they were desperate for the knowledge everything would be okay.

Certainty, to ease our fear.

I climbed the steps, gliding my fingers along the railing. Snow fell in wet clumps onto the porch. I kicked my boots to clean the treads and pushed open the door.

Inside, Tessa had stacked boxes of personal items that were to be stored until I could go through them. Every surface had been scrubbed clean and dusted. It smelled of pine and freshly laundered sheets. I couldn't help but smile.

"Even in death, you're getting everyone to do your chores, aren't you, Grandma? I still think it's genius."

Closing the door behind me, I headed for the kitchen and found a corkscrew, then placed my basket on the table near the hearth. I started a fire and lit the sconces. While Tessa had packed most of Winifred's things, she'd left her mirrors. They dotted the room like little windows into the future.

Digging into my basket, I removed a bottle of elderberry wine and a plate of scones. I poured two glasses, slid one in front of an empty chair, then took my place across from it.

Over the years, I'd had countless conversations with ghosts. Often, their unfinished business was simply telling their loved ones their last wishes and saying goodbye. This time, the unfinished business was mine, and even though I knew she couldn't hear it, some things needed to be said out loud before you could make peace with them.

"Hey, Grandma," I said softly. "The scones are your favorite. I didn't make them, before you get worried; Argus's cook Fiona did. They're amazing. I figured we should have one more chat, even if it's just me going through the motions." I took a sip from my glass, and the wine slid painfully around the lump in my throat.

Night had set in, deepening the shadows. The room was so quiet, the silence broken only by the flames crackling in the hearth. Breathing easier now I'd started, I settled back in my chair.

"If you were here, you'd be scolding me for all the crazy things I've done the past few weeks, and then we'd share a plate of scones and a bottle of wine until it was empty. By the end, you'd be laughing. I miss that. I miss a lot of things, but mostly, I miss hearing your voice telling me everything will be okay." I sighed and polished off a scone, adding another to my plate before I continued. "I met Melody the other day, and she shared the truth about what you did. You should have told me. Maybe we could have figured out something together. I understand why you did it and even why you didn't want me to know, but I still hate that you had to make that choice."

Running my finger along the wine stem, I stared into the ruby liquid. The room remained silent around me.

"I bet it was easy to choose though. I know when I saw Argus's death, taking his place wasn't even a question...but now, I don't think it's the right decision. I have to wonder if being an oracle makes us blind to the third choice, the one without any certainty. It's risky and terrifying, and we could lose everything, but there's also a chance we could win. Melody said the choices we make with our hearts change the future, and I'm counting on it."

Draining my drink, I stoppered the bottle and claimed the scone on my plate. I moved toward the fireplace and curled up in the armchair beside it. The warmth from the flames and the liquor flowing through my veins made me drowsy.

"The good news is, it hasn't all been doom and gloom. Tessa and I had a great time at the High Council gathering. That was some pretty strong punch, and I made some pretty poor choices. I don't think I'll be asked to play magical darts again. And then there was the time Argus drank a sleeping potion. Knocked him right out—it was hysterical. You would have loved it. He's a good man, Grandma. But something tells me you knew that."

I yawned, covering my mouth with the back of my hand, and stretched my toes out in front of me. Finishing the scone, I brushed the crumbs from my fingers. Heat warmed my skin, and I pulled a blanket off the top of a wooden trunk to drape over my shoulders.

"I miss you, Grandma, and I'll do my best to make you proud with all the time I have left. Hopefully, there's quite a bit. I still have a lot to learn about the mirror, and I hope I get that chance. Thank you for everything you did for me. I promise, when the time comes, I'll get top dollar for this house. You can rest easy on that one."

I snuggled deeper into the chair, feeling lighter than I did when I entered the cottage. This was my home for so many years, and I was thankful it still felt like one.

I closed my eyes, falling deeper under sleep's spell.

It was days since I last saw Argus, but like returning to the cottage, I couldn't put it off for much longer. Even if our relationship never went any further, I owed it to him to finish what we started.

The future might be dark, but I was ready to face it.

***

A step creaked.

I shifted in the chair, tugging the blanket under my chin.

The sound came again—a soft thump from outside, on the porch. I blinked my eyes open, squinting to see in the low light.

The front door was still closed, the latch drawn. But someone was out there. Maybe it was one of Argus's men? Against my wishes, he'd had someone stationed outside my house, and it was likely the man had followed me here to do his job.

Another creak. Whoever it was couldn't keep quiet. Tossing the blanket aside, I climbed to my feet and snatched the wine bottle off the table as a makeshift weapon. I tiptoed to the window and pushed aside the curtain. Faint moonlight revealed the figure.

It was Argus.

He rubbed his shoulders as he paced the porch. Every time he stepped on one of the loose boards, it creaked. *Unbelievable!* Did the man not understand normal calling hours?

I hurried to open the door.

"What are you doing out here? It's freezing!"

He halted mid-step. "I'm trying to decide if I should break in. You told me to stop doing that, but I didn't bring the right jacket for a night outdoors."

"Ever think of knocking? Or better yet, just go home. It's the middle of the night."

"I needed to see you." Feet planted like he wasn't going anywhere, his gaze raked over me. "Why did you come here?"

"Did you walk a mile through the woods to ask me that?"

He shivered inside his coat and gave me a half-smile. "No. I walked a mile to stand on your porch

JENNA COLLETT

and freeze to death."

"Get in here." I waved him through the door and thrust the wine bottle into his hands. "You're lucky you didn't try to break in. I would have hit you with that."

He tested the weight of it. "Beats getting hit with an iron candlestick, I guess." He moved toward the fire and grabbed a couple logs from the stack, then placed them in the hearth. His gaze roamed over the room, taking in the packed boxes and sparse interior. "You didn't have to do this by yourself." He gestured to the boxes. "I would have helped."

"Tessa and Derrick did everything."

An awkward silence fell. We stood there like two chess pieces, afraid to make a move that would leave either of us vulnerable.

Finally, I couldn't take it anymore. Hands on my hips, I let out a loud breath.

"Why are you here? Is this about the mirror? I know it's been a few days, but I'll hold up my end of the deal."

"You think I'm here to have you search the mirror?"

"Yes. Why else would you need me?"

"That's not fair," he said softly.

"It's not? I seem to recall a night very similar to this where you broke in and demanded I search the mirror. So, do you want me to start with that one over there, or the big oval one in the corner? Better yet, maybe you brought your own?"

He flexed his jaw. "I see how it is." Crossing the

326

room, his boots thudded on the floorboards. He looked angry, hands squeezed into fists as he walked past me. Stopping in front of a mirror, Argus gripped the frame and ripped it off the wall. He moved to the next one and the next, taking them all down, stacking two and three at a time. He flung the door open and charged outside.

I followed on his heels, staring open-mouthed at the mirrors he dropped into the snow. "What are you doing? Some of those are very expensive."

He wheeled me around and pushed me up the steps. "To hell with the mirrors. I'm not here for those. Get back inside—it's freezing."

The man had lost it! The cold must have addled his brain. He slammed the door closed behind us, and I couldn't take my eyes off the empty walls. In some places, the mirrors had been up so long they left a circular outline.

"Sit down," Argus said, scraping a chair across the floor.

"Argus—"

"I said, sit down."

Tossing up my hands, I obeyed, watching in confusion as he took the opposite seat and reached into his jacket. A rectangular object dropped onto the table between us, and a harsh laugh burst from my lips.

"You're joking! First, you toss all the mirrors outside, and now, you want to play cards? You've gone crazy."

"Yeah, but you already know you drive me crazy,"

he muttered as he shuffled the deck.

I crossed my arms and leaned back in my seat, tilting my chin higher. "I don't want to play."

"Too bad. I do." His gaze locked with mine, and the breath lodged in my throat.

Why was he looking at me like *that?* It was a mix of heat and barely leashed control crumbling by the second. I'd only seen that look once before, in my kitchen, right after I kissed him for the first time.

He broke the connection, leaving me reeling, and dealt the cards. They slapped against the table, and I didn't have any other choice but to play along. Pulling them to me, I kept them facedown, afraid to see what they were; afraid of where this game was going. It wasn't playful and teasing like it was the first time. This was intentional. A means to an end. I just didn't know what end or if I wanted to get there.

"Why are we doing this?"

"I found my sister tonight."

His answer startled me. After all this time, he'd finally found her. I breathed in relief. With the Grimm's blade in his possession, he had everything, so why was he rattled?

"Argus, that's good news. Is she okay? Where has she been?"

"Sarah helped her hide. She stayed away to make things easier on me. She thought she was a burden." He rubbed a hand over his face, his voice breaking low. "I did that. I pushed her away until she felt she had nowhere else to go. I made her feel like she didn't matter."

A lump formed in my throat. "I'm sure that's not true."

"Yes, it is. I did the same thing to you. When we were attacked after finding the Grimm's blade, you asked me a question. I didn't answer truthfully." He tapped his cards. "You're going to ask me again."

So, that was the game we were playing. My heart thudded painfully in my chest as the memory of that night replayed in my mind. The way he'd wrapped himself around me, keeping me safe, only to deny why it mattered. The pain was as real now as it was then.

I swallowed, my mouth suddenly dry. "Only if I win."

"You'll win."

"Did you cheat?"

His brow rose. "Did you see me cheat?"

No, I didn't, but there was something in his eyes that said he did. A flick of the wrist, maybe a card up his sleeve? I knew it with a certainty that surprised me. He wasn't willing to gamble with this hand.

I braved a glance at my cards.

Three kings.

He'd set me up. Fine. If he wanted to play, I would, but I wasn't going to make it easy on him. He was too confident I'd do exactly what he wanted; bend to his rules. That wasn't my style.

I tossed the cards down, watching him closely. "I'll take three."

The confident gleam in his eyes never faltered, and doubt crept in. He swept my three kings aside and dealt me new cards from the top of the deck, not taking any for himself. I was slow to react, already raw from the short time he'd been in my presence. What if the answer to the question was worse than his silence the day I left? His silence broke my heart. What would his words do?

The knot in my stomach tightened as I peeked at my cards.

Three queens.

"I knew you'd do that," he said. "You never back down from a challenge." Revealing his hand, he spread his cards faceup on the table. He had nothing.

"Cheater," I whispered.

"If it gets me what I want, then yeah. Whatever it takes. Ask the question, Vivian."

He might have forced my win, but I wasn't done playing. It wasn't fair he'd burst in here dredging up that night after I'd already relived it a thousand times. I tossed my queens onto the table and stood. His gaze followed me as I moved closer.

"Fine, but there's just one problem. The rules are, the winner chooses the question." My hand trailed along the back of his chair, then ghosted over his shoulder.

Argus clamped down on my wrist, halting the movement, his body tense and still. "Don't even think about it," he rasped.

Leaning forward, I brushed my mouth over his ear and whispered, "What's your favorite color?"

He growled in frustration and dragged me onto his lap. An arm banded around my waist, securing me in place.

"Bloody hell, woman, you never do what I say." His fingers threaded through my hair, and he pressed our foreheads together. "Ask me," he pleaded, his voice thick. "Ask me why I did it."

Our breath mingled, and for an endless moment, we stayed that way, at the very edge. The question felt too big to ask even though I'd wanted the answer for so long.

"Why did you do it?"

Air left him, and I felt relief course through his body. "Because I saw what my life would be like without you in it, and I hated it. I've never needed anyone until you. But it was easier to push you away than risk losing you." He paused to exhale a broken laugh. "Trouble is, since the moment you left, all I've thought about is how much I want you back."

Throat tight, I searched his gaze. "Tell me something you've never told anyone."

"That's two questions."

"I know. I'm greedy like that."

He framed my face with his hands, thumbs feathering over my cheekbones. His expression shifted from resistance to unwavering determination. Seeing him like this was worth the wait. Worth all the pain. It was everything.

"I love you, Vivian James. I've never said that to anyone. You're the first."

My voice shook as I asked my last question. "And what are you most afraid of?"

"Spiders," he deadpanned.

"Stop it." I dropped my head against his, laughter trembling my shoulders. "Be serious."

He lifted my chin, holding me in the intensity of his gaze. "I'm afraid I'm too late, and you won't love me back." His lips quirked. "But spiders are a close second."

I threw my arms around him and held him close. His heart pounded against mine. He cupped the back of my head with his palm, his embrace tightening to an almost painful degree.

"You're not too late. I love you back," I whispered against his ear.

"Finally. I thought I would have to answer more of your questions."

"Actually, I have one more—"

He silenced me with his mouth, kissing me thoroughly, sweeping his tongue against mine. A low rumble sounded in his chest as he angled his head to deepen the kiss. The sound sent a rush of heat through my body. I wound my arms around his neck, shifting more firmly against him, wanting him more with every demanding draw of his lips.

The chair creaked under our weight, threatening to end the kiss before we were ready.

Argus broke away with a groan. "We can't stay here."

"The room down the hall, first door on the right, is mine. But I have to warn you, it's a bit messy."

He laughed, slipping his arms under my legs, and locked me against his chest. "I knew you were messy."

I stifled a smile. "Yeah. My entire life is a lie."

"Let's see how bad it is." He moved swiftly down the hallway and toed open the door.

"Be careful. There might be spiders." I landed on the bed with a bounce, and then he was gone. The room was pitch dark, and I fumbled over the bedspread. Maybe spiders really were a close second? I didn't know whether to laugh or be horribly offended.

A match scraped, and a candle flame sputtered to life. His hand clamped around my ankle, and he dragged me under him, pressing me into the mattress.

"I'll take my chances with the spiders."

I wriggled my brow. "Famous last words."

His fingers brushed my cheek as he cupped my face. The laughter faded from his eyes, replaced with something raw and insistent. Argus's throat worked, and his voice was tight.

"I don't deserve you. I don't know if I ever will, but I'll try. I swear—"

"Hey, stop. If I have to spend all my time convincing you how wrong you are, I will, but I'm sick to death of promises. No more. Just show me."

A seductive smile curved his lips. "Now, that, I can do."

His head dipped, and he claimed my mouth. My heart fluttered as he laced his fingers with mine and drew them over my head. I breathed in his scent and arched my neck at the scrape of stubble over my jaw. Palms pressed together, Argus teased my lips, kissing me with a need that drove my senses wild. With deliberate slowness, he worked the ties on my dress. Cool air rushed in as he removed it, and his lips burned a path over the newly exposed skin.

His darkening gaze raked over my body. "Don't deserve you. But you're mine."

His broken whisper made me shiver. I closed my eyes as his tongue skillfully explored my breasts until sparks danced behind my eyelids. I moved beneath him, grinding my hips against his, and he bit back a moan, dragging his teeth lower.

Every place he touched was on fire. He removed his jacket, then his shirt, and then, splaying a hand against my back, he lifted me to my knees and drew me in for another urgent kiss.

Tentatively, my palms roamed over the ridges of his abdomen, soaking up the heat from his skin. The sound of approval in his throat sizzled through my body as every stroke of my fingers wound him tighter. He broke off with a curse when my touch grew bolder.

Seizing my hands, Argus's roughened voice made my stomach clench. "You're driving me crazy, love."

I smiled against his shoulder. "It's my favorite thing to do."

"Never stop."

He removed the last of our clothing and moved over me, gliding his roughened palms up my body. With every achingly tender stroke of his tongue, my pleasure coiled tighter. He worshiped my mouth, and even though I didn't want promises, he kept his, showing me with every possessive draw on my lips how much I meant to him.

I inhaled at the sharp pressure from his first slow thrust. He sank deeper, and my head arched on the pillow as the sensation grew into pleasure. The rhythm increased, and I met his gaze for a heart-splintering second. The fierce love in his eyes stole my breath, and he captured my mouth as I came apart.

Following seconds later, Argus drew me against him, curling his body around mine. The candlelight illuminated the tanned skin of his forearm anchored over my waist, and I linked our hands together. It was the safest I'd felt in my entire life. I breathed through the tightness in my throat, knowing he'd kept that promise too.

Our breaths evened. As the peaceful silence blanketed the room, a new worry crept in. I still had a terrible secret. I'd always planned on telling him, but now, every minute felt like a betrayal.

Turning in his arms, I leaned on my elbow. He brushed a wave of hair out of my face and smiled. The slow curl of his mouth made my heart twist, and I almost wavered. But I couldn't lie to him, not after he trusted me with his heart. It wasn't fair. We'd come so far, but there was still one dark obstacle to face.

"Argus?"

"Yes, love?"

"There's something I have to tell you. It's about the vision. I know who's going to die."

Chapter 32

ARGUS

Vivian rolled away from me and reached for her clothes. Her words echoed in my mind. She knew who died, and I knew the killer. The pieces of the puzzle were clicking together.

Dragging on my pants, I moved around the room, finding another candle and lighting it.

Vivian returned to the bed and sat cross-legged on the mattress. Her hair tangled in waves over her shoulders, and she looked so beautiful it made my chest ache. I didn't think I'd ever take a clean breath again. I wasn't sure I even wanted to if it meant I'd feel any less love for her than I did in that moment.

I'd told the truth during our game. No one had ever made me feel anything close to all I felt for her, and saying it out loud only reinforced it. Who knew cards could be so terrifying? I would never play them the same way.

The bed dipped as I sat next to her. "Tell me what happens."

She expelled a slow breath. "I don't know where to start. Just promise you'll let me finish telling you everything before…well, before you react."

Too late. I was already reacting to the hesitation in her voice. Icy dread slid through my veins. Somehow, I nodded, refusing to verbalize the promise knowing full well I'd never keep it.

"I guess I should start with Winifred. Argus…" Her hand reached for mine, her skin so cold. I rubbed her fingers between my palms to warm them. "We were wrong about what Winifred saw in the mirror before she died." Leaning forward, she gave me a wobbly smile and whispered, "This is the part where you have to let me finish." Another noncommittal nod, and she took a deep breath. "Winfred never saw her death. She saw mine."

A roaring overtook my ears. Vivian was still speaking, but I only heard parts of it. Winifred died in her place? Sent her away? A horrible understanding dawned, and my heart seized. She kept going, telling me about the vision and how when it cleared, she saw me lying dead in the snow.

"And then, it changed," she said. "The vision changed because I took your place, just like Winifred did, and that's when I realized—"

"No!"

She flinched at my harsh denial.

"That is *never* happening." I gripped her fingers so hard she pulled them away. Did she understand? Did she even have a clue what that would do to me?

"Argus, let me fin—"

"Damn it, Vivian!" I clenched my hands around her face. My entire body shook with uncontrollable fear as I pressed her forehead against mine. "Don't you dare." I choked on the words. "Don't you dare take my place."

Tears flowed unchecked from her eyes, and she wrapped her arms around my back, trying to soothe me. "You're supposed to let me finish. I thought I was very clear. That's only one version."

"And we're going with the original one. That's final."

"God, you're frustrating! Listen to me. Yes, the vision changed because I would go alone if that was my only option, but it's not. And you going alone isn't an option either. In one version, no one dies, and I think that's the one where we go together."

I shook my head. "It's too risky. I don't want you there at all. What if you're wrong?"

"I'm not wrong. I feel it. I don't know if it's intuition or what, but I'm certain." She placed her hand on my chest, palm flat against my heart, and pleaded. "At the memorial, I asked you to make a choice, and you said you'd stand with me. I'm asking you to do it again." My hesitation spurred her further. "If you say no, I won't go. I swear it. I'll let you lock me up and throw away the key. But we started this together, so let's finish it that way."

"It's a terrible plan."

"All good plans are terrible."

"No, they aren't! That doesn't even make sense."

She smiled and nudged me in the shoulder. "But

what if it *does* make sense?"

"Stop twisting everything I say. It's a terrible plan, and it doesn't make sense—but I trust you. So, if you think facing my father together will keep us both from dying, then fine. But I'm going on record that if you die, I will be furious."

She blinked, and her eyebrows drew together. "Wait… Did you say, your father?"

"Yeah." I scrubbed a hand through my hair, wincing as she leapt from the bed.

"The Red Wolf is your father? He's not dead?"

"Yes, he is. And no, he's not dead."

"So, what you're saying is, while I was over there spilling my dark secret and brilliant plan, you were hiding the fact the man who killed my grandmother is your father?"

"I wasn't hiding it. We just didn't get to it, what with everyone dying in your visions. If you ask me, not dying is more important than who does the killing."

She slashed her hand through the air, eyes flashing. "That doesn't even make sense!"

"It does too!" I roared.

She faced me, lips trembling. I cursed and climbed off the bed to reach for her.

"Viv, don't do that. I didn't mean—"

She laughed and slapped a hand over her mouth, but she couldn't contain it. A giggle escaped from between her fingers. Her eyes widened.

"I'm so sorry, but do you hear us? We're screaming about whose plan makes the least sense and whose secret is bigger. And then you tried to apologize." She snorted.

My lips twitched. "It's not funny. This is very serious."

"It's a little funny. Come here."

I closed the distance and wrapped my arms around her, resting my chin on top of her head. She sighed and locked her hands around my waist.

"It's late, and we're exhausted. There's nothing we can do tonight. Let's try to get some sleep and figure things out in the morning."

"That actually sounds like a good plan. One that makes sense," I grumbled, walking her backward toward the bed.

"I'm nothing if not practical."

Scooping her up, I laid her against the mattress and slid under the covers. I brushed my mouth against hers, lingering for a moment, still in awe that she was mine, then reached over her and pinched out the candle flame.

"You're a menace."

"You love it."

I did, and I had a feeling I always would.

Chapter 33

ARGUS

I stared at the Gothic arches of the Royal Agency and considered whether I'd truly lost my mind. Vivian's latest suggestion—the one that had a gangster standing on the steps of the police headquarters—was that we should ask for their help. Practical, my ass. The woman was downright impossible.

She bounced on her heels in the cold next to me, blowing into her hands for warmth. "Think of it this way: your father's built himself a werewolf army. We need one too. Your men, plus Derrick's officers. You know I'm a fan of hedging my bets."

"This isn't hedging our bets; it's a one-way ticket into a prison cell."

She scoffed. "Don't be ridiculous. They want to catch the Red Wolf as much as we do. Besides, how does that saying go? The enemy of my enemy is my friend. That applies here, doesn't it?"

"Don't quote wisdom when I'm feeling surly."

"You weren't surly this morning," she teased, flashing me a charming smile.

"That's exactly my point! You made your *suggestion* while we were otherwise occupied. I had no idea what I was agreeing to."

"It's not my fault if you can't pay attention."

"Bloody hell, woman."

"Oh, look! There's Tessa." She waved as the witch crossed the street. The day had started so well, and now it was spiraling downward.

"Good morning…" The witch swallowed like she tasted something sour. "Argus."

"Tessa, what a pleasure." My voice was pure sugar. Vivian pinched my side, and my grin widened, showing teeth. "A genuine pleasure."

"Oh, forget it," Vivian snarled. "I give up. I'll be dead and buried before you two get along. It's really not worth the effort. Come on—let's go. I'm sure Derrick's waiting."

We climbed the steps and entered the agency. The quick walk to Detective Chambers' office felt more like a walk to the gallows. The concessions I made for this woman. She had no idea.

When we were seated, Vivian rested her hand on my knee, probably thinking it would improve my mood. It did not—for the most part.

Detective Chambers leaned forward in his seat and eyed me from across his desk. My three-inch-thick file rested next to his elbow. I bet it made for some good reading.

"You're telling me Robert Lennox is not only alive

and back in the Kingdom of Ever, but he's the were-wolf responsible for the recent murders?"

Vivian nodded. "Yes. Sarah Remington can corroborate it's him. He approached her. She's one of his victims and has some knowledge of his plans. There's also Bowen MacKenzie's account that Robert visited a witch before he supposedly died. A witch Tessa confirmed performed a wolf transformation spell within the last few years."

"So, what does he want?" Detective Chambers asked.

"He wants what he's always wanted: complete control over the kingdom," I said bluntly, folding my arms over my chest. "Sarah says the wolves will overrun the village and head inward toward the castle. When it's over, we'll be under his rule."

The detective leaned forward, bracing his arms on his desk. "How do we stop it?"

"The Grimm's blade. If we kill Robert, the rest of the wolves will fall. They'll lose the tie that binds them along with the wolf's curse."

Vivian squeezed my knee as she got to the point she knew I wasn't sold on. "And that brings us to my visions. They're getting stronger, revealing more each time. The one I had this morning showed a clearing in the woods near a large cave system. He might be hiding out there. In the vision, there's a confrontation, and we're asking for the agency's help to fight him."

"Vivian, you know the agency will do everything in its power to bring your grandmother's killer to justice and keep this kingdom safe."

Tessa grinned and patted the detective's shoulder. "What Derrick's saying is, we'd love to help. I've been practicing a few spells that would be perfect for this situation. You'll love this. Watch." She curled her fingers into a fist and shot her arm out, sending a stream of sparks into the bookcase.

The dry parchment ignited, and Detective Chambers lunged from his desk, throwing a basin of water onto the fire. It hissed and went out, sending little curls of smoke into the air. I suddenly noticed he had quite a few basins of water placed around the office. Fire must be a common occurrence.

The witch bit her thumbnail. "I was aiming for the metal grate. It's a work in progress. But we'd still love to help."

The detective groaned and rubbed the bridge of his nose. "Tessa, you're not traipsing through the woods hunting werewolves."

"Why not? I have fire skills."

He looked incredulous and lifted his palms in disbelief. "Not good ones! It's too dangerous. I won't risk it."

"You're being unreasonable."

They stood toe-to-toe having the same kind of argument Vivian and I had every time she wanted to leap into danger. I felt bad for the guy. It was... relatable.

Vivian rolled her eyes. "Can you believe these two? We're nothing like them."

A bark of laughter sprang from my throat. "Love,

we *are* them."

"No, we're not. I'm way better at dangerous missions than Tessa. Fact: I fought off a wild animal inside Bowen's manor all by myself."

"It was a dog," I grated. "Hastings told me. You can't keep using that one. Need I remind you, a fury statue almost impaled you to the wall, and a werewolf nearly mauled you?"

She curled her lip and looked away, slinging her arms over her chest. The witch had slumped into a chair of her own and was mimicking the same posture. Detective Chambers caught my gaze and angled his head toward the door. Neither woman cared when we stepped into the hallway. They'd already begun to fight between them over who was the better wolf tracker. I wouldn't place my bet on either of them. They were impossible.

The detective mumbled under his breath, "That woman will be the death of me."

I smirked. "Don't worry, we'll have matching graves."

"The two of them are unbelievable. Tessa lit the bookcase on fire and thinks I'll be fine with her going one-on-one with a werewolf."

"She'll do it no matter what you say. 'Stay home and wait,' isn't exactly in their vocabulary. Believe me, I've tried."

He nodded. "I've tried that too, with poor results. Look, if Robert Lennox has returned, we need to take care of him. This kingdom isn't going back to the way it was when he ruled the streets. We will not be overrun by those creatures. You have the Grimm's blade, so let's kill him."

"Agreed. We need to locate the cave system and bring the fight to him."

"I'll send some officers to scout the location. You do the same and see if Vivian can get anything else from the mirror. We don't have a lot of time. They could attack at any point, and we have to be ready." He held out his hand. "For the kingdom."

"For the kingdom." I clasped his hand, and we shook.

Look at that, the enemy of my enemy really is my friend.

Vivian would be so pleased she was right. There was definitely an "I told you so" in my future, I knew that much. No mirror required.

***

Over the next few days, our plan came together. Derrick's men located the cave system and put eyes on my father. We would attack the following night— all of us, both sides coming together to take down a common enemy.

It felt surreal.

My gaze roamed over the scene in my office. Everyone closest to me had gathered together, even the ones I tried so hard to keep away. Adella and Wade talked in the corner, Hastings sat on the sofa polishing knives, and Vivian stood out among them all, telling Hastings some ridiculous story about how she almost won a game of magical darts.

"I had my shot all lined up, but the bull's-eye moved at the last moment, and the stupid dart struck a glass display of potions. They made me pay for the entire thing! Apparently, if you break it, you buy it," she grumbled, slumping against the seat cushion.

Hastings chuckled. "Did the bull's-eye move, or were you seeing things from too much mystical punch?"

She cringed and picked at a phantom piece of lint. "I stand by my story. It moved." Catching my eye across the room, she smiled and left Hastings to his task. "You believe me, don't you?" Vivian asked as she sauntered over.

"I believe you believe it moved."

Smothering a grin, she wrapped her arms around my waist and rested her head on my chest. "You're quiet tonight. Everything okay?"

My hands sifted through her hair. "Yeah, I'm just ready for this to be over."

"Me too." Her voice dropped, and she slid her hands up my back. "Argus, if something happens tomorrow, I want you to know—"

"Hey, no, we're not doing that." I leaned back and captured her face in my hands. "No goodbyes."

She made a face. "It's what normal people do. They get their affairs in order."

"You and I are not normal people. You especially." My thumbs brushed her temples. "Tomorrow, we're going to kill a werewolf with a mystical blade and end an uprising to overthrow the kingdom. After that, we'll come home and have dinner. That's it."

A laugh shook her shoulders. "You're right, that doesn't sound normal at all. We'll be fine."

My throat closed. We had to be. I met Wade's gaze over her shoulder, and a look passed between us. He nodded. Our plan was in place, and he'd do what was necessary.

No matter what.

Adella clapped her hands together, claiming everyone's attention. "What should we do to pass the time and take our minds off things? How about a game?"

"Argus has a deck of cards lying around here somewhere," Wade said, searching the bookshelves.

I glanced at Vivian, and she gave me a knowing smile. "Pick something else," I said. Cards were our game, and I didn't want to share it with anyone.

Adella tapped her foot. "How about charades? Hastings, put away those weapons. Argus, Wade, help me move this sofa." She hurried to one end, while Hastings gathered up his knives.

"Duty calls, love." I unwound her arms and went to lift the other end of the sofa.

Vivian wandered to the sideboard and set out a line of glasses.

"Are you any good at charades?" Wade asked Adella, moving her aside to help me shift the furniture.

"Yes, I'm very good." She nodded solemnly.

He winked. "You can be my partner then. Those two won't stand a chance."

With the floor cleared, my gaze drifted back to Vivian. She was still in front of the sideboard, but she'd left the glasses empty and paused to stare into the mirror. There was something about her absolute stillness that made my stomach drop. She was transfixed, caught in its grasp. The visions had started to come more frequently, almost relentless whenever she looked into the mirror. What was I thinking leaving that one up? When this was over, they were all coming down except for a single designated one for her to use. No more running into visions by accident.

Her chest rose on quick inhales, and her lips parted.

"Viv, what's wrong? What do you see?"

My hands clasped around her shoulders, but she still didn't break away. Our reflections stared back, mine wide-eyed as panic slid through my veins. A vicious crack split the mirror, racing through the center. I dragged her away, shielding her face from any flying shards.

Vivian blinked and looked up at me. The room went deathly quiet. Then, I heard footsteps racing down the hall, and the witch appeared in the doorway gasping for air. She held the doorframe and bent at the waist, a sheen of sweat coating her brow.

"I came as fast as I could," she rasped. "The wolves are here. They're attacking the kingdom tonight. Derrick's men are holding them off."

Vivian's voice was shaky as she nodded. "I saw it too. The vision—it's happening now. We have to prevent Robert from reaching town. If we wait any longer, we'll be too late."

Chapter 34

ARGUS

We moved through the trees, sticking to the shadows. I'd gathered everyone I could, leaving some of my men behind to deal with the wolves attacking in the streets. The witch promised Derrick's officers were on their way and would be the reinforcement we needed.

The Grimm's blade radiated power where it was sheathed at my waist. A calmness had settled in my chest even though we were a day early and caught off-guard. It would be over tonight.

Vivian walked beside me just as she had since we started our search. She swore this was the right decision; that her grandmother had taken her place out of love but that standing together was just as heartfelt. In fact, it was more so, a decision based on trust and faith in the other person. It went against everything I'd known until the day Vivian appeared in my office with a blade pointed at my back. Even though I'd spent weeks with her grandmother consulting the mirror, Vivian was a future I never saw coming.

We paused at the edge of the clearing, the cave system straight ahead. It was quiet except for the wind rustling through the bare trees. Overhead, the sky was cloudless, and the moon hovered over us like a spotlight on our final confrontation.

"We need to wait," the witch whispered. "They'll be here. Derrick won't leave us defenseless."

Vivian laced her hand through Tessa's and nodded. "He'll come. I know he will. We'll wait."

There wasn't much choice. We might hold off my father's wolves for a little while, maybe even get close enough to take a shot at killing him, but without the agency, things were bleak. I almost had to laugh at the irony. Without them and everyone at my side, this would be a suicide mission. It still might be—but at least now, we had a chance.

I locked gazes with Vivian, and her soft smile illuminated only by moonlight filled me with purpose. We had more than a chance. We were going to win.

A commotion behind us made my shoulders tighten. Had Derrick's men arrived?

The wait was over. It was time.

I turned, and my heart slowed to a sluggish beat. Wolves filled the forest. Their silver eyes glowed in a half-circle around us. They were tall, hulking beasts, hunched on their hind legs in anticipation of a strike. Matted fur covered their muscled bodies, extending down their arms toward razor-tipped claws.

Vivian stumbled back, pulling the mace from her bag. On my left, the witch cursed and lifted her palms. Orbs of fire appeared, hovering over her skin. Wade and the rest of my men unsheathed their weapons and faced the wolves, ready to attack.

A man weaved through the throng. He didn't shift, instead remaining in human form. My father paused in front of us, his vast army of wolves at his back.

Lips curling into a malicious sneer, he said, "Hello, son. I was hoping you'd come. Destroying the kingdom won't be the same unless I destroy you first." He shook his head, teeth flashing as his sneer widened. "You look a bit outnumbered. This pathetic show of force won't stop me. Neither will your worthless weapons. Unlike before, this time, I'm impossible to kill."

I tensed. He didn't know I'd found the Grimm's blade, so we had one advantage among a sea of disadvantages. It wasn't ideal, but it was something.

"Tell you what…" His voice cut through the trees. "It almost doesn't seem worth the fight. I'll make you a deal: I'll kill you, and then I'll kill the witch. They're a dime a dozen, but I'll keep the oracle for myself and let the rest of your men join my side." His leering gaze raked over Vivian. "What do you think, pet? Will you tell me my future after I turn you? I can be quite persuasive. I'll even let you stay at the Lennox mansion seeing as how you're already used to it."

Fury hardened the lines of her face. "I'll tell you your future right now. I'm going to kill you for what you did to my grandmother."

Robert laughed, the sound a harsh echo. "Has the oracle seen my demise? Visions didn't help your grandmother. Her blood spilled beneath my claws whether or not she saw it coming."

Vivian made a sound in the back of her throat, and I reached for her, holding her back with my outstretched hand.

"Easy, love. He's baiting you."

"He's a dead man."

"That's the idea, but we need to stall. We can't fight them alone." I lifted my hands, palms out, and addressed my father. "You shouldn't have come back here."

"Why not? This is my kingdom. Things will go back to the way they were—except, this time, my power will be absolute. It's amazing what you can accomplish when you show people your claws. You can smell the fear on them." He sniffed the air. "It's my favorite scent."

A string of howls resonated through the trees. The wolves edged closer, scratching their claws in the snow. We couldn't hold them off much longer.

Robert chuckled. "I can smell the oracle's fear. I hope you run, pet. I love a good chase. I'll run you to the ground and take my first bite." His grin widened. "I'm tired of waiting. Reunion's over, son." Hair sprouted along his arms, and his body curled inward. Robert roared through the transformation, clothes ripping into shreds and fluttering to the ground. His eyes flashed silver, and he bared his teeth, letting loose a guttural growl.

The wolves advanced.

"Time to see what those spells can do, witch! Aim for the heart."

"One set of fire skills coming your way," Tessa shouted, thrusting her arms out.

The last thing I saw before the light blinded me was a wolf leaping through the air, claws targeting my throat.

Chapter 35

VIVIAN

Light from Tessa's magic filled the clearing and sliced through the wolves as they charged. Some fell; others dug their hindquarters into the snow and pushed forward. I spun, slashing the mace through the air, as a wolf's claws sank into the fabric of my cloak, nearly tearing it from my back. Ripping free, I stumbled, my knees going down in the snow before I recovered and swung the mace a second time. It made contact with the wolf, and blood splattered across the white landscape. The copper scent flooded my senses, churning my stomach.

I could hardly catch my breath, there were so many of them.

Tessa whirled, sending magic into anything that got too close, and Argus and Wade positioned themselves at my back, their blades glinting in the moonlight before sinking into the attacking wolves. Howls drowned out everything else. When one fell, it seemed another rose to take its place.

A wolf came up on my side and raked its claws. I ducked, but the tips grazed my shoulder and sliced through my arm. Fiery pain burned my skin, and I bit back a sob. We weren't going to win. Bile climbed my throat, the bitterness choking me. I was so sure facing the wolves together was the right plan. It had to be! We were stronger together than alone, which was a perfectly fine saying so long as the other side didn't have the bigger army.

It seemed adages worked both ways.

This was my fault. Instead of one, there'd be many losses. Argus would fall along with his men, and so would Tessa. I wanted to rail at the helplessness caged inside me. But most of all, I was sorry. Sorry I'd made things worse, and sorry I hadn't been good enough to change the vision.

Another flash of light shot through the trees as Tessa's magic went wide. A wolf leapt through the air to take her down. She landed on her back, arms crossed over her face.

The wolf roared, baring its teeth. A stream of spittle oozed from its mouth.

I lunged for her, my boots sliding in the wet snow. The wolf saw me coming and barely made it out of striking distance before I swung the mace. Tessa rolled to the side, her features contorted in fear. I grabbed her hand, and our fingers locked together. The residual heat from her magic scalded my palm, but I squeezed tighter, giving her the leverage she needed to get back on her feet.

Snarling, the wolf sank its claws into Tessa's ankle.

She screamed, the sound ringing in my ears and stalling my heart. The wolf jerked her back, ripping her hand from mine. Tessa scrambled for purchase in the snow, snagging roots and branches as the wolf dragged her by the foot into the trees. Her wide, terrified eyes met mine.

Then, she was gone.

"Tess!" I raced after her, leaping over a stump.

"Viv, no!" Argus shouted from somewhere behind me, but I didn't stop.

Low-hanging branches tried to slow me down, snagging my cloak and whipping my exposed skin. My heart cracked painfully against my rib cage, and the icy wind froze my lungs as I gulped in air. Skidding to a stop, I searched the forest. Moonlight cast rays of silver against the snow, but the dense trees provided too much cover and darkness.

Tessa had vanished, her cries lost among the many others ringing through the clearing behind me. A wolf growled, the sound too close for me to do anything but dodge behind the nearest tree. Its claws slashed the bark and sent chucks spitting into the air.

I squeezed my eyes shut and pressed myself against the trunk, a whimper lodged in the back of my throat.

We were going to die.

My legs were weak as I staggered from the tree and followed the tracks in the snow. The darkness deepened, only hints of light creeping through the thick branches. My eyesight blurred through a mixture of tears and the panic swamping my body.

"Tess, where are you?" My hands shook so hard around the mace that the spiked ball shuddered. Every one of my muscles ached with tension and the fear I was already too late. I crept around another tree and spotted her lying on the ground. The wolf swiped at her as she tried to summon a final stream of magic. Fire sizzled and went out in her hands, and in a last-ditch effort, she kicked her boot into the wolf's middle.

"Get off me!" she shrieked, rearing back to kick it again.

Something whistled past my ear. A bolt thunked into the wolf's chest. The beast froze for a heart-stopping moment, then collapsed on its side.

Tessa crawled to her feet, staring at the bolt sticking out of the wolf's matted fur. A whoop of cries filled the air, and we both spun toward the sound. Men raced through the trees, raising their weapons to attack the wolves. Tessa sagged in relief and braced herself against a tree trunk.

"They're here. Derrick must have finally found us."

And then, there he was. Derrick ran at Tessa, scooping her up in his arms before dropping her to her feet and searching for injuries. His features were pale, eyes glazed with concern. She tried to capture his hands.

"I'm fine. It's okay."

He bent to examine her ankle, hissing in a breath at the bloody puncture wound. "You should have waited! What were you thinking?"

"Everything happened too fast. They cornered us. I'm glad you're here. We were not doing well." She tried to laugh, but there was a note of terror lurking in her tone.

Derrick heard it, and he pulled her tight against his chest, banding his arms around her. He whispered urgently in her ear, and Tessa nodded, clinging to him with everything she had. He looked at me over her shoulder. I was afraid to meet his eyes, certain they were filled with hostility for putting Tessa in danger, but when I finally looked, I only saw relief.

"Are you hurt, Vivian?" he asked.

"I don't think so. Scratches, mostly. Nothing Tessa's noxious salve won't heal."

"I made extra especially for the occasion," she said as she turned in Derrick's arms. "Stank up the whole shop. I hope you're happy. I won't have customers for weeks until the smell fades."

I wouldn't be happy until this was over.

"I have to get back. I need to find Argus." I backed away toward the clearing. Tessa must have tried to follow, but Derrick's voice stopped her.

"Oh, no, you don't. You're a distance shooter now."

I couldn't help but smile. Tessa would be all right. Derrick would make sure of it.

I raced through the trees and came to the clearing. The wolves were being held off by the newcomers as both of our groups came together. I searched for

Argus but couldn't find him. My heart kicked against my chest as I panicked.

A wolf launched through the air, aiming for me, but Wade was already at my side taking the brunt of the hit. They crashed to the ground. The force of their collision clipped me, knocking the mace from my grip.

My weapon rolled down an embankment and disappeared.

Wade fought viciously in the snow, getting enough momentum to sink a dagger in the wolf's chest. He rolled from underneath it, blood soaking through his clothes.

"Where's Argus?" I helped him to his feet, and he jerked his head.

There he was, circling one of the remaining wolves. I knew instantly it was his father.

Wade held me back as I went for him.

"What are you doing? Let me go!"

"Sorry, I can't. Argus doesn't want you intervening. I'm supposed to stop you whatever it takes."

I bucked against him. "No! I have to help. Don't do this."

"He's not taking any chances with you. He made me promise." Wade dragged me away, and I ground my boots into the snow. It didn't do much.

I couldn't believe this! We were so close. I wanted to scream. Men and their protective instincts were the worst! It was ruining everything.

Robert backed Argus up against the rock face, and there was nowhere for him to go. The vision assailed me, and all I could see was Argus's vacant gaze, blood pooled around his body. I refused to let that happen.

"All right, fine. I won't help, but you're holding me right where a wolf sliced my arm. Please, let go. It hurts." I whimpered, and his grip instantly loosened.

He muttered an apology.

Wow. I didn't expect that to work.

I whirled and did exactly what Argus taught me to do: I didn't hesitate. Putting my entire body into it, I swung a right hook into Wade's face. My knuckles cracked against his cheekbone.

He staggered back, his hand reflexively covering his eye. "Damn it! What is it with women giving me a black eye?"

"Sorry, Wade." I dodged as he tried to grab me again and ran for Argus, weaving through the fighters and the last of the wolves.

Staggering to a stop, I reached for the only weapon I had left. Good thing I'd brought two. My fingers delved into my boot, pulling out the vial of yellow powder. I popped the cork and poured a handful into my palm, closing my fingers around the fine dust. It burned my skin, but I hardly noticed.

The Red Wolf roared, the sound triumphant as he dove into Argus, thrusting them both against the jagged rock. Argus lost his grip on the Grimm's blade, and it sank into the snow. Rearing back, his father raised his claws, preparing to deliver the final blow.

Argus dropped to his knees and strained to reach

the blade. His head came up, his search stalling when he saw me approach.

"No," he mouthed, his eyes widening. Fury flattened his lips and darkened his gaze, and I felt a little guilty I'd ruined his plan. But that wasn't how this was supposed to go. I'd had to cheat to get Wade to release me, and I wasn't stopping until I won.

Robert swung his head, silver eyes centering on me. I swear, he smiled—if a wolf could smile. Either way, it was an evil snarl loaded with the knowledge I was weaponless and vulnerable.

Blood rushed behind my ears, drowning out all sound. This man killed my grandmother. He'd taken everything from me. A calm feeling settled inside my body.

I was going to kill him.

The wolf lurched until he was mere inches away. Argus's frantic shout almost distracted me, but I held my ground. Robert's foul breath assailed my nostrils. Blood dripped from his teeth. There was a gleam in his eyes, and I saw my reflection in their silver depths. They were like mirrors, except this time, I decided the future.

Lifting my palm, I unfurled my fingers and blew the powder into his face.

The beast breathed it in, taking it into his lungs and through the eyes. He jerked in surprise and blinked, trying to clear the lingering dust. The silver in his eyes dimmed, and a milky film spread, growing thicker as it formed underneath his lids. He swung his arm, missing me completely. Another swipe landed a foot from my shoulder.

His bellow shook the ground.

Robert sniffed the air, trying to scent me. That might have worked, except Argus gained his footing. Our eyes locked, admiration blazing in his gaze. He nodded and tossed me the Grimm's blade.

It was almost like coming full-circle. My hand wrapped around the hilt, and the memory of Argus pressing my fingers against my ribs, showing me the way, filled my mind.

Aim here.

I thrust the blade into the Red Wolf's heart.

A sound like thunder cracked the air.

The dagger protruded from the wolf's chest. It turned molten orange, glowing brighter and brighter, and I shielded my eyes from the vivid light. Suddenly, the light winked out, plunging me into darkness until my eyes readjusted.

Robert lay on his side, his wolf form gone. The milky film still covered his unseeing eyes.

With their master defeated, the remaining wolves fell, transforming back to humans in the snow.

"It's over," I whispered. "We did it."

Argus reached me in three steps and dragged me to him. "That was incredible. You didn't hesitate."

"I told you the third time I stabbed something would be the charm." Frowning, I beat his shoulder. "You had Wade restrain me. I'm furious with you. I had to give him a black eye, and my fist really hurts."

"You hit him?"

"Yes! And I'm debating taking a swing at you too.

I'm very wound up."

"Ah, love—"

"Don't defend yourself. I saved the day. Me! This was my plan, and I'm going to remind you of it every chance I get. Prepare to be worn out on it." I shook him off and turned on my heel.

He hauled me back, capturing my face in his hands, and kissed me. *Not fair!* His mouth moved over mine, and I clung to his shoulders, my anger draining away.

Resting his forehead against mine, Argus smiled that cocky grin I loved, and I scrunched my nose. "You're such a cheater."

"Argus!" Wade shouted, claiming his attention. "Help me get the last of these guys rounded up."

He brushed the hair out of my face. "Why don't you go relax, hero? I'll just clean up."

"Good idea," I grumbled, still trying to cling to the last of my irritation.

"I love you," he said, his grin widening as he walked backward.

My frown wobbled as a stupid smile broke through. His attention shifted to Wade, and the two of them helped Derrick's officers with the rest of the fallen men. I blew out a breath and kicked my boot through the snow.

Well, that was immensely satisfying.

The vision had changed, and we'd picked the correct path. I sent up a word of thanks to my grandmother for everything she taught me.

When my toe connected with something solid, I

looked down. A round object was partly buried in the snow. *That's odd...* It resembled the same mysterious object I saw in the original vision, the one my future self found next to the body and pressed against her heart. Ice flooded my veins as I reached for it.

The medallion fit perfectly in my palm. Turning it over, I bit back a moan. An insignia for Ashworth Shipping was etched into the metal. I'd seen the same medallion before, in the maze with Jason the night he died.

I stopped breathing. How could I have missed this? There was more to the vision than I realized. Not one killer, but two.

Ashworth was here.

The threat hadn't passed. He still intended to avenge his son's death. I scanned the crowd, searching through Derrick's officers and Argus's men. Where was he?

"Argus!" I shouted. "We missed something."

He looked over at the same time a figure emerged from the trees. The man drew back his hood, and I recognized Ashworth's grim features. Rage hardened the lines of his face as he lifted a crossbow, aiming at Argus.

"No. Don't move!" I shouted.

Argus paused, confusion in his gaze. He hadn't noticed Ashworth. No one had. But Argus was still among a group of officers, and Ashworth didn't have a clear shot. Relief swamped me only to turn to horror as Ashworth realized the same thing, and the crossbow shifted direction, aiming at me.

Bellowing his son's name, he fired the bolt.

It struck me in an instant, so fast my mind didn't register the pain. Then, the fiery torment speared through me, and I sank to my knees in the snow.

Everything was so loud. I wanted to cover my ears, but I couldn't lift my arms. Numbness spread like the widening pool of blood beneath me.

I blinked. Somehow, I'd ended up on my back staring at the sky. The moon was a giant silver sphere that grew fainter with each second.

It vanished, obscured by Argus's distraught features. He leaned over me, lips moving, but I couldn't decipher the words. I focused on his face, and when my eyes drifted shut, I swore I could still see it.

Then, it was gone.

Along with the pain…and my future.

Chapter 36

ARGUS

Ashworth shot Vivian.

My mind rebelled at the scene in front of me, her blood melting the snow and running red. A crushing failure stole my breath. *I did this.* I should have been more careful, handled Ashworth myself.

My hands hovered over her wound, afraid to touch her and make it worse. Vivian gasped when I pressed down on her chest to stem the flow of blood that ran between my fingers. Pain glazed her eyes, her sight unfocused and fading.

"Witch!" I shouted, frantically searching the crowd. The chaos that erupted when Ashworth took his shot had ended in a terrifying stillness as everyone watched. "Get the witch," I growled at the man standing over me.

He stumbled back, making a path through the crowd.

Vivian's eyes fluttered as I leaned over her, still

pressing against the wound. "Hang on, love. Tessa's coming." Panic choked my voice as more blood pooled through my fingers. "Don't leave me."

Another set of hands pressed against mine, and I looked up into Tessa's tear-stained face.

"Do something. Save her."

Her lips trembled. "Argus, I can't. I don't know how."

"Save her, damn you!" I lunged, fisting her cloak and dragging her to her feet.

Rough hands gripped my shoulders and shoved me away. When I charged for her again, Derrick twisted my arm behind my back.

"Let go," I snarled.

"Not until you calm down."

Calm down? A harsh laugh escaped my lips. There was no calming down.

He held me another moment, then relaxed his grip. I caught the look on his face, and it gutted me. Pity. Horrible pity.

I turned on Tessa. "You're a witch. What good are you if you can't heal your friend?" She flinched, and her body caved inward. "Do something—anything! I'm begging."

"I don't know what to do!" she cried. "I make salves and headache potions. She's dying! There's..." She sucked in a breath as a look passed between her and the detective, and then she whispered, "I know what I have to do."

"Do it," I snarled.

Tessa whirled and pushed her way through the

crowd, disappearing into the trees. I sank to my knees beside Vivian. Her blood coated my hands, and I rinsed them off in the snow before cupping her cheek, needing to touch her.

She didn't move. Her skin was deathly pale.

My lungs burned. I wasn't even sure I was still breathing. Everything ached with such a fierce agony, I wanted it all to end.

Tessa returned and knelt beside me. She held a short branch between her fingers. Closing her hand around the tip, she whispered an incantation, then opened her palm.

The tip of the branch had turned razor-sharp.

"Quick—give me her hand."

I held Vivian's icy fingers in mine as the witch sent me one last unreadable look, then used the point of the stick to prick her finger. A small bead of blood welled on the surface of her skin. Tessa continued to chant, closing her eyes, her voice the only sound in the unbearable stillness. When she finished, her eyes flew open, and she gestured to Derrick.

"Remove the bolt."

The detective gently wrapped his hand around the end protruding from Vivian's chest and pulled. The bleeding stopped, and the wound slowly mended. Vivian's cool skin warmed with life.

It's working! Hope bloomed in my chest, burning away the anguish.

"You did it. You healed her." I stared at the witch, my voice cracking. "Thank you."

"Don't thank me." A fresh wave of tears spilled

from her eyes, and I glanced down at Vivian. She was so still, her eyes closed. Shouldn't she be awake?

With each second, more of my hope withered.

"What did you do, Tessa?" Derrick asked, wrapping his arms around her.

She broke into a sob and turned her face into his chest.

My throat tightened. "Witch, what did you do? Why hasn't she opened her eyes?"

Tessa inhaled a shuddering breath. "I'm sorry. It was the only thing I could think of. She was going to die. There was no time. It's called sleeping death. I didn't save her; I cursed her."

A curse?

"How do we break it?"

"I don't know. I only know of one other case, and she still sleeps."

"For how long?" I asked, my voice thick.

Tessa's features crumbled, tears streaming down her cheeks.

"Witch, tell me how long the other woman has been cursed."

She brushed her fingers over Vivian's brow, not looking at me as she answered. "It's been over fifty years, and no one can wake her. The curse stands."

Chapter 37

ARGUS

Three weeks later...

"Pass me that book over there, the one with the orchid on the cover." Tessa pointed to a thick volume stacked on top of ten others.

"You read it already," I said, turning the wispy-thin parchment of the book on my desk.

"Are you sure? They're all starting to look alike." Slumped in her chair, she rubbed her bleary eyes and sighed. "This is impossible."

"Keep looking. We haven't gone through them all. There has to be something in one of these books about the curse."

"We've been reading nonstop for three weeks—"

"And we'll read for one hundred more until we find it. Keep looking." I pushed out of my chair and stalked toward the sideboard, nearly tripping over a four-foot stack of spellbooks.

We weren't getting anywhere. Tessa had sent missives to the High Council, and they'd sent new books every week, but it didn't matter. They were useless. None of the other witches knew how to break the curse, and I was beginning to wonder if it was even possible.

Splashing an inch of whiskey into a glass, I threw it back and stared at the space on the wall where the mirror had been. They were all gone, every last one. I couldn't look at them. Not only because they had a hand in Vivian's fate, but because I couldn't stand to see my reflection.

I didn't keep the promise I made to her grandmother. At night, when I shut my eyes, it wasn't Vivian's smiling face I saw; it was her pale skin, eyes closed, still as death. A sleeping beauty I'd failed to protect. It was my fault, and the nightmares barely scratched the surface of the punishment that came with daylight.

Tessa came up beside me and poured herself a drink. "Argus, I'm not suggesting we stop looking."

"Good, because we're not giving up."

"No, never. I just…" She winced as she drained her drink. "I'm worried about you. We all are. Your sister, Hastings—we just want you to be okay in case…"

"In case, what? In case we can't wake her up? In case I spend the rest of my life searching for answers and never get them? In case, what, witch?" I curled my hand around the rocks glass and hurled it into the hearth.

Tessa flinched as it shattered in the grate. She moved her glass out of my reach and went to collect her bag.

"There's a new shipment of books getting delivered to the magic shop. I'll bring a few back here and have these other ones returned. We'll find something." She lingered by the door for a long moment, and when she spoke, her voice was thick with unshed tears. "Argus, did I do the right thing? Would she have wanted this? I know you blame yourself, but I blame myself too. I should have been able to do more. I just miss her so much."

So did I. Every day a little more.

"You did the right thing. It's not over."

"I hope you're right." The door closed softly behind her.

An hour passed, maybe two. It was hard to tell. The words on the page blurred, and I closed the volume I was reading.

"Sir?" The door creaked as Hastings entered. He carried a covered plate to the sideboard, not even acknowledging when his boots crunched over broken glass. "It's lunchtime. Fiona prepared your favorite."

"I'm not hungry. Have you seen that smaller book with the leather pages? I can't find it." I sifted through a stack by my elbow.

"No, sir, but I'll look for it." He stood near the corner of the desk, hands clasped at his waist.

"You're hovering, Hastings."

"I am, sir. The shipment you ordered came in today." He placed a slip of paper next to the ink blotter.

I stared at it, feeling my heart slow to a sluggish beat. "Tell them to send it back."

"You should go pick it up."

"What's the point?" I shoved the stack in front of me, and books toppled to the floor.

"Because she would have wanted you to."

"After everything that happened? I doubt it."

Hastings furrowed his brow and smoothed the buttons down the front of his vest. "I got to spend a lot of time with Miss James while she was here. We had many lengthy conversations, and I know you're wrong, but if you're not interested, then maybe I'll tell my friend about it. You remember the butler at the Tomalsens', don't you? Well, he was telling me their son was in the market, and it just makes more sense than sending it back."

My chair scraped across the floor. I thrust my arm into my jacket.

"The hell you will. Prepare the carriage."

"Right away, sir." Hastings spun on his heel and strode toward the door, but not before I caught the hint of a smile.

***

Standing in front of the counter at Relics and Rarities, I tapped the bell and waited. Andrew Billings emerged from the back room, a wide smile on his face. It faltered when he spotted me.

"Mr. Ward, a pleasure to see you again." He ran a finger under his collar, pulling at the fabric, and cleared his throat. "You'll be happy to know there have been no other undocumented shipments coming through my shop since the last time. I'm sure you'll find everything above reproach."

"That's good to hear." I surveyed the shop, making him sweat while I took stock of his inventory. He had a decent collection, mostly rare antiquities shipped from overseas. It could be better though. With the right investor, he could expand and afford higher quality merchandise. I drummed my fingers on the counter. "How much do you owe me, Andrew?"

The man visibly swallowed. "S—sir, I've been making payments and haven't missed a single one."

"No, you haven't. But that's not what I asked."

He angled his head, doing the calculations. "Well, there's the loan I took out to cover storm damage, and then the second, to pay for that lost shipment. Rents have gone up, so I needed the third loan to cover the difference for a few months. I don't have the total figure in front of me, but it's quite a lot."

"That's what I thought."

Andrew paled. This was kind of fun, and it was three long weeks since I'd had any of that. I felt like a cat toying with a mouse, except said cat had already eaten his last meal.

"I'm thinking of clearing your debt."

The man was stunned into silence. A clock on the wall chimed, and a little wooden bird trundled out, chirped, then went back inside. It was comical. The bird, and the look on Andrew's face.

"Mr. Ward, I don't understand."

"It's simple. I'm looking to invest in a shop, and I think I can make a larger profit taking a share of your sales than I can from your loan payments, especially if we spruce things up. I'm a businessman after all, not a gangster." I flashed my teeth.

Andrew's skin turned from ash to red. "Certainly not, Mr. Ward. No one has ever said that."

"Ah, well, let's not start our collaboration with lies, Andrew."

"No. What I meant was, we've always thought that. I even came up with a nickname for you—"

I lifted my brow, and his skin was back to ash. Yeah, this would be fun.

"Well, as an investor, I'm sure another nickname will be in order."

"Partner?" Andrew's smile was strained.

"Partner. I'll draw up a contract. I'm sure we can work out an agreement that will benefit us both and make us a ton of money."

"Mr. Ward, you don't know what this means!" Genuine excitement spread across his features.

"Actually, I do," I said, slipping him the piece of paper Hastings gave me earlier. "I'm also here for this."

Andrew grinned and tapped the paper with his finger. "I think you'll be very pleased. I apologize for how long it took to come in, but these things can take time." He bent to retrieve a wooden box from beneath the counter and placed it in front of me.

I stared at it, half-afraid it would be empty when I opened it, the contents missing like the Grimm's blade had been. Gathering the courage, I unhooked the metal claps and flipped the lid.

"Isn't it great?" Andrew beamed.

I snapped the lid closed, causing Andrew to jump.

"If you're unhappy..."

"I'll have the contract sent over." Picking up the box, I walked out of the store, leaving Andrew gaping behind the counter.

Chapter 38

ARGUS

By the time I returned home, evening had given way to night. It felt strange to be out, setting things into motion and planning for a future that might look different from what I wanted it to.

I had my dinner sent to Vivian's room and went to sit with her before I returned to the spellbooks. As I approached her door, I heard the soft tones of my sister from inside.

With the wolf connection severed between her and Robert, Adella didn't have to worry about turning anymore. She and I had started a new normal, and, surprisingly, we had a fair amount in common. In a way, I was glad she'd escaped that night because it gave us the chance to express things neither of us were aware of. We might still be leading separate lives, oblivious to the fact we could actually be a family.

I knocked on the door and peeked inside. Adella

looked up from the book she was reading to Vivian and smiled. Her eyes were bright with excitement.

"Argus, did you know, there are many common household items that can pick a lock?"

"Adella, what are you reading?"

She held up the book, and I groaned.

"It's titled 'A Mastery of Thieves.' Tessa brought it over. She said it's one of Vivian's favorites. It's so informative. I'd like to try a few of these techniques."

"What did I tell you about accepting offerings from the witch?"

She pouted and set the book on the nightstand. "Next, you'll be telling me I shouldn't attend the potions lessons she offered. Really, brother, you're awful stuffy for a gangster."

Potions lessons? The witch was a bad influence. At the rate things were going, Adella would be setting things on fire left and right.

"Speaking of gangsters, I have some news for you about my current occupation. I've decided to turn over a new leaf." I placed a hand on my heart. "I'm going to invest in an antiquities shop."

Her face fell. "Can we still keep the house?"

"What? Yes, we can still keep the house. I'm not broke. I plan on making more from this venture than I currently do."

"Oh, well, that's a relief."

I rolled my eyes and went to examine the tray of food Fiona had set up in the corner.

Adella leaned over Vivian and fixed her pillows. "You know, I was talking to Tessa, and she explained everything that happened with Vivian's visions. I know you don't like to talk about it, but I can't believe what her grandmother did. It's amazing how an act of love can change someone's future and even prevent their death. I think it's beautiful."

I scowled and picked at the food on the tray, not bothering with any of it. "An act of love didn't prevent Vivian's vision from happening. It didn't stop anything. She was wrong about all of that."

Adella frowned and crossed the room, her hands fisted on her hips. "That's not true. Vivian would have died if Tessa didn't perform the curse. Think about how hard that must have been for her, knowing she might condemn her friend but loving her so much she had to try. If you ask me, an act of love absolutely saved Vivian's life." She placed her arm on my shoulder and sighed. "I'm sorry. I won't mention the visions again. I know it upsets you. Don't stay up too late reading those books, and eat something. Try, at least."

I nodded and took a bite of chicken for her benefit. She gave me a sad smile and checked to make sure Vivian looked comfortable one more time before heading to bed.

It was always the quietest when it was just the two of us, almost as if the whole world had fallen asleep right along with Vivian. I lowered myself into the chair beside her bed and ran my hand over her fingers.

"It's been three weeks, love. Still not rested enough?" I didn't expect an answer, but I still waited just in case. "Well, thanks to that book of yours, my sister will probably be able to pick every lock in the kingdom." I cleared the tightness from my throat and dropped my head into my hands. Adella's words kept replaying in my mind. I couldn't focus. Why did she have to bring up the visions? She knew I hated them.

Maybe I couldn't get them out of my head because she had a point about the witch. I didn't stop to think about how cursing Vivian might have affected her. She'd had to risk knowing her curse could leave Vivian in a sleeping state forever, never giving her the chance to cross over; an eternity of nothingness, all for the slim chance maybe one day, we'd be able to wake her. Adella was right: an act of love had saved Vivian's life. Just like Winifred. Just like...

No.

It couldn't be that simple. People had been trying for fifty years to wake the other girl. There was no way my foolish thought could be the answer.

Although, the curse was called the sleeping death...

Coincidence? Maybe. But what if it wasn't? What if we had the answer all along and didn't realize it?

My hands trembled as I brought my gaze up to Vivian's face. Did I dare? It was only a kiss. I'd kissed her before, planned to keep doing it if the curse didn't happen. It wasn't a big deal.

It was *everything.*

And it could work.

I felt like I should warn her.

"I'm going to try something here, and, to tell you the truth, it's a bit unorthodox. It would probably get me punched in the face if it was anyone but you. Hell, it could still get me punched in the face if you wake up to some guy leaning over you, but you know I'm a bit of a risk-taker."

I inched closer, cursing myself for being a crazy fool thinking something like this could work and also dying for it to be the answer. Heart cracking against my rib cage, I tucked a strand of hair behind her ear.

"Viv, I did a thing today. I started a new future. For you, even if you don't get to see it. But I hope you do because I love you, and you're the one I want to share it with. And don't worry. We can still keep the house."

Leaning in, I kissed her.

Her lips were soft against mine. The faint scent of lavender filled my senses, and I cupped my hand against her cheek. When I pulled back, her eyes were still closed, and my heart sank.

What a stupid idea. Good thing no one saw it. They'd think I'd gone off the deep end.

Her fingers twitched, and I froze.

Slowly, Vivian turned her cheek into the pillow, stretching her arms over her head like a cat waking from a long nap. Then, her eyes opened, and she smiled.

"Hi," she said.

I tried to find my voice, but it seemed lost somewhere in the back of my throat. When I didn't answer, her smile dimmed.

"Why are you looking at me like you've seen a ghost? Oh, no!" She pressed her hand against the spot where the bolt struck her, searching for the wound. Her eyes went wide. "Am I dead? Can you see me?"

"I can see you."

"Jeez!" She smacked my arm. "Don't scare me like that. I thought I was a ghost. The last thing I remember is getting shot, and it *really* hurt. I do not recommend it. How long was I out? Man, I am starving!" She pointed to the tray in the corner. "Is that dinner? It smells like chick—"

"God, I missed you." I dragged her into my lap and kissed her again. This time, she kissed me back, wrapping her arms around my neck. Everything else faded away.

Until the door cracked against the wall.

"Argus! I figured it out. You need to ki—" Tessa burst into the room, coming to a stop when she spotted us. Her gaze landed on Vivian, and she shrieked. "You're awake!" Then, she frowned. "Which means you already figured it out. Huh. It's just kind of anti-climactic for me. I had to read a five-hundred-page book from cover to cover, and I've been at it all day."

"Figured what out?" Vivian asked.

"I cursed you. You've been asleep for three weeks. Argus and I practically worked our way through the entire mystical library to figure out how to break it."

"You did?" Vivian searched my gaze, and I nodded.

Tessa smiled and wiped at her suspiciously wet

lashes. "I'm so happy you're awake. We all missed you." Her gaze met mine, and she smiled, moving toward the door. "I'll give you guys some time alone and come back in the morning. I should probably go write a letter to that other girl's family to tell them how it's done. Fifty years and they never figured out how to break the curse when we did it in three weeks. I'm not saying we're better, but read the tea leaves, am I right?"

I cleared the thickness from my throat. "Thank you, Tessa. For everything."

"You too, Argus. I'll see you both in the morning." She closed the door softly behind her.

Vivian fell back against her pillow and stared up at the canopy. "What is happening? Now, I really don't know what to think. I must be dead because you two are getting along."

Stretching out next to her, I rolled onto my side. "You're not dead, and she's not so bad. For a witch. She actually helped a lot. These past three weeks have been the worst of my life."

"I'm sorry I scared you," she whispered.

"You did scare me, and you're going to have to make it up to me."

She chuckled and moved closer, sliding her palm over my chest and wriggling her eyebrows. "Oh, yeah? And what did you have in mind?"

"How about we start with this?" I reached into my pocket and pulled out the box I picked up earlier. The laughter died on Vivian's face as I placed it into her hands. Her breath caught, and her slender fingers shook as they traced the lid.

"Is this what I hope it is?"

"Depends on what you're hoping for. Open it." The thickness in my voice was back, and there was no getting rid of it.

She lifted the lid and pulled the ring from the velvet lining, holding it to the light. Angling her head, she peered at the inscription engraved on the inside.

I promise.

Her eyes met mine. "You promise, huh? What are you promising this time?"

"I already told you. Everything. I just want to make it official."

"That will be a lot of work." She lowered her voice to a whisper. "I've been told I'm a menace."

"No? Who would dare? Do they want to get stabbed?"

She lifted her shoulders. "It's crazy, right?"

I cupped her face and took a shaky breath. "Marry me, Viv."

Tears streamed down her cheeks, dropping onto the bedspread. She wiped them away and slipped the ring onto her finger.

"Yes, I'll marry you. And I don't even have to look in the mirror to know it's the right answer." She kissed me, sealing the deal, then leaned back, shaking her head. "An ex-ghost hunter-turned-oracle falls in love with a gangster. That will make for some interesting stories to tell our children."

I laughed and held up my hands. "Not so fast. You've been asleep for three weeks, and things have changed around here. I'm not a gangster anymore."

Her brow furrowed. "You're not?"

"I've become an investor. In antiquities."

A slow smiled spread across her face. "So, what you're telling me is, we get to hunt treasure now?"

"Well, not exactly. Think more ancient pottery and less gold doubloons."

Her grin widened, and she nudged my side. "Are you sure? Because I heard treasure."

"You drive me crazy. Do you know that?"

Flattening her palms on my chest, she rolled on top of me and planted a kiss on my mouth. "I know. And you love it."

I do.

And I always would.

Epilogue

VIVIAN

Eight years later…

"**S**ebastian Lucas Ward, put that down."

Sebastian plunked the crystal statue back on the shelf and jammed his tiny fists into his pockets. His gaze darted sheepishly to the floor, and he pouted.

"But, Mom, Fredrick wanted a closer look."

I smiled knowingly at my son. "Tell Fredrick I have no intention of reimbursing Mr. Billings for broken statues, not unless he has the means to pay. Maybe he'd be willing to dip into his winnings?"

Sebastian burst into a fit of giggles and whispered something to the space beside him. After conferring with the ghost, he nodded solemnly.

"Don't be silly, Mommy. You know Fredrick is saving his winnings for something big."

"I do know. I just wish he'd tell us what it is."

Andrew Billings cleared his throat from behind the counter. "Ghosts? There's a ghost in my shop?" His skin paled as he searched the room for the invisible specter.

Sebastian giggled again, covering his mouth with his fingers. "Don't worry, Mr. Billings. Fredrick is a friendly ghost. He says you and my dad have the best antiquities shop in town."

"That's right, we do," Argus said from the entrance to his office. He leaned against the doorframe, arms folded across his chest, and winked at Sebastian.

"Dad!" Sebastian hurtled his small body across the shop and wrapped his skinny arms around Argus's waist. "Mom and I came for a visit."

Argus grinned and ruffled Sebastian's dark hair. I might have seen it a million times, but my heart still swelled at the sight of father and son. Sebastian was a mini Argus, sly smile and all.

Kneeling, Argus came even with Sebastian's height and straightened the lapels on his fitted jacket. "Fredrick, huh? What happened to Ruby?"

Sebastian shrugged. "Ruby said Traders and Treasures was a better shop, so now I'm pretending I can't see her." He leaned close and stage-whispered, "It's driving her mad."

I laughed. Poor Ruby. The spirits were no match for my little ghost hunter.

It didn't surprise me to learn Sebastian had inherited my old ability. He'd taken to it quite well. It was Argus who had his hands full with the kingdom's oracle and a budding necromancer. To say the supernatural surrounded him was an understatement, but he swore he wouldn't have it any other way. He claimed magic saved my life, and for that, he'd be forever grateful. But I felt like the grateful one. Grateful for Winifred's sacrifice, and for the second chance I never took for granted.

Argus chuckled. "There's no loyalty among ghosts. Andrew, watch Sebastian for a bit, will you? I'd like a moment alone with my wife."

Sebastian wrinkled his nose and spoke to his left. "Stick with me, Fredrick. They're probably going to kiss again. It's so gross."

Andrew rolled his eyes and rounded the counter, taking Sebastian's hand. He led him into the back room muttering something about making sure the ghost kept his distance. I stifled a grin and followed Argus into his office, where I placed the lunch basket Fiona had packed on a stack of invoices. Argus closed the distance and trapped me against the edge of his desk.

Wrapping my arms around his neck, I sighed dramatically. "I'm the one who's supposed to see the future, yet our son is quite good at it too. You really should try to hide your love for me more, difficult as it must be."

The corner of his mouth hitched, and his fingers sifted through my hair, sliding down my back. "That was me trying to hide it."

"Well, you're terrible at it. Really awful. You're fooling no one."

His head dipped, and he trailed a kiss along my jawline. "I'll try harder, I promise."

"No, you won't," I murmured, angling my head so he could reach the sensitive spot behind my ear.

"No, I won't." He found the spot, and my eyes drifted shut.

"We can't stay long. I have clients all afternoon."

He answered by framing my face with his hands. His lips found mine, and he wasted no time deepening the kiss.

I pushed against him. "I mean it! We can't stay."

"Reschedule. I'm sure their futures can wait. I want to spend the afternoon with my wife. Hastings can babysit."

Laughing, I smacked him lightly on the chest. "Hastings is busy. He's taking Fiona out for the evening."

Argus groaned. "Hastings is a traitor. He abandons me in my time of need to go enjoy himself."

"Well," I said, running my finger along his collarbone, "maybe if you'd paid him better all these years, things would have turned out differently."

He snagged my fingers. "That man is richer than Midas. All those raises you wrangle out of me every time he does anything even remotely well..." His voice rose, mimicking my pitch. "Look how perfectly Hastings opens the door, Argus. Have you ever seen such grand posture?"

I bit my lip to contain a laugh. "I don't remember that one."

"Your memory is funny like that, love."

JENNA COLLETT

I shrugged. "It doesn't matter. I can't cancel today. I have a special case—a child from the orphanage. The headmistress is concerned for the girl's well-being and hopes a consultation with the mirror will shed some light on her situation."

Argus frowned. "A child from the orphanage? That's unusual."

"Exactly, so you're on your own for this evening. But I promise to make it up to you when I get home." I wriggled my eyebrows. "Cards tonight?"

"I'll start making my list of questions now."

"Ha. It's cute you think we'll get to them. I'm on a winning streak."

"Two wins is not a streak."

I scrunched my nose and curled my lip. "Maybe it's the start of one?"

He chuckled. "I doubt it. Want me to watch Sebastian while you're with your clients?"

"No. I think the girl might be more comfortable to have someone there her age. Besides, Andrew can only handle the ghosts for so long before he gets twitchy."

"That's true." Argus rounded his desk and pulled his jacket from the coat stand. He slipped it on and closed the account book he'd been working in.

"What are you doing?"

"Walking you and Sebastian to your shop."

I rolled my eyes. "It's barely two blocks from here. You're busy, and the lunch Fiona packed will get cold. Honestly, there's no need."

He placed a hand over his chest in mock horror.

"There's every need. How can you compare my work to spending time with you? Fiona's lunch might be tempting…" His voice faded as he opened the basket and peeked inside. Breathing deep at the heavenly scent, he nodded, making his choice. "No, you're right. Off you go. Safe travels."

"Argus!" My cheeks ached from smiling, but we'd played this game before. I spun on my heel toward the door, counting only two steps before his arm snaked around my waist to pull me back against him. His head dropped to the crook of my neck.

"I changed my mind. I choose you."

"Even if she packed scones?"

"Still you."

"Good, because Sebastian and I ate them on our way here."

"All of them?"

"Every last one."

Taking advantage of his shock, I wriggled out of his embrace, laughing as he chased me into the shop.

***

A brief two-block stroll later, and the three of us stood in front of my shop. It hadn't changed much since the days I used to summon spirits. Now, instead of ghosts, I consulted mirrors.

Sebastian bounced from foot to foot, his hand swinging in Argus's larger one. "Mom, do I have to stay here while you work? It's so boring. You put Fredrick to sleep last time, and I had no one to talk to."

"My work is not boring. It wasn't my fault Mrs. Clarkson spent three hours at my table wanting a description of every gown she'd wear this season."

Sebastian threw back his head in pained irritation. "It was awful."

Argus lifted a brow. "You put a ghost to sleep? That's a new low."

"You're one to talk. My eyes glaze over every time you ramble on about ancient pottery."

"Your words wound me, love. That pottery is worth a fortune."

"Well, so is showing Mrs. Clarkson her gowns. She pays above the going rate."

Argus gave Sebastian a pitying look. "Sorry, son. We go where the fortunes are. But you're in luck. Today's client is a girl about your age. Maybe you'll make a new friend. One who's still living."

Sebastian's features scrunched together, and he visibly shuddered. "Friends with a girl? They're so boring. Nothing but tea and dresses. I'll stick with Fredrick."

"You know, one day, you won't mind so much." Argus clapped him on the shoulder. "Besides, girls aren't boring. They can pick locks, scale buildings, and wield weapons. I've seen it happen."

I scoffed. "We do it better than some men. But none of your complaining today, Sebastian. You will be polite to the young lady while we try to help her." I took his hand, and he nodded sulkily.

"If you say so."

"Run inside and light the candles. They'll be here

shortly." I gave him a nudge, and he trudged up the steps grumbling something to Fredrick along the way.

"I'm afraid to look into that boy's future. I can just see him sitting in some dark room playing cards with a bunch of ghosts while actual people outside live their lives." I scrubbed a hand over my face in frustration. "At that age, at least I had Tessa. I don't want people to judge him like they judged me. They look at him like he's crazy."

Argus placed his hands on my shoulders and squeezed. "Viv, it will be fine. He's still young. Give him time. Everything will sort itself out. You'll show him how, and I'll be there to teach him how important real relationships are. I'm kind of an expert."

"An expert, huh?"

"No one's better at it than me, love."

"Oh, please. Your charm is so thick we could spread it on Fiona's toast."

His eyes went wide at Fiona's name. "Speaking of… You don't think Andrew will get into the basket and eat my lunch, do you?"

"Not if he values his life. But I wouldn't risk it." Going up on my toes, I gave him a quick kiss. "Go. We'll be home before dinner."

He waited until I reached the top of the steps, watching me with a look I knew I'd never grow tired of. Maybe he was right, and everything would work out? Steeling myself, I entered the shop and prepared to look into a young girl's future.

***

The child peered at me from beneath a wave of blonde hair. Her gaze was striking, deep green like a valley in springtime. She had rosy cheeks and a pert nose that turned up when I asked her name.

"Answer the question, dear," the headmistress said, nudging the girl in the shoulder.

"It's Alice." She lowered her green gaze to the tabletop.

"It's nice to meet you, Alice. My name's Vivian, and this is my son, Sebastian. He's only a few years older than you."

Sebastian gave her a bored look, then turned to his left and spoke to an empty chair. "I'm not asking her that, Fredrick."

Alice lifted a brow. "He talks funny. Is he crazy like me?"

The headmistress gasped. "Alice, don't be rude. No one thinks you're crazy. We just want to understand you better. That's why we're here."

"Where did you live before you came to the orphanage, sweetheart?" I asked.

She cocked her head, and a blonde curl swung across her cheek. "I can't find it. I want to go back, but it's hiding. I look for it all the time."

The headmistress sighed. "Alice has run away five times since she arrived. We found her in the woods last time, chasing a rabbit of all things!"

"Fredrick likes rabbits," Sebastian said.

I bit my tongue. Maybe bringing Sebastian wasn't

the best idea.

"Alice, why do you run away so often, and why did you go into the woods?"

"Because I can't be late! No. Not ever. I can't be late."

The headmistress met my gaze from across the table. I could read the sadness darkening her features. There was a desperation to help the poor girl who seemed so confused. I wasn't sure how I could help her, but maybe the mirror would reveal something useful. I placed my hands on the glass when Alice jerked her head toward Sebastian.

"Sebastian, don't be late. When it's time, you can't be late."

He froze, struck by the fierce look in her eyes. The ghost forgotten, he slowly reached across the table as if he meant to take her hand.

I'd never seen Sebastian initiate contact with anyone except for Argus and myself. When she didn't return the gesture, he left his hand where it was, his interest drawn to the little blonde girl. My throat felt tight, but I returned to the mirror and stared into its depths.

The reflection swirled as I chanted, changing into smoke, then darkness. Complete darkness. Heart thudding painfully, I moved further through the timeline of the vision, swiping my hand along the glass.

There was only darkness. It was endless; the kind associated with death. Alice's death. I inhaled a shuddering breath and looked at the girl.

Green eyes stared back.

I dropped my gaze and caught a tiny flash of light in the mirror. Slowly, the darkness cleared. Years after she was supposed to be dead, there was life.

Resurrection? Was that even possible? I tried to make sense of what I saw, and then the smoke converged again, swirling until I saw a figure walking among it. A man called her name. He shouted it, searching. His features made my heart twist because I knew that face. I would recognize it anywhere, even though it was years into the future and he was no longer a child but a man.

Sebastian.

The vision faded, and I stared at my son. How had fate intertwined them? It revealed nothing else, and the mirror went dark again as if the future had ended a second time—not in death, but distance.

The headmistress interrupted my thoughts as she leaned across the table to ask, "Did you see anything that will help her?"

Alice moved then. She finally reached the few inches to Sebastian's outstretched hand and covered it with her own.

"They'll try to keep me away, but Sebastian will help me find it."

"Help you find what, Alice?" I asked.

The little girl smiled, her green eyes sparkling. "Wonderland."

The end...for now.

***

Dear reader,

Thank you so much for reading Wolfish Charms. I hope you enjoyed Vivian and Argus's journey. If you'd like to share your thoughts with other readers, please consider leaving a review or rating on Amazon.

Next up, I'm really excited to bring you Alice and Sebastian's story, titled, Edge of Wonder. It will release on December 7th, 2020.

Synopsis:

It was a simple plan.

Alice Montgomery has spent her entire life hiding from the mercenaries dispatched to kill Wonderland royals. Still years away from claiming her birthright, she follows through on a risky plan to trick them into thinking she's dead. Unfortunately, it works a little too well, and now she's trapped, haunting an old clockmaker's cottage.

Better late than never. Try telling that to the dead girl.

Sebastian Ward doesn't give a damn about the

prophecy that says he'll aid a princess in claiming her throne. He has better things to do, like making a name for himself as a kingdom renowned ghost hunter. Dodging fate for years, his latest haunting brings him face to face with a ghost from the past.

Their paths are on a collision course, and when Sebastian is forced to fulfill his part of the prophecy, it triggers the mercenaries to resume their hunt. Now on a quest through a ruined kingdom where nothing is what it seems, he must decide whether guarding the last princess of Wonderland is worth losing the only thing he's ever wanted, his freedom.

- Thank you again for reading. Till next time!
Jenna Collett

Acknowledgement

I wanted to take a moment to thank a few people who have helped me along the way. I'm grateful to my family who continuously encourage me to keep writing. My husband who always gives me the "Don't you have a deadline?" look, my sister who is an amazing support system, and my mom, who starts almost every conversation with, "When is your next book coming out? When can I read it?"

I also want to mention another sort of family that has been with me through the years as this series has morphed into the books they are today. Thank you to my Wattpad readers who have supported me from the beginning. You read the early stuff, and you always put a smile on my face. These books are for you.

Thank you!
Jenna

Books In This Series

Ever Dark, Ever Deadly

Spellbound After Midnight

Wolfish Charms

Edge Of Wonder

Printed in Great Britain
by Amazon

27485689R00233